Nothing is more precious than independence and liberty.
Ho Chi Minh

About the Author
John Pullinger is a former Travel writer, English teacher and hotelier born and educated in Brisbane, Australia. He has worked in and out of Southeast Asia for over 20 years and lives on the Sunshine Coast of Queensland, Australia.

The Last Cyclo to Thanh da

John J Pullinger

Copyright © 2012 John J. Pullinger
Published by Vivid Publishing
Fremantle, Western Australia
www.vividpublishing.com.au

Cover design by Amazink, Maleny Qld

National Library of Australia Cataloguing-in-Publication data:
Author: Pullinger, John J. (John Julian)
Title: The last cyclo to Thanh Da / John J. Pullinger.
ISBN: 9781921787218 (pbk.)
Dewey Number: A823.

For information about the author, and to purchase more copies of this book, please visit:
www.vividpublishing.com.au/lastcyclo

This book is dedicated to the people of Vietnam with love.

1

'Where is she?'

Steve Conway walked slowly from the arrival hall of Tan Son Nhat International Airport and squinted into the burning sunshine of a Saigon morning looking for a woman he'd never met. His flight from Manila had arrived on time; he'd cleared immigration and customs quickly and now stood scanning the milling crowd.

He searched the sea of eager, expectant faces crowding the barriers and apart from a few friendly smiles from a number of local lovelies no one seemed interested in this foreigner.

He carried his suitcase past the steel barriers into the open area beyond and waited amongst the mob, trying to ignore excited little men in white, short-sleeved shirts and black pants yelling and pointing toward their waiting taxis. His shirt clung like a second skin and he could feel rivulets of sweat running down his back. He took out a handkerchief and mopped his brow. Same old 'Nam, still hot as hell; at least they're not shooting at me this time.

Suddenly to his right he heard a soft voice tinged with anxiety.

'Mr Steve, is that you?'

He turned to see a slightly built young woman, probably mid twenties, wearing a dark green *ao dai* the traditional silk dress of Vietnamese women, walking quickly toward him with a worried expression.

'Hi Kim Anh, yes, it's me,' he grinned, hiding his relief.

* * *

She had spotted him in the distance after parking her motorcycle. It had to be him. He was standing alone, the only foreigner, slowly looking back and forth among the dwindling crowd obviously searching for someone. He was reasonably tall, not quite six foot, rather well built, nice looking she told herself, dark brown hair cut short above a tanned, open face.

She had lain awake the previous night thinking about him, secretly excited about their meeting, now butterflies began to take flight in her stomach.

I hope he won't be cross with me for being late but he sounded nice on the phone, his voice soft, reassuring and friendly. She was not used to speaking with foreigners, they made her uncomfortable and she always felt her English was never adequate. And now here he was…just a few yards away. The butterflies were fluttering madly.

She smiled shyly brushing away an unruly lock of shoulder-length dark hair from her face and said quietly, 'Welcome to Vietnam sir, please forgive me for being late.'

Conway nodded and returned her smile.

'No worries Miss Kim Anh,' he replied gallantly. 'Thank you, it was good of you to come and meet me. I appreciate it very much.'

'You must be tired from your flight sir,' she said, trying to hide her nervousness. 'There is a hotel car coming. It should be here now,' she said, frowning slightly. It was late too, making the butterflies flutter even more madly. My goodness, I am late and so is the hotel car, what will he think of us?

'I will wait for your car sir then I'll meet you at the hotel because I have my motorbike and…' at that moment, another attractive young woman clad in a white *ao dai* joined them and introduced herself.

'Hello sir, Mr Conway? I am Lisa from the Le Le Hotel, your car is over here sir,' she said nodding to Kim and pointing to a waiting white Toyota Crown.

Kim Anh acknowledged Lisa then turned to Conway.

'Bye sir, I will see you back at the hotel,' she said and hurried away across the car park, her *ao dai* billowing in the slight breeze.

She was relieved. 'He's very nice…and handsome,' she giggled to herself. 'I hope he will allow me to show him around my city.'

'Friendly girl,' Conway said to himself, watching her small figure now at the far side of the airport concourse.

Kim Anh kick-started her motorbike and stood for a moment looking back as his car merged with the traffic heading into the city. The first meeting was over; the butterflies had flitted to the ether and were replaced by a delicious excitement. Why did she have this uncanny feeling that her life was about to change…Forever.

2

Conway looked out on the frenetic, ever changing scene of a Saigon morning as his vehicle threaded its way slowly through the traffic. 'Well, here I am again in 'Nam, I wonder what awaits this time?'

The drive from the airport took him along neat, clean tree-lined avenues with median strips a riot of brightly coloured flowers. Conway didn't know much about flora but the variety in these gardens was simply stunning. What a great impression for any newcomer to the "New Saigon". This once war-torn city was now a booming, free-wheeling metropolis powered by the God Honda. The world which had once fled Vietnam in terror had now returned with dollars and expectations. Capitalism was king and the brakes on a free market economy were most certainly...off!

The roads were choked with motor scooters, ridden barely inches apart by an eclectic group of citizens young and old. From very old grandmotherly types to entire families with new-borns perched front and back. Daring young blades weaved in and out attempting to strike up conversations with beautiful young women; some straight-backed and proud in their traditional dress but most in the western attire of blue jeans and designer tops.

The motor scooter had become the beast of burden. There seemed to be no end to what the resourceful Vietnamese could fit on to these small machines. He shook his head in disbelief at this procession of humanity carrying things large and small of every description; from refrigerators to huge panes of glass, wire cages of squealing pigs, wicker baskets of fruit and vegetables, tyres, large cardboard boxes of goods, not to mention the human cargo.

It was the normal, busy, daily scene of any Asian city with everyone going about their business. There were no signs of the previous conflict, confirming that Saigon had been spared the devastation wrought on many other cities in Vietnam.

* * *

Thirty minutes later they arrived at a cream, narrow, French-style hotel in Pham Ngu Lao, a central area of Saigon popular with backpackers. Conway checked in and was shown to a spacious air-conditioned room on the third floor, a pleasant relief from the furnace-like heat outside.

It was tastefully furnished with Doric columns in each corner and cream walls adorned with prints of Vietnamese village life. There were the usual fittings, television, phone, bar-fridge and a rather unique French-style bathroom complete with bidet.

On a small teak writing desk beside a large bay window stood a huge vase of flowers and a bowl of fresh fruit. A *very* comfortable looking double bed suddenly made him realise how tired he was. It had been an early morning flight from Manila which necessitated a pre-dawn drive to the airport. He was about to unpack when his phone rang with a message from the front desk telling him Kim Anh was waiting in the lobby.

She smiled as he emerged from the elevator and after more pleasantries asked if he would like to "have a look at my city". Yes of course he did, and followed her downstairs to where her Honda motor scooter was parked.

She put on a light brown, small-brimmed hat, turned up the front, then pulled on a pair of long white gloves to her elbows and tied a pink silk handkerchief across her face for protection from the motorized pollution. She mounted her trusty steed and turned to him with laughing eyes.

'Have you ever ridden on the back of a motor bike before sir?'

'Not for a very long time Kim but I am game if you are,' he grinned uncertainly, then looking at the heavy traffic flying past, his confidence waned more than a little.

'Well, here goes,' he thought, gingerly taking his place behind her and placing his hands either side of her slim waist.

She took off slowly and surely down Pham Ngu Lao Street, turning left at the traffic lights across a wave of motorbikes, cars and heavy vehicles which seemed to be heading straight for them and an inevitable accident, but somehow at the last moment a path opened allowing them through.

At a steady pace they skirted anti-clockwise around a huge roundabout in front of a large building he was to come to know as the Ben Thanh market. Scooters came flashing past from every direction, across, in front and behind, from right and left, all impatient to get somewhere. Cars, buses, heavy goods vehicles rumbled by within inches, horns blaring, roaring, snarling, wheezing in a dangerous dance where one misstep meant a trip to Saigon hospital or the morgue. Death was indeed a hair's breadth away but adrenalin kicked in and he found he was actually enjoying the thrill of it all.

They swept down into the divided expanse of Le Loi Street in District One, the virtual heart of Saigon, and turned left off Le Loi into further heavy traffic on Pasteur Street. Several hundred yards later she smoothly guided the little scooter into a parking area in front of the former Presidential Palace, the scene of the end of the war on the 30th April 1975 when North Vietnamese troops smashed through the tall iron front gates.

She bought two tickets for their entry, and they strolled along the gravel drive to the imposing front entrance of the palace. They tagged onto the end of a tour group and followed them through the various ornate and beautifully furnished conference and reception rooms featuring wonderful murals depicting Vietnamese history through the centuries.

From there down to an underground bunker deep below the palace, where on the wall were posted lists of the foreign combatants. Conway said nothing when he noticed the list included 7000+ Australians. They passed banks of old-fashioned grey teletype machines and were taken to a small theatre to be shown a black and white propaganda video on the fall of Saigon.

As they sat in the darkness, without thinking, he reached to his left and took her hand. It felt soft and warm…and she did not pull away. He glanced sideways at her but she was looking straight ahead at the movie, expressionless. He knew at that moment, a bond had formed with this quiet, gentle Vietnamese girl. It was a bond that would have consequences, over which he would have no control.

The tour finished with a mini concert of Vietnamese music featuring the *dan bau* a traditional instrument unique to Vietnam made of a single steel string stretched over a gourd with one end attached to a piece of wood equipped with a flexible handle. Conway looked on fascinated as the player plucked the string at its harmonic nodes using the handle to vary the tension. The sound was haunting and beautiful.

Upstairs on the way out he stood on an open verandah looking down at the well maintained bright green lawn, where over to the left proud and gleaming in the midday sun stood two of the tanks that crashed through the gates at 11.00 am on that fateful day.

For lunch, she took him to a restaurant appropriately named *Nice*. It was bustling and crowded with neatly dressed office workers. They squeezed into a small table by a window. She scanned the menu all in Vietnamese and on his bidding, ordered for both of them. He sensed Kim Anh was not completely at ease. It was obvious she was not used to the company of foreign men.

She ordered coconut juice for him and orange juice for herself and they sat chatting while waiting for their meal. She listened carefully as he told her a little about the Down Under Hotel in Manila, and she responded by saying her uncle had phoned her and told her how well he had been looked after during his stay there.

She was a secretary for a water park resort in the Thu Duc area on the outskirts of Saigon, a joint venture between an Australian and Vietnamese group, had been there for a year, enjoyed the work and offered to take him to visit during his stay.

'It is a place of fun sir,' she smiled, 'with large swimming and wave pools, a great place for families, I am sure you would love it.' He was about to ask about her family when their meal arrived.

The food was tasty and being unfamiliar with the etiquette of eating in Vietnam (the Army never taught him that in Nui Dat and the cuisine was a hell of a lot different) he watched and followed what she did. She identified each dish for him; the sour soup, boiled chicken, fried fish, assorted vegetables and the ubiquitous bowl of rice without which, no Vietnamese meal would be complete. She daintily filled his small bowl with rice then added chicken and fish.

'I hope you like our food sir, I know it is quite different from yours,' she said, watching him take a morsel with his chopsticks and clumsily bring it to his mouth. The Army never taught him how to use chopsticks either.

'Delicious,' he said, his face breaking into a broad smile, bringing an almost audible sigh of relief from her.

As they ate he looked at her as if he was seeing her for the first time. She was good looking, some would say beautiful. Large, dark, intelligent eyes were set above a strong, straight, slightly flared nose in a heart-shaped face framed by thick, glossy black hair which curved up slightly as it hit her shoulders. The beautifully shaped lips were inviting. 'Stop dreaming Conway,' he said to himself.

As she lowered her head to take a piece of fish, her long eyelashes gave the appearance of an angel in repose. Her skin was smooth, flawless, the colour of light copper and had a slight sheen to it. He glanced around at other women in the restaurant and noticed most seemed white of skin and there was a similarity in the planes of their high cheek boned faces. Kim Anh was different, darker, and to him, more attractive.

At the end of the meal she surprised him by insisting on paying. In Vietnam she said, the tradition is that the party who invites, pays for the meal. He was a little embarrassed and tried to pay but she would not hear of it. She dropped him back at his hotel promising to come back at 6.00 pm. He thanked her and watched as she sped off, then went upstairs for a nap on that comfortable bed.

* * *

Exactly at 6 o'clock Kim Anh appeared in the lobby. She had changed from her *ao dai* into a simple white top and dark grey slacks. She wore no makeup and looked so young and fresh he couldn't help smiling. Suddenly he remembered something and asking her to wait, turned and hurried back to the elevator. She stood mildly surprised, a smile hovering on her lips as he disappeared. A few minutes late he returned with a small gift-wrapped parcel and handed it to her.

'Sorry Kim I forgot to give you this. Your uncle asked me to bring this back to you, and I have something for you as well,' he said, reaching into his shirt pocket and producing a tiny, gold kangaroo pin. Her mouth fell open in surprise, delight and a hint of embarrassment. Kim Anh had never been given many gifts in her life and *never* from a foreign male.

She looked at it gleaming in the palm of her hand and shook her head in wonderment. 'Oh, thank you so much, it is beautiful.' She looked up at Conway, her smile radiant. 'I will treasure this always,' she said, carefully pinning it to the left breast of her blouse. 'And my uncle too, he is so thoughtful.' She brushed away that disobedient lock of hair and placed the small package into her handbag.

'As I said at lunch,' she continued, 'he enjoyed being a guest in your hotel, the service and staff, were excellent. What I didn't tell you was that he told me you were a very good man and that I was to take good care of you when you came to Ho Chi Minh City.'

'I am very glad to hear that, and now, Miss Kim Anh,' said Conway, as they walked down the front steps of the hotel out on to Pham Ngu Lao Street. 'Lunch was great however I insist it is my turn to return the compliment and take you to dinner. But,' he grinned, 'I'm sorry, I will have to leave the choice of restaurant to you.'

They made their way among the evening crowd of what seemed mostly office workers returning home and a sprinkling of tourists, mainly young backpackers. Vietnam had recently opened its doors again to tourism and this area with its cheap accommodation, cafes, restaurants, bars and travel agencies, was a magnet for the young and adventurous during their tour of 'Nam.

She led him left down a narrow alley off Pham Ngu Lao Street lined with small hotels and bars until they came to a tiny restaurant. It was a simple place, pure basic Vietnamese with small, metal topped tables and low plastic stools. The menu again was in Vietnamese but this time with each item numbered. With Kim's guidance he chose the chicken curry while she settled for sautéed beef with noodles and rice. The food though simple, was excellent and he toasted her with coconut juice while she smiled happily sipping her usual *nuoc cam* (orange juice).

The meal was ridiculously cheap and had he paid with a two dollar bill he would have received change. The piastre, a legacy of French rule, had been replaced by the Vietnamese dong. He smiled to himself as he sorted through the notes in his wallet remembering the ditty the bar girls of Saigon would sing scornfully to the relatively poorly paid Australian soldiers.

'Uc da loi cheap Charlie
He not buy me Saigon tea
Saigon tea just twenty 'P'
Uc da loi cheap Charlie'

He also remembered the friendly villagers in Phuoc Tuy Province, who would smile at the Australians, give them the thumbs up and say, *'Uc da loi number one, VC number ten!'*

The night air had become surprisingly cool and pleasant after the heat of the day; for Conway, a most welcome change as they strolled along among the markets of Pham Ngu Lao stopping occasionally to look at the vast array of goods for sale. There were ceramics from Hanoi, artifacts from Sapa on the Chinese border, colorful hand-made cloth bags, hats from the Mekong Delta, wood carvings and fruit from Central Vietnam together with the usual touristy tee shirts, flower stalls, hand-made leather sandals, rubber slippers, flick knives, watches, gold and silver plated rings. The list was endless.

The quality of most items was surprisingly good, the prices more than reasonable. Outside a travel agency they stopped and read advertisements for the various tours available. The fares were so cheap he had to look twice: *City Tour $US 6.00*: *Cu Chi Tunnel Tour $US 4.00*: *Nha Trang $US 7.00*. The last one was incredible value because the seaside resort of Nha Trang was at least 8 hours by bus.

They sat at coffee in a small open-air bistro in De Tham Street watching the passing parade. There was plenty to see; and not all of it pleasant.

Apart from the never ending stream of wandering backpackers in their beards, tie-dyed shorts, skirts and Jesus sandals, there were book vendors; young girls with vertical piles of novels, cheap photocopies of the originals. Among them skinny, pitifully dressed beggars, cripples and amputees and others their bodies twisted and misshapen, necks at unnatural angles obviously the victims of the war. Conway had seen it before…the terrible legacy of *agent orange*.

Young shoeshine boys with large brown eyes hopefully holding out their cleaning brushes, motor bike taxis waving expectantly and the strident call from slow moving cyclos. 'One dollah! I take you round Saigon!' Among this mix of humanity was also a sight that would amaze any tourist: Old women in conical hats hurrying by, their backs bent by large overloaded baskets of fruit hanging from a wooden yoke across their shoulders. The place was alive. There was so much energy, so unlike the relatively staid conservative suburban markets of Western cities.

They sipped their coffee, making small talk until Kim glanced at her watch and with a start, stood up and told him she had to leave. It was nine o'clock. Her older sister had apparently placed a curfew on her nighttime activities and it was time to return home. They walked back to his hotel where on the front steps, she gave him another of her shy smiles and said goodbye. There was no embrace or touch of the hand so he thanked her again for her hospitality, but she shook her head.

'Sir Steve, it was my honour to show you around and have you as my guest for lunch.' She mounted her motorbike and went through the routine of putting on the long gloves and handkerchief across her face. She sat for a moment then with a hesitant wave, kicked the engine into life and eased out into the heavy traffic where she was quickly lost to sight.

Stifling a yawn and nodding to the smiling security guard he walked back up the steps to reception where a young desk clerk, wearing a figure hugging, royal blue *ao dai* flashed him a dazzling smile as she handed him his room key. 'Such friendly people, how different these days,' he said to himself as he waited for the elevator.

In his room his thoughts went back over what had been a long but interesting day and...Kim Anh, a rather intriguing young woman. She seemed a very nice person but there was something about her he could not quite put his finger on. Yawning, he took a towel from the end of the bed and headed for the fancy, French-style shower. The sharp cold needles of the shower invigorated him. He climbed into bed and was tempted to read a paperback he'd bought in Manila airport but decided against it.

Sleep came almost instantly.

3

The early morning sun streamed in on Conway as he awoke from a good eight hours sleep. He blinked and looked around for a few seconds wondering where he was. Yawning, he pulled himself out of bed, grabbed a towel and staggered to the bathroom to shower and shave before breakfast. As he passed reception on the way to the dining room he was surprised to see Kim Anh sitting there. She smiled at the look on his face and rose to greet him.

'I thought I would come to see you before I started work,' she said, 'and if you don't mind, I will ask my boss if I can have a few days off to spend time with you and show you more of Saigon...'

He smiled at her in appreciation. She looked gorgeous in a lightweight pink cotton blouse and grey slacks and pink open-toed sandals. Again she wore no makeup and like many Asian women, didn't really need to. He could not hide his delight at her suggestion.

'That's wonderful, I hope he says yes,' he said, taking her hand and leading her into the dining room. She surprised him again by saying she had already taken her breakfast at home in Thanh Da; which she had mentioned the night before, was on the far north eastern edge of the city. But yes, she would like *tra da,* the traditional Vietnamese cold tea served free of charge in virtually every restaurant and hotel in Saigon.

Conway nodded to a waitress and Kim ordered in Vietnamese. While her tea was poured he perused the menu, settling for a crusty French bread roll with a block of cheddar cheese, strawberry jam, a plate of pineapple pieces, banana and dragon fruit followed by hot black tea in a quart glass mug.

'What would you like to do today?' she asked, watching with great interest as he spread the strawberry jam on to the roll and placed some sliced cheese between the two halves. This was a rather different breakfast than the normal fare of a Vietnamese which usually consisted of *Pho* or *Bun*, beef or chicken noodle soup. He cut the roll in half, pausing before he answered.

'Well, first of all I have to make a phone call back to Manila to see how the troops are behaving. Then, I would like to find out the best way to get down to Phuoc Tuy, and thirdly,' he grinned, 'Miss Kim Anh; I would like the pleasure of your company.' She blushed and lowered her head, trying to hide her own grin.

'I will call you here later and let you know,' she said, sipping her tea. 'My boss is a nice man I think he will give me the time off.' While he ate they chatted about the places she had taken him to the previous day then she casually glanced at her watch and her eyes widened.

'Oh my goodness I forgot the time again. I am so sorry Mr Steve, but I must go or I will be late for work,' she exclaimed, pushing the cup away and getting to her feet: 'Thank you for the tea, bye bye now sir.'

'Kim,' he said, rising from his chair and taking her hand, 'please call me Steve and I will call you Kim, or Kim Anh, is that a deal?'

She started to laugh. It was the first time he had seen her completely at ease. 'Oh, I'm sorry. I'm so formal aren't I? Thank you si…Steve.'

She was still smiling as she hurried down the front stairs of the hotel to her motorbike, left in the care of the hotel security guard. Conway waved as she rode away then went back and finished breakfast.

'She's quite a girl,' he said to himself as he drained the last of his coffee, 'now I'd better make that call to the Philippines.' In his room he sat on the side of the bed and was about to reach over to pick up the phone when he began to reflect on the events of recent months in his Down Under Hotel in Manila.[1]

---

1 *The Last Jeep to Baclaran*

With an injection of capital from Australian shareholders the hotel had undergone extensive renovations since the departure of the Pricketts, the major one being a rooftop swimming pool. The rooms had all been renovated and upgraded, a new kitchen had been installed and the travel desk modernized with a new computer reservation system. All rooms had been fitted with IDD telephones and cable television. The hallways and common areas had been re-carpeted throughout. Many of the old staff had been replaced. Imelda Prickett's relatives had either left or been dismissed and their positions taken by qualified and dedicated staff.

Zeny Diaz the accountant from the sister hotel, the Billabong in Angeles City, had settled in well taking over Susan Santos' position as Chief Accountant and proved to be a capable and popular replacement.

Ang, the wife of Jumbo Keyes his American assistant manager, had given birth to another child, a beautiful little girl they named Nemencia quickly nicknamed "Menchie", and Keyes declared himself "the happiest man in all of the 7,107 Philippine islands".

The Down Under Hotel now exuded a whole new atmosphere of professionalism, dedication and spirit of cooperation, which led to happy and contented guests who spread the word. Occupancy rate and profits soared. The shareholders were happy and Steve Conway was a proud man.

Lily Li had returned to Manila on a flying visit to check on her restaurant and they spent a night of passion together. She regaled him with stories of Shanghai saying how much she loved the vibrant and exciting lifestyle. Her restaurant on the Bund was a big hit with the locals and she had already covered her initial investment.

'Darling please come. I know you will love it too, it's such an interesting and great city, it's already taken over from Hong Kong in importance as the major seaport.' He had assured her he would, and smiled at her reply to his question about her current love life.

'Mmmm, I've had a couple of "encounters",' she said unabashed. 'But nothing serious, no one to compare with you lover,' she said, giving him that familiar wicked grin, 'if you know what I mean?'

Susan had phoned from Hong Kong and although she said she missed him, the calls were often short because as usual, she was "loaded" with her work. His friends and colleagues all seemed to be doing well but there was one whose story was disturbing.

Two months ago he had received a letter from Sally, a former lover and employee of the *Black Jack* bar. She had married her Marine and at first all seemed to be "wonderful". However, over time things began to change and he became increasingly moody and withdrawn. And, although she did not say so, reading between the lines, he suspected there was violence. The whole tone of the letter was one of unspoken desperation, hinting at a return to the Philippines...alone.

The Manila newspapers had given banner headlines to the trial and conviction of Ramon Sanchez. He had been sentenced to a long stretch in Muntinlupa prison. But within days of his confinement early one morning, he was found dead in his cell from multiple knife wounds. Goal is no place for a crooked cop. Retribution had been swift and final. There had been no further word on the fate of the Pricketts or Bert Groyne and Barney Lawson. Conway presumed justice had taken its course.

* * *

He dialed the number of the Down Under Hotel, promptly answered by an operator he knew as Annie.

'Hi Annie, Steve here, can I speak to Mr Keyes please?'

'Ooohhh...hello sir, how is my favourite boss?' replied Annie cheekily.

Conway grinned. She was a cute and cheerful girl, typical of the new breed of friendly and efficient staff in the Down Under.

'I am well Annie, are you behaving yourself there?'

'Oh course sir,' replied Annie archly. 'Always sir, you know I am a good girl,' she giggled emphasizing *good*. 'I will put you through now sir.'

'Keyes.' The deep, familiar, rumbling tones of Jumbo Keyes brought a smile to Conway's lips. Apart from being a terrific assistant manager, the big black man was also Conway's best friend.

'Hi Jumbo, Steve, how are things, anything important I should know about?'

'Hey man, great to hear from you. How are you? Been wondering how you were getting on in 'Nam. Things are pretty normal here. Apart from "Weasel" boring the backside off me with his phoney sexual exploits and complaints, everything's under control. You'll be pleased to know the hotel is full, as are many of the guests, but most of them are behaving for a change,' he chuckled. 'And best of all, little Menchie is beginning to allow me to have a full night's sleep. Anything of note happening there buddy?'

Conway smiled to himself, "Weasel" was one of the Down Under's long time guests who had retired from the Australian public service and spent most of the year in the Philippines and the Down Under in particular. He was known for his outlandish stories and those who knew him well gave him a wide berth.

He told of his meeting with Kim Anh and how she had shown him some of the sights and even paid for lunch.

'Yeah, I remember that being a Vietnamese custom from my time there. How's the hotel accommodation Steve?'

'Fine. Clean, comfortable, well furnished, staff friendly and efficient, no complaints, I'm enjoying the break.'

'And Kim Anh…what about her?'

The tone of his friend begged the question. Had Conway and Kim Anh hit it off? Conway played it cool. 'Nice girl, friendly, simple, smart, works as a secretary at a water park, going to show me more of the city later today if she can get time off from work.'

'A looker?'

'Yes, she certainly passes muster. I like her; seems very genuine and rather innocent.'

'Watch out buddy,' laughed Keyes. 'There are some stunningly beautiful women in that town. Elegance personified, and when they wear those ao dais, wow! What about Phuoc Tuy and Long Tan. Made any arrangements to visit yet?'

'Not yet. I will, but right now I just want to get to know the city a bit more. I've hardly scratched the surface but I've got a great little guide in Kim. It's a good looking city these days without all the military crap we used to see. I'm impressed so far with what I have seen. When I was here during the war I never saw much of the place, they kept me in the province, only came here once or twice and both times briefly.'

'Yeah, me too,' said Keyes, 'I was stationed up in the highlands around places like Pleiku, Quang Tri and Danang, never spent a lot of time in Saigon. I've heard nowadays with all the new investment, it's probably one of the better cities in South East Asia.'

They continued to chat about a variety of matters and Conway was about to hang up when Keyes gave him some surprising news.

'Sally is back in town!'

'Really? When? How is she? That letter she sent me was a worry.'

Keyes didn't answer immediately, seeming to choose his words carefully.

'Ah,' then a pause. 'I don't think she's too well, she's not quite the same Sally but still lovely. She didn't say much, just came in looking for you and seemed disappointed when I told her you were in Vietnam and asked when you would be back.'

'What about her husband, what's happening there?'

'I don't know, she didn't say anything about him, somehow I don't think he's in the Philippines. You can ask her when you get back Steve. She left a phone number.'

'Ok, thanks, here's my hotel number, call me if you need me. If I leave town for a few days I'll get the hotel staff here to hold any messages. Ok Jumbo, bye now mate, and you have my permission to turf "Weasel" out if he gets on your nerves too much.'

'No,' laughed Keyes, 'he's harmless enough and a good paying guest and as a matter of fact, I feel a bit sorry for him. You stay out of harm's way there buddy.'

Conway sat for a minute or two thinking about Sally. They had been lovers and if Marvin the Marine had not come back on the scene there was a possibility their relationship could have developed into something more permanent.

* * *

Kim Anh rang just after lunch and said she had been given permission to take the rest of the week off from tomorrow and would see him at the usual time of 6.00 p.m.

'My boss wants me to bring my work up to date, I'm sorry I can't see you earlier.'

'No worries Kim there is something I have to attend to so I'll see you at six.'

With Kim not available till the evening it was a good opportunity to make enquiries about going to Phuoc Tuy, but first things first. He called the front desk and asked for the phone number of the Australian Embassy.

His call to the Embassy was put through to a youngish sounding Australian who informed him the best way to get to Phuoc Tuy and Long Tan was to join a "Battleground tour" run by one of the local travel agencies. Several visits to travel agencies in Pham Ngu Lao made him think twice and perhaps consider a different approach. The fees they wanted to charge were exorbitant with figures of $US250.00 being bandied around for a day trip which included lunch and "entrance" to the areas.

'That's a bit expensive,' he told the last agent, a skinny, smooth talking, cigar chomping Vietnamese. 'I think I'll find my own way thanks.'

'Ah, sorry but it is our government who decides the fees and conditions of these tours and in any case, you won't be able to find the place,' said the skinny one smugly, blowing a smoke ring and watching it curl into the air.

'Don't bet on it sport,' said Conway on his way out the door. He went to *Allez Boo* a restaurant on the corner of Pham Ngu Lao and De Tham Streets which catered for tourists and backpackers. He ordered coffee while he thought about his next move and his reasons for being back in a country which held so many traumatic memories.

This was his first time back in 'Nam since serving with the Australian Army during the war. A journey he hoped would bury the demons he still carried from that time – and there was another reason – more important to him than his own emotional issues; and that was to revisit a special Vietnamese friend in Phouc Tuy province where the Australian task force had been based. But that was more than twenty years ago; his friend would be quite old now and there was no guarantee he had survived the war; the chances of finding him alive Conway knew, were slim at best.

Kim's a bright girl, I bet she could and would show me the way, and I should ask her, but not just yet, don't want to wear out my welcome too soon. It was mid afternoon and there weren't many customers. Probably out touring somewhere he thought, as his Vietnamese coffee dripped slowly from the top of the small, cylindrical stainless steel filter into the bowl holding the sweet condensed milk.

Out in the street a few *xe om* (motor bike taxis) boys lazed on their bikes in the heat, the occasional long-haired grubby backpacker wandered past and the "hurtling hordes" of motorcycles continued their endless procession.

He opened his map which covered the area south from Ho Chi Minh City, as the whole metropolitan area was now called, to Vung Tau on the coast. In the middle was Phuoc Tuy renamed the province of Vung Tau/ Baria. He traced a line on route 51 down to Baria then north on route 766 past Long Tan, the site of the most celebrated battle fought by the Australians during the war, to a point which would bring him he surmised, within walking distance of Nui Dat.

Looking at the map brought back the memories. He closed his eyes and the images came back like some long forgotten newsreel. Images of battles fought and good mates lost. There was the terrible heat, the thunderous monsoon rains and the stinking mud. The welcome sound of the *whap whap whap* of the helicopters; the care of the wonderful Australian nurses at the hospital in Vung Tau and the thick, treacherous, and at times almost impenetrable jungle. The blood, the screams of wounded men reminding him of the line of the song, *I was only nineteen,* the anthem of the Australian soldier in Vietnam, which intoned:

When every step on two feet could be your last.

But there were good times too. He smiled remembering the nights carousing in the Grand Hotel in Vung Tau, where the legendary Kevin "Dasher" Wheatley is supposed to have swallowed a frog to win a bet from an American Marine. How could he forget the sudden rattle of small arms fire; and mortars; the gut wrenching fear – and the sound of men dying. He glanced back down at the map and those familiar names, *Long Tan, Nui Dat, Dat Do, Binh Ba, Xuyen Moc.* It all seemed like yesterday.

'Would you like another coffee sir?' asked a sweet-faced young Vietnamese waitress, startling him out of his reverie.

'Huh? Oh, no thanks. No more...how much?' He paid the bill and walked out into the afternoon sunshine trying to clear his head. He never spoke about those horrors of war to anyone. How could he? Only the vets would understand and even then it was hard to talk about it openly. These demons were a very private thing and he, like so many Australians who had served in Vietnam, had to cope with them in his own way.

* * *

The sun was burning and the humidity must have been up near 100%. His cotton shirt was wet, clinging to him like a second skin, but suddenly he stopped and shivered. Should I have come back here? He looked down at his hands and saw they were trembling. The memories, the fear, it was always there but always, he tried to suppress, keep it in the far recesses of his mind, never let it take over. But now back in Vietnam he knew he was losing this internal battle.

The truth was...he was scared to go back to Nui Dat. Even now just thinking about it tightened his gut. But he had to go. He had to pay his respects. He owed it to his mates.

'Snap out of it Conway,' he told himself. 'That's the past, you cannot and will not forget, but you have to deal with it.' He walked back to his hotel wishing Kim was there waiting for him, but she wasn't due for an hour or more. He wanted her company so much just then. He needed to sit and talk with that quiet, gentle, intelligent Vietnamese girl, to see her smile and hear her voice. Six o'clock could not come quickly enough.

* * *

As usual, right on time, she appeared in the hotel foyer carrying a parcel the size of an A4 sheet, wrapped in dark blue paper, tied with a light blue ribbon. Conway happened to be at the front desk chatting to one of the front desk staff, an older lady named Eliane who was telling him of her experiences during and after the war. He turned at the quiet, 'hello Steve,' and his first reaction was to rush over and give her a huge hug, but formality forbade that, so he simply smiled and glanced down at the package.

She smiled a little self-consciously. 'I hope you don't mind, I thought I would repay your kindness and bring you something, this is for you,' she said, quickly pushing the parcel into his hands.

He stood looking at it for a few moments not knowing what to say.

'Er, thank you,' he stammered. 'May I open it now?' the urge to kiss her now greater than ever. 'Of course,' she said shyly. 'I hope you like it.'

The last person to give him a gift was his late wife. He tried not to show it but he felt as excited as a child opening a birthday or Christmas present.

He slowly and carefully unwrapped it. Inside written in neat copperplate, was a small card which said, *To Steve, my Australian friend, from your Vietnamese friend, Kim Anh xxx.* His eyes lit up and he smiled in disbelief at a beautifully bound coffee table book of photos taken all over Vietnam.

There were quirky street scenes, stunning landscapes, village life and the best photos of all; the people of Vietnam themselves; all brilliantly photographed by a photographer, Kim said was Vietnam's finest. He shook his head as he leafed through the book. It was a stunning work… and expensive.

'I don't know what to say,' said Conway, trying to stifle his emotions. 'This is a very special book and I will treasure it always.' This girl had probably spent a large part of her wages on this gift and yet he knew there should be no mention of cost so he accepted it in the spirit with which it had been given. Before Kim could react he leant over and kissed her lightly on the cheek.

'Oh,' she said blushing, 'thank you…sir…Steve, I am glad you like it.'

'I love it,' he said, flipping through the book again. 'What magnificent photographs, I may not get the chance to see these places this time, but I am sure I will return to explore your beautiful country, thank you again for this.' He handed the book to the care of the front desk staff and turned to a beaming Kim. He took her hand and led her to the front door. 'Now Miss Kim Anh, let's go and have a look at more of this lovely city, but only after I have taken you for dinner, ok?'

'Ok Mr. Steve,' she laughed, 'where would you like to go tonight?'

'I thought a leisurely cyclo ride from here to say, the middle of District 1. I want to visit the Rex Hotel, it's quite famous for reasons I will tell you about later. Do you know it?'

'Of course,' replied Kim. 'It is a lovely hotel but too expensive for me,' she laughed. 'It is in a triangle with the Caravelle Hotel and the Continental Hotel, I am sure you have heard of them too.'

'Yes I certainly have,' he replied. 'The Caravelle was made famous for the same reasons as the Rex and the Continental was where Graham Greene lived and wrote, *The Quiet American*. I think we should have a look at them too if we have time.'

They caught a cyclo from just outside *Allez Boo* and after a bit of haggling by Kim, the driver agreed to the price and there followed a slow, smooth ride through the thick peak hour traffic. Hundreds of motorbikes flew past within an inch of the slow moving cyclo but somehow Conway felt completely safe. It was all in the lap of the Gods as far as he was concerned. Kim sat quietly beside him occasionally pointing out various landmarks as they glided around the huge roundabout at the top end of Le Loi Street.

Passenger seating in these three wheeled pedicabs is small and can be uncomfortable for two depending on the size of the occupants and Kim had to almost sit on top of Conway but he didn't mind, she felt soft and warm and sat there calmly, completely relaxed and obviously enjoying the ride. He certainly was.

They looped around between the impressive Opera House and the Caravelle Hotel then around and back past the Continental and came to a halt outside the Rex. Conway slipped the guy a few extra dong and they walked up several steps to be welcomed through the huge ornate glass doors by a smiling, young Vietnamese girl, looking cool and elegant in a mauve and white *ao dai*. An elevator took them to the fifth floor open-air garden bar/restaurant where they were taken to a table which had a wonderful view down the broad, flowered Boulevard of Nguyen Hue.

It was mutually agreed to have a drink and dinner at the Rex and explore the other hotels at leisure. A white-coated waiter arrived to take their order and stood patiently as they checked the menu with Kim ordering a Vietnamese dish of steamed fish, vegetable and rice while Conway decided to go Western and settled for a rump steak, salad and chips. He ordered a local beer 333 and Kim a coconut milk.

There were few other diners. The stars shone on a beautiful balmy evening with a slight breeze rustling the flower bedecked terrace and small coloured lights among the topiaries and shrubs created a romantic, tropical atmosphere.

Conway looked around. So this is where it all happened?

'You were too young to know about this place Kim,' Conway said, 'but during the war this place was where each night at 5pm they held, *The Five O'clock Follies*.'

She looked at him quizzically? '*The Five O'clock Follies*. What does it mean?' He explained that at five o'clock each night the American military high command would give a daily briefing on the progress of the war, usually very upbeat. However the journalists covering the conflict knew it to be a version where the allied successes were exaggerated, and the losses minimized, so much so that at times the truth became so twisted as to be laughable; thus these briefings came to be known by the cynics among the Fourth Estate as, *The Five O'clock Follies*.

She listened intently then looking Conway in the eye said softly, 'I have never heard of this, and besides, I come from North Vietnam.' There was an edge to her voice he'd never heard before. Conway hid his surprise at her change of tone and changed the subject.

Something tells me it's just as well I haven't mentioned my involvement in the war yet, he thought. She is too young to have been involved, but being from the north, may have had relatives who were killed. I'd better be careful, I do need to ask her about Phuoc Tuy, but I don't want to spoil the evening so I'll leave it till later.

Kim had become rather quiet and although he changed the subject to a lighter note and told her again how much he liked her city, her contribution to the conversation was monosyllabic. She seemed uninterested and just nibbled at her food.

Conway became uneasy and put her change of mood down to a long day at work, but still, the mention of the war had touched a nerve. He would let it drop for now, but it was obvious there was much more to Kim Anh than he realized, and whatever had changed her, he had to find out… and fast.

4

Back in his hotel Conway showered and lay awake for hours thinking about the extraordinary change in Kim Anh at the Rex Hotel. They had left after dinner, one that he didn't particularly enjoy given her mood, and walked the short distance to the Caravelle Hotel.

The Caravelle's *Saigon Saigon* bar on the ninth floor offered spectacular views of the brightly lit city but her moody silence spoilt the atmosphere between them and he was glad to leave after one drink.

Not to be deterred, he kept his chat light-hearted and on his suggestion, she reluctantly, agreed to cross the square to the venerable and stylish Continental Hotel, famous for once being the residence of author Graham Greene. Conway felt he had gone back in time as they wandered around a lobby which bespoke a more genteel era. He gazed in fascination at the various sepia photos on the wall of the old pre World War II days and more recently during the Vietnam War or as the Vietnamese called it, "The American War".

There were faded copies of news stories mainly about the history of the hotel which made interesting reading for Conway, but not for Kim Anh who seemed preoccupied with her own thoughts.

On the spur of the moment he went to the front desk and asked if it was possible to see the room where Greene had lived and where in 1955 he had written *The Quiet American*.

His request was granted with a smile from the pretty desk clerk. She gestured to a footman who took them to room 214 on the second floor. It was a corner room overlooking Lamson Square and the Caravelle opposite, and had a wonderful view along Dong Khoi Street with its classy restaurants and chic boutiques.

As Conway stood looking down from the balcony of the celebrated author's old room he wondered what Greene would make of his beloved Saigon today. In Greene's time, Dong Khoi Street was known as Rue Catinat and the view then would have been quite different.

The famous author probably stood and watched pith-helmeted men in horse-drawn carriages leisurely ferrying people and merchandise down to the docks of Saigon Port. French soldiers on leave strolling with beautiful *ao dai*-clad Vietnamese women along the tamarind tree-lined avenue ignoring the cries of street hawkers, beggars, orphans and cyclo drivers.

Today, he would see a never-ending stream of *Honda Dreams* speeding down Dong Khoi ridden by sporty, well-dressed young Vietnamese men carrying beautiful young women in *ao dais*, who in this new "enlightened" Vietnam, rode with their arms around their beaus in a bold show of affection; something the authorities in the fairly recent past would have frowned upon.

There is no doubt it would leave The Great Man a little perplexed, but he would have approved of the $US3 million dollar makeover the *"The Grand Dame of Saigon"* had received. A newspaper clipping proudly declared how the restoration had been done without any foreign investment and had, *importantly maintained the beautiful French Colonial style of the original building which has left many of our guests feeling they have gone back in time "temps perdu", as the French say.*

They sat under the stars in the Continental's Orchid Garden lounge, he sipping a cold beer wondering how to cheer her up and bring her out of this mood; she toying with her mineral water continuing to say nothing. In exasperation he had leaned over and said,

'Kim dear, what's the matter? Have I said something to offend you? Please tell me.'

But she just shook her head and remained silent. They returned to his hotel by taxi and neither spoke a word during the journey until they alighted outside the front. He helped her from the back seat and said "goodnight". She said something inaudible, mounted her bike and left him standing on the sidewalk shaking his head.

He could only conclude that his remarks about the war had triggered her negative mood. She had changed so quickly from a sweet, warm person to a sullen, unpleasant creature he hardly recognized. Something traumatic had happened to her...or her family, of that he was sure. But how could he get her to speak about it? The last thing he wanted to do was to open a can of worms and revive old and painful memories.

It was past midnight when his telephone rang. He jerked upright and reached over to pick it up to stop the jangling which seemed twice as loud at that time of night.

A small, quiet, familiar voice said, 'h...hello...is that you...Steve, sir?'

What now? He waited a few seconds before answering.

'Yes Kim, what on earth are you doing ringing me at this time of night? Are you ok?' he asked with more concern than anger.

There was a long pause and a sniffle. Had she been crying? Finally she began to speak again...very softly. 'I am so sorry for my behaviour tonight, you must think I am a terrible girl....' her voice trailed off.

'No, no,' he said soothingly, 'there was obviously something on your mind. I was just worried I had said something which offended you. I think you are a lovely girl and I wouldn't knowingly say anything to hurt you. If you want to talk about it, I'm here to listen.'

'You are such a nice, kind man,' she said so quietly, he found it hard to hear her. Then heartened by his friendly tone, she continued in a stronger voice.

'I must apologise for the way I acted. It is not the Vietnamese way. We are a polite, friendly people, and I was very impolite. I am ashamed of myself,' then again lowering her tone, 'will you forgive me please?'

'Oh Kim, there is no need to apologise,' replied Conway gallantly. He did not press her about the reason for her change in mood, but thanked her for calling and said he looked forward to seeing her in the morning. Her relief was palpable as she hung up promising to call early so they could have a full day together. He had invited her for breakfast but she declined, saying she had a few things to do at home before coming to see him.

He replaced the receiver and slumped back on his pillow. She hadn't told him what caused her sudden change of attitude, but as far as he was concerned, it was probably just a problem at work or at home that had been bothering her and was obviously nothing (he hoped) to do with him. He reminded himself she was Vietnamese and came from a culture very different from his own. Tolerance and understanding was what was needed. God knows what the poor girl had suffered in the past. Now more relaxed, sleep came quickly.

* * *

At breakfast he started to think about his journey to Nui Dat and wondered if his friend Mr Loc was still living in the village on the perimeter of the Australian Task Force base. For some reason Mr Loc had taken a liking to the young Australian soldier and would often wave to Conway as he passed on patrol.

One day as his platoon was skirting the village, Mr. Loc was tending his small garden. Conway had walked over with his hand outstretched. The old Vietnamese took it with a broad toothless smile. Conway reached into his pack and produced a packet of cigarettes and handed them to him. Mr Loc looked at them for a moment then back up at Conway. He smiled and put them in the pocket of his faded white shirt. As Conway turned to leave, Mr Loc said, '*Uc da loi la so mot....*

His Vietnamese was limited to say the least but he knew what Mr Loc was saying, "*Australians number one*". For all Steve knew, Mr Loc could have been a Viet Cong sympathizer. The fact that he had survived so long being relatively close to the Australian Base was food for thought, but without any evidence, Conway treated him with respect and as a friend.

Several weeks later as he passed by Mr Loc's house the Vietnamese called out and gestured for him to come over. Beside him stood a fresh-faced young girl of around eight years old, slim, with glossy dark hair falling below her shoulders. Even at this tender age, her golden skin, huge almond eyes, high cheek bones and full lips promised great beauty within a few years.

Turning to her, the old man said a few words in Vietnamese then, the usually smiling Mr Loc looked back at Conway with an expression that was a mixture of sadness and despair.

The girl nodded and looking up at the Australian said in surprisingly good English.

'Sir, my grandfather wishes to tell you, he is going away. It is too dangerous here for him, he is going to Chau Doc near the border with Cambodia and if he survives the war, he will come back to his house. He wants to tell you, he thinks Australian soldiers are good men who have treated his people with respect and kindness and he thanks you.'

She looked down shyly and took her grandfather's hand. Conway thanked her and asked her to tell the old man he wished him a safe journey. He then shook Mr Loc's hand, and told the girl that he would return again that night.

On dusk, as Conway and his men moved out on patrol he returned to the house and presented the old man him with a carton of *Lucky Strike* cigarettes he'd bought from the American PX in Bien Hoa the previous week and a box of chocolates for the little girl whose name she said, was Mai.

Mr Loc kept looking at the cigarettes, then reached up and took Conway's hand in a surprisingly firm grip. There were tears in his eyes. He said something in rapid Vietnamese then hugged the Australian. Little Mai smiled and said in her quiet, sweet voice, 'My grandfather very sad, he will miss you and hope he can see you again one day.'

The tough, battle-hardened soldier was touched much more than he let on. He knelt down on one knee and drew the little girl to him.

'Mai, tell your grandfather that one day this war will be over and I will come back to see him. Will you do that?'

Mai threw her arms around him and began to cry. 'Oh yes I will! I will!...I hope you come back to us sir, please come back to us,' she sobbed. Conway held her tight. 'One day I will come back,' he said softly.

'Nice old man Sarge, what's with him and the little girl?' asked his corporal.

'Just saying goodbye,' grunted Conway giving a hand signal for silence as they moved quietly into the jungle dark.

* * *

Back in his room after breakfast Conway pored over the map again. Maybe I might be better off going straight to Vung Tau and heading back up to Nui Dat from there, stop at the Long Tan Cross, pay my respects then call at the old Grand Hotel and have a beer.

He was smiling to himself thinking about old times and good mates at the Grand when his phone rang with a message from the front desk.

'Miss Kim Anh is here sir.'

She was sitting in a lounge chair by the window when he came down and rose, greeting him with a nervous smile.

'Hi Kim, how's the best and most beautiful guide in Saigon this morning?' smiled Conway, immediately trying to put her at ease. She sighed with relief at his words and their tone.

'I am very fine this morning...thank you,' she said. Her face glowed, and to his surprise (and secret delight) reached for his right hand with both of hers and gave it a gentle squeeze.

It was the old Kim; gone was the unhappy, silent, morose girl of the previous night. He looked down into those large, beautifully shaped, now sparkling brown eyes. It was hard to tell who was the most relieved.

Saigon blessed them with a cloudless, breezy morning as they whizzed down past the flower gardens of Le Loi Street. Kim's sure and steady, small brown hands skillfully guided them through the traffic with Conway on the pillion, now quite unconcerned about the blaring noisy tumult around him.

Except for an ear-shattering blast from an 18 wheeler driven by what looked like a skinny kid of fourteen, his nerves remained steady. In fact, he was beginning to enjoy the experience and wondered what his staff at the Down Under would make of it if they could see him now.

It was Kim's "Ho Chi Minh City Mystery Tour", a city rich in history with much to offer the tourist. For starters there was the lavish architecture of elegant commercial and government buildings, wide boulevards and grand plazas, courtesy of the French. They passed classy boutiques, beautiful parklands and botanical gardens ablaze with flowers flourishing beneath towering tamarind trees where couples sat holding hands, gazing into each other's eyes in the unspoken words of love.

They visited the wonderful French-built General Post Office and the heart-wrenching "War Remnants Museum" a testimony to man's inhumanity to man. The Jade Pagoda, then the huge Binh Tay market in Cholon. 'Unbelievable!' he gasped, at the size of the place and the extraordinary variety of goods on sale.

They finished with a tour of a lacquerware factory watching artisans fashion their exquisite wares, all sold at affordable prices.

At lunch she took him to a small, cosy French restaurant in District 3 where they were fussed over by mine host, Jean-Pierre. Conway decided on a tomato salad with goat's cheese to be followed by seared spring lamb chops, coffee and cheese. Kim chose a main course of grilled chicken with rosemary. While Conway sipped a chilled white wine from Bordeaux, Kim settled for a tall glass of soda with lime juice.

'Love this intimate French atmosphere,' smiled Conway, looking at pen and ink washes on the walls of Parisian scenes and a brass bust of Napoleon just inside the front door. 'How did you find this place?'

'My boss took me here just before Tet, our Vietnamese new year festival and I always wanted to come back but could never afford it,' she giggled.

'Well it was a terrific choice, and I'm glad we came. What shall we do this afternoon my little guide?'

'I would like to show you where I work at Waterworld then, if you wish, I will take you to a restaurant which is very famous,' she said eagerly. 'It is called Nha La and has the reputation of being the best duck restaurant in Ho Chi Minh City and it is also very close to where I live and...' she paused as if not really wanting to say what she had on her mind, 'there is something else.'

'Go on,' he urged.

'Would you like to come to see my house and meet my family?'

Conway knew enough about Vietnamese culture to know this was an honour being bestowed upon him.

'I would love to, thank you very much.'

Kim beamed and attacked her chicken with relish. She had obviously been worried about asking Conway to her home thinking he might reject her after last night's episode, and now with that weight lifted from her small shoulders, her appetite returned with a vengeance.

Conway smiled watching her eat then when she finished, raised his glass.

'I give a toast to Vietnam and to you dear Kim!'

She smiled and bowed graciously. 'I am honoured to be with you Sir Steve and the pleasure is mine,' she replied, elegantly lifting her own glass, 'to Australia and to Mr Steve Conway, the nicest man I have ever known.'

It was Conway's turn to bow and he raised his glass again, 'to the most beautiful guide in Saigon,' he grinned. She blushed prettily. 'Oh thank you, I am so happy now.'

'There is something that has surprised me about this city Kim,' said Conway, with a broad smile.

'Oh, what is that?'

'I understood in this rather strict Communist society, public petting was frowned upon but since I've been here I have seen many young couples kissing and fondling each other on park benches. Admittedly,' he went on, 'it has been in the evening but it's much more overt than even in Australia, so what's going on?'

'Times have changed,' she smiled. 'Does it bother you?'

'No of course not, it's just not what I expected.'

'Since *Doi Moi*, which you would call "renovation", this country has loosened up in many ways and has now begun to allow such things. The authorities don't really like it, but,' she paused to take a sip of her soda, 'so long as they do not try to have open sex, a blind eye is turned.'

'Seems like they might be a bit more enlightened here than where I come from. If fifty couples sat cuddling in a park in Australia there would be headlines in the local papers, it would be all over television, you wouldn't believe the commotion it would cause.'

'I'm glad that we can teach you something. Personally I would not do it I am too shy… but then…I have never been in love…'

They stared at each other for a long moment.

'Let's go to Waterworld Miss Kim Anh.'

They took a shuttle bus from opposite the Ben Thanh market and forty-five minutes later arrived at the huge Waterworld complex, a joint Vietnamese/Australian venture in the Thu Duc district on the northern rim of Ho Chi Minh City beside the banks of the Saigon River.

Waterworld was a revelation to Conway. It resembled a huge oasis in a hot and sprawling city. It was a weekend and crowded with families and their screaming, laughing children running in and out of the pools, sliding down the water slides and being happily dunked in the large wave pool.

Everyone was having so much fun Conway wished he'd brought his swimming togs so he could join them. Kim shrieked with laughter and grabbed hold of him as a little boy splashed her when she walked too close to a pool chock full of kids. They strolled along well maintained paths shaded by overhanging tamarind trees and shrubs, crossing ornate wooden bridges placed throughout the park to allow visitors to move from one attraction to another.

As they passed by a number of low set buildings she stopped.

'This is the admin block where I work.' Taking his hand she led him across to a window. Peering in he could see a small, modern, open-plan office with glass partitions, a number of computer workstations, filing cabinets and desks piled with accounting documents and files.

She pointed to a workstation near a drink fountain and proudly declared, 'that's my desk,' she said, squeezing his hand. He looked down at her, returning the squeeze.

Leaving the admin block they walked over to a small restaurant by the river and sat sipping soft drinks and chatting to the occasional staff member who upon recognizing Kim, came over to say 'hello'. She seemed pleased to introduce her "foreign guest". Conway noticed knowing smiles on the lips of the staff as they returned to their duties. It was obvious they saw Conway as more than her "guest".

As evening drew nigh she suggested a taxi to the duck restaurant in Thanh Da for dinner then home to meet her family.

The restaurant was a large, unpretentious, simple, double-story place full of diners on the ground floor so they took a table upstairs in the open air. Thanh Da is a relatively poor suburb of Ho Chi Minh City and the place was pretty basic with square metal tables set with plastic containers of chopsticks and spoons.

They sipped mineral water while waiting for their meals which as usual, Kim ordered in her polite Vietnamese way. Although the place was packed with early evening diners, two large bowls of steaming duck soup meals came promptly. She looked on with a slight frown as Conway took his first sip. It was delicious. She smiled with relief as he gave her the thumbs up.

'Never tasted better duck soup,' he said sincerely. 'No wonder this place has such a good reputation.' Much to her delight, he ordered a second helping. They followed with a small plate each of fruit salad and finished with a cup of Vietnamese coffee. It was dark by the time they left to take the short journey to Kim's home.

She shared a small, two-bedroom apartment in a large run-down tower block with her older sister Ngoc, brother-in- law Tran and their two small children. Nugyen, a shy five year old boy and a cute little girl of three named Trinh. They gave Conway a warm, if diffident welcome and the children looked up at him with awe. They had never laid eyes on a white man before and little Trinh kept giggling and peeking at Conway from behind her mother's skirt.

Kim, the only English speaker, interpreted for Conway and told her family how happy he was to meet them and they responded with warm smiles. Conway suggested a photo and they posed for a family group among much giggling from little Trinh and shy smiles from Nguyen.

Ngoc insisted on making green tea for Conway and ushered him to their small kitchen table. While he drank his tea the rest of the family stood or sat opposite, saying nothing, just gazing fixedly as he took each sip. Conway found it hard to keep a straight face and not spill his tea. *Uc da loi* was a curiosity indeed.

Kim stood to one side smiling at this little pantomime. When he had finished, she rescued him by suggesting they go for a walk around Thanh Da. Conway thanked her family and followed Kim downstairs into the warm night air.

5

Thanh Da at night teemed with life. A few yards from Kim's apartment they turned left into a street which she said would lead down to the Saigon River. There they could sit and chat undisturbed. The weak overhead street lights cast shadows on families out and about after their evening meal.

Groups of women holding babies stood chatting outside a small playground watching their children chase each other yelling and shouting happily. Other kids screamed and laughed as they flew down a slippery slide on their backsides and bellies.

They watched this joyful scene for a few minutes before moving on past a busy Night market. Although Thanh Da is one of the poorer areas of Ho Chi Minh City, to Conway's eyes it represented a wonderful microcosm of Vietnamese life.

Men sat in small groups on plastic stools chatting, some drinking coffee, others, green tea or beer. Smiling old gap-toothed women implored them to buy bunches of flowers wrapped in paper cones; grizzled war veterans ('they fought for the South,' said Kim) hunched over portable ice boxes offered cold soft drinks while others sat impassively in front of cardboard boxes of cigarettes and watches: middle aged matrons invited them to try on racks of second-hand clothing; others tempted them with sticky rice cakes. The tantalizing aromas of stir-fried beef, pork and noodles wafted through the night air from several small, bubbling braziers tempting their taste buds while several women energetically turned and stirred the steaming ingredients.

'It's a pity we've had dinner,' laughed Conway, 'that food looks and smells delicious.'

'Next time dear, I will treat you,' she said taking his hand. He smiled to himself at her endearment. They strolled on past colourful pyramids of fruit and vegetables in a variety as good as he had seen anywhere. Oranges, apples, limes, strawberries, dragon fruit, grapes, rambutan and durian were plentiful, together with an equally tempting array of healthy looking tomatoes, cabbages, lettuce, carrots and potatoes, most of which Kim told him, came from Dalat in the central highlands of Vietnam.

Skinny young men covered in grease crouched over motor cycles in various states of repair, while pretty young girls in pairs, held hands as they walked laughing and chatting to each other, pretending to ignore the hopeful smiles and comments of eager young paramours. All the while, motorbikes, scooters, cars and three-wheeler vehicles carrying all manner of goods sped back and forth in a noisy, never-ending procession.

Conway looked on all this with pleasure. This was life! The kind of community interaction lost in affluent Western countries where at night in suburbia, citizens remain isolated within their modern, remote castles, watching television or glued to computer screens, often too frightened to venture out onto increasingly violent streets.

They came to the river where yet another vendor was selling soft drinks. He bought a couple and Kim led him to plastic chairs lined up along the river wall, placed there by the People's Committee for the locals to chat (and at night for young couples to cuddle) and mingle.

They sat beneath a full moon watching the river traffic of heavily laden barges, sampans and a variety of small craft, with phosphorescent wakes gleaming in the moonlight, sipping their drinks and talking of many things; of life, love, Vietnam… and its future.

She spoke of her early life growing up in a small village outside Hanoi. It was a grim and dark time. The war with America and its allies had not long finished, and the economy of North Vietnam was in ruins. Like everyone else, her family was unimaginably poor.

There was no running water or electricity. Crops were ruined, food was scarce. It was a desperate daily struggle for her family of six children to survive. Each day her parents would join long queues to collect what was little more than a hand full of rice. It was beyond subsistence and many starved. This was victory?

At age five she would accompany her father to pick peanuts. They sold the edible peanuts to the market for next to nothing and ate the rest.

'Many we could not eat because the soil was poisoned from what had been dropped from the air during the war,' she said, unable to hide the bitterness in her voice; something that did not escape Conway's notice.

Beneath her quiet exterior lurked another Kim Anh; a different Kim Anh whom she tried to suppress, but unable to at times when the war was mentioned. Conway looked at her thoughtfully but held his peace and let her continue.

Illness and starvation eventually claimed her youngest sister and further tragedy struck when her father was electrocuted putting up coloured lights for a party to celebrate her tenth birthday.

Somehow, her mother kept the family together by doing menial housekeeping jobs and selling hand-made clothes in the market. Kim, stubborn, bright and determined to escape this poverty, studied English and her other high school subjects diligently in the hope it would gain her entry to a tertiary institution.

Her efforts were rewarded when she was awarded a scholarship to one of Hanoi's leading universities where she graduated with honours in commerce and linguistics. Saigon was beginning to boom with foreign investment and the doors were beginning to open on a free market economy. That's where the good jobs and big salaries were on offer and that's where Kim Anh headed to achieve her goal of finding a better life.

Her eldest sister Ngoc had already moved to Saigon some years before and invited Kim to join her family in their small apartment in Thanh Da.

Kim's commercial knowledge, secretarial skills and good English quickly found her employment but most jobs were boring and poorly paid until her current position as secretary to the Sales Manager of Waterworld. The salary was comparatively high; she enjoyed the work and her colleagues. Life at last was beginning to look a whole lot brighter.

She spoke of the pain of loneliness and a desire for love and although many of her friends were married, she had seen much unhappiness and despair in marriage where economics and not love, had too often been the reason for the union.

'But what about boyfriends?' he asked. 'You are a very attractive girl, surely there have been…'

'There is one, but I don't really like him. He's very jealous. He wants to be my boyfriend. I work with him but he gets mad if he sees me talking to other guys. We went to Vung Tau once for the day, on a company picnic and he sat on a rock on the beach and sulked because I played on the beach with my colleagues and didn't pay any attention to him.'

'He sounds like a boy, not a man.'

'Yes, and I will *only* marry a man I truly love and definitely not for money,' she said gazing out at the moonlit river. Conway was impressed by her quiet sincerity. This was a true Vietnamese girl; a woman of dignity, intelligence and high morals. Beside the river under the stars that night, despite some tiny misgivings, he could feel the bond between them growing. He looked at her sitting there, the moonlight illuminating partly the planes of her strong face. She looked so peaceful. No one would know, looking at this young woman, the terrible privations she had suffered in her childhood and teen years.

How could we have waged war on these gentle people? He reached over and touched her hand. She turned to him and smiled, her small white teeth gleaming in the darkness. Then to his mild surprise, she turned away as if embarrassed.

Kim Anh was essentially a private person and had opened up to him speaking of events in her past she had never before mentioned to anyone.

A past she was desperately trying to forget.

They arrived back at his hotel later than usual but unlike the previous night, she was in no hurry to leave and smiled when he held her hand as they stood talking on the front steps of the hotel.

'I loved being with you today,' she said quietly. Again, he had an overwhelming desire to kiss her, but resisted the urge and simply thanked her for 'such an enjoyable day and evening'.

He was watching a movie on television when his phone rang. He looked at his watch, nearly midnight. Who could this be? Probably someone phoning the wrong room?

It was her.

She told him again how much she enjoyed the day and his company. He smiled to himself. Perhaps this growing bond *is* a two-way thing?

It must have been about 6.00 am when she phoned again apologizing profusely, saying her sister had asked her to visit a relative in Bien Hoa. They would be there all day and wouldn't be able to see him until the evening.

This suited Conway. He wanted to go to Nui Dat and Long Tan and had decided not to say anything to her, but wasn't sure how to explain his absence. He was still a bit wary of her attitude to the war and was loath to mention his part in it.

'Ok, that's fine, I'm sure I can find things to see and do in your fine city, see you tonight.' They agreed to meet at his hotel at 7.30 pm which Conway believed would allow him to visit his old war zone and be back in plenty of time.

He took his map of the area downstairs to the front desk and asked to speak to Michael the bright, 20-something manager. He told Michael briefly what he had in mind and spread his map out on a table in a small ante room off the foyer. He pointed out the area he wanted to visit and asked the young manager if he knew anyone who could take him.

Michael pored over the map for a minute, frowned, scratched his head and asked Conway to wait while he made a phone call. Ten minutes later he returned, all smiles.

'I have a friend who can take you.'

'Can he take me today? I'd like to go this morning if possible.'

'He is still on the phone sir, just wait for a minute and I will ask him.'

Conway waited impatiently until Michael returned still smiling, 'yes, he can take you this morning Mr Steve.'

Half an hour later a Mr Tam arrived to take Conway to Nui Dat. He was resplendent in a rumpled light grey suit, white shirt, and wide, garish tie (he'd been told the passenger was a foreigner and wanted to make a good impression; it helped get him healthy tips). A slightly built man in his fifties Mr Tam's English was about as good as Conway's Vietnamese. As a friend of Michael, he was prepared to offer a "very special price" which Conway accepted without bothering to haggle, and with map and a bottle of water in hand followed Mr Tam to his Toyota sedan; a chariot which like his suit, had seen better days.

The bodywork was dinted front, back and sides. It didn't engender much confidence in Mr. Tam's driving skills. The paintwork once bright red was now dull and worn through to bare metal in places. Adding to the overall dismal picture were the windows and the tyres. Only one window was operational and that was on the driver's side. Of the four tyres only one showed any semblance of a tread. Although Phuoc Tuy was a relatively short drive south-east of Saigon, Conway looked dubiously at his transportation and wondered if it would last the distance to Nui Dat and back. Or worse still, if he would even get there. The odds seemed against it.

His fears were compounded when they set off with a crash of gears and a backfire which nearly blew the backside out of the old bomb, bringing a sheepish grin from Mr Tam. Conway sighed, it was going to be a long journey to Nui Dat and back…a return by 7.30 pm seemed wishful thinking.

6

They rattled off across the centre of Saigon, through the teeming residential and traffic-infested Binh Thanh district and headed north east passing Thanh Da before turning right from the road to Bien Hoa, and heading south on highway 51 toward Baria the provincial capital; from there he would begin his search for the old Australian base at Nui Dat and the Long Tan Cross.

The sprawling, dilapidated residential areas and factories finally gave way to green paddy fields and vegetation. A few miles from Baria they came upon a layby where a number of taxis and *xe om* stood waiting for passengers. Tam pulled up, jumped out and engaged a couple of the taxi drivers in animated conversation, asking directions to Nui Dat and Long Tan.

He brought two of them over and laid Conway's map across the bonnet of his vehicle. The three of them pored over it with much shaking of heads and pointing. A *ex om* tried to get in on the act but slunk off back to his battered motor scooter after copping a torrent of abuse.

Finally, the little Vietnamese nodded his head, shook hands with the smiling taxi drivers and excitedly signaled to a bemused Conway that they were to continue their journey.

'You know where to go?' asked his doubtful passenger.

'Yes sir, yes sir,' said Tam, confidently, jumping in behind the wheel, then, with the usual crash and grinding of gears, they were off again.

On the outskirts of Baria they turned left and headed along a sealed bitumen road which ended after a couple of miles. From there on they bumped, bounced and fishtailed along muddy, red, furrowed tracks, slippery from recent monsoon rain; exactly the time of year when the battle of Long Tan had been fought.

Today, the sky was cerulean and cloudless and the countryside was straight from a Vietnamese postcard with emerald green paddies on one side and rubber plantations on the other. Occasionally a farmer up to his knees in a rice paddy sloshed along behind his buffalo while small children waved gaily as they passed.

Conway looked at this scene, now so peaceful. But the memories were returning, more vividly than ever. He felt the tension mounting. His gut began to tighten and his throat became dry. His hands began to tremble involuntarily. The images, the memories, the nightmares that woke him in a lather of sweat; it was all coming back!

After a few wrong turns they finally arrived at Nui Dat. Taking a deep breath he opened the car door but did not alight. He sat for a couple of minutes gathering his thoughts before easing himself out. Not surprisingly, there was nothing left of the old task force base. It was hot, bloody hot; just as it was during those far off days. The sweat rolled down his cheeks and the middle of his back as he walked slowly across what was now, just a deserted, uninviting landscape.

He stood and shook his head slowly as he took in the scene. Here and there lay patches of broken concrete slabs, once walkways and the base of operational buildings and living quarters. The remains of the old helicopter pad was still visible, but not much else. A few trees on scrubby, dried grassland were all that remained of what was the home of a proud Australian fighting force.

Conway could hear the voices of his men laughing and ribbing each other as they returned from an operation. Humour that couldn't disguise the relief of knowing they'd made it back in one piece...again. But underlying the bravado were the words unsaid about those who hadn't returned...Mick, Dave, "Thommo", Les; too many of them were his close mates.

He walked all over the former area of the base and across to Luscombe airfield which had served them so well. Now it lay barren and neglected. He stayed for many minutes thinking, remembering.

Looking at this flat, quiet emptiness it was hard to imagine the frantic military activity that took place there. It seemed like only yesterday he would wait with his fellow soldiers on Luscombe, tense, armed and ready to be airlifted by Iroquois helicopters to an operation somewhere out beyond the wire.

There were always the butterflies. Brave? Bullshit! They were all scared but it made them careful; made them concentrate on the job in hand; made them bloody good soldiers. In his mind and no doubt those of the others, was always the ever present thought. Will I make it back this time?

Barely able to keep his emotions under control, he said a quick prayer and returned to Tam, directing him to backtrack a little further south toward Long Tan which they'd passed on the way. But before Long Tan, he had another call to make.

Just over a mile down the road he asked the little man to stop.

'Wait here, I won't be long,' he said, setting off across flat country, skirting paddy fields and through knee high grass toward a collection of simple dwellings roughly 200 yards away in front of the tree line; the village of Mr Loc.

As he approached, a couple of dogs began to bark a warning. Small groups of men sat around outside a leaning, tin-roofed shanty serving as a simple eatery. One group sat in a circle squatting on small plastic stools some drinking coffee others eating bowls of noodles. Another two were engaged in what looked like serious discussion, while a third smoked and watched a couple playing checkers. As one, they turned and stared at the approaching foreigner. He had to be either Russian or American. Neither was particularly welcome: White men usually brought trouble.

A few children, braver or perhaps more intrigued than the adults, ran to Conway, looked up at him, one even pulled at his trousers then giggled and scuttled away. Visitors were rare and the word was quickly passed that a stranger had arrived, a foreigner. From the houses a few more men and women came to look.

Conway approached with what he hoped was a winning smile. As one they stopped eating and drinking and stared unblinking in his direction. Their expressions indicated neither fear nor favour. He directed a question to a scholarly looking middle-aged man wearing wire-rimmed glasses. Conway remembered a phrase in Vietnamese he had found in his guidebook. One he knew would come in very handy, especially when traveling in the countryside where English was rarely spoken.

"Co ai o day biet noi tieng Anh khong?" 'Does anyone here speak English?'

The scholar's mouth dropped open upon hearing his language, albeit poorly, coming from the mouth of this foreigner, then shook his head sheepishly in unison with the others. Conway scratched his head trying to figure out his next move. The answer it seemed was to return to the vehicle and bring back Mr Tam. He was about to leave when a soft female voice said.

'I speak English sir. Can I help you?'

Conway turned to see a slim young woman he guessed late twenties, in a simple white house dress. She somehow looked familiar. He took in the high cheek bones, the beautiful almond eyes, full lips and was about to say something when the young woman's eyes widened and her mouth fell open in surprise. 'Mr Steve! Mr Steve!' she cried, and to the amazement of the onlookers threw her arms around him. He held her back at arm's length then pulled her close again.

'Hey Mai, you are so beautiful, I didn't recognize you,' he said, looking in wonder at this lovely, now grown up woman. 'Is Mr. Loc still alive, is he here?' asked Conway fearing the worst.

'Yes! Yes! He is here! He is here! He is blind now but when he knows you are here it will make him so very happy!' She stepped back to look at Conway, shaking her head in disbelief, laughing and crying at the same time.

'Oh Mr. Steve, Mr. Steve, I never thought you would come back, I thought you had forgotten us,' she said through her tears. 'I cannot tell you how happy I am to see you, please you must come with me now!' Taking his hand, half walking, half running, she pulled him across to a small, thatched-roof dwelling, little more than a shack…the house of Mr Loc.

It was dark inside the little hut and coming from the bright sunshine outside, it was at first difficult to see. As Conway's eyes became accustomed to the gloom, he saw in the corner lying on a simple bamboo mattress, a very old, now very frail Mr Loc, looking up with unseeing eyes. His cheeks were sunken, the skin a sickly yellow and tight over high cheekbones, his body skeletal. My Loc was dying.

'Grandfather,' said Mai softly, 'I have very, very, good news, it is Mr Steve, Mr Steve, *uc da loi*, come to see you!'

Mr Loc's head jerked upwards at her words and he tried to rise from his bed but the effort was too much. He gave a deep, racking cough and fell back onto his cot. Steve sat down beside the old man and took his hand. 'It is me Mr Loc, your Australian friend, I told you I would come back one day. I am so glad to see you my dear Vietnamese friend?' Mai translated and Mr Loc gripped Conway's hand, his wizened old face breaking into that toothless smile Conway remembered so well. The old man struggled for breath as he spoke a few halting words which Mai translated.

'He can't believe it's you Mr Steve,' whispered Mai, 'you have made him so happy. He said he can go to meet his ancestors now.'

'Tell him I am also very happy to see him Mai but I don't want him to meet his ancestors just yet,' grinned Conway, continuing to hold the old man's hand. 'You must tell me what has happened to both of you since I have been away.'

She questioned Mr. Loc and translated his answers into English. It appeared that Mr Loc had made it to Chau Doc safely and stayed there for two years after the war had ended, eventually returning to his old home to see out the rest of his days. He had been lucky and escaped the re-education camps the Communists had set up in the area for anyone thought to be a friend of the Americans or the previous regime.

Mai whose parents had both been killed during the war remained in his home during his absence and had been caring for the old man since his return.

Conway stayed by his old friend's bedside for well over an hour then looked at his watch. He had to leave if he was to visit Long Tan and return to Saigon in time to meet Kim Anh.

Reluctantly he said his goodbyes but just as he left the little room he noticed a faded black and white photo on a small dresser in the corner. It was of a young man, no more than eighteen. It was the kind of photo you would see in the home of many Vietnamese but there was something about this photo that made Conway look twice.

It was a photo he did not expect to see in the home of Mr Loc and he wished he hadn't. It was of an unsmiling young man dressed in loose fitting black pyjamas holding an AK47; the common outfit and weapon of the National Liberation Front. Conway suddenly felt sick. He turned to Mai with a stony face.

'Who is this?'

Mai's radiant smile vanished when she saw his expression and heard the tone of his voice. She stood there for a moment not knowing what to do or say then motioned to him to come outside. He followed her to a roughly hewn bench beside a small stream out of earshot of Mr Loc's house.

'The person in that photo was my brother, Son.'

'VC?' asked Conway abruptly.

Mai lowered her head and replied in almost a whisper.

'Yes.'

Conway looked down at her. His reaction had been one of shock. But then why should he have been so surprised? This was VC country in those days and this woman, then a young girl, was an innocent victim. Like millions of Vietnamese, she'd lost her whole family...her home... everything. He could not and should not, hold any anger or bitterness toward her. In fact in his view now, it should be the other way around.

'The war is over now Mai, but tell me all about him, where is he now?' Conway's voice softened taking her hand, drawing her down beside him on the bench.

'He's dead.'

She looked at him, her eyes brimming with tears.

'He was killed in the battle with the Australians at Long Tan. He was only nineteen,' she said quietly.

There was a long silence. If only she knew what she had just said, thought Conway. All he could think of to say was, 'I was not in that battle Mai. I was in hospital in Vung Tau,' as if this was some kind of excuse for what had happened. He felt stupid as soon as he said it.

'It doesn't matter now, war is war,' she said dully. 'He was a very gentle boy but he wanted our country to be free of "foreign invaders" as he called them. I know that many of your young soldiers were forced by your government to come here. I wish none of you had come, it only brought us heartbreak and misery,' she said, looking away.

'And Son was the same,' she continued, her breasts heaving with emotion, 'he didn't really want to fight but he had no choice! All our young men around here were either taken into the Army or by the National Liberation Front whom you call the VC. Most were simple farm boys, they knew nothing of politics! They just wanted to work in the fields, find a nice girl, marry and have children. So many of them died...and for what?' she said bitterly.

He put his arms around her. 'We asked the same question Mai, we wondered why also. You were very young when I first knew you, how do you really feel about me now...being an enemy at that time?'

'Oh Mr Steve,' she replied with some passion, 'you were *never* the enemy. My grandfather told me many times what a good man you were. I never hated you. I hated the war and the killing and the tragedy it brought to so many families and I am sure it was the same for your people. Sir Steve,' she looked up at him with those beautiful, intelligent eyes. 'We are a nation who has been at war for centuries and we know that soldiers have to do their master's bidding. But it is wrong to take young men who are not soldiers, away from their families and force them to fight without giving them a choice.'

Conway nodded. Although he had been a regular soldier he had seen first hand the terrible stress the Australian National Servicemen had been placed under, exactly the same as the young Vietnamese men of Long Tan. Innocent boys forced to fight and kill each other. He shook his head at the memory.

'I am sorry Mai, but I have to ask you this question.'

'What do you wish to know now?' Their conversation had momentarily replaced her radiant beauty with that of the misery of a much older woman; a woman who had witnessed too much tragedy, heartache and loss.

'Mr Loc…was he VC?'

She looked at him for a few seconds before answering.

'No, he wasn't,' she sighed, 'but I can tell you now the real reason he left to go to Chau Doc.'

Conway was almost afraid to hear what she had to say.

'What was the real reason Mai? I remember he told me it was too dangerous here and that's why he was going away. Was there something else?'

'Yes and no,' she replied taking a deep breath. 'What he told you was the truth. It *was* too dangerous for him to stay here and the reason was because Son told him, the local Viet Cong of the D445 regiment with the help of North Vietnamese regular soldiers were going to attack the Australians and drive them from Phuoc Tuy.' She looked down at her lap twisting a small handkerchief between her fingers.

'Your Army,'…she paused not knowing whether to continue. 'Your Army,' she said again slowly, 'had become a big problem for them in this province and they were determined to attack and destroy you and drive you out of here. They were going to inflict such a devastating and humiliating defeat that you would be finished in this province.'

'Well, it might have worked,' he said grimly, 'if it hadn't been for a chance encounter with a platoon of ours from Delta Company, 6 RAR, that's when it all began. It was a pretty terrible afternoon for all concerned Mai, your people and ours…I'm very sorry about Son,' he said, placing his hand on her shoulder.

She just stared at him for a moment then looked away again, her shoulders slumped. She kept shaking her head as if wanting to be rid of the terrible memory. His hand dropped from her shoulder and they stood silently facing each other. There was nothing more to say.

They walked slowly back to the village. She was close to tears again and said softly, *'hen gap lai,'* (see you again). He groped for words but all he could come up with was a muttered, 'goodbye Mai.' He walked out of the village and hadn't gone more than 30 yards when he suddenly stopped, and looked back.

She was still standing there waving; a small, sad, lonely figure. On an impulse he ran back and drew her to him. They stood for a long moment with their arms around each other.

'I *will* come back, I promise,' he said, then turned and left her, stunned and open mouthed. The patient Mr Tam welcomed him back with a toothy smile. Conway ripped open the passenger side door. 'Ok let's go to Long Tan.'

7

Further down the road it deteriorated again into a series of narrow, red mud tracks. They came to an intersection in thick jungle. Where to now? There were no signs and no indication where the Long Tan Cross memorial built by the Australian troops was located.

A young girl on a bicycle appeared from nowhere. Tam jumped out and ran after her waving his arms and shouting. She stopped. They spoke briefly. She pointed and they headed off again…in the wrong direction.

Along another slippery track barely wide enough for their vehicle, they came upon a clearing, in the middle of which stood a motley collection of wooden shacks. A young man came out to investigate and once again the erstwhile Mr Tam engaged in more hand waving and nodding before returning with a wide smile.

'I know,' he said.

Conway looked at his watch and started to worry. If they didn't find the Cross soon he would be late getting back to Saigon.

Mr Tam ripped the old chariot in a tight 360 degree sweep and roared back down the way they had come then turned right along another track where he slowed down. This time they were among a plantation of rubber trees all neatly aligned, symmetrical, row after row. Conway could feel they were close. Then he saw it! Through the slim, green trees maybe 100 metres away to his left like a white apparition, stood a lone white post in the shape of a cross.

The Long Tan Cross!

They pulled up beside a narrow track which dipped down to the left. Conway got out and stood for a moment looking around. Apart from Mr Tam he was alone on that track. Or was he? In that moment he could feel the ghosts of fallen comrades. He began to walk slowly down through the scrub, the red soil, muddy from recent rains, sticking to his boots as he approached this sacred place.

It was late August. The battle of Long Tan had taken place on the 18th August 1966 and scattered on the ground in front of the Cross were the remains of the recent anniversary service. Wreaths, flowers and hand-written notes from former veterans lay there as mute testament to fallen comrades. Abruptly the clearing was cloaked in darkness for a moment as a large nimbus cloud blotted out the sun adding to the eeriness of the scene.

It was deathly quiet as he stood, head bowed.

So tranquil, so different from that terrible afternoon when the air was ripped asunder with the roar of a monsoon storm, the scream and thump of artillery from the Nui Dat batteries. The barking of the Australian *slrs* and the heavy, unrelenting small arms, rocket-propelled grenades and machine gun fire of the D445 Viet Cong battalion and North Vietnamese forces.

But now the guns were silent and Vietnam was at peace. In that lonely, isolated glade all that remained of a gallant effort by a small group of brave men, was a lone white cross.

Although not a burial site, Conway repeated *The Ode to the Fallen* and prayed for many minutes trying to comprehend what it had all been about. When he opened his eyes he still couldn't understand why. But a purple ribbon on one wreath at his feet said it all: *Lest We Forget.*

The sun suddenly reappeared, its golden rays slanting down through the trees bathing the scene and the lone figure in an ethereal light. It was almost as if the footlights had come up in a darkened theatre to signal the end of a performance.

He glanced at his watch. Not enough time for Vung Tau and the Grand Hotel so it was back to Saigon where against all odds, the old vehicle pulled up outside the hotel just before 7.00 pm.

* * *

He had showered and just finished shaving when a phone call came to tell him Kim was waiting downstairs. She rose from the settee in the lobby as he stepped out of the elevator and gave him the kind of smile a woman gives a man she has special feelings for. He pulled her to him and pecked her on the side of the cheek. She felt so good he would have gone further but felt her stiffen slightly.

The two female front desk staff looked at each other with big grins then called out. 'Yes sir!' and gave him the thumbs up. Conway's friendly manner had won them over and they had formed a warm kinship with Kim Anh.

They took a cyclo to Givral coffee shop opposite the Continental and had a light meal. He had never seen her so animated and joyful. She was blooming, full of questions about his day and nearly spilt her orange juice in her eagerness to find out how he had spent it. Her enthusiasm was infectious and he was tempted to tell her where he'd been but sensed it was not a good idea and simply said he'd done some more sightseeing.

'I missed you today darling,' she said. He smiled to himself. *Darling.* Things really were looking up. He let it pass without comment and simply replied, 'I missed you too Kimmee. By the way, what did your family think of me?'

She hesitated, seeming to consider her answer carefully. Taking a sip of her coffee she replaced her cup in its saucer and said slowly, 'they thought…you, were very friendly.'

'Oh really? Just friendly…nothing else? They didn't say, "we liked him, he's a great guy, hope you stay with him"…just…very friendly?' She leaned across the table and took his hand.

'No, they just said you were a very friendly guy but I know they liked you.'

He squeezed her hand, 'I liked them too. And those kids are so cute. Please thank them for their hospitality, I really appreciated it,' he replied, hiding his disappointment.

If anyone had asked him later what he ate that night he could not have told them. Love was in the air and they scarcely touched their food. They sat for a long time looking into each other's eyes. Finally he broke the spell.

'Where can we go that's quiet and private?'

She had to think about it for a while. It was obvious Kim Anh had not been involved in any quiet smooching around District 1 and if Conway's guess was right, no where else either.

'Perhaps we could go down to Saigon Port. It's quiet by the river and there are nice gardens. There is some privacy, not much, but we can sit there if you wish?'

Ten minutes later they sat holding hands on a bench among a tree-lined garden beside the broad Saigon River.

'It's Saturday tomorrow I'd like to spend the weekend at Vung Tau, would you care to …ah…join me?' he asked. He expected her to refuse. Although their relationship was now warm and more than friendly, she had generally kept him at arm's length. There was a long pause. She had been to Vung Tau many times with relatives and work colleagues. To go there alone, with a man, was unthinkable.

'I would love too,' she replied softly.

He tried to hide his surprise and delight…unsuccessfully.

'You mean it?'

'Yes, I mean it.'

He sighed with relief and slipped his arm around her, his face splitting in a wide grin. She leant into him. They sat watching the river and its ever changing moods until it was time for her to return to Thanh Da. He wanted to kiss her. They had privacy and he felt she wouldn't have resisted, but somehow it seemed not the right time.

They took a taxi back to his hotel. Emboldened by her acceptance of his offer to Vung Tau, he suggested she come to his room but she just gave him an enigmatic smile and politely declined. 'It's a bit late and my sister might be worried. They say you are friendly but I don't know if they trust you,' she laughed.

'Ok,' grinned Conway crookedly, covering his embarrassment at the rejection. She sensed his discomfort and leant up and gave him a light peck on the cheek.

'I really am sorry darling but I must go, see you tomorrow.'

Despite the trauma of his day, Conway was a very happy man as he dozed off that night.

* * *

Saturday dawned bright, sunny and cloudless; a perfect day for the beach. He woke early, and was talking to the front desk staff when Kim arrived. She was wearing a pink, cotton top, blue jeans and open-toed sandals, her shiny, jet black hair held by a matching pink bandeau. Conway smiled and gave a low whistle. She looked gorgeous.

They had breakfast of *Pho*, a beef or chicken noodle soup, a Vietnamese staple, in a small eatery before catching a taxi to Saigon Port. He bought their tickets at a small office opposite the wharf and they sat on a wooden bench chatting happily, like a couple of excited kids waiting to go on school excursion.

With the Vietnamese penchant for strict timekeeping right on 8.00 am they were signaled to board. As Conway helped her to navigate the narrow plank to the deck of the hydrofoil for the 75 minute journey to Vung Tau, neither noticed a Vietnamese male sitting on a motor scooter watching them from beside the ticket office. He waited until the hydrofoil had roared into life and moved away into midstream, then turned and rode away toward the east of the city.

* * *

The hydrofoil glided along the coffee-coloured Saigon River quickly leaving the city behind. On either side all Conway could see were mangroves and small narrow tributaries leading off into the scrub. To his surprise they were handed a cold towel and a bottle of water free of charge by a smiling young female crew member, reinforcing Conway's already favorable impression of the Vietnamese he had met this time round; a far cry from dodging their bullets in Phuoc Tuy.

An hour in and the wide expanse of the river mouth appeared. They went up on deck and stood in the cool breeze as the distant outline of Vung Tau slowly appeared on the left. Fifteen minutes later the hydrofoil wheeled in a wide semi-circle and berthed beside the concrete wharf right on schedule. Conway shook his head in admiration. The Communists could teach the Democrats in the Philippines a thing or two about punctuality.

He followed Kim across another rickety, narrow plank to the dock where a gaggle of taxi drivers and *ex oms* shouted, waved and tugged the clothes of the arriving passengers. Grabbing Kim's hand he looked around ignoring the unruly mob and waved to a good looking young taxi driver standing diffidently at the back. The young guy's face lit up and he hurriedly pushed and shoved his way through to them.

'Yes sir, can I help you sir?'

'*Bai Sau,*' said Conway, handing him their luggage.

'Back Beach sir, very good sir, follow me sir, ma'am,' he said excitedly, leading them back through the crowd to his immaculate white Toyota Corolla. He carefully placed their belongings in the boot and opened the back door for them with a smile from ear to ear.

'I am Mr Thang sir and Madame, and I am pleased to be of service to you,' he said, nosing the vehicle through the crowd and accelerating away toward Back Beach. They hadn't made any bookings so it took a couple of enquiries with Thang's help before finding a small, comfortable, reasonably priced guest house, overlooking the beach. Conway handed in his passport as part of the usual police requirement and paid the accommodation for two rooms.

Kim's moral values and strict Northern culture would not permit her to share a room with a man to whom she was not married. They had discussed this on the way down and although Conway was disappointed, he didn't show it and secretly admired her stance.

He quickly unpacked, donned a pair of navy blue shorts and white tee shirt, cleaned his teeth then knocked on her door. She was in the bathroom but called out for him to enter.

Her room was similar to his. Small, basic and a little gloomy with dark green walls relieved by a double window and a tiny balcony with a view across the road of a fairly large open air restaurant, a couple of nondescript little shops and the beach beyond.

Beside the window was a lumpy looking double bed. He touched one of the pillows; hard as a rock. In the corner stood an ancient black and white television, and against the far wall, a small white dresser and wooden chair. It was no honeymoon suite. Kim came from the tiny white-tiled bathroom. She had changed into a cotton top of pale lemon and a pair of white shorts. The outfit contrasted beautifully with her golden skin. She looked good enough to eat.

They locked up and walked across the road down on to a white sandy beach. There was surf but the waves were small and didn't appear dangerous. A few fishing boats plied their trade about a mile offshore and further out an old steam packet beat its way south.

They strolled along the water's edge letting the gentle waves wash around their bare feet. Families sat beneath umbrellas eating and drinking. Others stood watching their little ones frolic in the shallows while seagulls soared in the sky above them, occasionally swooping onto the beach to steal a tasty morsel then take off chased by squealing, laughing kids. It could have been a beach scene from an Australian summer.

They laughed and splashed each other on their way to where the beach ended in a rocky headland. Further just inland on a high hill with a commanding view up and down the coast stood a huge statue of Jesus, said to be blessing the South China Sea. During the war it was the site of an American artillery battery but Conway kept that to himself.

A narrow creek below the headland carved small rivulets in the sand to the shoreline. Kim crouched and spent a few minutes looking for small fish in these streams, like a happy child on the first day of her holidays. Conway smiled benignly and took a couple of photos of her. So far this was the most relaxed she had been in his company.

They had lunch at a small open-air place beside the beach then decided to go back to their "little dump" as Conway nicknamed it for an afternoon nap. At her door she hesitated and he said, 'can I come in for a few minutes?'

She smiled and said nothing which he took to be a 'yes'. He went to her balcony and stood looking out across to the beach. She came and stood beside him. For a whole minute nothing was said. He placed his left arm around her waist. She didn't resist. He led her back to the bed and they sat for a moment beside each other. Then he kissed her. She returned his kiss with a passion that surprised him. They gently fell back to the pillows still locked in an embrace their lips eagerly seeking each others.

His hand slid up her back feeling the velvety skin until he came to her bra strap but he didn't attempt to undo it. His hand hovered there then returned to their embrace. They continued to kiss with increasing urgency, their bodies still joined with Conway fighting to control his emotions.

He wanted her. He wanted her badly. He wanted her naked, to hear her moan with pleasure as he ran his hands tenderly over her body before he took her. But he couldn't! From their previous conversations he knew she was a virgin and he didn't want to be the one to spoil her.

He had read somewhere that Vietnamese girls were expected to be virgins when they married. A voice in his head kept repeating, *'you cannot dishonour her Conway, you must not!'* Exercising self control he never knew he possessed, he reluctantly broke the spell ending the kiss and stroking her hair as she buried her head into the crook between his shoulder and neck. They lay there, bodies heaving for many minutes, until their emotions settled allowing them to drift off into a deep slumber.

That night they had dinner under the stars at another small beachside restaurant. She had changed into a blue scooped neck, light blue dress and strapped white shoes. The dress was a first. Apart from the *ao dai* she had worn on his arrival, he had never seen her in anything but slacks and a top.

He had always been amazed how women could look so different and so beautiful with just a simple change of clothes and there was no doubt about it, Kim Anh looked beautiful! He smiled and shook his head in admiration. Was it the sea air or something else that had her looking so radiant?

They ordered seafood and she taught him how to attract the young male waiter's attention by calling, '*anh oi*'. She explained the hierarchical way the Vietnamese addressed each other from the oldest to the youngest and since the waiter was male and younger than either of them the correct form of address was *anh oi* (young man). Had it been a waitress younger, she would have used the words, *em oi.* (young sister). An older woman would have been addressed, *chi oi* (older sister).

Anh oi assured them the fish was fresh and caught that afternoon. He was telling the truth. It literally melted in the mouth. Conway washed his down with a Tiger beer while Kim stuck to her usual orange juice. Although the food was simple and tasty they enjoyed the meal simply because of their own company. Even a raucous group of men at a nearby table, whom Kim said were teachers from North Vietnam, did not destroy the loving atmosphere between them.

The night air was cool, too good to resist, so hand in hand they began to walk, and walk...and walk. They took a route along the concrete beachfront path past well tended flower gardens. It led them back around to Front Beach where they had arrived in the hydrofoil.

The stars blazed out of an inky sky and lights of small vessels far out at sea winked in the darkness. They stopped in the shadows of a clump of palm trees and kissed and if anything, their passion was greater than it had been that afternoon.

It was late when they returned to their accommodation and after one last kiss they reluctantly said goodnight and went to their separate rooms. It took Conway a long time to get to sleep that night. He was sorely tempted to get up and knock on her door but in the end fell asleep still thinking about it.

After a leisurely breakfast of *Pho*, orange juice and coffee at a beachside restaurant they took a taxi around to Front Beach for Conway to check out The Grand Hotel. To his disappointment it was closed and the whole frontage was covered in scaffolding and hessian bags. The Grand Hotel was undergoing renovations. A workman informed Kim it would not be finished for some months. They returned to Back Beach where Conway, a keen surfer rode a few waves watched from the shore by an admiring Kim sitting under an umbrella swathed in a towel, shielded from the burning sun.

Back in "the little dump" they showered, packed their gear and prepared to leave shortly after lunch, this time returning to Saigon by road.

Kim phoned a bus company and arranged for 2.30 pm pick up. The next hour was spent in yet another passionate session followed by lunch at the same restaurant they had eaten on arrival.

The bus company proved to be unreliable and didn't arrive until 3.00 pm. What followed was a slow, cramped and extremely uncomfortable 120 kilometer ride back to Saigon in a grossly overloaded, unmarked mini bus which stopped and started picking up and dropping off passengers almost all the way back to the city.

By the time they got back to Saigon the Australian would have happily strangled the fat woman who sat beside the driver. She was obviously the owner and Conway's blood pressure rose as she kept inviting more passengers into the already overloaded vehicle.

'How can the authorities allow this?' complained Conway, as they sat squashed among 25 sweating bodies in a vehicle where ten was a tight fit.

'The traffic police don't work on Sundays so these bus drivers can do what they like,' gasped Kim, as the bus hit a pothole and threw him against her.

Finally, thankfully, they were dropped off at Saigon port. They took a taxi to his hotel arriving much later than expected. She looked at her watch, grimaced then told him reluctantly that she could not stay, but would have to leave for home immediately.

'Darling, that was the most wonderful time I have ever had in Vung Tau, thank you so much,' she said, as the security guard brought her motorbike from where she had left it in an underground car park.

'It was certainly better than last...' He suddenly realized what he was saying and quickly continued, 'glad you enjoyed it darling, let's get back there again soon.' She appeared not to notice his stumble and leaned a little toward him as if she wanted him to kiss her, but then pulled back and kicked her little motorbike into life.

'Bye darling, see you in the morning,' she called, blowing him a kiss and heading into the traffic toward District 1. He watched till she was out of sight then went to his room.

Neither realized they were being watched from across the street.

He thought about having dinner out but in the end decided to eat in the hotel. After a meal of pasta and a couple of cold Tigers he watched a movie on television then lay on his bed reviewing the weekend. Five minutes later with a smile still on his face he was asleep.

* * *

Back in Manila, Jumbo Keyes received a disturbing phone call.

8

The next morning Conway had breakfast alone. Kim had phoned saying she was busy with a few domestic things and would see him at lunch time. He called Keyes again and received an update on the hotel operations. Everything was going smoothly but they were all looking forward to his return.

'I'm booked to fly back on Tuesday morning Jumbo see you then,' said Conway hanging up. Although he had mentioned to Kim his visit to Saigon would be brief, he hadn't said anything about returning to Manila and wondered how she would take it. As he replaced the phone it occurred to him that he hadn't thought much about leaving Saigon either.

His feelings for Kim Anh had grown and it was obvious she felt the same way toward him. He never intended to stay more than a week and the last thing he expected was to become romantically involved with her or anyone else.

He was in Saigon for a brief holiday and a chance to try and find an old friend, nothing more. So he had to go back to Manila. Or did he? He knew in his heart, what he really wanted to do was to stay in Saigon... with her.

They met for lunch at a small café in De Tham Street not far from his hotel. She arrived all smiles, still wouldn't let him hug her in public but instead, took both his hands and squeezed them warmly. Conway could only manage a weak smile.

'Darling, I think I like your western food,' she laughed, flicking past the extensive Vietnamese selection to the pasta. 'I think I'll try this…er… spaghetti bolognese.'

He followed suit ordering the carbonara, both deciding on coconut juice. They sat facing each other across one of the small booths which lay along the left side of the narrow elongated restaurant. Her beautiful dark eyes glowed with happiness as she leant across the table and took his hand.

'How are you today my Steve?' she asked merrily.

He looked at her for a few moments before replying. She looked so happy, so lovely, so thrilled to be with him. Shit! How can I tell her?

'I'm fine,' he lied.

She was hungry and attacked her food with relish. He had a few mouthfuls which he couldn't taste and had trouble swallowing. He put down his fork and said, quietly but just a little too quickly, 'Kimmee, I have to return to Manila, I have to go back to work…Tuesday.'

She looked at him as if she'd been struck. Her mouth fell open, the fork she held dropped from her grasp, hitting the side of the enamel plate with a clatter bouncing onto the table cloth. Her shoulders slumped. She lowered her head then looked back up at him for a moment, tears welling in her eyes. In a heartbeat she had changed from a blissfully happy young woman, to one whose whole world had come crashing down.

She pushed the spaghetti away and sat staring at her plate. After what seemed like an eternity, she spoke, haltingly, barely above a whisper.

'If you leave, please do not come back, or if you do, please, please do not tell me, I could not bear for you to leave me again,' she said brokenly. There was more pain in her words than he had ever heard from another human being. He sat there miserably, not knowing what to say. She was inconsolable anything he said would only make things worse.

Her reaction was exactly what he feared. They continued to sit in silence. Neither could find words that would alleviate the pain of the moment. He had known great pain in the past with the loss of his wife and child in tragic circumstances. No pain could equal that. But what he felt at that moment came pretty close. She lowered her head again and said in a muffled voice, '*Em yeu anh.*'

'I love you too Kim Anh,' he replied quietly.

She sat very still, desolate, downcast, her cheeks now wet with tears. He handed her his handkerchief and said softly, 'let's go.' He called for the bill and they left with her walking in front of him seemingly oblivious to his presence. He took her across to a park nearby where they found a quiet spot on a small wooden bench beneath a clump of flowering tamarinds.

The slight breeze cooled them but her attitude was much cooler. He tried to make conversation and explain his position, but she sat saying nothing, twisting his handkerchief in her small hands, occasionally dabbing her eyes. He tried to put his arm around her but she shrugged it off.

Long minutes past until suddenly she stood up and said curtly, 'I'm going home.' Without another word, she stalked off making it obvious she did not want him to accompany her.

He watched as she left the park and crossed the street to where her motorbike was parked outside his hotel. She went through the routine of the gloves and face mask then rode away without looking in his direction.

He walked slowly back to his hotel feeling sick and empty. Is this how it's going to end? He lay awake for a long time that night wanting to call her. Twice he picked up the phone but then dropped it back in its cradle. He was hoping she would phone him. He fell asleep still hoping.

* * *

In Thanh Da Kim lay awake in her tiny room. She tossed and turned in the darkness. Sleep was impossible. She knew she shouldn't have reacted so emotionally. Of course she knew he had to return to Manila, she was not a stupid lovesick schoolgirl. But he could have told her more tactfully. Why couldn't he have given more thought to his words, been a little gentler, more sensitive, instead of just blurting them out like that? Surely he knew how she felt about him? Why are men so stupid and unfeeling?

But for all her recriminations, she was too embarrassed to call him and apologize. She was afraid of what he would say. This was the second time within a few days she had reacted badly to his words. There was no way he would forgive her this time.

The house was deathly quiet. She could hear the even breathing of her sister, brother in law and their children sleeping peacefully in the room adjoining hers. They were poor but happy together. She felt the tears roll down her cheeks. Why can't I find happiness? She silently cursed her emotions. They had caused trouble in her personal life in the past and she hated herself for it. But just before sleep descended she knew she had to see him one more time. She would go to him in the morning and apologize, accept his rebuke and say goodbye.

* * *

Conway was walking past the front desk after a breakfast he hardly touched, when Michael called to him. 'Sir, you have a call?' His heart leapt, Kim! He grabbed the phone from Michael's outstretched hand.

'Hello! Kim?'

But it was only the travel agency confirming his flight to Manila. He returned to his room and began to pack. He wasn't leaving for another day but he had nothing better to do. His thoughts were of her and he kept looking at the phone hoping she would call to say sorry and that she understood: It remained silent.

He packed everything except a fresh change of clothes, shaving gear and a toothbrush then went to the window and looked out on a blue sky broken only by a couple of wispy cirrus clouds. A lovely day, too nice to feel the way he did. What to do? Then he remembered he had to buy a couple of gifts to take back to Manila for the wife of Jumbo Keyes and his secretary Gina.

He thought about the lacquer factory; no, maybe next time. If there is a next time, it seemed highly unlikely now. He left the hotel and walked around to De Tham Street where he remembered there were a number of small gift shops selling souvenirs and local bric-a-brac.

He began to browse in one trying to decide between hand-made leather purses, silk scarves and a showcase of ornate bracelets. He had a scarf for Ang and was looking at a bracelet for Gina when he felt a light tap on his arm.

He turned and standing there looking at him with a mixture of trepidation, embarrassment and uncertainty…Kim Anh. For a few seconds they just looked at each other. Then his face split into a wide grin of relief. He pulled her into his arms, bent her head back and kissed her fully on the lips, long and passionately ignoring the consternation of the elderly matron behind the counter.

When they finally broke apart she stepped back for a moment to catch her breath then threw her arms around him again, as if she was afraid he would run away. No chance. Then she began to sob uncontrollably. He held her and let her cry herself out then wiped away her tears and gave her another hug.

'What do you think of these Kimmee?' he said, holding out the things he had selected. 'They're a couple of presents for people back in Manila?'

She shook her tear-stained face; a face now glowing with happiness and relief.

'No darling let me choose for you,' she said, handing them back to the shopkeeper who snatched them back, her face a mask of disapproval. Like many of her vintage, she was conservative in the extreme. Foreigners passionately kissing local young ladies in her establishment was totally unacceptable and a breach of Vietnamese social mores. In the past, Kim Anh probably would have agreed with her.

Women are innately better at this kind of shopping and after lengthy consideration Kim chose another scarf and bracelets, more stylish and colourful than he would have bought. The scarf was pink silk, embroidered with an intricate gold weave; Ang would love it. The bracelets were made of clear, brightly coloured cut stones with facets that gleamed and sparkled in the light.

To his eyes they were exquisite. He offered to buy her one which caught his eye more than the others. She refused but he bought it anyway. She gave him a hug and kept looking at it as they strolled back along De Tham.

On the spur of the moment they decided to have coffee in *Allez Boo* where she sat all smiles, still admiring the bracelet.

She looked at him across the small wicker table for a moment weighing up what she had to say then drawing a deep breath said. 'Darling, I know I acted like a silly schoolgirl yesterday, I just don't want to lose you. Please forgive me.'

'Forget it Kimmee.' He leant across the table and took her hands. 'The truth is, I don't want to lose you either but I have a hotel to run. I've been thinking, and, from what I've seen, there's a need for a good expat bar-cum hotel in this town. I'm going to talk to my shareholders about it, so you haven't got rid of me yet darling.'

She let out a huge sigh of relief. 'I hope you will come back soon my Steve and, oh, if you don't mind, I want to take you somewhere special this afternoon.'

'Where love? Can you tell me now or is it another one of your mystery destinations?' he laughed. It was so good to see her. He didn't care if they did nothing but sit there all day.

She smiled at him coquettishly. 'Mmmm, don't you like my mystery tours darling? Just wait and see. I have to go home now but will be back to pick you up about one o'clock, ok?'

'It sounds intriguing…I'm looking forward to it.'

He looked past her to an individual in the far corner of the small restaurant who seemed to be showing more than a passing interest in their presence.

He was carrying a newspaper and had taken up a position in the opposite corner of the small restaurant and kept sneaking glances at them over the top of his newspaper.

He was Vietnamese, short, a little overweight, probably mid-thirties. His face was pudgy and a pencil-thin moustache beneath narrow eyes and a broad nose gave him a rather shifty look. But it was the expression on his face that got Conway's attention. His mouth was set in a thin, grim line. The eyes were black, deep set…and baleful.

He wore a white shirt and tie, common attire of the local office workers. He could be anything. A clerk, maybe a government official, a plain clothes cop, unlikely…But whatever he was, what was his interest in them?

Conway looked straight at him then turned and glanced back over his own shoulder in case this fellow was looking at someone else. There was nothing behind them but an open window. Conway turned and looked back frowning. The guy's eyes widened at the expression on Conway's face and quickly looked back down at his newspaper. The act was laughable, but what was his game?

This bloke's no professional, he's too obvious. I should go and find out what he's about thought Conway then decided against it. Kim was still smiling and checking out her bracelet. With her back to their observer, didn't notice anything amiss.

They finished their coffee and began to walk back to his hotel when Conway suddenly stopped and bent down pretending to tie a loose shoe lace. He turned and looked back and there he was, on the sidewalk outside *Allez Boo* watching them.

'You know this guy Kim?' She had taken the opportunity to buy some fruit for her sister while he tied his shoe lace and was checking the change given.

'Who darling? Where?'

Conway looked back. The man had gone.

'A Vietnamese guy was checking us out in *Allez Boo* he looked very, very unhappy. I've never seen him before I thought you might know him.'

'What was he like darling?'

Conway described him and Kim thought for a few moments then shook her head.

'He sounds like a million Vietnamese men maybe he mistook us for someone else?'

'Maybe.' But Conway knew there was no mistake. It was *them* he was following, but why? Who was he? And what was he? The look on his face *was* cause for concern. They came to the hotel and for the first time, she let him give her a hug in public, while a smiling security guard looked on.

As she rode away he turned to Conway. 'She's a special girl isn't she sir?' The Australian returned his smile. 'She certainly is,' he said, walking back up the steps into the hotel still thinking about the Vietnamese guy in *Allez Boo*.

As good as her word, Kim appeared as the clock in the foyer ticked over onto one o'clock. She still refused to tell him their destination so Conway just smiled good-naturedly and climbed on the pillion of her trusty little Honda.

They sped off across Saigon, Kim expertly weaving through the heavy traffic in the Binh Thanh district when Conway suddenly realized they were taking the same route toward Thu Duc on the day he'd gone to Baria. The highway divided on the outskirts of Saigon and Kim turned right, away from Thu Duc and crossed the well-worn bridge into the pot-holed streets toward Thanh Da.

Bumping along on the back Conway began to wonder. 'Is she taking me home again? If so, where's the mystery?' Her apartment block loomed up on their right but they kept on going along a road which narrowed considerably with heavy undergrowth closing in on both sides.

Just over a mile past Kim's house the scrub on the left cleared and he could see well tended thatched bungalows, green lawns and gardens in between a few ponds. She slowed up and turned into a parking lot above which was a sign, *Binh Quoi Tourist Village*

'Here it is darling, I hope you like it,' she said as they dismounted.

It was Monday afternoon. The place seemed uninhabited; maybe siesta time. No one stopped them as they strolled in. Immediately Conway was enchanted.

'Hey this place is beautiful, it's a real oasis. I'd never have found it without you,' he said, taking in the neat bungalows, landscaped green lawns, lush tropical gardens on their left and ponds of lilac and pink lotus flowers on their right. It was an amazing contrast to the noisy, urban sprawl of nearby Thanh Da.

They stopped for a moment while Conway snapped a few photos of Kim in these lovely surrounds. A few yards further on they came to a lotus pond spanned by a narrow log serving as a bridge. Another skinny log served as a handrail. She squealed with laughter as she took a photo of him skylarking; pretending to wobble and nearly fall as he gingerly made his way across.

'How long has this place been here? he asked, stepping down beside her.

'Not long, SaigonTourist, the government tourist agency built it and it's proved quite popular. She pointed to a small jetty. Occasionally I come here with my sister and brother in law to fish or take a ferry ride on the river. We enjoy doing that usually on a Sunday afternoon. It's also a favourite spot for wedding ceremonies,' she said shyly. 'Brides love having their photos taken in their wedding gowns among the gardens, maybe one day I will…'

Conway nodded in agreement. For a moment he imagined Kim in this idyllic setting wearing a white wedding gown, flowers in her long dark hair, holding a bouquet, happily posing for photographs; she would look so beautiful…He snapped out of his reverie when he felt her tug at his arm.

'Are you hungry darling? You can have something to eat here.'

He looked around. There was no restaurant or anything that looked like an eatery.

She pointed out an open-sided thatched rotunda beside the river some thirty or forty yards away. 'That building is part of the resort's restaurant, it's different isn't it, but I think rather romantic.' He agreed, but it *was* an odd set up. The restaurant was almost hidden in the trees well away from where they stood, but he still couldn't see anything that resembled a kitchen.

'Don't worry they will come,' she smiled, taking his hand and leading him to the rotunda.

They sat beside each other at one of the several small bamboo tables and waited, and waited. Finally, a teenage waiter in spotless white shirt and dark pants spotted them waving and sprinted over.

'I am very sorry sir…ma'am…forgive me I did not see you. We do not get many guests on a Monday,' he gasped, trying to hide his embarrassment, handing them each a menu.

Kim wasn't hungry and after a quick scan handed back the menu and asked for an orange juice. Conway ordered the citronella chicken and a bottle of Tiger beer.

Given the tardiness of the waiter, their orders arrived promptly. They sat quietly while he ate, each knowing the other was thinking about his departure the next morning.

He finished his meal and reached over and put his arm around her. She leaned into him and shivered a little as he kissed her lightly on the neck. The waiter had disappeared and apart from the occasional trill of a native bird there was complete silence. They seemed to have the whole complex to themselves.

On arrival it had been a glorious day of bright sunshine broken only by a few cumulus clouds. But now as Conway glanced at the sky he saw large, black storm clouds tinged with green gathering.

Monsoon rain was imminent.

Within half an hour the sun disappeared behind a dark curtain leaving a narrow sliver of light beneath earth and sky. They were suddenly sitting in a deepening gloom. A few minutes later the rains came. It began with a spatter followed by the terrifying, ear-splitting boom of thunder then wind whipping across the rotunda blowing paper serviettes, Conway's plate and Kim's glass from their table.

'This is just a rainy season storm, it will pass soon,' said Kim, with more hope than conviction in her voice. 'We can stay here.' That was fine by Conway. He was content to stay with her, rain or no rain.

She cried out and grabbed his arm as without warning, jagged flashes of lightning ripped across the sky and the storm increased in intensity. The rain began to pour in great vertical sheets. The noise was deafening…and frightening.

Conway felt her shiver as the temperature dropped and the hot Saigon afternoon amazingly now became a damp chill. They moved to the centre of the rotunda and sat huddled together with him trying to protect her from occasional gusts of rain driven across their unprotected refuge by the powerful wind. Visibility was now down to no more than a few metres from their flimsy haven. Conway had seen monsoon rain in Manila…but nothing as fierce as this.

The storm roared on unabated all through the afternoon into the evening battering their little refuge but the little rotunda stood firm: testimony to ingenious Vietnamese construction. Kim leant against him her head on his chest, saying nothing her breathing steady and even. He looked down and stroked the glossy black hair, then realized that despite the tempest, she had fallen asleep! He grinned and kissed the top of her head. There's no doubt about Asian people, they can sleep anywhere, through anything.

It was beginning to look as if they'd be there all night but gradually the rain began to ease, slightly, then more so, and finally into a drizzle until just before nine o'clock, it stopped.

'Wake up sleepy head, we'll have to leave soon,' he said softly into her ear. She yawned, blinked a few times then stretched her arms looking around for a moment wondering where she was.

'Sorry darling, what time is it?'

'Nearly nine o'clock, we better make tracks out of here.' They waited for a few more minutes until certain it was over, then hand in hand, squelched across the waterlogged lawn in the darkness to a gravel path which led to the exit.

Fortunately, the path was lit by oil lamps in the trees creating weird, ghostly shadows in the bush either side and in front of them. Vietnamese have a reputation for superstition, so believing she would want to leave what was now a rather surreal and somewhat scary scene, he increased his pace. But a little further on, she surprised him by stopping and pulling him off the path across to a low wooden bench beside a lotus pool lit by beams from a pale moon breaking through scudding clouds.

They sat gazing out into the darkness for a few moments. Then he kissed her. It was gentle at first then became simple, unbridled passion. Hands clawed frantically at clothing on top, then beneath, seeking, exploring bare flesh. Buttons and zippers were undone but the damp ground prevented anything further than heavy petting.

They remained glued together until finally, she broke away, her breath coming in short, uneven gasps. 'You love me…but you are leaving me,' she sobbed, her small shoulders heaving with emotion. He took her again in his arms and kissed her again…tenderly.

'Do you *really* think I want to leave you? It's the *last* thing I want to do!' he said, placing his hand beneath her chin, lifting it so she was looking up at him through tear-stained eyes. 'I *will* come back for you darling… I promise!'

She hugged him for many minutes in silence. 'Please come back, my Steve, please! I can't bear to be without you.' Her voice was muffled against his chest.

'Darling, *nothing* will keep me from returning to you,' he said quietly.

They kissed again. Then, both knowing the time had come, they slowly walked back with heavy hearts to her motor bike, now standing alone in the parking lot. One last kiss in the darkness then it was a slow journey to Thanh Da to rejoin the torrent of heavy, city-bound traffic to his hotel.

Years later, he was to recall that afternoon and evening in Binh Quoi to be the most bitter-sweet interlude of his life. In his quiet moments of reflection it seemed almost like a scene from a Jane Austen novel, yet it happened...and he would cherish that magic afternoon and evening forever.

* * *

The next morning she arrived early and joined him for his last breakfast. They took a taxi together to Tan Son Nhat airport; a journey during which no words were spoken. She sat beside him gripping his hand staring straight ahead.

They stood outside the departure gate holding hands looking into each other's eyes. Hers were full of tears and the lump in his throat threatened to choke him. Neither was able to speak.

She could not bring herself to embrace him in such a crowded public area and stood there fighting unsuccessfully to stop the tears. She reached into a small calico bag and took out an envelope, a small handkerchief, to replace one he had given her the previous night to wipe her tears, and a tiny, gift-wrapped package.

'For you,' she murmured.

'For me?'

'Yes, I want you to have these, as a memory of your visit to my country.'

He looked down at the small package then back up at her his voice cracking with emotion. 'Thank you darling...I will keep this forever.' He took a deep breath and squeezed her hand. 'This is not goodbye darling.' Then he turned and walked away through the departure gate, almost immediately lost to her inside the crowd of departing passengers. '*Tam biet, hen gap lai* (goodbye, see you again) *darling,*' she called out softly. The tears rolled unchecked down her cheeks.

After check-in he looked hopefully across through the large plate glass windows and was relieved to see her still waiting. She was looking desperately back and forth trying to see him one last time. Finally she spied him and waved frantically. She was still waving as he looked back down from the escalator taking him to immigration on the first floor. Even from that distance he could see the tears streaming down her face. Then she was lost to sight.

As he sat waiting in the departure lounge he opened the envelope. Inside was a letter written in her neat, precise hand.

> *My Darling Steve*
>
> *I have known you for only a short time but I feel I have known you all my life. You have brought into my life sunshine and love I never thought could exist. I am sorry I have caused you some pain and I hope from the bottom of my heart you forgive me. I know I have not shown you as much of my city as I should have. But that is because I want you to come back my darling. Please let it not be too long. I will count the days until you are in my arms again.*
>
> *Love*
>
> *Your Kimmee. xxx*

He opened the package to find a small pink, quartz stone within which were embossed in gold lettering the words... *I love you.*

He sat looking at it his mind a maelstrom of emotions and memories until his thoughts were broken by his flight's boarding call. He kissed the stone reverently, put it in his pocket and walked toward the departure gate.

9

As the Philippine airline flight was pushed back for takeoff, Conway sat thinking…looking out across to the airport building. She had probably left by now and was on her way to work weaving through the heavy traffic on the long journey across the city to Thu Duc.

He had an overwhelming desire to unbuckle his seatbelt and rush to the door of the aircraft, rip it open and run back to her. Instead, he just sat there emotionally drained, oblivious of the safety instructions given by the aircrew. He never heard the mighty roar of the engines as the captain opened the throttle of the silver bird allowing it to race down the runway and lift effortlessly into the cloudless blue sky; he just kept staring at the small stone in his hand…

* * *

Jumbo Keyes flashing a smile like a row of piano keys shook Conway's hand and grabbed his suitcase as he emerged from the arrival hall of the Manila International Airport into a typical steamy afternoon. Thunderheads over Manila bay suggested the arrival of a late storm.

'Welcome back boss, our hotel vehicle is in the car park it'll be here in a few minutes,' said the big black American, producing a well-used handkerchief to wipe perspiration from his brow.

Conway was laughing at some story Keyes was relating when the hotel coaster arrived. Mario the driver, hopped down from behind the wheel his face creased in a huge smile grabbing Conway's suitcase and placing it carefully in the back of the vehicle.

'Welcome back sir,' he said holding open the passenger door for his boss. Ah, there was nothing like the smile of a Filipino.

Traffic inbound along Roxas Boulevard was light allowing them to make good time to the Down Under Hotel in Ermita, a bayside suburb of Manila. Thirty minutes later, Conway was met in the foyer of the Down Under by a phalanx of staff waiting to welcome him back and find out about his trip to Vietnam.

'Where are our *pasalubongs* sir?' Annie called out cheekily from her switchboard.

'I only bring presents for *good* girls Annie,' grinned Conway, bringing a roar of laughter from everyone.

'Oh sir,' said Annie, in a tone of mock disappointment and affronted dignity. 'You know I am a *good* girl sir...well sometimes,' she said wickedly, amid another round of laughter.

'How about a party instead?' suggested Conway, 'Friday night in *Barrio Fiesta*, 7.00 pm, all welcome; happy now Annie?'

'Yes, sir, thank you sir, I know we will all come,' she giggled.

At the door to his office Conway almost collided with Zeny Diaz. 'Oh sorry! Oh! Hello sir, welcome back, we missed you sir,' said Zeny smiling sweetly, stepping back, allowing him to pass.

'Thanks Zeny, any problems in your department?'

'No sir, we have our accounts up to date, I have left them on your desk,' she said proudly. Susan Santos had left behind an enviable reputation for efficiency; Zeny, for professional, and more importantly, personal reasons, was determined to maintain the high standards set by her predecessor.

Conway looked at the neat piles of paperwork on his desk and smiled ruefully. 'Well, I know how the rest of my day is going to be spent.' Zeny laughed, told him again how good it was to see him back and hurried off down the hallway to her office.

His secretary Gina appeared at his door lighting up the room with her bright Filipina smile. Small in stature but big in the efficiency department, she was a relatively new addition. Conway had found the ever increasing amount of management paperwork correspondence and appointments necessitated another pair of hands.

Gina, a graduate of the Philippine National University was an excellent choice and Conway often wondered how he had ever managed without her.

He produced her gift and in her surprise and delight she impulsively gave him a big hug then stepped back, embarrassed at what she'd done.

'Oh, I am sorry sir,' she said, not knowing where to look.

'Hey Gina, that's the nicest thing that's happened to me since I arrived, I hope you like it.'

'Sir, may I open it please?'

Conway nodded and smiled as his bubbly secretary quickly unwrapped the gift and held up the bracelet.

'Oh sir, it's beautiful,' she squealed, just stopping herself from giving him another hug. 'Sir, I have to show it to some of the other girls. May I sir?' Conway nodded and wondered how much jealousy he had probably inadvertently caused as Gina rushed out of his office.

He sat down behind his desk, picked up the phone, leaned back and asked Annie to get him a number in Saigon. It took a few minutes but finally the operator of Waterworld answered. Conway decided to try out his Vietnamese.

'*Cho gap Kim Anh?*' *(may I speak to Kim Anh)*

A few moments later a familiar voice said softly, '*Kim Anh nghe.*'

'Guess who?'

'Oh darling this is so lovely, so quick, you back in Manila already?'

'Yes in the hotel sweetheart, just thought I'd give you a call to let you know I arrived ok and miss you already.'

'I am the same my dear Steve, I am so happy you phoned. I have been missing you from the moment you left me at the airport. I can't wait for you to come back to me my darling.'

They chatted for a few more minutes then Conway glanced at the pile of paper on his desk. 'I have to go but will keep in touch. Please take care in that Saigon traffic it worries me, must go, bye now darling.' As he replaced the receiver Jumbo Keyes appeared at his door. Keyes' big grin betrayed the fact he'd heard some of the conversation.

'What can I do for you Mr Keyes?' asked Conway a little self consciously.

'Your Vietnamese friend?' winked Keyes.

'You know bloody well it was,' smiled Conway. 'What's up?'

The grin on Keyes' face disappeared and was replaced by a frown. 'Steve, remember I told you about Sally being back here in Manila?' Conway nodded.

'She rang again a couple of days ago and said she needed to see you urgently when you got back here.'

'Did she say why?'

'No, but from the tone of her voice it's important, she sounded scared. I told her you would arrive today, ok boss?'

'No problem. I owe Sally. Did she leave a contact number?'

Keyes shook his head. 'No, she said she'd contact you...and Steve, I think it'll be pretty soon.'

Conway rubbed a furrowed brow. 'She's obviously in some kind of trouble. My guess is marital problems. I got a letter from her some time ago and reading between the lines, things weren't going too well on the home front.'

'Wouldn't be the first time a marriage between a Filipina and foreigner hit the rocks, they're not all married to great guys like me,' grinned the big guy.

Conway rolled his eyes. 'How *is* Ang and the new arrival? Oh, by the way, I've got something for her.' He reached down into a carrier bag and handed Keyes the gift. 'Here's a little something I got in Saigon.'

'Hey, thanks buddy, that's very thoughtful, she'll love it whatever it is. Ang's great and Menchie's cute as a button. Ang brought her in here one day and the staff wanted to steal her. You know how crazy Filipinas are about kids?'

A shadow passed over Conway's face.

'Yeah, they love kids,' he said quietly.

The big man instantly realized his mistake. His happy remark had apparently brought back memories of the infant Conway had lost so tragically.

'Ah, ok Steve,' said Keyes with a hint of embarrassment. 'Thanks again for the present. I'd better let you get on with it. As you would say man, a kangaroo couldn't jump over that lot,' he smiled, pointing to the pile of paperwork Zeny had left.

'Yeah,' Conway said, staring into space.

* * *

At 9.00 pm that night he yawned and rubbed his eyes. The rest of day and evening had been spent checking income statements, signing cheques; replying to correspondence from suppliers and local government departments and sundry other documents in addition to taking many internal and external phone calls. It had been a long day and time to have a late dinner and get an early night. He was half-way out the door when his phone rang. Now what? He stood for a moment undecided. Should I, or shouldn't I? No choice.

'Hello...hello... is that you...sir Steve?' said a small voice...Sally!

Conway groaned inwardly wishing he'd let the phone ring.

'Hi Sally, Mr. Keyes told me you were back in town. How are things?'

'I must see you! Can we meet tonight? Please!'

He was dog-tired. The last thing he needed was someone with an emotional problem, but it *was* Sally. She'd been a good friend and lover and...she sounded desperate.

'Ok, *Guernicas* restaurant in Del Pilar, you know it don't you?' he said wearily.

'Yes, I know it, what time?'

'I'll be there in thirty minutes.'

'Ok sir...thank you,' she said, the relief in her voice palpable.

'And Sally.'

'Yes.'

'My name is still Steve...not sir,' he said, softening his tone.

'Sorry...Steve.'

Guernicas is an institution in Manila; a restaurant known throughout the Philippines and loved by the old Spanish families of Ermita fond of saying, *it evokes the sunny Spain of bullfights and flamenco.*

Conway sat in an intimate dining area of crystal chandeliers, and tables set with red and white tablecloths. Whitewashed walls were adorned with large posters of bullfights and flamenco dancers. The windows were enclosed by curved, black wrought iron grills; all very Spanish. He was checking the menu when Sally appeared at the arched front entrance. It was a busy night and she stood for a moment, hesitant, her eyes flitting nervously from table to table.

He stood and waved nearly knocking the food from the tray of a passing waiter. Her face lit up in recognition and relief. She quickly made her way through the crowd and threw her arms around him to the amusement of diners nearby.

'Oh darling Steve, it's so good to see you again,' she exclaimed, as if she couldn't believe he was actually standing in front of her.

'Likewise Sally, take a seat and tell me what this is all about, I never expected to see you back in Manila again,' he said, easing her into a chair opposite.

'It's a long story but I'll try and make it as brief as I can si...Steve.'

'Ok, are you hungry? I am. Let's eat first. I've heard the paella here is sensational.' He handed her a menu. She quickly scanned it, her mind obviously on more important things.

He ordered the *paella* and she settled for '*longestinos* themidor to be accompanied by a carafe of vintage Spanish red. The wine arrived, Conway filled her goblet and she began her story.

'You received my letter didn't you?'

He nodded, filled his own glass and came straight to the point. 'Sure, but to be honest I detected you weren't entirely happy with the marriage?'

Her eyebrows lifted. 'Was it obvious?' She paused and sipped her wine. 'Yes, you are right. We married a month after I arrived in the States and lived in San Diego. The house was nice, even had a swimming pool. He was a loving husband, couldn't do enough for me, so attentive, so caring. For months it was wonderful; what I always wanted, then'...her voice trailed away and she looked down at her glass toying with it for a minute or two. He said nothing, letting her collect her thoughts.

'Almost over night he changed.'

'How?'

She grimaced and looked back up at him, the strain of what had been going on in her life clearly showing in the lines on her face.

'He became moody, withdrawn, began to find fault with everything I did. I could not seem to please him. He started to fly into violent rages for almost no reason. Steve, I was scared, I thought he would kill me.'

'Ok, for no apparent reason his personality changed but, he was in Vietnam wasn't he?'

'Yes he was.'

'So didn't he get professional help? There are organizations that help Vietnam vets.'

'Yes he did. The military sent him to psychologists, psychiatrists, all kinds of counselling. They put him on medication and it seemed to help for a while but he would forget to take it and the old violence would return.'

She gave away the sipping and took a gulp of her wine. Her hands trembled, her voice shook with emotion. This was a Sally he had never seen before. He couldn't help noticing the drawn face and nervous manner when she first arrived. There were lines that weren't there before; the incipient crow's feet, the legacy of many stressful days and sleepless nights.

But she was still a very attractive woman. The heart-shaped face with its large sloe eyes, framed by glossy shoulder length black hair, the shapely figure, now a little thinner but still able to attract admiring glances from other male diners.

But it was the haunted look that set her apart from the Sally he once knew. She had aged in the relatively short time since he'd last seen her. Gone was the sweet, cheerful Sally, now replaced by a strained, nervous, agitated woman who had undergone a traumatic experience of which he was about to hear more.

'Once he held a rifle to my head,' she said, taking another gulp of her wine. 'I was sure he was going to kill me. His whole body was shaking. His face was red and twisted and the hatred in his eyes, My God! I've never been so frightened in all my life! I have never seen hate like I saw in that man's eyes that night.'

The hand that held her glass continued to shake. Conway reached over and gently took it from her.

'Slow down. What happened then?'

'I closed my eyes expecting a bullet. I was sure I was about to die. Then…nothing happened. Maybe 30 seconds later I opened my eyes and he was gone. My legs gave way and I collapsed onto the floor. Then I vomited Steve. I kept vomiting until my belly was aching and I couldn't vomit any more. It was horrible. I lay there in it for a long time then I got up and phoned the police.'

'Did he come back?'

'No, not that night,' she said tiredly. 'He didn't, thank God, but then I did a silly thing.'

'Like what?'

'Suddenly I had this feeling of contrition. I knew I couldn't turn him in. Steve, he was my husband! I knew he'd been through a terrible time in Vietnam. He'd been wounded, seen his best friends blown up and shot, seen so many awful things. I knew he was suffering from post traumatic stress. So…I lied to the police and said it was an intruder and gave them a false description.'

'Did they buy it?'

'I don't think they did but what else could they do? They told me they would put out an all points bulletin. They asked if I wanted protection or go to the hospital, stuff like that, but I told them I'd be ok. I could tell one of the cops an older guy didn't really believe me, but they left saying they would have a car cruise my neighborhood for the rest of the night.'

Their meals arrived, glasses were refilled but given the circumstances there was no *joi de vivre*. They ate in a gloomy silence. When Conway finished his meal he dabbed his lips with a napkin and took another sip of wine. 'So, tell me, what happened after that night…and why are you back in the Philippines?'

She avoided his eyes for a moment then let out a huge sigh.

'I didn't know what to do. Should I run? Should I hide? It's so hard being a foreigner in another country, especially when there is no family support. Mine are here in the Philippines, but my parents are dead and the others are scattered. I haven't seen most of them for years except an uncle here in Antipolo. In the end I phoned an Army buddy of his, explained what had happened and asked for his advice and help.'

'And?'

'He said he would help but he had to report the incident to the military authorities and see if they could do something. He said he thought he knew where to find Marvin. There was a vet's refuge in north California. They'd both spent time there when they came back from Vietnam. It was a good bet he'd head for there.'

Conway signaled for their carafe to be refilled. 'Go on.'

The carafe arrived and she swallowed a mouthful too quickly, bringing on a violent coughing fit. Conway patted her gently on the back until it stopped. She sat for a couple of minutes to regain her composure then continued her story.

'The one thing I knew I had to do immediately was to go into hiding. I was terrified. I knew Marvin in his present state would kill me sooner or later if he didn't get further treatment. I decided the safest place for me was the Philippines. I would tell no one, just pack up and leave. That's what I did…and here I am.'

'So no one in the States knows you are back here?'

'No one. But…I have a few close Filipina friends in San Diego and you know what the Filipino network is like. They will figure it out. I'm still worried that he'll find out and come looking for me.'

'Where are you staying here?'

'Antipolo, it's on the outskirts of Manila. I'm staying with the uncle I told you about. Marvin doesn't know of him but Steve, I'm still scared.'

'So how can I help?'

'I'm not sure you can, but I just wanted to see you again and tell you my story. I have missed you so much, I….' She blushed and lowered her head. Conway was nonplussed. He wanted to help her but how? Did he really want to become involved with a woman on the run from a psychotic and potentially murderous husband?

He paid the bill and they stood outside Guernicas on M H Del Pilar waiting for a jeepney to take her back to Antipolo. It was late, the street almost deserted and traffic was now almost non-existent. She tentatively took his hand.

'Steve, I don't think I'll be able to get jeepneys all the way to Antipolo at this time of night and I can't afford a taxi fare. Would you...' she hesitated for a moment. 'Would you mind...if I stayed with you tonight. I promise I will leave first thing in the morning?'

It was now Conway's turn to hesitate. He remembered only too well their passionate affair. She was now married and off limits as far as he was concerned. But, what she said was correct. Antipolo was a long way from Ermita. She would need to catch at least two jeepneys to Antipolo and most had finished for the night. He could give her taxi fare but they were few and far between. What she said made sense...and he did have a spare bed.

'Ok, but you must leave in the morning, come on,' he said gruffly, striding off on the ten minute walk to his apartment.

* * *

Kim Anh looked up from her computer to see Dung staring at her from the far side of the office. She flashed him a quick smile and returned to her work but a few seconds later felt a tap on her shoulder, Dung.

'Hello Miss Kim Anh,' he said with a nervous smile. His tone was formal, one he seemed to always use in her presence but not when speaking to others. Before she could reply he rushed on. 'Miss Kim Anh, I wonder...' he stopped for a few seconds and coughed, trying to clear his throat and cover his nervousness. 'Would you be so kind as to have coffee with me this evening?'

Kim was only too well aware of his feelings for her. He had made that abundantly clear by often trying to engage her in conversation at work and on the staff bus which took them back to the city after work. But his manner unsettled her. It was unnecessarily possessive. After all, he was not her boyfriend; they'd never even been on a date. He seemed to become jealous to the point of anger if he saw her talking to other male members of the staff, especially if she was laughing and enjoying the conversation.

She remembered his behaviour on the weekend the company had taken the staff on an expenses paid trip to Vung Tau. As she told Conway that night beside the river in Thanh Da, Dung had sat on a rock and sulked as Kim chatted and played on the beach with some of her colleagues. Finally she had come and asked him to join them but he mumbled a refusal and wandered off. Now he was asking her for a date! She didn't want to hurt him, but she had given her heart to another man.

'Thank you so much Mr Dung, I appreciate your kind offer but I am sorry, I am busy tonight,' she said kindly, trying to let him down as softly as possible. Dung's expression changed. The smile disappeared instantly. His lips twisted in an ugly sneer. He seemed about to say something but changed his mind. His black eyes bored into her for a second then he turned and stalked off.

Kim shivered as she watched him walk back to his office.

She knew he was terribly hurt and thought about going after him to apologize but decided against it. His sudden change frightened her. She sat there staring at her computer keyboard for a while. Vietnamese men could be insanely jealous when rejected. Had she made an enemy?

10

Conway unlocked the door of his apartment and ushered Sally inside. He left the main overhead lights off and flicked on the red wall bracket lamps, the glow creating an atmosphere of warm intimacy.

Her eyes swept around an apartment that was well kept and spacious. The living area contained dark, highly polished *narra* furniture contrasting with brightly coloured scatter rugs on the parquet floor. Lemon and cream walls hung with watercolor originals of Filipino life and the open plan kitchen with its stone bench top, modern gas stove and stainless steel utensils reminded her of her own home in San Diego.

She walked out to the small balcony and looked for a few moments at the city lights far below then came back inside. 'I always loved your place,' she said, lightly rubbing a finger over the bench top and glancing across at an ornately carved wooden coffee table where magazines were stacked in a neat pile. 'You keep it nice, do you have a maid?'

He shook his head. 'Not on a permanent basis but usually once a month I get someone in to give the place a spring clean.' She came and stood in front of him; a little too close, and took both of his hands in hers.

'The only time I was here before was the night I told you I was going back to Marvin,' she said quietly. 'I didn't stay long and was so emotional I had forgotten what a nice apartment you had...remember?'

'I remember,' he replied, more abruptly than he intended.

'Sally, it's late. I've an early start in the morning, you can sleep in my bedroom,' he said, leading her down a hallway.

'Oh lovely, I was hoping for that.' She broke into a broad smile which vanished as he turned away at the bedroom door.

'Oh…you don't…where will you sleep?' her face mirroring surprise and disappointment. They'd been lovers and she had always felt and hoped, it would lead to something more permanent; that was until Marvin came back into her life.

'I'll sleep in the spare bedroom. Have a shower if you wish. Towels are in the bathroom.' He went to a dark panelled linen cupboard and took out a blue, long-sleeved cotton shirt. 'You can wear this.' She held it up in front of her and tried to hide her feelings with a weak smile.

'Thank you sir, you are so kind, but it's *so big*! I think I will get lost in this, I hope you can find me in the morning.'

He ignored her attempt at humour. 'Just help yourself to anything. If you're awake before me, there's plenty of food in the fridge, good night.' He turned and left her standing beside the bed feeling downcast and foolish. She went to the bathroom and stripped off in front of a floor to ceiling mirror and checked out her image. Doesn't he find me attractive anymore?

She stretched and fluffed the hair at the back of her head letting it fall back to her shoulders a motion which uplifted her still, full, dark-nippled breasts. They now had the slight sag of maturity, but were still good enough to attract most men when she cared to wear low-cut dresses or tops. Her olive skinned body was still slim; concave belly and shapely legs. Like most Filipino women she tried to look after her figure even to the extent of trimming her pubic hair into a neat vee.

She poked her tongue out at the figure looking back at her and stepped into the shower letting the warm spray cleanse her body, but it did little to soothe her troubled mind.

When she finished, she felt like a new woman…almost; towelled herself dry, glanced again in the mirror and wrapped the towel around her body. She spent a few minutes combing her long dark tresses then moved silently out into the darkened hallway. As she tiptoed past the closed door of his bedroom she stopped for a few seconds. There was this almost overwhelming desire to knock, but given his attitude, thought better of it.

It was a warm night. She picked up his shirt from the bed then tossed it away in a combination of anger and frustration, climbed naked into the king-sized bed and pulled up the covers. Although dog-tired after a stress-filled day, sleep was a long time coming.

In America she'd realized her big mistake. She'd been in love with Conway before leaving the Philippines; but the promise of a new life in America with her former lover was too great an opportunity to pass up.

An added incentive was the money she could make by working in the States. This would allow her to help provide a better life for the rest of her dirt-poor family in the province. Had she been so wrong?

Sure, the truth was she was fleeing from Marvin but there were a thousand places she could have hidden in the US. The real reason she was back in the Philippines was the secret hope, now a seemingly forlorn one, of reviving the relationship with Conway.

She lay in the dark hoping he would change his mind and come and make love to her and for a few precious moments take her into a realm somewhere she could forget the pain, torment and fear she had endured these past months. What the hell, she didn't care anymore! She hadn't been with a man for a long time, sex with Marvin had been brutal and a chore. What she longed for more than anything was a little tenderness, if not…love.

Her thoughts drifted back to the sweet times in Manila with Conway. The passion they'd once shared and here he was, just a few yards away, treating her as if she didn't exist.

He had changed; his manner now cool and indifferent. She couldn't blame him. She'd rejected him and gambled in the hope of a better life… and lost. The game of life plays some cruel tricks at times. Hot tears rolled down her cheeks.

What the hell is wrong with this guy? Maybe he's got another woman? The thought made her suddenly sit bolt upright in bed. Maybe it's that restaurant bitch! That Lily Li! She's rich and sexy. I'm sure they were lovers, it was written all over her face the day we met her outside Robinson's department store. So damn superior! I hate her!

She fell back to the pillow and stared at the ceiling her mind whirling around with all kinds of possibilities. When I contacted the hotel looking for Conway no one said anything. Knowing Filipinos, and their insatiable appetite for gossip, someone would have said something; especially if it involved the flamboyant and exotic Lily. I know I hurt him and he has a right to be angry but there was a time when he couldn't wait to get me into his bed? Something or someone has changed him but what?

She was still wondering as she drifted off into a dreamless sleep.

* * *

Conway yawned, stretched and blinked as the early morning sun streamed in through his window. The apartment was quiet. He got up and padded down the hallway to her bedroom. The bed was neatly made; the room empty. He went to the kitchen and noticed a scrap of paper on the bench; a note, from Sally. He held it in one hand and began reading as he switched on the electric kettle to make coffee.

Dear Steve,

Thank you for letting me stay the night and please forgive me for burdening you with my troubles. You were the only one I thought I could rely on for help. It seems I was wrong. I don't blame you for turning away from me, after all it was me who turned away from you at a time we had become very close. I hope you can find it in your heart to forgive me for that also. Thank you for your love and everything you had done for me in the past. I will not trouble you again.

Love always

Sally xxx

He read the note several times before placing it back on the bench. 'Shit Sal, I'm sorry. I was bloody rude. You deserved better than that!'

He heaped a teaspoon of coffee into a mug and filled it with boiling water added milk and sat at his kitchen table trying to think what he should do about her.

He had no idea where she lived other than Antipolo, a long way from Ermita. The chances of going there on spec and finding her were remote. The Black Jack bar where she once worked had been closed for over a year since the owner Bert Groyne had been deported to Australia. Questioning the neighbours of her old apartment might be worth a try, but in the meantime I've got a hotel to run and I need to speak to the shareholders in Australia about a Down Under operation in Saigon.

He had a shower and a quick breakfast of fruit, cereal and more coffee before walking to work on a bright sun-filled Manila morning, still unable to shake an uneasy feeling about Sally.

He put a call through to James Sinclair the managing director of the Down Under group and waited. Thirty seconds later his phone rang and Annie chirped, 'Mr Sinclair for you sir.'

'Hi Steve, welcome back, how was Saigon?'

'Very interesting James.' He liked the ebullient Scottish MD, a man of excellent judgement with a keen eye for a deal and a dollar. 'I've got an idea you might be interested in, an expansion of our operation.'

'What've you got in mind?'

Conway outlined his thoughts about looking for either a small hotel or opening a bar/restaurant bar in Saigon.

'From what I could see, there's a need for a decent expat operation in Saigon also catering for tourists, similar to what we have here. There's a couple of bars catering for foreigners but they're small, pretty low key and boring, the service is often indifferent and too many staff are disinterested to the point of rudeness. With Vietnam opening up and tourism on the boil there, with our expertise and experience, an operation like we have in Manila would be a winner. I'm sure of it!'

'As a matter of fact, I've been thinking about exactly the same thing too,' agreed Sinclair excitedly. 'As you say that country is on the move and you're right, tourism is going gangbusters and foreign investment is coming in from all over! Do we have any contacts there? You know we need a local, one who's on the ball, knows the local business ropes and most importantly, has got the right connections in high places. You and I both know how easy it is to fall in a heap investing in that part of the world Steve.'

'Well, I don't have anyone specifically at the moment but there is at least one person I feel could lead me to the right people.'

'Ok, put your thoughts on paper; costs, location, company set up, investment rules, potential, you know the sort of thing I need to put to the other shareholders. Then let's do what the Yanks say and *run it up the flagpole.*'

'Will do. How're things in The Land Down Under?'

'Same old, same old Steve, you know how it is,' he chuckled. 'More rules, more regulations, more dickheads pretending to govern the country. Greatest place on earth to live, but they're trying to bore us to death here. I look forward to your report. Keep up the good work son.'

Conway replaced the phone, with a smile of satisfaction. 'Thanks James, Saigon here we come!'

* * *

Lily Li was horny, very horny…thinking about Steve Conway. She stood gazing out through the floor to ceiling window of her Shanghai apartment on the Bund across at the silver-blue space-age spire of the Pearl TV tower and the magic surrealism of the skyscrapers dominating the Pudong area on the other side of the busy Huangpu River.

Her lovers had been few and far between in recent times. She'd come to Shanghai on the advice of relatives to set up a restaurant similar to the successful *Lily Li's Teahouse* in Manila. A sensual woman, she'd been too busy finding a location for her restaurant to concern herself about finding a man. Finally after weeks of searching she found the ideal site on the top floor of a building leased by a bank with a magnificent view of the Bund promenade and beyond.

Tough negotiations followed and the local bureaucracy had been a nightmare, but in the end Lily's innate combination of business acumen and more than a little cunning had secured the site with a long lease at an acceptable rental.

She brought in the best interior designer in Shanghai and transformed what was a bare shell into an elaborate 100 seat bar and restaurant in an ultramodern, futuristic style. All soaring glass chrome and stainless steel furniture set on two levels. A large circular bar on the top level was staffed by bright young men in black shirts and tight shiny black pants while the restaurant below under the control of a team of hard-working gourmet chefs, was served by beautiful, young Chinese women in figure-hugging, bright red ankle-length gowns.

The atmosphere evoked class, money and restrained sophistication but lively enough to appeal to the young (and not so young) Chinese *noveau riche* who packed the place most nights especially Fridays, after a week of frantic deal making. China was booming and no more so than in Shanghai, *The New York of China*.

Every night Lily would smile with satisfaction at the packed restaurant and frenetic bar trade and bless the relatives who advised her to come to Shanghai and try her luck. But she missed male company; in particular, that of a certain Australian. She picked up the phone and asked the operator to get her a Manila number and smiled as Conway's familiar Australian accent came down the line.

'Hello lover,' cooed Lily.

'Hey Lily, how's things in *The New China*?'

'Wonderful darling, but be much better if you were here. When are you coming to see your Lily? You know she misses *everything* about you darling, if you know what I mean?'

Conway found it hard not to laugh; same old Lily, great fun, in and out of bed. She was pretty transparent but he knew her feelings for him were genuine, even if she was a bit over the top at times.

'I've just returned from Vietnam, so you above all people, would know the amount of work I have in front of me. No rest for the wicked.'

'Yes, and I know you are wicked darling,' she said evilly. 'But seriously darling,' she dropped Lily the libertine and became Lily the business woman. 'Is there a chance you can come here? I do want to talk to you about a few things. There are great opportunities opening up which I am sure would interest you, and your company.'

'I haven't forgotten our previous conversations about Shanghai and there is interest among our shareholders, but right now we are looking at a Vietnamese operation. If that doesn't pan out, I promise you we'll definitely look at China.'

'Ok lover, it looks like I'll have to come to the mountain if Mahomet won't come to me. As a matter of fact, I *do* have to come to Manila for a few days to talk to a lawyer about the lease on my restaurant and visit my mother, so I hope to see you soon. Ok lover?'

'Always great to see you Lily, look forward to catching up again. By the way, when will this be?'

'Within the next two weeks darling, so keep your bed warm,' she laughed, hanging up. Conway grinned. Kim Anh, Lily, Sally, maybe the smart thing is to head for the mountains and become a monk. Suddenly he remembered something. He picked the phone again and called Keyes.

'Mate, when I called you from Saigon you said Sally had left a phone number. Do you still have it?' Keyes didn't answer immediately obviously trying to remember where it was. Finally, 'ah, yes, I put it somewhere, will have a look and bring it up to you buddy.'

Five minutes later Keyes walked in and handed Conway a slip of paper with Sally's phone number. Conway took it and waved Keyes to a chair. Keyes sat with a quizzical look on his face.

Conway glanced at the note then put it under a small jade paperweight beside his phone.

'I met Sally last night Jumbo and things aren't good with her.' Keyes was fond of Sally and listened intently as Conway told of his meeting with her. He frowned when Conway came to the part about the threat with the rifle.

'The guy's a psycho Steve. He was in Vietnam; it's post traumatic stress syndrome.'

'No doubt about it, that's why she's back here, she's afraid for her life and who could blame her.'

'Hasn't he been receiving treatment? There's a lot that can be done these days for these guys and America is finally trying to make amends for the shit treatment they handed out to their Vietnam vets…'

'He has had some, and apparently is on medication but he forgets to take it and then the trouble starts. There is a buddy, Sally tells me, who's trying to get him help but in the meantime she's hiding here.'

'What are you going to do Steve?'

Conway clasped both hands behind his head and leaned back in his chair. 'I don't know. I don't really want to get involved, but I do owe her. I'll give her a call and tell her to keep in touch and let me know if she needs anything. Other than that, I don't know what else I can do.'

'You two were pretty sweet once weren't you man?'

'Yes, we were, but she made her decision…' Conway let his words hang in the air, his tone indicating the matter was closed so they discussed hotel matters.

When the Saigon proposal was mentioned, Keyes' eyes widened.

'Hey man, that could be a smart move right now. Let's get in before America lifts the embargo and all those greedy Yank corporations come in with all their money and beat us out of it.' Conway smiled inwardly at his American assistant manager's disdainful reference to *greedy Yank corporations.*

'My thoughts too, but it means I'll have to go back there for a while, you'll be minding the fort again, ok?'

Keyes rubbed his hands. 'Hey, I love being king pin and throwing my weight around, go for it buddy.'

Conway smiled. He knew Keyes the gentle giant, was loved and respected by all the staff for his professional manner, consideration and good humor. The Down Under was in good hands when Jumbo Keyes was in charge.

'By the way, I got a call from Lily this morning…she's coming back to Manila for a few days.'

The big man rolled his eyes and flashed his piano keys smile. 'Good luck!'

He dialed Sally's number and the voice that answered was male, old and tired. Sally came to the phone, her voice timid and fearful. Very few people knew her phone number now. When she realized who it was, her tone became cold and bitter.

'What do you want? You made it clear to me last night I was a burden to you.'

'I'm sorry for my behaviour last night. I was rude, you have every right to be angry,' Conway replied calmly. 'I want to tell you that I am here for you, if you need me Sally.' There was a long silence and he thought she had hung up until she said quietly, 'thank you but I…I…don't want to be a burden but you were the only one I…' her tone now one of sadness and resignation.

He wasn't sure what to say next; except he knew he would be only fooling himself if he tried to fight the fact that he still had feelings for her, and they were stronger than he cared to admit.

'Sally, I meant what I said. I have never forgotten what you did for me…and what we meant to each other.'

'Me too,' she replied, brightening a little. 'Would you mind if I called to see you again one time?'

'Of course not but I have to go back to Vietnam for a while. Keep in touch and next time you're in town let's have lunch or dinner together, ok?'

'That would be lovely. Can we make it soon?'

'Sure, give me a call first huh?'

'I will, thank you so much, dar…Steve, see you soon.'

Conway replaced the receiver and sat deep in thought for a few minutes then got up, stretched and walked downstairs to talk to his front desk staff.

* * *

At midnight in San Diego, a tall, thickset individual crept up the concrete driveway of a neat, low set white stucco house, then straightened up and hammered on the front door. The house was in darkness. He waited for a few moments and with no response or sound from within he went around the back and smashed the glass of a window off the back porch; still nothing.

He reached through carefully and unhooked the catch, eased up the window and crawled in. He switched on lights in the kitchen, living room then went to the main bedroom. Back in the kitchen he opened the refrigerator. No food. No smell. He checked the trash can in the kitchen… empty. The house had been unoccupied for some time.

He went back to the bedroom and began frantically rummaging through drawers and cupboards, hurling the contents on the floor in frustration. Leaving the mess on the floor he returned to a second bedroom used as a study and continued the hunt through the drawers of a credenza ripping out papers and household documents and throwing them around the room. No luck!

Back in the kitchen he stood pulling at his hair and mouthing obscenities. Then a thought! He unlocked the back door and went to an Otto bin and hauled it into the living room and upended the contents. It hadn't been emptied and overflowed with trash. The carpeted floor became an evil smelling mess of rotten food scraps, egg shells, fruit skins, paper, plastic containers and an infestation of maggots. He bent down clawing wildly among the foulness for several minutes hurling rubbish around the room in ever increasing fury. Then, he found the evidence he was looking for...a crumpled, soiled copy of an airline flight schedule and something else...a business card with the name *Steve Conway*...and an address in Manila.

11

Kim Anh pulled into the ground floor basement of her house in Thanh Da. It had been a long hard day at work. She'd had words with Dung over a trivial matter concerning the double booking of a family. It had left her tired and stressed and she was looking forward to having a short nap before dinner.

She parked her motorbike against the side wall and went upstairs where to her surprise and chagrin, found Dung sitting with her older sister Ngoc at a table in their tiny living room. He looked up as she walked in his expression a mixture of anxiety and guilt. He put down the cup of tea he was drinking and rose offering a half smile.

She glared back at him. 'What are you doing here?'

He was taken aback by her hostile tone and stood uncomfortably, his sallow face reddening, mouth open and closing like a fish gasping for air, trying to find a reply. He gave up after a few moments and reached down beside the table and from a large plastic bag produced a bouquet of flowers and held them out to her.

'For…for you,' he stammered, 'a peace offering.'

Kim ignored the flowers and continued to look daggers at him.

Ngoc looked up from the table, her eyes pleading with her young sister to accept the bouquet. Reluctantly, Kim took them and muttered an unconvincing 'thank you.' Ngoc motioned her to sit down beside Dung.

'Kim Anh.' Ngoc always used Kim's full name when she wanted to say something of significance. 'Mr Dung has something to say to you and I think you should listen.'

'Mr Dung has already said enough to me today *chi oi*,' retorted Kim.

'No please listen to him,' pleaded Ngoc. Kim knew Ngoc wanted her for Dung. He had a good job at Waterworld "with prospects", she kept reminding Kim, 'and his family was said to be quite wealthy.' But it fell on deaf ears and right now the younger sibling refused to sit and continued glaring at their extremely uncomfortable visitor.

Dung cleared his throat and licked his lips nervously. 'Miss Kim Anh, er, ah, I want to apologise for our conflict today. I accept the blame, it was a silly misunderstanding. I hope you will forgive me.'

Kim said nothing.

'Em, Mr. Dung is a good man, hear him out,' pleaded Ngoc.

Kim continued to stare at him, her face a stone mask.

'Ah...er...Miss Kim Anh,' he gulped, 'I...er...have been invited to a wedding this Saturday evening, a wedding of a friend who was...is... a very important man in Saigon society, and I would formally like to invite you to come with me. Will you please do me that honour?'

Her reply was short and to the point.

'No,' she said, pushing past him to her bedroom slamming the door behind her. Ngoc and Dung looked at each other in dismay. Ngoc shook her head and touched his hand reassuringly.

'Don't worry,' she said in a low voice so Kim could not hear. 'I will talk with her. She will see my way, I promise you. I do not want her with that foreigner.' Dung rose, his face flushed. '*Cam on*,' (thank you), '*hen gap lai*,' he muttered and made his way to the front door.

A few minutes later, Kim emerged from her bedroom, having changed into a light blue cotton housedress. 'Has he gone?'

Now it was Ngoc's turn to be angry. 'You were very impolite and rude to him, you must apologise.'

'I will not! He is the rude one, and very jealous, I do not like him.'

'He is right for you,' insisted Ngoc. 'He is well educated, your own age and has a good job, even you told me that,' she said, picking up the empty tea cups and taking them to the sink.

'Mr Dung would make an ideal husband for you,' she said over her shoulder, 'you would be stupid not to consider him.'

'Let me tell you something,' replied Kim hotly, 'Mr Dung followed Steve and I to a restaurant in Pham Ngu Lao one day. I did not see him but Steve described a man who kept looking at us in a very unfriendly way. I knew it was Mr Dung but I said nothing at the time, I did not want any trouble.'

Ngoc would not accept any negative talk of Dung and ignored the comment.

'This Mr Steve,' she said turning to Kim, 'this foreigner!' she almost spat the words. 'He is much older than you and after what they have done to us in the past, we Northerners do not trust foreigners.'

Ngoc's tone then softened. She stopped washing the cups, wiped her hands on a towel then went across to her sister and hugged her. But Kim stood straight and unyielding. 'Please,' Ngoc said, holding her close. 'This Australian seems friendly enough but you do not know this man, and I can tell you this…your life would be better if you married your own kind. You know I only want the best for you, and our mother would not be happy if you married a foreigner, you know that don't you?'

'I have not discussed Steve with mother,' replied Kim, pulling away defiantly. 'What are you telling me? I have not heard this before! I do intend to write to mother and tell her about Steve and then we will see how she feels. Now, please, I have had enough of this. I am tired, I want to have a nap, call me when dinner is ready!' Ngoc was about to say something but thought better of it. Kim returned to her bedroom and slammed the door again leaving her sister seething.

Kim was the stubborn one in the family and in one of her impossible moods. But the older sister would not give up on Dung, not yet anyway. Her husband's voice downstairs told of his arrival from work; he expected his evening meal to be waiting for him. She hurried to their small gas stove and began preparing the food.

* * *

Instead of returning home, Dung decided to have his dinner at a small, open-air café around the corner from Kim's house; the same street where she and Conway had strolled a few weeks before. He finished a bowl of noodles and signaled to the middle aged woman who had served him to bring a can of beer and a glass mug.

He emptied the beer into the mug, took a huge gulp and sat staring sullenly, immersed in his thoughts. He had hoped to make up with Kim after their angry words at work but her cold rejection in front of Ngoc had humiliated him and caused him to lose face; a dangerous thing to do to a Vietnamese male.

A proud man, he was firstly insulted that a Vietnamese woman would choose a foreigner over one of her own kind and secondly, this guy's intrusion into Kim's life had now made it that much harder for him to win her, something he had been trying to do unsuccessfully for some time. His hatred of the foreigner now knew no bounds. He took the empty can, bent it in half, dropped it to the floor and ground it viciously beneath his heel.

He gulped down the last dregs of the beer, ordered another, ripped it open and not bothering with a glass emptied it in one long swallow. Then he ordered another, and another giving it the same treatment. Not being a regular drinker the sudden ingestion of so much alcohol was already beginning to have an effect on him; a bad effect.

He had to find out what Kim and this foreigner had planned. Kim Anh had informed Ngoc that Conway had returned to Manila and Ngoc had eagerly passed this on to Dung. But, was he coming back to Vietnam? Surely she would not marry him? Ngoc would see to that! But if he does come back I will do something, I will not let him take her from me! I will kill him first!

He continued to sit there hunched over his beer brooding until he had finished then pushed himself to his feet, paid the bill and walked unsteadily across the street to his motorcycle fumbling with the keys. His vision was slightly blurred; he felt dizzy and was now having trouble walking in a straight line, causing him to be nearly barreled by a motorcyclist confused by Dung's weaving gait, had to swerve at the last moment to avoid hitting him.

Somehow he made it to his bike, gave a few dong to the small boy who'd been the bike's minder and waited while the kid fitted the key in the ignition. He was in no condition to do it himself. The boy held the bike while Dung mounted, steadied himself, then looking back with a scowl toward Kim's apartment, slipped the clutch and roared off into the humid Saigon night.

* * *

Two weeks later, Lily Li's flight touched down into Manila's International Airport at exactly 7.15 pm. She waited impatiently beside the carousel until her luggage appeared then flashed her passport to a disinterested customs officer and walked through the large glass doors onto the airport concourse where to her extreme annoyance, she was delayed by a zealous official who made her fumble through her purse for the baggage receipt attached to her airline ticket.

It never happened at other international airports and was a constant source of irritation. She finally found it and glared while he slowly peeled it from the ticket and handed it back with a smile. She ignored his 'thank you ma'am' and rushed beyond the steel barrier across to her driver waiting beside a black limousine.

Just over half an hour later she arrived at her Spanish style mansion in Malate where waiting on the steps were her aged mother Maria Victoria and her pretty, ever-smiling maid, Binky. There were hugs all round as they trooped into the house leaving the chauffeur to stagger in with the heavy luggage. His boss was never one to travel lightly.

Lily smiled with appreciation as she entered the large dining room with its white marble floor, large crystal chandelier and ornate furniture and fittings. She was hungry and dinner had been set at the long mahogany table with crystal goblets, silverware and flowers. Binky filled their glasses with expensive white French wine then whizzed off to the kitchen for their first course.

Lily and her mother took their places at either end of the table and immediately got down to business discussing the lease and the options on her restaurant in Manila and various other business matters.

Binky appeared with their entrée of white fish and green salad, followed by a main course of chicken adobo and sinigang. They took their time over the meal and discussed whether to renew the lease on Lily's restaurant or put the business up for sale. They were still undecided as they worked through a tropical fruit salad before finishing with a platter of imported cheeses and tiny cups of strong Turkish coffee.

The little maid brought in another small bottle of vintage French and filled their glasses before flashing a huge smile and skipping from the room. Lily watched her leave.

'She's a gem isn't she?'

'I don't know what I would do without her dear,' replied Maria Victoria. 'I'm only afraid that one day she will meet a man and leave. She will be hard to replace but my darling, it is you I am concerned about. Are you really happy in Shanghai dear?'

Lily's mother had been concerned about her daughter for some years. She felt Lily worked too hard and put too much effort into her business enterprises and not enough into finding someone to replace her late husband. Lily glanced down at her wine glass then looked up with a wan smile.

'Yes…and no, Mama,' she sighed.

'Oh, my dear, what do you mean?' Lily had always been a bright, outgoing woman, positive and forthright, ready to take on the world; her manner this evening seemed sad and introspective. Maria Victoria frowned. This was not her Lily.

'Mama, the restaurant is going well. We are making money, I'm meeting some very influential people and there's a possibility in the future I may open a *Lilys* in Beijing, Guangzhou and perhaps even Hong Kong but…'

'But what darling? What is the problem?'

Lily and Maria Victoria were close. Always had been and she could, and had, confided in her mother about most things in the past, but when it came to personal relationships there was hesitation.

Lily was more than attractive, men seemed to agree she was beautiful, even exotic and there had been no shortage of offers. But since her husband died there had been emptiness inside her. A feeling she had kept well hidden. A feeling she did not wish to talk about to anyone, least of all her mother, until now. To a proud woman like Lily it almost seemed like failure that she had not been able to find another suitable man...but there was one.

Lily drained the rest of her glass, 'Mama, I have been successful, I *am* successful but...I need someone, I think you know what I mean...'

'Yes, you are beautiful, you are successful my daughter, but do you really mean to tell me there is no one yet in your heart?'

'There is someone mama,' sighed Lily again, feeling guilt she did not understand. Was it an admission of failure? 'But,' she said, sipping her wine, 'I don't know what his true feelings toward me are. We have been...close but since I've been away I feel the distance has ruined our relationship.' Her mother leaned forward eager to learn more.

'Who is this man dear, is he Filipino? Chinese? Where is he and what is he?'

'He's an Australian, Mama. He's the boss of a hotel here in Manila.'

'Will you see him this time you are here dear?'

Lily paused with the glass at her lips then placed it back on the table.

'Yes, I phoned him from Shanghai, we agreed to meet but Mama it's so frustrating. He told me he's going back to Vietnam on another project. His company is apparently looking at starting something there...I don't know Mama, what do you think?'

'Do you love him dear?'

Again Lily took her time before replying.

'Yes...I think so...but as I said, I don't really know what his feelings for me are, and Mama, I can't wait forever.' The almost plaintive tone was so unlike her proud Lily.

Maria Victoria, a tiny, elegant woman in her late seventies, had lost her husband many years ago in a traffic accident. He was the love of her life but she had shed her tears in private. She had watched with pride as Lily had overcome the tragic loss of her husband also and built a highly successful and respected business in Manila. She was well aware that her daughter too, had kept her grief well hidden.

The old lady smiled reassuringly at her daughter. 'God will decide my child, if you are meant to be with this man, it will happen.'

'You are right of course Mama,' smiled Lily, raising her glass in salute. 'Let's go out and sit by the pool and enjoy this lovely Manila night.'

* * *

Conway put the finishing touches to his Saigon proposal for submission to the Down Under shareholders and called Gina to his office.

'I'd like to get this off to Australia tonight, so please make this a priority,' he said handing her the document. His hand-written proposal was long and detailed. It outlined the reasons for the project emphasizing the need for such an operation which he'd expressed to Sinclair, an expected location and a projected first year budget which was more of a guesstimate, based on calculations from his recent visit.

He wrote of the huge potential in the emerging Vietnamese tourist market and the relative low cost of overheads in rental, labour, electricity, water and sundry set-up costs including legal and accounting, which made it a very attractive destination. If his submission was accepted he proposed undertaking a feasibility study and reporting back as soon as possible.

The report was the result of many phone calls back and forth to Vietnam firstly with Kim who had been a big help in providing basic vital information including costs of renting properties around District 1 where it was deemed to be the most suitable venue for such an operation.

She had also given him the name of several accounting and legal firms with English speaking staff and the most important contact, an Australian expat named Jack Malone who had lived in Saigon for ten years and was heavily involved in the booming building industry. Conway and Malone had numerous phone conversations and arranged to meet when and if Conway returned to Saigon. Now it was simply a waiting game.

Conway's phone rang. It was his bar cashier Jackie, she sounded nervous. 'Sir..ah...there is someone in the bar...wants to speak to you, he says it's urgent.'

Conway looked at the pile of paperwork on his desk and grimaced.

'Ok Jackie, tell him I'll be there in a few minutes.'

He made a couple of phone calls, signed a few cheques for Zeny, finished a memo for housekeeping then went down into the bar on the floor below. It was mid-morning and quiet with little trade. Apart from a young male guest and his Filipino girlfriend, the only other person in the bar was a large male. He was sitting at a table in the far corner with his back to Conway. Jackie pointed and mouthed 'that's him.'

'Can I help you sir?' asked Conway politely.

'Conway, Steve Conway?' said the stranger, turning and getting to his feet. Conway could see now why Jackie was nervous. This guy's whole attitude was intimidating. He was about Conway's age, and where the Australian was just on six feet, this guy was easily six feet five. His once fit body was now fighting an incipient paunch, the result of two many boozy nights and bad food. The short sleeved khaki shirt revealed forearms that were thick and hairy. He stood arms akimbo in a stance suggesting imminent violence.

He looked down at Conway, eyes pale blue and cold. The thick-lipped mouth turned down in a scowl. The close shaved skull said it all. Marine hair cut. Even when they left the service, old habits die hard. Conway suddenly recognized him. It was the face in the photo he'd seen in Sally's apartment shortly after they had met. How different from the clean cut young Marine in the photo, but it was the same guy; Marvin, Sally's husband.

'Sally Reyes,' his tone deep and menacing; 'you know her?' He made the question sound like an accusation.

'Who are you?' asked Conway quietly.

'You don't need to know,' growled Marvin, 'just answer my question.'

The hairs stood up on the back of Conway's neck. 'Mate, I don't know who you are, I don't like your tone, and if I knew this Sally, you'd be the last person I'd tell.'

The big guy clenched his fists, the eyes wide, the pupils dilated. He was obviously having trouble keeping his temper under control.

'Ok smart ass, my name is Marvin Legrand and I'm her fucking husband and I *know* you know her. Don't lie to me or you'll wish you'd never been born! The bitch's run out on me and I found your name on a card…this!' he snarled pulling Conway's business card from the top pocket of his shirt.

'As well, I found details of an airline schedule indicating she was coming back to the Philippines. I knew she would, and for all I know, the bitch was coming back to you, asshole!'

This guy was dangerous. The heavy breathing, the flared nostrils, the stance, the intimidating manner; he was on a knife edge, and it wouldn't take much to push him over the abyss. 'Ok Marvin,' replied Conway coolly. 'I knew Sally when she worked here in Manila. The last time I saw her she told me she was leaving the Philippines to live in America and marry you! That's all I know. Sorry I can't help you.' Conway turned to walk away but Marvin grabbed his arm and swung him around…a bad move.

'You know more than that you bastard you…' that's all Marvin got out before a savage left rip into the soft paunch bent him double. He'd hardly emitted a loud "Ooohhh" before a crunching right cross spun him across the bar and dropped him face first onto the carpeted bar floor, out cold.

Conway turned to a shocked and open-mouthed Jackie. 'Get the guards to throw this arsehole out…and never let him in this hotel ever again…he's barred!' Then turning on his heel he returned to his office, breathing on his knuckles. Marvin had a soft belly but a hard chin. He called Jumbo Keyes to his office and told him what had happened.

'He's bad news Jumbo and he's got murder in his eyes, I can understand now why Sally is so frightened. Anyway, he's barred. I don't want him back in the place.'

'Got a description for me Steve? I'll memo all staff and make sure they all know.'

'He's a white guy, heavily built, 6 feet plus, paunchy but still in reasonable shape I would say. The face is broad, long nose, full pouty type lips, bit like a woman but make no mistake, he's a mean looking bastard. The almost shaven skull with the Marine hair cut gives him away. I'm a bit of an artist,' grinned Conway, 'I'll give you a bit of an identikit…it may help.'

'What about Sally Steve?'

'I'll get in touch and let her know the situation. She needs to be warned, pronto!'

'Ok, I'll get on to it straight away.'

Conway called Sally.

She was terrified. 'Oh my God! I knew he would somehow find out I had come back here. What am I to do? I know he will kill me if he finds me.'

'Who else apart from your uncle in Antipolo knows you're back here?'

'No one, oh God, I am so scared…'

'He doesn't know the whereabouts of your uncle does he? Do you have any other place to go? Are there any relatives in a far away province he doesn't know about?'

Sally thought for a few moments.

'I have an aunt in Isabella, it's in the far north, but Steve, I am sure one day he will somehow find me. He is crazy, I know he is.'

'Sally for the time being lay low. Get the hell out of here, go to Isabella. I'll have a word with the American Embassy I've got a good friend there. I'll explain the situation they may be able to help. If in the meantime Marvin breaks the law here, he could be thrown out of the country and not allowed back in…and the way he's acting that's a distinct possibility.'

'Oh God,' she said, her voice shaking. 'I hope he does something like that…but not with me. Thank you Steve darling, I would love to see you before I go but…'

'Get out of Manila now…today!'

'I will. Can I stay in touch? Leave you a contact address or phone number please?'

'Yes of course, do that and if I hear anything or can help further I'll let you know.'

'I will, thank you so much darling, I still love you,' she said, paused, waiting for a reaction which didn't come and when it didn't, she hung up. Conway let out a huge sigh and began to attack the paperwork on his desk. Ten minutes later the phone rang. What now?

'Hello lover, I'm back!' said a familiar female voice.

Holy hell what a morning! A brawl in the bar; Sally nearly hysterical and now Lily. 'You sound like Arnold Schwarzenegger Lily but I think I'm more scared of you,' he laughed.

'Mmmmm, darling that's not the impression I got last time we were together,' she cooed.

'When can we meet? I'm dying to see you again lover. I want to tell you all about Shanghai. And you know my darling Steve, I often think of our little interlude on Boracay. So romantic, we must do that again, sooner rather than later, what do you think?'

'Er, ah, yeah ok. I'm attending a local Chamber of Commerce meeting here at 6.30 pm. I'll be free after that.'

'Great, let's meet in the lounge bar of the Manila Hilton on UN Avenue at say, 7.30 pm darling, does that suit?'

'Done, see you then Lily.' Conway hung up but his mind was still on Marvin and his conversation with Sally. This guy was capable of anything and Marines were taught to be resourceful. Sally's life was in danger while Marvin was still in the Philippines. He picked up his phone and phoned the American Embassy and asked for Chuck McGaw, an old friend who happened to be a liaison officer with the FBI.

'Hey man, nice to hear from you, long time no see…to what do I owe the dubious pleasure of this call?' asked a clearly delighted McGaw. Agent McGaw together with his Australian counterpart Detective Chief Superintendent Jack Roberts had been responsible for rescuing Conway from a sticky situation involving a drug running syndicate headed by a local police chief and they had become firm friends and occasional drinking buddies.

McGaw a tough, no nonsense professional, hid it behind a smiling easy-going manner but in a tight situation Conway could think of no one else he'd rather have on his side. He quickly outlined the story of Sally and Marvin and his encounter with the latter that morning.

'Chuck, this guy is dangerous, psychotic, he's out to kill her. What can be done, if anything?'

McGaw had listened patiently without interruption. He didn't answer immediately, taking his time to consider Conway's story.

'Steve, there's not a lot we can do at this point. We can take action if one of our citizens misbehaves here but as I'm sure you'll understand, we are limited and have to tread very carefully in whatever action we take.

I'll have him checked out to see if he's on the run from anything in the US. If so, we can grab him and send him home. He's under Philippines jurisdiction here and again, if he commits a felony here he can be deported. Anyway I'll follow this up and get back to you. Let's have a beer buddy, 'bout time you bought me one.'

'Any time Chuck! Anytime! Come and see me soon, ok?'

'Will do man, bye now,' said McGaw hanging up.

* * *

Conway rose from his seat in the plush lounge bar of the Hilton Hotel as Lily entered, sashaying across the scarlet carpet toward him. Heads turned as this exotic creature in a figure hugging, low-cut, French-designed black number, threw her arms out in a theatrical gesture and hugged him for well over a minute to the amusement of the watching bar staff. A waiter in black bow tie, white shirt and perfectly creased dark pants waited until the clinch ended then glided to their table a millisecond after they sat down.

Conway was about to order drinks when Lily waved him off and demanded, *champagne cocktails with the best French you have.* 'Let me be the first to buy the drinks darling,' she smiled, leaning over allowing him a view of a generous cleavage. There was nothing subtle about Lily Li. 'It is so good to see you it's been such a long time so I want this to be a night to remember.' Conway grinned to himself. It usually was with Lily.

* * *

Somewhere in Manila a heavily built white man flagged down a taxi. He ripped open the front door but didn't get in. 'Know where I can buy a hunting rifle?' he growled at the driver. Ricky Tan had been pushing his hack around Manila for over twenty years. He knew where to buy anything in that sprawling metropolis; legal or otherwise.

'Sure sir, Quiapo sir, I take you there,' Ricky replied, flashing a huge toothpaste smile.

'Where's Quiapo?'

'Not far sir, ten minutes maybe, just over the bridge.'

'Ok, and step on it, I'm in a hurry.'

Ricky's judgement was spot on. Ten minutes later the taxi stopped outside a small, dilapidated shop in a dark, narrow, rubbish strewn lane in Quiapo, a squalid area of grey ugly, concrete streets, home to hundreds of small shops, supermarkets, movie theatres and a place no self respecting Filipino would wander around alone at night. The shabby wooden hoarding above the shop declared in faded black lettering, *Tito's Military Hardware.* The big guy frowned and turned to the taxi driver.

'This shit little place? You sure they got rifles here, and ammo?'

'Sure sir, I guarantee, I wait you sir, ok?' asked Ricky with a nervous smile. A typically gregarious Filipino, Ricky had tried to make conversation during the journey but had been ignored. His passenger sat there staring straight ahead.

'No,' was the curt reply. Ricky caught the 100 peso note that was thrown offhandedly at him and watched with relief, as his passenger heaved his bulk from the taxi and lumbered into the shop.

12

The bow-tied waiter hovering nearby swooped in, took their empty glasses and stepped back with a questioning look...'Sir...Madame...more?'

Conway looked over at Lily. Her eyes were wide and bright. In the past ten minutes her smile had become a giggle. The champagne cocktails were having an effect despite the sumptuous meal. Her speech was beginning to slur slightly, the full bottom lip now drooping loosely. One more champagne cocktail and Lily would be unable to leave the restaurant unassisted.

'I think that will be all,' he told the waiter, 'but coffee for both of us...' then glancing at Lily, 'make it black...and strong.'

'Oh darling,' she pouted, 'your Lily would *love* another cocktail, don't be a spoilsport darling, I'm having such a good time.'

What she said was true. They were enjoying each other's company. Lily had made him laugh as she regaled him with stories of the misadventures of setting up her restaurant in Shanghai. Despite the frustrating and overbearing bureaucracy and endless meetings and mountains of paperwork, she had succeeded and made it sound fun into the bargain.

Lily was indeed a remarkable woman and he couldn't help but admire her. He let her do most of the talking and didn't say much about Vietnam other than his meeting with Mr Loc.

He leaned over and moved her glass out of arm's reach.

'Lily dear, I want to get you home in one piece. You said your mother is living with you now. From what you told me, she's a rather matriarchal lady. What would she think of me if I brought you home drunk?'

Lily blinked and thought about that for a moment. Her eyes were beginning to glaze. Conway began to worry. She seemed to be rapidly losing it. 'She'sh wouldn't care darling, she'sh a woman of the world,' gurgled Lily, the slur now more pronounced. Conway insisted she drink both coffees. She could only manage one and part of the second, spilling the remainder across the spotless white linen tablecloth. It was time to leave. He paid the bill and with Lily clutching his arm and beginning to stagger, they headed for the door which a smiling livery coated doorman held open.

His smile vanished when immediately Lily stepped out into the cool night air she let out a low moan and her legs gave way. She would have collapsed onto the sidewalk if a very aware Conway hadn't grabbed her.

Both men held up the rubber-legged glamour girl as her chauffeur George came running. The three of them bundled her into the limo where she slumped like a rag doll against Conway as they sped off down UN Avenue.

He looked down at Lily. What a difference from the sexy, sophisticated woman of a few hours ago! Gone was any semblance of elegance and style. The expensively coiffured hair lay in tousled disarray. Dark tendrils lay crookedly across her face, spittle oozed from the now smeared, carefully painted red lips and the French number now hung crushed and rumpled on her limp body, and to make matters worse she'd lost one of her outrageously priced Italian shoes as they shoved her ingloriously into the limo.

Conway shuddered. He now had on his hands, a helplessly drunken woman. What a wonderful first impression he was going to create with her mother.

'Good evening ma'am, lovely to meet you. Please forgive me for carrying your daughter in over my shoulder but, she's blind drunk...'

George ripped the big limo in through the large wrought iron gates and brought it to a skidding halt on the gravel drive at the foot of the imposing front steps. With great difficulty they eased the *non compos* Lily from the vehicle and half-carried her up to the front door. The chauffeur knocked lightly, tentatively. He and Conway praying Maria Victoria wouldn't be the one to greet them. Luckily, it was little Binky, who took one look at the trio and nearly fainted.

Conway quickly explained the situation and was relieved to learn that Lily's mother had retired several hours earlier. With Binky fussing around them like a mini blow fly, they carefully and quietly hauled her boss, legs dragging, up the winding staircase to her first floor bedroom and set her down on a large Victorian four poster. Mmmm, new bed, not the one we last had fun in, mused Conway, carefully laying her down on the silken quilt.

During dinner Lily had invited Conway home to meet her mother making it abundantly clear she expected him to stay around to indulge in some fun and frolic in her boudoir. How the best laid plans can go astray…

Conway's last view of his exotic playmate was of her sprawled on her back, arms and legs spread wide, eyes closed, mouth open, snoring loudly. He shook his head and couldn't help a little grin as he tiptoed back downstairs where George, unable to hide a similar grin, was waiting to take him to his apartment in Ermita.

* * *

'Steve, the board has approved your submission,' James Sinclair shouted down the phone line. It had been only ten days since he'd sent his submission and the speed of the acceptance was a pleasant surprise.

Conway breathed a sigh of relief. With Sinclair's enthusiasm and the green light given by the other shareholders, funds for the project would be swiftly forthcoming. They discussed the submission at length ending with Sinclair assuring Conway of his total support and urging him to leave Keyes in charge and return to Saigon as soon as possible.

Conway needed no second bidding. He drafted a letter to the staff advising of his imminent departure, buzzed Gina to book a flight for a few days hence then called Keyes to his office. 'Saigon is a go mate,' he said, as Keyes came in and sat down. A broad grin spread across the big man's face. He listened intently as Conway outlined the project in detail then they discussed management arrangements in Steve's absence.

Keyes would become acting General Manager, a role he was now accustomed to, but, would report regularly to Conway in Saigon, who in turn would be advising his progress there to management in Australia.

Next he called Lily to give her the news. He'd phoned her the day after their disastrous dinner date to check on her condition. A very hung over and chastened Lily had answered the phone and apologized profusely and informed him most emphatically she had taken the pledge. Conway laughed and made light of it. 'We must have lunch before you return to Shanghai,' he had told her, 'but this time, let's both stick to mineral water.'

'Thank you darling,' replied Lily with relief. She was still mortified and had spent many hours wondering about Conway's reaction to her embarrassing behaviour. 'I will be busy for the next week at least,' she said. 'Can you give me a call then?' Steve agreed, but a combination of work problems and nighttime meetings caused him to completely forget the arrangement until now.

Binky answered the phone and to his surprise, said Lily had returned to Shanghai urgently. She hadn't given Binky any details of the reason except to say that it was serious and needed her urgent attention. Binky was to apologise to Conway and tell him she would contact him as soon as "she had the situation under control". A bemused Conway replaced the receiver.

The unpredictable Lily had struck again.

Sally phoned from Isabella to ask if he'd heard anymore about Marvin and was somewhat relieved to learn about Conway's phone call to McGaw. She had settled in well with relatives and was enjoying the peaceful provincial life, but saddened to hear of his departure for Vietnam.

'How long…will you be there?' she asked with a catch in her voice.

'I can't say, but give me your address and I'll write and give you my contact details there if you need me, ok?' She did so and they left it at that but, there was a long pause before Sally replaced the receiver.

'I will miss you,' were her last words.

Dung looked out of his office window across at Kim Anh chatting and laughing with colleagues near the front gate of Waterworld. Work had finished for the day and she and her co workers were waiting for the company bus to take them back to the city.

Kim Anh would be dropped off at Thanh Da on the way. Dung often used the same bus but on this evening he was required to stay behind to finish some reports. He gazed disconsolately at the happy little group, a wave of frustration sweeping over him.

At that moment Kim turned with a shriek of laughter at something one of her colleagues had said and noticed Dung at his window. Her laughter vanished immediately, replaced by an expression of contempt.

Dung half raised his hand to wave but dropped it when he saw the look on her face. She turned back to her friends and began again to speak animatedly. It seemed as if she was deliberately scorning him.

She was still chatting and laughing when the bus arrived and boarded it without a backward glance. Dung returned to his desk simmering. He felt as if he'd been slapped in the face. 'I will kill that foreigner if he comes back here,' he grated, wheeling around and smashing his fist against the nearest wall.

* * *

In Manila Marvin watched the gunsmith place a rifle carefully into a leather pouch and wrapped several boxes of ammunition in old newspaper. The shop didn't have a great range of rifles, most old and dusty, like the shop and its owner. He'd finally chosen a ruger m40 semi-automatic model.

It wasn't exactly what he was looking for but was in good condition. He checked the bolt action, smooth as silk. All components had that black, glossy unused appearance. The sight was perfectly in line and the balance was right. It would do the job.

He paid in US dollars and didn't bother with a receipt. In fact, he made sure one was not written. He wanted no trace of the transaction. The old man, shifty and unsmiling, nodded and took the cash without a word slipping it quickly into the pocket of his ill-fitting brown trousers. Marvin left and walked quickly up the narrow lane to the busy main road looking for a taxi.

* * *

It was ten minutes to midnight in an almost empty bar of the Down Under. Jumbo Keyes finished reading the *Stars and Stripes* and was about to order a beer when Conway walked in.

'Make that two Jackie,' he said, turning to the Australian, 'what's happening boss?'

'No beer for me thanks,' Conway said waving off the order. 'It's been a long day. I'm off home for a good night's sleep. You can steer the ship, see you in the morning mate.' The night was cool and dark and a few street lights needed replacing, same old Ermita, thought Conway as he strolled into M H Del Pilar. On the spur of the moment he decided to have a nightcap at *Nightbirds* now under new management since Barney Lawson had been deported to Australia to face the long overdue music.

His mind was full of thoughts of Saigon and expectation of seeing Kim again when a friendly voice called out from across the street. 'Hey! Mr Kangaroo!' It came from Ronnie the young doorman of *Romeos* a small bar Conway occasionally dropped into after work. The beer was always cold and the staff friendly, especially Beth the 40 something Mama San and her small coterie of "lovelies". He turned to wave and promptly fell into a hole in the sidewalk he'd been carefully stepping around for months.

It saved his life.

A shot rang out smashing into the spot exactly where a second before he'd been walking. Conway scrabbled around knee deep and half bent over in the hole full of vile smelling filth and assorted rubbish.

Bang! Another shot. Ronnie screamed and glass shattered.

People came running from everywhere white faced and shouting. The shooter having missed Conway had seemingly taken his frustration out on the young doorman who now lay on his back covered in blood among the shattered glass of the front window of the bar.

While Conway was helped from the hole a noisy crowd gathered around Ronnie. He limped over and shouldered his way to where Beth was crouching beside her young doorman, screaming and sobbing. Her shoulders heaved with convulsions as she tried to comfort the youth. It was useless. Ronnie was dead. The right side of his head had been blown off.

Conway pulled Beth to her feet. 'Find out if anyone saw who did this. Use Tagalog, English, whatever, we've got to find who's responsible!' he yelled above the pandemonium. Beth and her girls began questioning the mob and a few minutes later she pushed her way back through to Conway.

'Several people saw a big white man running away from the park opposite the church, up MH Del Pilar carrying a rifle, he jumped into a taxi and headed down Del Pilar,' she said.

'Try and get me a better description than that? Big is not enough,' gasped Conway, still shaken from his close call. Beth went off again and came back with a slightly better description of the shooter; shaved head fattish face, khaki shirt and pants. It could only be one man…Marvin.

As a group of uniformed police and an ambulance arrived, the Australian eased back out of the crowd and slipped away down a side street. Within ten minutes he was back in his apartment. He ripped off his filthy, foul smelling clothes and had a long hot shower. He treated several small cuts on his knees with iodine, grabbed a bottle of Jack Daniels, a tall glass, threw in some ice and poured himself a decent slug.

He sat on his settee for a long time thinking and emptying the bottle of Jack. Fucking Marvin! The man's a psycho! If he's not caught, sooner or later he'll find Sally and kill her. He must be in this area somewhere, a white man that size stands out. If there is good press and TV coverage, someone will see him and a reward should pay dividends. I'll phone McGaw in the morning but Sally doesn't need to know about this.

It was nearly 2.00 am when he staggered to his feet, put the bottle back on the sideboard, rinsed the glass and fell into bed, asleep before his head hit the pillow.

* * *

It was a woozy Steve Conway who phoned McGaw next morning. As usual the American listened carefully and didn't interrupt as he was given details of the previous night's events.

'It's a local matter at the moment Steve,' said McGaw, 'but I'll check with the cops at the Western Police District and see what they've come up with. I agree with you, a white guy built like Marvin should be easy to run down but you never know my friend. This is a big town: There's plenty of places to hide.'

McGaw paused, considering Marvin's options. 'He'll go to ground Steve. An ex Marine, he'll know a few tricks about concealment and will lie low for the moment but once he puts his head up we'll grab him,' he said confidently. 'In the meantime you better watch yourself.'

'Yeah Chuck I'll be careful. I'm leaving for Saigon in a couple of days so if anything comes up before then I'm on this number, after that let Jumbo Keyes know and he'll pass it on to me.'

'Roger that, enjoy Saigon, it's a great town.'

'Thanks Chuck, somehow I think I will.'

Two days later, he flew to Saigon.

* * *

Marvin hid in a squalid boarding house in Blumentritt on the outskirts of Manila. No one seemed the slightest bit interested in the burly, unsmiling white man whose only conversation was a surly grunt. He ventured out only after dark and that was just for a quick meal and a beer in a tiny cafe a few yards from his bolt hole. The boarding house was located at the end of a long, dark, rat-infested alley where no foreigner would ever seek accommodation; except someone on the run.

The owner, an old woman of indeterminate age and ancestry didn't look surprised or ask any questions when Marvin arrived carrying an elongated parcel, and asked for accommodation.

Two hundred pesos a night got him a squalid, windowless room. There was no floor covering, just bare pitted cement. Paint was peeling off the walls as if it was in a hurry to leave this hell hole. A bed with a lumpy mattress and a filthy grey sheet stood uninvitingly in a corner. A tiny putrid bathroom and toilet completed the luxurious abode. Marvin didn't care. He'd lived in worse. He was out of sight and it would serve his purpose while he figured out his next move.

* * *

Philippine airlines flight PR 751 touched down right on time at Saigon's Tan Son Nhat International Airport. Conway cleared immigration and customs quickly and stepped out into the sunshine where Kim Anh stood on her tip toes among the dense crowd pressing against the steel barriers, waving frantically, trying to attract his attention.

His face lit up when he saw her, again wearing the green *ao dai*. This time she gave no thought to her cultural restrictions. As he put his suitcase down, she threw her arms around him and they hugged oblivious of onlookers, before she stepped back her eyes shining. To his surprise, she pulled him to her again. Kim's cultural disposition forbade a kiss but he didn't care. The hugs were wonderful, but in the end he was the one to break the embrace.

'Hey, I'm not going to run away,' he laughed.

'Sorry darling,' she said, a little embarrassed at her uncharacteristic public display of affection, 'but I'm just so happy to see you again, I've missed you so much.'

'Believe me Kimmee, the feeling is mutual, it's so good to be back here again,' he said as they walked across the concourse to a line of waiting taxis.

They piled into a taxi and headed for District 1 where, in an enthusiastic phone call just before he left Manila, she'd told of an apartment she'd found for him.

'I hope you like it darling,' she said, taking his hand. 'I tried to find one which had all the things you asked for. It is centrally located I hope....'

'I'm sure it'll be fine darling, I've every confidence in you,' he said, giving her hand a little squeeze. For once the usual frenetic traffic was light, and in no time the taxi rolled down Dong Khoi Street, turned left around Lamson Square and crossed into a small side street off the main thoroughfare of Hai Ba Trung Street.

'Here we are,' she smiled, as the taxi turned into a narrow alley lined with small shops on the left. On their right occupying most of the alley, was the back wall of a large restaurant where at a staff entrance, a number of attractive young female staff in white tops and white mini dresses squatted, chatting and drinking coffee.

Kim directed the driver to stop at the end in front of the entrance to a shop on their left. 'Please wait,' she said, getting out and hurrying inside, returning a few minutes later with a pleasant faced, rotund woman in her early forties and a handsome, slightly built man of the same age and a youth of around nineteen.

Kim introduced Conway to Mr and Mrs Thanh, the owners of the apartment he was to rent. The Thanhs gave him a friendly smile and gestured to the youth to take charge of Conway's luggage.

Conway paid off the driver with dong he'd kept from his previous visit and followed Kim and the others up a narrow, winding, terrazzo staircase to an apartment on the first floor, his new home in Vietnam; Nguyen Sieu Street, District 1, Ho Chi Minh City.

Outside on the street looking down the alley unnoticed by Conway and his group, was a black clad figure sitting astride a motorcycle.

13

Conway's eyes lit up as he inspected the apartment. Kim Anh had chosen well. The place was spotless and welcoming.

The large cream-walled lounge/dining room featured a comfortable maroon futon beside which a white telephone sat within easy reach on a small, round, yellow silk-covered table. To his surprise, a wide-screen television filled the space in one corner.

The comfortable, homely atmosphere was further enhanced by a large vase of freshly picked flowers sitting on a teak coffee table in the middle of the room, while an expensive looking multi-coloured rug on the sparkling, white tiled floor added a sense of style. Across the width of one wall was a print of an autumn scene from the Canadian Rockies while opposite, small watercolours of Vietnamese landscapes added a local touch. But the *piece de resistance*, to Conway's amazement, was the crystal chandelier. Who would have expected it in this neighbourhood?

The kitchen was tiny but functional with a two burner gas stove and mini oven. He opened the small refrigerator and another surprise. It was well stocked with *Trung Ngyen* the local coffee, condensed milk, ingredients for the popular local beverage, French cheddar, tomatoes, ham, green vegetables, milk, crusty bread rolls and fruit; Kim Anh had been shopping.

There was plenty of good quality crockery and cutlery and he nodded in approval at the bathroom tiled in royal blue. It was fitted in the French style with two shower roses, one for conventional use and the other which emitted a fine spray. A bidet accompanied the standard white toilet and then there was the bedroom…

A shaft of early evening sunlight streamed in through a large window giving the room a golden glow. The double bed was adorned with a quilt of red and gold squares adding to the atmosphere created by the sunlight. Beside it stood a small teak cupboard, on top of which was a brass reading lamp: A 6-drawer writing desk and lamp sat by the window.

There was ample cupboard space for his clothes and the aircon above the window looked brand new. This bedroom was cosy and more than adequate. He turned to the rotund, smiling Mrs Thanh and an anxious Kim Anh.

'I like, I'll take it,' he said smiling broadly, causing an audible sigh of relief from Kim. Mrs Thanh put her arm around Kim. 'Miss Kim Anh has been here many times,' she said, giving her a motherly squeeze.

'I was worried, I just wanted to make sure it was good enough for you,' Kim said shyly, avoiding his gaze.

There was no contract and the Thanhs simply asked for two months rent in advance which Conway agreed to pay the following morning when the banks opened. There were handshakes all around and the Vietnamese landlords left assuring Conway they would be available for him at any time.

As soon as the door closed behind them they fell into each other's arms. Their kiss long and hungry. Many minutes passed before they broke away and stepped back, both breathing heavily.

'Welcome back,' she said and he burst out laughing.

She gave him a puzzled look. 'Why darling?'

He shook his head. 'Darling, it's just wonderful to be back, I'm so very, very happy. I love the place, I love you and I love Vietnam.' He gave her another hug and hand in hand they returned to the lounge room where the boy had placed his luggage.

'Ok, let's unpack this lot than go out somewhere nice for dinner, what say you *em oi?*' She smiled at his Vietnamese reference to her age and position.

'Ok, *Anh oi*,' she replied cheekily, 'good idea. You just relax, I will unpack for you.' He sat on the bed smiling as she unpacked and carefully hung shirts and trousers in a cupboard, stored socks, underclothes, shorts, tee shirts and other bits and pieces in drawers. His shaving gear was placed neatly in the bathroom and his spare pair of shoes and trainers put side by side on a rack just inside the front door.

Conway showered, changed his clothes and they headed up town to an open air restaurant, one of a series which set up each evening in a street beside the huge Ben Thanh market. Although the place was packed with tourists they soon found a spot on a table occupied by a young Vietnamese couple who offered a friendly smile and shifted along to make room.

Conway was ravenous and went for the chilli con carne while Kim chose *ca ri ga + banh mi* which she interpreted as chicken curry and bread. Both chose fruit shakes for which this restaurant was famous. While waiting for their order she listened intently as he brought her up to date with his mission.

'I would like to help you darling, is there anything I can do?' She said reaching across the narrow metal topped table and taking his hand.

'Thank you love, one of the first things I have to do is find a suitable site. So if you could scan the Vietnamese language newspapers for commercial sites for rent, preferably in District 1 that would be a big help. Tomorrow I'll give Jack Malone a call and have a chat to the people in Austrade in the Australian Embassy, oh, here's our food.'

They attacked their meals and it seemed Kim was as hungry as he was. He stopped eating for a moment and looked at her as she picked daintily at her food. She had a different hairstyle now. It was cut short in a cute urchin style. Those lovely eyes with the long lashes entranced him.

Women had many physical attributes that made up their beauty, but to him, none more so than a beautiful pair of eyes. He had never seen her look happier and more content than at that moment.

They followed the meal with a stroll down Le Loi Street past the sidewalk vendors with their touristy wares until Kim reminded him of the time. It was the witching hour of 9.00 pm so they returned to her motor bike parked beside the Ben Thanh market. She dropped him back at Nguyen Sieu Street and after a quick peck on the cheek, sped off into the night.

The combination of a new bed and the many things on his mind made it difficult for Conway to find sleep that night but around midnight after much tossing and turning and trying to belt his pillow into a comfortable shape, he finally dozed off.

The days that followed for Conway and Kim Anh were blissful. At evening they would eat at any number of classy, well-priced restaurants big and small, throughout the city usually followed by a walk in a park to watch families with their children at play and lovers cuddling in the shadows. Conway would rib Kim about this and suggest they do the same only to be met with a shy smile and silence. It was the typical Vietnamese woman's way of reacting when she did not want to answer a sensitive question.

Occasionally she would come to the apartment laden with food and prepare meals of tasty Vietnamese cuisine, spring rolls, *Pho, Bun bo*, and his particular favorite, *Cha ca*, filleted fish slices broiled and served with noodles, green salad, roasted peanuts and a sauce made from *nuoc mam* (fish sauce) lemon and a special (and secret) volatile oil.

'Do you know that Vietnam has nearly 500 different traditional dishes?' she told him one night as she set about preparing his evening meal. 'So I have about another 499 to go,' he laughed, spooning rice into a small bowl, Vietnamese style. Now that he was actually living in her country, she had shown him the etiquette and way to dine Vietnamese.

He learnt the correct way to eat the local food was to take rice from a shared dish (eating Vietnamese style is usually a communal affair, they hate doing anything alone; it's a cultural thing) put it in your rice bowl then use your chopsticks to select whatever meat, fish or vegetables you want from serving dishes and place it all in your rice bowl before eating.

There were a couple of no, nos. Never pour sauces directly into your bowl and it is regarded as ungracious to pierce food on communal plates. The rice bowl should be held close to the mouth. It makes use of chopsticks easier. Vietnamese are often amused watching foreigners unused to chopsticks, trying to transfer food all the way from the table to their mouth.

'Darling, another thing, you should always use both hands when passing or taking something and it is polite to acknowledge this with a small nod,' she said. 'And don't be surprised, if when you are invited to a meal, someone eating with you puts some food in your bowl. It will be the best looking piece and they will be honouring you as a distinguished guest.'

'You have a lovely culture Kim. We Westerners could take a few lessons in etiquette and courtesy from your people,' he said, as she placed a steaming bowl of *Pho* on the table in front of him.

There was no doubt about it, Vietnamese love to feed their guests, as Conway soon found out. He learnt to turn up hungry when invited for a meal at the home of Vietnamese friends. They always stuffed him to the gills and smiled with satisfaction as he put away plate after plate of various dishes.

'Please come again to our house Mr Steve,' a delighted Mrs Thanh told him, when he used the phrase, *ngon qua* to compliment her on a delicious and sumptuous meal she had cooked in his honour. He meant it. She was a great cook and his stomach felt about to explode as he said good night and staggered off to his apartment on the floor below.

* * *

The business of finding a suitable site for a Down Under operation began to take most of his time. Each day he set off exploring the central Districts 1 and 3 for suitable sites for a bar/restaurant or small hotel. Kim's help was invaluable feeding him information from the pages of various Vietnamese language newspapers and in her free time, accompanying him as an interpreter.

The Australian Embassy weren't too interested. Their focus it seemed was on bigger projects than his. Jack Malone proved to be more useful. Over a beer in an inner city bar he gave Conway the names of a number of Vietnamese well connected in the property field.

'I agree with you Steve, this town's crying out for a decent water hole. The expats here are pretty cliquey. In some bars, it's like walking into a private club, and the service is…well, to put it mildly, bloody near non-existent. The staff in this joint are too busy chatting among themselves to bother about the customers,' said Malone angrily, trying to attract attention of a bar attendant who had her back to him, while she chatted to another girl crouched down behind the bar.

'Look at this mate,' he continued, shaking his head. 'I want another bloody beer and this sheila is too busy yapping to her mate, they don't give a damn. I'd sack the lot of them. Let's piss off and go somewhere else. I've got a driver but where we're going is walking distance so he can follow.'

They left and crossed Hai Ba Truong Street, turned right at Thi Sach Street and came upon *Apocalypse Now*, a large, rowdy bar crowded with young expats, tourists and locals where the service was quick and the beer cold. Conway grinned when he noticed hung on one wall, a life size, bright yellow surfboard, with the words emblazoned in red, *Charlie don't surf.*

'Have to be donated by an American serviceman. "Charlie" was their favourite expression for the VC,' said Conway, nodding at the surfboard. 'Yeah, I'd say so,' replied Malone, sipping his *Tiger* beer. 'It would have to be a recent addition. This joint's been around a while but I don't think the Commies in the early days would've been too happy to see that, but who knows? Maybe they never woke to the subtle insult.'

They had another beer then Malone put his empty bottle on the bar. 'Mate, sorry but this head banging stuff's too noisy for an old bloke like me, let's go somewhere quieter, I know another place within walking distance, we can go there and chat in peace. I want to tell you a bit about the pitfalls of doing business in this country, and this town in particular.'

They finished their drinks, and headed up Thi Sach to *Le Figaro,* an old-styled French villa, stunningly restored as a restaurant.

Five minutes later they entered *Le Figaro* through black wrought iron gates past overhanging tamarind trees and climbed the stone steps to be met by a slim, striking French/Vietnamese woman in her mid forties wearing a figure hugging, off-the-shoulder white number, which showed off her deep tan superbly as a counterpoint to her disturbingly beautiful green eyes.

Conway took in the glossy, shoulder length dark hair, jutting breasts, the shapely, brown legs and dainty feet clad in thin golden sandals...this was all woman!

'Yes gentlemen, can I help you?' she asked in a low, smoky French accent. Conway nodded and couldn't help smiling. It seemed everywhere he went in Saigon there were women who wouldn't be out of place on a

Paris or New York catwalk. As for this woman's voice, it was extraordinary; he'd never heard anything so innately sensual. Was he imagining it or did he detect a flash of interest in those green eyes? Neither was particularly hungry so they ordered plate of mixed sandwiches and two beers.

'I will return with your meal very soon, *mai oui,*' she said in that wonderful voice and favoured them with the kind of smile that makes men want to leave home.

'Yes, please come back soon,' joked Malone, 'I'll still be here.'

'Amen to that,' Conway said giving a low whistle, watching her rolling hips all the way across the restaurant to the kitchen in the far corner.

'Now, where were we?' said Malone, but Conway's gaze was still transfixed in the direction of the kitchen.

'Ok Steve, to put your mind at rest,' chuckled Malone. 'That's Juliette the owner…a looker isn't she? It's Monday night, usually quiet so most of the staff are off and she runs the place almost single handed.'

'She's something else alright,' agreed Conway. Her figure and sexy aura reminded Conway of Lily. For a moment his thoughts were comparing the attributes of the exotic Chinese Filipina and Juliette but he was quickly brought back to earth by Malone.

'Now mate listen to me. I'm going to give you a run down on the pitfalls of doing business in this town. To say it can be tricky is an understatement and you have to know the right people. I guess that applies anywhere but more so in this neck of the woods where the language barrier is against you for a start. It's tonal and you'll never understand what they're saying even if you have a few language lessons, because the accent differs depending on what part of the country you are from. You'd need to be here for quite a while to get the hang of the lingo.'

'I'm all ears Jack. It was difficult in the Philippines but at least there, English is widely spoken. In that sense here I'm really behind the 8 ball. The Aussie Embassy wasn't much help.'

Malone took a packet of *Marlboros* from his shirt and lit one when Conway declined.

'Useless bastards,' he snorted. 'Only want to know you if you have a very big wallet and a government contract or know some big shot in the

Party here. What you need first of all is a *good* Vietnamese connection and I can help you there mate.'

'How's that Jack?'

Malone looked around almost furtively and leaned across the table.

'Those other guys I mentioned are in the government and handy to know of course, but the person who you should meet, is a lady called, Tran Thi Thuc Linh. She's a widow who's been in business here most of her life. Comes from the North, knows everyone worth knowing, said to be a relative of General Vo Nguyen Giap the guy who kicked the yanks' arses in the war.'

He took a deep draw of his cigarette, his craggy face broke into a broad grin.

'I love her, she's a real sweetheart, heart of gold and she's helped a lot of foreigners find their business feet in this town.'

'How can I get in touch with this lady?'

Malone took a pen and notebook from his shirt pocket and scribbled her name and phone number and handed it to Conway.

'Give her a call, tell her I sent you. Take her for dinner and get to know her. Tell her what you want, what you are looking for and I'm sure she'll steer you in the right direction.'

'What about her Jack? Nice lady? How old?' asked Conway, as Juliette arrived with their beer and sandwiches. She placed their order in front of them with a flourish and a smile then sashayed back to the kitchen with the eyes of both men firmly glued to her swaying hips.

'Ah…where was I?' grinned Malone. 'Oh yes, Mrs Linh, a nice lady. She's middle-aged, has worn well, but not into any funny stuff…you know what I mean Steve?'

'Sure, no worries, but I wasn't really meaning anything personal, I'm taken care of in that department,' smiled Conway, taking a sip of his *Tiger* beer and a sandwich from the heaped plate.

'Steve I better give you a bit of run down on how things work in this town. I don't want to tell you to suck eggs mate because you have already been involved in business here in South East Asia but Vietnam is a different animal from the Philippines. They are only just getting used to a free market economy and you have to be wary of the *red capitalists.*'

'*Red capitalists*?' Conway paused between bites.

Malone stubbed out his cigarette and grabbed a sandwich.

'The Commies have embraced this new style of economic socialism and wealth, and those in power or those with powerful friends are rushing in to make as much money as quickly as possible and don't care how they do it or who gets hurt along the way. More than one foreign investor has had his nose bloodied trying to do business in the new "enlightened" Vietnam.'

Malone paused to emphasize the point. 'So mate, I've been in this town ten years and I can tell you, when doing business here, the old *caveat emptor* "buyer beware" applies in spades, got it? There's a huge bureaucracy, corruption is rife, and why not? Who can blame them? These poor bastards are paid a pittance. We'd do the same if we were in their shoes right?'

Conway nodded. 'Yes, we would. I've seen the same thing in the Philippines. Tell me more. I can do with all the advice I can get.'

'As I said, it's easy to get burnt, the law is complex and if things go wrong you've got *Buckley's chance* if you try to take anyone to court, especially if it's a state run institution.' He lit another cigarette and continued. 'Mrs Linh will be able to introduce you to a decent lawyer, there's not many around at the moment but she knows the good ones.'

'She will,' he paused, taking a deep draw of his cigarette, 'also help you find a suitable place for your enterprise but you will have to be patient… and keep a low profile, ok?' Malone rubbed his chin between thumb and forefinger. 'Listen to this. They reckon there are five things you've got to be if you want to do business here mate…determined, resourceful, flexible, ingenious and patient.'

'Shit Jack, a piece of cake,' laughed Conway. 'But frankly, I'm under no illusions, I never expected an easy road. As you say, I've done business in the Philippines and I have been here before, not in a business capacity but I have a feel for the people and the place.'

Malone's eyebrows shot up. He stubbed out his cigarette and looked at Conway with renewed interest. 'Whaddya mean? You in the war?'

'Yeah, came in from Malaya posted to I RAR, finished up in 6 RAR.'

'Long Tan?'

'Missed that one, I was on short holiday in a hospital in Vung Tau. I had an argument with VC shrapnel, and lost.'

'Yeah, well mate,' Malone said, taking another sandwich, 'some of these jokers here running things are probably ex VC and they can still be dangerous…if you get on the wrong side of them, so just go with the flow ok?' They continued to discuss the idiosyncrasies of doing business in Vietnam then at Conway's request Malone gave some insight into his own background.

At 45, made redundant from a large building company in Sydney, with no wife or dependents, he decided it was time to live a little and travel the world. After spending a long, cold winter on building sites in the north of England then wandering around the capitals of Europe, the seemingly never-ending grim, grey clouds chased him south looking for warmer climes.

India didn't appeal, Singapore, too expensive, Bangkok ok for a while but rampant commercialism had virtually destroyed Thai culture leaving him casting around for somewhere else. An American in a Bangkok bar suggested Vietnam.

'Buddy, living's cheap, girls are truly beautiful, still feminine and the people are wonderful.' That was enough for the footloose Malone and a week later he was checked through immigration at Tan Son Nhat airport.

'That was ten years ago mate, and never left the joint since, best decision I ever made.' He lit up another cigarette, blew a smoke ring and watched it curl lazily toward a slow moving overhead fan. 'Yeah, it's a great place Vietnam.'

Malone looked every bit his 55 years. Short, stocky, weather beaten and tough, his round tanned face had laugh lines around the eyes which became slits when he smiled. A good man Conway decided. Thanks again Kim Anh.

It was midnight and time to leave. They thanked the beautiful Juliette and made their way toward the door. She turned from clearing a table and flashed her megawatt smile which seemed to focus on Conway for just a few seconds longer than necessary. She was still watching as they disappeared down the steps into the night. Then smiling to herself, she continued resetting the table.

Malone's vehicle was waiting outside. He offered to drive Conway home but with his apartment only a few minutes away the offer was declined.

'I'll walk thanks mate.' They shook hands and agreed to meet again soon. It was a pleasant night and a cool breeze had sprung up as he strolled through the quiet, darkened streets and for once he could see a few stars glittering through the smoggy Saigon night.

He looked up at a pale moon peeping through scudding clouds. Could be more rain tomorrow, at least it'd keep the fearsome daytime temperature down a bit. There was something to be said for the monsoon season in South East Asia. There was little traffic but as he was about to cross Thi Sach he noticed a black four-wheel drive without lights, approaching at speed.

It was the only vehicle in sight and far enough away for him to beat it to the other side but for some reason he decided to stop and let it pass. As it got closer the driver appeared to be accelerating. At almost the last second it veered, mounted the sidewalk and headed straight for him.

He had no time to think and acted instinctively. Instead of diving back to his right he threw himself to the left but not far enough. It clipped him with the bumper and flipped him into the air. He landed heavily on his side, rolled onto his face and lay still. The vehicle careered along the sidewalk smashing into a low concrete garden bed before bouncing back onto Thi Sach and roaring off into the night.

He lay in the middle of the road ignored by several passing motorbikes. They slowed up but then weaved around his inert body and kept going. It was a few minutes before he recovered consciousness and slowly pushed himself to his feet, took a few steps before collapsing and rolling into the gutter.

He stirred as he felt two pair of hands bring him to his feet where he stood on jelly legs trying to make sense of what had just happened. His hands were bleeding where he'd tried to stop his fall; his shirt was torn and his pants were ripped and filthy.

The good Samaritans were two young Vietnamese men heading home after a night out. They were a little drunk and neither could speak much English but were very concerned about his welfare and with hand gestures and a mixture of English and Vietnamese, indicated they wanted to take him to a *benh vien* (hospital). He thanked them but shakily refused, told them he'd be ok, and limped off home.

It was a long, slow, painful walk up the steps to his apartment. He had to stop several times and lean against the wall for support. He fumbled around for his keys, taking several attempts before he was able to unlock his door.

He staggered into his bedroom, took off his clothes slowly and painfully, and left them on the floor. In the bathroom he stood with head down and both arms outstretched against the wall letting the soothing warm spray of the shower wash over his body. Thank God, he didn't seem to have any broken bones.

The Thanhs had thoughtfully provided a small glass medical cabinet fitted to the dining room wall of his apartment. Sorting through the pills, bandages and assorted ointments, he found a small bottle of iodine which he applied to the cuts on his face, hands and other abrasions on both knees. What he needed most of all was a stiff drink but the cupboard was bare so he made a cup of hot tea and took it into the bedroom.

He sat on the bed sipping the tea trying to get his head around what had happened. What the fuck is going on in my life? Someone tries to shoot me in Manila now some idiot tries to run me down in Saigon. Was that vehicle really aiming for him? Was it deliberate or just a drunk driver? He knew very few people in Saigon. He hadn't been there long enough to make enemies, so who would want to run him over?

It had to be some crazy young guy full of booze who'd momentarily lost control. After the way he'd seen some of them ride their motorbikes around Saigon it made sense. He washed a couple of panadol down with a glass of water and eased his aching limbs into bed, still wondering when, as a blessed relief, sleep finally arrived.

* * *

Next morning when he woke his entire body screamed in protest; when he tried to rise. He cried out and dropped back onto mattress. Every joint was stiff and sore. It seemed there wasn't a bone in his body that didn't ache.

He winced when he touched his left shoulder where he'd hit the rock hard road. Both knees, his back, elbows, his whole body throbbed. He'd forgotten to turn the aircon on when he went to bed and the room was like a furnace. Sweat poured out of him as he lay there, unable, and unwilling to move. There'd be no scouting around for a site for at least one day, maybe more.

He went back over again what had happened. Sure, it could have been a drunken driver but he kept coming back to this nagging, sickening thought.

Someone had tried to kill him!

14

Kim Anh came to his apartment the next evening throwing her arms around him when he opened the door. She jumped back in shock as he flinched, involuntarily, his face a mask of pain.

'Darling what's wrong? What did I do?' she cried, seeing his face twisted in agony. He led her to his bedroom and they sat down on the side of his bed. She listened, her mouth open in horror as he told her what had happened and his suspicions.

'Oh my God, you could have been killed! I must take you to the hospital.'

'No, I'm ok, just a few scratches and bruises, nothing too serious, I was lucky.'

'But who would want to do that? It must have been a drunken driver.'

Conway shook his head. 'I've been thinking about it and I'm not so sure,' he said grimly.

'When I think about what actually happened…it was just a bit too deliberate.'

'Darling, please take off your clothes.'

'Huh?'

'Oh don't worry,' she giggled. 'I just want to attend to your hurts.' She went to the kitchen and heated water in a ceramic bowl. Taking a few balls of cotton wool from the medicine cabinet she returned to the bedroom, nearly dropping the bowl when she saw the cuts and bruises on his body. 'Oh my God, you poor man, I must take care of you.'

Conway looked up at her with a cheeky grin as he shed his clothes.

'What are you going to bathe first?' Kim coloured, but couldn't help a smile as she set about tenderly bathing his wounds.

When she finished he dressed, gave her a peck on the cheek and suggested they look for somewhere to have dinner.

'Are you sure you will be able to walk? We could stay here. I can cook or go out for some takeaway?'

'I'm fine. I know somewhere nice, we haven't been before.' She reluctantly agreed. With Kim holding an arm in support he gingerly took the stairs down to her motorbike and ten minutes later they were sitting under the stars in the cool garden setting of *Tropica* restaurant in District 3.

The menu was a mixture of Vietnamese and European. They both ordered Vietnamese with Conway going for the grilled fish marinated in hot sauce plus *coi om*, sea snails grilled in chilli salt, while kim ordered a plate of star crabs, fresh cuttlefish and mango shrimp salad. He washed his down with a bottle of ice-cold Tiger beer; she stayed with her usual orange juice.

He told her about his meeting with Malone; of the advice and warning from the long-time expat about doing business in Saigon. She was more worried about the incident with the vehicle and was only half listening until he mentioned Mrs Linh, then her ears pricked up; another woman? 'Who is she and what is she?' Kim asked with a frown, her chopsticks half way to her mouth.

The look on her face told Conway she suspected a rival? He smiled and patted her hand.

'Darling, she's a middle-aged matron from your part of the world who apparently has helped quite a few foreigners find their feet in business here.'

'Oh, and what can this Mrs Linh do for you?' Kim feigned nonchalance but there was an edge to her voice.

'Hopefully she will help me find the site I am looking for. Malone says she knows everyone, and has some powerful contacts. She's said to be related to the famous General Giap.'

'I would like to meet her,' murmured Kim, head down picking at her meal, all the while thinking to herself, who is this Mrs Linh? Foreigners, especially first timers who cannot speak the language, are unaware of the subtleties of the culture and can be fair game for the plausible and avaricious.

'Sure, I want you to meet her,' Conway said, pouring himself a glass of beer. 'I'll try and set up a meeting as soon as possible; now, what do you want for dessert?'

After the meal they returned to Conway's apartment but his injuries prevented anything more than a couple of light kisses. She made him a cup of tea, leaving with a promise to call him in the morning.

He looked at his watch, too late to phone Mrs Linh. He finished the tea, washed up the cup, placed it on the sink and grabbed a towel for a shower. Thirty minutes later the novel he was reading slipped from his hands to the floor as he dozed off.

* * *

Rogelio Cardenas sat in his cane chair, yawned and looked at the luminous dial of his watch; another hour till dawn, then two hours until the end of his shift as a security guard at Manila port. Then thankfully, he could return to his small house in Quezon City. He smiled to himself thinking about his upcoming trip to the United States to visit his daughter.

A widower for many years the 76 year old had very few joys in life but his beautiful daughter Diane was one of them. She'd married well to an American computer whiz and they'd settled happily in Seattle. With one daughter and another child on the way the family was excited at the prospect of granddad Rogelio's visit.

It would be his first and probably last to the U.S. and he'd been promised in many letters, of a huge and loving welcome. Rogelio smiled at the memory of those words. He missed his Diane so much. She was his only child and had always been the apple of his eye. The thought of seeing her and hugging his three year old granddaughter Chloe filled him with joy.

He took a photo from his top pocket and the dim glow of the overhead lamp showed a beautiful child with big black eyes and a cute, mischievous smile. Aah to be young again, he sighed, kissing the photo and returning it to his pocket.

It had been a long night and thankfully without incident. Roistering merchant seamen had weaved along the wharf shouting and singing drunken refrains. Some, had arms around painted, mini-skirted women trying to keep their paramours upright as they staggered up ill-lit gangplanks into the darkness of their vessels. Most had waved to him as they passed, one sailor even offering him a drink from a half-empty bottle of rum but took the refusal in good part and wobbled back to his friends.

Rogelio fingered the butt of his Smith and Wesson.38. There had been no need to threaten anyone with it on this night. Not that he was likely to use it. The old man abhorred violence of any kind and he had never actually fired a shot in anger. On numerous occasions he'd drawn the weapon but only for show and fortunately it had been enough to persuade the miscreant to behave.

His head dropped and he began to doze. He never heard the footfall behind him but the soft curse and the noise of an empty tin rolling across the wharf brought him half awake.

His eyes were only half open as his hand went to the holster of his revolver but a grip of steel held the old man's wrist fast. He felt his gun being removed. He attempted to rise and cried out in pain, slumping to the ground as he was savagely pistol whipped. Blood streamed from a gash across his cheek and again he tried to grab at his assailant's legs only to receive another vicious blow across the side of the head which dropped him face down unconscious on to the dirty, oil-stained concrete.

Rogelio never felt himself being lifted and carried across the few yards to the edge of the wharf where he was dropped into the murky waters of Manila harbour, disappearing with a soft splash. The heavily built white man checked the revolver and clip of bullets then ghosted back into the shadows.

Rogelio Cardenas' body was found almost a week later by scavengers as they scrounged among the filthy shores of Manila bay; just another victim of a mean city. One crone went through the pockets of the old man and withdrew a soggy photograph of a little girl. She glanced at it for a second then tossed it into the water. In the U.S. an increasingly worried Diane waited for news from her father…

* * *

Marvin stood hidden in the darkness of an alley, looking across UN Avenue at the brightly-lit front entrance of the Down Under Hotel. He noticed with satisfaction the gun toting guard at the front door was different from the one on duty the day he was thrown out by Conway.

He lit a cigarette and crossed dodging the traffic, stopping near the guard pretending to check out the hotel frontage as if he was a prospective customer.

'*Pare*', Marvin motioned to the guard offering him a cigarette. 'I'm looking for a friend; I hope you can help me.'

'Yes sir, thank you sir,' said Roland the 21 year old guard, slinging the shotgun over his right shoulder and gratefully accepting the smoke. He was bored stiff. No one apart from Mary the front desk clerk ever showed the slightest interest let alone acknowledge him, so he appreciated the offer and the chance of a chat with someone, anyone, even this big, tough-looking white guy. He cupped his hands as Marvin lit his cigarette then blew a smoke ring.

'How can I help you sir?'

Marvin smiled and effected a jovial manner which, given his basic dour personality, didn't quite come off. 'Hey, I'm looking for a guy I knew in Vietnam, Steve Conway, I believe he works here. Is he in?'

'Mr Conway sir,' said Roland enthusiastically, 'yes, he's my boss sir, but I'm sorry sir, he's in Vietnam.' Marvin's eyes narrowed. He stifled a curse, his smile now fixed and phony, but the young guard didn't seem to notice.

'Vietnam! When'd he go? How long will he be there?'

Roland hesitated. He wasn't sure if he should tell this stranger anything. The deep-set black eyes were cold behind that smile. Roland was young but he'd been brought up in the tough suburbs of Tondo and Quiapo, where life was cheap and a wrong move or word out of place could mean a knife or a bullet. He'd seen plenty of bad guys and these were the eyes of a killer.

Seeing Roland's reticence, Marvin handed him the rest of his cigarettes; the pack was almost full. Roland's eyes lit up. 'Thank you sir, he left over a week ago sir, I don't know how long he will be away.'

'Reckon you could find out how long he'll be there and more importantly, where he is, Saigon? Hanoi?' Again, Roland shuffled his feet and hesitated.

'There's a carton in it for you kid,' urged Marvin. 'If you can find out, I'd be much obliged. We're old buddies, haven't seen each other since the war, I owe him, if you know what I mean?'

Roland nodded as if he understood, and gave a half grin. He didn't have a clue what this guy meant but if there was a carton of foreign cigarettes on offer…The stranger smiled again. It wasn't a friendly smile. There was an unspoken threat in those frightening eyes. Roland felt his sphincter contract involuntarily.

'Er…ah…yes, ok sir, come back here same time tomorrow and I will see what I can do…ok sir?'

'Gotta better idea; what's your name kid?'

'Roland…sir'

'Ok Roland, what time do you knock off here?'

'Eleven pm sir…why sir?' asked Roland, a little nervously.

'You know a little bar called *Madames* just off Adriatico Street?' *Madames* was a tiny bar at the end of a dark alley rarely frequented by law abiding citizens.

'Yes, I do sir, sometimes the owner Danny Mondelo comes and drinks here in the Down Under.'

'Ok, get that information for me and meet me at *Madames* tomorrow night after you finish here. There could be more in for you than a carton of smokes…if you get my drift,' grunted Marvin touching his nose with his forefinger. His tone left no doubt that the guard better be there…or else.

Roland watched the tall stranger turn and lumber away toward MH Del Pilar. He waited till Marvin had turned the corner, then dropped the butt of his cigarette, stamped on it and went back inside the hotel; if Mary was alone, maybe they could have a quick chat.

At 11.15 pm the next evening Marvin glanced at his watch in *Madames* and, was about to curse Roland when the young guard pushed his way past the tattered curtain inside the front door and eased up onto a stool at the bar beside him.

'Waddya got for me?' asked the American from the corner of his mouth, looking straight ahead at the mirror behind the bar.

Roland ordered a San Miguel from the ancient barman. He was pissed off. The big guy hadn't acknowledged him or offered to buy a drink. The old barman scribbled out a chit for the newcomer's drink and was about to put it into a small cup and place it in front of him when Marvin grabbed his arm and grunted, 'mine,' took the chit and put it into his own cup. The old man grimaced in pain and retreated to the far end of the bar.

Roland looked around the bar. There were two other customers, at the far end out of earshot, a Filipino and a foreigner; both very drunk. They were arguing and too far gone to notice Marvin and Roland. Several young women, employed to attract the clientele, were asleep on a couch near the other two drinkers.

'Well?' growled Marvin, still looking straight ahead.

'Mr Conway's in Saigon, he's looking for a place to put another Down Under Hotel. It seems he will be there for a few weeks, maybe longer.' Roland took a long swig of his beer. He just wanted to give Marvin the information, grab the cigarettes and get the hell out of there. This guy scared him.

'Where's he staying in Saigon?'

'I was told he has rented an apartment in the middle of a place called District 1. They wouldn't tell me exactly where. Look, this information cost me you know…'

'Keep your shirt on kid, I'll look after you. So you don't know exactly where he is in Saigon?' muttered Marvin, looking as if he wanted to chew his bottle of San Mig.

'As I said sir, I don't know exactly but I did hear someone say he is near a hotel called the Carabille or Cara…something.'

Marvin's grim expression broke into a crooked smile. Conway was living somewhere near the Caravelle Hotel. He knew the area from his time as a Marine sergeant based at the US Embassy. He swallowed the rest of his beer and looked down the bar.

'Hey you. Another two beers!' The old barman put down the glass he was polishing and hurried down to serve them.

Roland started to loosen up after another couple of drinks and with four more inside him, euphoria took over and he began to giggle. Marvin hit him with a couple of shooters and by the time they left, Roland was legless.

Marvin didn't ask for a bill, instead, tossed a few hundred pesos on the bar. That would cover it in a dump like this and besides, he was feeling a bit expansive after Roland's information.

'Come on *Pare*, time to go,' he said, lifting Roland from the stool where he now lay slumped and dragged him through the front door under the impassive gaze of the old barman.

Outside it was almost pitch black. The only light was a weak bulb above the door of *Madames*. It was virtually useless as a means of lighting the way and the crescent-shaped fluoro sign which once used to illuminate the entrance, had long ceased to operate.

Instead of taking him up the alley in the direction of the traffic and activity of Mabini Street, Marvin half carried the young man to the far end into a tiny ginnell.

With one hand around Roland's jaw and the other his forehead, Marvin wrenched his head in opposite directions. There was a sharp crack as the neck broke. Marvin lowered the limp body to the ground and taking a small flashlight from his pocket, checked that the material he had seen during the day was still there.

He dragged the body into the end of the small recess and carefully covered it with a couple of sheets of corrugated iron and a few old worn planks of timber and rags. A large rat came out to see what was happening, its red eyes glowing in the dark. Marvin squashed it with the heel of a heavy duty boot then stood still listening for any sound or movement nearby. No grave was quieter.

He came out of the ginnell and stood in the shadows for a minute or two waiting. Keeping to the shadows he stole back up the alley and out into the bright lights of Ermita where he hailed a passing taxi. Thirty minutes later he was back in his hovel in Blumentritt.

Twenty four hours later he caught a flight to Saigon.

* * *

'Hello, you are Mr Conway?'

A trim, petite 50-something woman made her way past mid-morning diners to Conway and extended a bejeweled hand. He rose smiling from the table where he sat with Kim.

'Yes, Mrs Linh, pleased to meet you. This is my friend Miss Kim Anh,' he said, ushering the newcomer to a seat.

He'd phoned Mrs Linh the previous evening and explained who he was and the reason for calling, mentioning Malone's name which immediately elicited a warm and animated response; enough to make Conway wonder just how close Malone was to this lady.

Mrs Linh said she would be happy to discuss the matter and suggested they meet the following day at Café Central on Nguyen Hue Boulevard in the heart of District 1.

Mrs Linh was, as Malone described her, a slim, well preserved, smartly dressed woman, wearing a stylish pale pink, linen business suit over a white silk blouse. Her shiny, black hair was upswept and worn in a chignon. Large dark eyes twinkled from an unlined, heart-shaped face.

There was an aura of elegance and class about her. She took Conway's hand and nodded to Kim who gave a half smile. This was a woman of substance and style, obviously from a high class Vietnamese family. Kim Anh never felt comfortable in the presence of such people.

'Coffee?' asked Conway with raised eyebrows. Both women nodded. Kim didn't want to appear like a peasant and drink simple orange juice in front of this woman. He looked askance at her then gave the order to a passing waitress.

While waiting Conway and Mrs Linh exchanged pleasantries enquiring about the well-being of each other's families, something Conway had learned was often the basis of conversation in Vietnam.

She was a widow with two sons and a daughter, all doing well. Her eldest son lived in Hanoi, she said, "working for the government". The other son, who seemed to be the favourite from the look in her eyes, had recently taken a position as an engineer with a foreign-owned company building high-rise apartments in District 2, while her daughter, the youngest of the trio, was an exchange student in Boston and, "loving it". 'Too much I think,' she smiled, somewhat ruefully.

'You are very handsome Mr Conway, I am very surprised you have no family but maybe…' she said archly, stealing a glance at an impassive Kim. Conway mumbled something about being "too busy" and moved to the subject of their meeting.

He gave a detailed outline of what his company was looking for, explaining that initially, they wanted an existing site in District 1 which could be renovated and converted into a bar/restaurant with enough room to expand upwards and on either side.

'If it all works,' he continued, 'later, we would want to provide basic, comfortable accommodation for travellers, more upmarket than a backpacker hostel, and probably around 20 to 30 rooms.'

She listened carefully, nodding occasionally, asking about a proposed budget, estimated staff numbers, the type and length of lease required as she explained, owning real property by foreigners was not allowed at this time. They covered a number of other legal and corporate matters until finally Mrs. Linh nodded and seemed satisfied that his proposal was serious and viable.

'Thank you Mr Conway I believe from what you have told me, you are acting for a very professional organization, I think I can help you. I know of a number of locations that might be suitable. I will contact these people first and then if they agree, we can visit and you can make your judgement. If you find something you like, we can begin from there. Is that ok with you?'

'Yes of course, thank you very much, you are very kind.'

She gave a small smile of appreciation then turning to Kim who had been sitting quietly and looking decidedly uncomfortable, asked about her family and work.

Fifty something or not, Kim noted, Mrs Linh was a striking woman, very personable and in good shape. She couldn't help a tinge of jealousy as she watched her animated conversation with Conway. They did not include her and she began to feel more than a little irritated.

Kim gave a forced smile and replied in Vietnamese. Because they both came from the North after a few minutes the barriers came down and they began to engage in friendly conversation.

Although Conway could not understand their Northern patois, he could sense the initial cool response of Kim to the older woman, but the eventual exchange of smiles told him the ice had been broken and in the end it was him who was excluded.

It was now almost lunchtime. Conway invited Mrs Linh to stay but she politely declined, saying she had another appointment but would be in touch again soon. She stood and extended her hand to Conway, smiled at Kim and with a quick glance at her watch, hurried from the restaurant.

'Nice lady, good contact. See...nothing to worry about,' grinned Conway, reaching over to touch Kim's hand.

'Yes, I liked her, she is a genuine person, I think she will be a big help to you,' Kim replied, ignoring Conway's little jibe. They lingered over lunch during which to Conway's delight Kim said, 'darling, I'd like to go to Vung Tau again. Would you like?'

'When did you have in mind?'

'This weekend...if you can...'

'I'd love to but let's see first what Mrs Linh comes up with, if there's nothing on...'

'Ah...yes...Mrs Linh.'

Conway was unable to read her expression but knew she was not happy and for all the friendly chatter between them, he realized Kim saw the elegant Mrs Linh as competition.

She had nothing to worry about in that respect but he decided not to pursue conversation in that direction. After she went back to work Conway bought an English language newspaper and checked out the few real estate ads for commercial properties for rent. There weren't many and it was obvious that at this stage, the Mrs Linhs and Jack Malones were going to be his best bet to find a suitable site.

* * *

In Shanghai Lily Li stormed in circles around her office stopping occasionally to glare at a small, fat Chinese man who sat behind her desk following her movements with an inscrutable expression. 'You bastard, I can't believe you have done this,' she raged, turning and slamming her fist on the desk within an inch from his nose.

15

The skinny, middle-aged, immigration officer at Tan Son Naht airport scanned Marvin's passport with a wrinkled brown brow, then looked back up at him with cold expressionless eyes.

'American?'

Marvin said nothing. It was just as well the Vietnamese couldn't read his thoughts.

Stamp the passport you little bastard before I reach over and screw your scrawny neck. It wasn't long ago I was wasting little shits like you...

He snatched the passport as it was handed back and gave the official one last glare before turning and heading downstairs where his black sports bag lay among a huge pile of suitcases, boxes and assorted other bags strewn around and on top of a stationary carousel.

* * *

Kim Anh dismounted and parked her motorbike against the wall beside the steps leading up to the entrance of her small apartment. It was Friday evening and after a long week at work she was looking forward to seeing

Conway later that night and arranging their trip tomorrow to Vung Tau. As she came to the top of the stairs she looked to her right and saw a bouquet of red roses on the small dining table. She smiled, 'my Steve, how thoughtful.' She picked up the blooms and read the note attached. Her expression changed as she read the words...

My dear Kim Anh,

These flowers are a measure of my esteem for you. I hope that we can put behind our past unfortunate misunderstandings and begin to understand each other more. I admire and respect you very much and I know that if you will give me a chance you will realise I am a much better man than you think.

Your true friend always

Dung

Her first thought was to take the bouquet downstairs and trash them but then, a feeling she didn't expect came over her. It was a thoughtful and caring gesture and perhaps she had been too harsh on Dung in the past.

He was awkward in her presence and a pain in the neck at times. His pedantic manner at work had driven her to anger on occasions nitpicking tiny, perceived grammatical errors in her work. Their personalities did clash, but there was no doubt, he was basically a very shy person. He had gone to some trouble and expense; it would be churlish of her to reject his flowers this time...and they were beautiful. Even Steve, although he had given her gifts, had never sent her flowers. She frowned. Surely something a man should do for the girl he loved?

She found a vase and arranged the flowers placing them in the middle of the dining table. They brightened the small room immediately. Kim smiled to herself. No doubt Ngoc would be pleased. Taking a towel from her bedroom she went to the bathroom a smile still on her lips. It was a lovely and unexpected gesture from Dung; this time, she would thank him.

Ngoc and her husband with the two children in tow arrived as Kim Anh came from the shower. The older sister had the vase in her hands. She had obviously read the card and was all smiles.

'Ah, how kind of Mr Dung, they are so beautiful.'

'Yes, they are, it was thoughtful of him,' Kim said quietly. Ngoc noticed the smile hovering on her younger sister's lips and glanced knowingly at her husband. Kim Anh's tone toward Dung had softened. Perhaps there was hope after all. Maybe she would warm to him now and turn away from the foreigner?

'Here is a letter for you from our mother, it arrived today,' Ngoc said, handing Kim a small blue envelope addressed in her mother's distinctive scrawl. It was postmarked just outside Hanoi and had taken several days to reach them.

Glowing with happiness, Kim took the letter to her bedroom, tore it open eagerly and began to read. Many minutes passed with Kim still in her bedroom. Impatient to learn their mother's news, Ngoc tapped lightly on her door and entered. She was shocked to find her young sister sitting on the side of the bed shoulders slumped, her face wet with tears; the letter lying in her lap.

Kim didn't move as Ngoc reached down and gently took the letter. She turned away from her sister and began to read their mother's words. The first three pages said how happy she was to hear from Kim again after so long and glad that she was enjoying her job and her life in Ho Chi Minh City. The mother as a true Northerner would never refer to it as Saigon. She went on to talk about minor details of her personal life and those of her friends in Hanoi then came to a part which brought a small smile to Ngoc's lips.

Your sister tells me you have a suitor in a young man at your work. He sounds suitable. Ngoc says he is from a rich family with good prospects. I hope you will consider him because I am not happy about your liaison with this foreigner you told me about in your last letter.

The age gap between you and this man is not acceptable in Vietnamese society. Believe me daughter foreigners will only cause you unhappiness and heartbreak. I once had a relationship with a man from America and my mother intervened and stopped it. At first, I hated her for breaking us up but in the end I knew she was right. Soon after, I met your father and we had a very happy life before he was killed. I learned to hate the Americans during the war and I am so glad I did not marry that man. Look what they have done to our country? It is ruined now. They had no right to be here. Your grandmother was very wise. I love you my daughter and want only the best for you which I believe the young man can give you. For your own sake, I beg you from the bottom of my heart, please give up this foreigner!

With all my love

Mother

Ngoc sat down beside Kim and tried to comfort her but to no avail. Kim pushed her away and remained staring at the floor.

* * *

Binky rushed to open the door to find out who was trying to break it down with repeated loud, impatient knocking. She opened it and stumbled backwards as Lily pushed past her and stormed upstairs to her bedroom. 'What is wrong, why is ma'am like that?' cried the little maid to George staggering past with Lily's luggage. The chauffeur shook his head and struggled upstairs in his mistress's wake.

Binky stood bewildered and hurt, tears welling in her big brown eyes. Her boss had always treated her with great kindness and respect. It was rare for Lily to direct any anger toward her employees and on those rare occasions it was over quickly.

She could be haughty and arrogant to others but she never used a condescending or sharp tone to her staff. Lily was excitable at times, it was part of her mixed race personality, but again, it was usually because of a business problem, or on occasions; a personal difference with a male admirer. To her staff she was the epitome of the perfect boss. What also puzzled Binky was Lily's arrival without any prior warning; unheard of in the past when she normally gave several days' notice of her impending homecoming.

It was twenty four hours before a pale and haggard Lily emerged from her bedroom and told her mother the reason for her sudden return to

Manila. Maria Victoria listened with troubled eyes as the story unfolded.

When she arrived back in Shanghai to her amazement, Lily found the doors to her restaurant locked and bolted and guarded by two armed security men. They refused to tell the angry and increasingly distraught owner what was going on and why her restaurant was closed. Panic-stricken, she rushed to her downtown office to phone her Chinese partner, Wang Ho, only to find him ensconced behind her desk. She was blandly told that he had taken a court order and sequestered all assets and title of the business.

The agreements between them had been rendered void and she now no longer had any control or ownership in the restaurant. Furthermore, he had terminated their association and deposited an amount of money (which she later found to be a pittance) in her bank account. The name was in the process of being changed, current staff had been sacked and renovations had begun which would alter the style and ambience to a traditional Shanghai-style Chinese restaurant. It was a classic case of a newcomer investing in a foreign country making good and then having it all taken away by the local partner. Lily had been well and truly burnt.

Wang Ho had leant across the desk and handed her a folder. Inside there were a number of legal documents confirming the awful truth and a plane ticket to Manila. She had stopped storming around her office for a moment and looked at it dumbfounded trying desperately to stem the flow of tears trickling down her cheeks.

Her world had come crashing down around her. She was shattered and for once in her life, Lily Li was speechless. In a daze she had stumbled from her office into a bathroom in the corridor where she bent over a basin and vomited until she could bring up nothing but green bile.

Shocked and sickened, she staggered to the elevator and out on the street, hailed a taxi to her apartment where she had lain staring at the ceiling for hours before falling into a sleep of nightmares. In the morning she handed in the keys of her apartment to the agent, took a taxi to the airport and flew back to Manila, a broken woman.

* * *

Marvin booked into a small hotel in District 1 around the corner from the Caravelle and hit the streets looking for Conway. His first stop was Dong Du Street just behind the Caravelle where he'd been told there were a couple of popular expat bars. Sooner or later he was certain Conway would appear in one of them.

In *Café Latino* he nursed a beer and checked out the surroundings. It was a long, narrow-gutted place and he would have to be careful. If Conway was there he would spot a guy as big as Marvin almost immediately. The other bar, *Heatwave* was even smaller, and impossible for Marvin to be inconspicuous. What to do? There was one option. He could observe both places from a French restaurant across the street.

Rene's had floor to ceiling windows which would give him an uninterrupted view of those entering and leaving either establishment. It might take a while, but he was patient. Time was no object and besides, he could always chat up one of the pretty Vietnamese waitresses while waiting for his prey.

As usual, his mood was black. Despite showing an official looking fake FBI identification card at Manila airport, an unsmiling security guard had taken the revolver and ammunition from him with the assurance he could collect it in Saigon.

No such luck. His enquiries on arrival had been met with a blank stare and no amount of shouting and protests had moved the uniformed official to action. Finally, sans revolver, he stormed out into the sauna of a Saigon afternoon frightening the life out of a taxi driver who approached all smiles, until he saw the look on Marvin's face.

The journey to his hotel was taken in silence. The cabbie checked his passenger out in the rear vision mirror a number of times and didn't like what he saw. When they arrived at the hotel he didn't bother to count the fare Marvin threw at him. He simply breathed a sigh of relief and roared off down Hai Ba Trung Street.

Marvin ordered another beer and continued to brood. Ok, so he had no gun but there were other ways of terminating someone. He was an ex Marine. It would be easy. The quicker he found this guy and killed him, the sooner he could go back to the Philippines and find that bitch and eliminate her also.

In a small apartment behind Marvin's hotel, Conway and Kim were preparing to leave for Vung Tau.

* * *

Steve watched Kim Anh finish packing their gear into a sports bag for their trip. She had surprised him this morning when he opened the door to her knock. He didn't get the chance to say 'hello' before she threw her arms around him and burst into tears. She stayed in his arms sobbing for many minutes before he was able to calm her down. She added to his bewilderment by doggedly refusing to tell him the reason for her distress.

He held her until she settled down and recovered her composure then handed her a handkerchief. She wiped her tear-stained face and asked a still puzzled Conway where his clothes were to take to Vung Tau.

He took her to the bedroom and pointed to clothing and shaving gear laid out on the bed. She handed him back his handkerchief and set about the packing.

They left the apartment and went out into Nguyen Sieu Street and turned left into Hai Ba Trung. They'd decided on the hydrofoil again. After their last return journey from Vung Tau, he'd had enough of Vietnam's mini buses and no way was he going to face another torturous four hour bus trip. And besides, the hydrofoil was the quickest and most comfortable, albeit more expensive method of getting there.

Their luggage was light so they decided to walk the relatively short distance to the hydrofoil wharf. As they passed the corner of Hai Ba Trung and Dong Du Streets they never noticed a heavily built man in *Rene's* restaurant jump to his feet knocking a full cup of coffee from his table in the process and rush to the door, where he stood staring at the two figures as they disappeared around into Me Linh square.

Conway bought their tickets and boarded as the crew unhooked the mooring ropes. On the wharf a tall figure watched in the shadow of a stand of tamarind trees while not fifty feet further along a black clad figure astride a black motor bike, also watched with interest.

With practiced ease, the skipper of the hydrofoil backed it smoothly away from the wharf into the centre of the river and set course for the 75 minute journey to Vung Tau. Kim sat silently holding his hand for the entire journey while his mind was a whirl of confusing thoughts.

Sometimes Kim Anh was impossible to understand.

* * *

They sat late on a balmy evening eating from a bowl of tangerines on a balcony of their hotel overlooking the South China Sea. It had been a happy day on the beach, devouring succulent fresh seafood and noodles at lunch, wandering among the markets and a pleasant, late-evening after dinner stroll along the seashore but now they were both engrossed in private thoughts. He handed her a tangerine and tried to make conversation but she seemed reluctant and distant.

Was it a trait of Vietnamese women that if something worried them they clammed up? It was irritating because he desperately wanted to help with whatever was troubling her. The girl was an enigma. She sat quietly, peeling the tangerine and placing the skin on a plate before slowly putting it into her mouth seemingly unaware of what she was doing.

He stood up and reached over to take her hand. 'Come on darling, let's turn in,' but she shook her head. 'No, no, you go ahead, I will come later.' Puzzled, his irritation growing, he left her staring out to sea. He was still awake when she crawled in beside him. He attempted to reach out for her but she pulled up a sheet and turned her back.

She lay there in the darkness, her mind in turmoil. She loved him so much but...her family forbade the relationship. Even her friends and colleagues had also warned her against involvement with a foreigner. Was this relationship so wrong? Why did everyone, her mother, sister, friends, colleagues all seem to be against it?

What was she to do? Tears rolled down her cheeks. He was a wonderful man and had shown her more love than any person she had ever known. He was kind, considerate and he genuinely cared for her. But how could she turn against the wishes of her family and the advice of friends? And could she accept his culture, so different from her own? What would happen if she married him, where would they live? She loved her country. I am Vietnamese, I could not live anywhere else, she told herself. There were too many questions and not enough answers. Sleep did not come until just before dawn.

He woke around 6.00 am and looked across at her. She looked so peaceful and yet beneath that exterior there was a complex and troubled girl...but what was it? Her mood swings worried him. If she would only tell him what the problem was, he could at least begin to help her and try to understand.

He felt so damn helpless and her stubborn refusal to enlighten him simply made him frustrated and annoyed. Maybe he just didn't understand Vietnamese women. Maybe it was something he'd done? If so why the hell wouldn't she tell him? He leant over and kissed her gently on the cheek then slipped out of bed, dressed quickly and quietly and headed downstairs for a walk on the beach to try and clear his head.

A gentle offshore breeze cooled him as he walked in the shallows. He skirted around children and families out for an early morning paddle and splashed a couple of cute little ones who squealed with delight and made funny faces at him as they rushed back to the safety of their parents. He smiled wryly; kids were the same all over, so beautiful and innocent. Would've been nice to have had a couple of my own...

He walked up to a rock wall bordering the road parallel to the beach and sat there gazing out to sea. He was lost in thought when he felt a gentle tap on his shoulder. He turned to see her standing there with a hesitant smile. She put her hand on his arm. 'Hello darling,' she said quietly.

'Hi, how are you this morning Kim?'

The implication was in his tone. Have you got over your mood?

'I'm ok,' she replied, a little too quickly. 'Let's go for a walk.' She took his hand and pointed toward the shoreline. He helped her down onto the sand and they strolled along hand in hand in the gentle waves of low tide.

Her mood had changed. It was like nothing had happened. They had gone nearly a mile when she drew him up the beach toward a large rock formation in the middle of which, nature had created a small cave. She suggested they go inside.

'It's nice and cool darling, come...' At that time of day there was no one around. They had this private little cave to themselves.

At first it was a comfortable height but further in it became lower and began to brush their heads. She turned and leaned back against a wall and pulled him to her. After last night's episode, the passion of her kiss surprised him. He returned it with interest and they remained glued together for many minutes. Finally she pulled away breathing heavily and said something which, on later reflection, he felt he should have given more thought.

'Whatever happens, I want you to know that I love you…more than any man I have ever known.'

This time he kissed her almost savagely. He never really knew why. Maybe it was anger at her moods, perhaps it was the frustration of not knowing how to cope with her at times, or more likely, the real reason was that he loved her to distraction…but at the same time, a little voice in his head said; *you will never understand her Steve.*

After lunch they had several hours to kill so it was back to the hotel room, a big improvement on the 'little dump' of their previous visit. He took her in his arms and although she seemed willing he detected a slight resistance which thankfully, soon melted. They fell on the bed and slowly undressed each other.

As his lips and hands roamed over her naked body past her belly to her womanhood she writhed and gasped as she felt his tongue. 'Oh darling, that is so wonderful. Darling, you are the first man to explore my body, I love it…please do it to me.' She was his for the taking. But again the words came back to him; '*she's a virgin Steve, don't spoil her.*'

'I'm sorry, I can't,' he said rolling off her. He had promised he would not dishonour her and tarnish her reputation. He wanted her more than he had ever wanted any woman, but he loved her and it was a promise he intended to keep! With great reluctance, he brought her down from the euphoria of the moment without completing the act. Was he being honourable in her eyes, or plain stupid?

She lay there on her side propped up on one elbow looking at him with an expression he could not fathom. He reached over to her but she rolled away from him and turned her back and curled up into a foetal position. He moved closer and put his right arm across encircling her waist to try to turn her back to him but she remained stiff and unyielding.

'For Christ's sake, what the hell's wrong now?' he said angrily. For several minutes she said nothing then very quietly said, 'why have you never asked me to marry you?'

The 64 dollar question and it took him completely by surprise. He had no immediate answer. Suddenly many questions about their relationship whirled around in his head. They had been there at the back of his mind for some time nagging…like festering sores. The truth was, he was afraid of the answers. It was easier to enjoy the present and not think about the future. But now he had to face the reality of the situation between them.

Of one thing he was certain; he loved her, there was no question about that. But could he embrace her society? Could he live in Vietnam? He had once told her that should he marry an Asian girl he would live with her in her own country and not take her from the environment she had grown up in; her family, her friends and everything that was precious to her. He had seen too many disasters in cross cultural marriages.

What could he say that didn't sound like a cop out? He got out of bed and walked to the window and looked out on to Back Beach, sparkling in the afternoon sunshine.

'Darling, I have not been back long and have had a lot on my mind,' he said, turning back into the room. 'As you know, I'm trying to set up a hotel or restaurant for my company; it's occupied a lot of my thoughts. The accident deliberate or otherwise has also been on my mind a lot. I still believe someone tried to kill me. I guess I just didn't get around to thinking about this subject. I always thought we would take our time and look to the future when I get organized here. We've got time haven't we?'

She said nothing.

He went over and stood looking down at her. He knew his answer sounded pathetic, weak, unsatisfactory, and was the kind of answer a politician would give; or an answer from someone not sure of himself. He felt ashamed; she was entitled to something better than that.

'Please give me a little more time darling.' He leant over and kissed her cheek. 'I will have things sorted with this project soon then we can make plans. I love you Kim Anh. I know we can make it together…please believe me.'

She remained silent.

They left Vung Tau on the late afternoon ferry. As they were about to board Conway stopped and looked back and forth at the crowd gathered around them on the wharf. Puzzled, she tugged his arm. 'What's wrong, what are you looking for?'

He continued to scan the crowd I like this place, I just wanted one last look; I hope we come back soon, it has lovely memories for us, don't you think?' but she had already stepped aboard and gone below.

The journey back to Saigon by hydrofoil was again uncomfortable. His attempts to make light hearted conversation were met with either a weak smile or silence. It was dark when they reached his apartment. She prepared a meal of spring rolls, salad and Vietnamese coffee but it was hurried and he got the distinct impression she wanted to leave as soon as possible. As they finished washing the dishes Conway reached for her but she stepped back, her hands up.

'I have to return home now Steve,' she said, her voice clipped. 'But before I leave there is something I have to tell you.' Her tone worried him. He had a sense of foreboding.

'That sounds ominous, what is it darling?' he forced a smile and tossed the tea towel onto the sink trying to lift the cloud that had once again descended over them.

'Steve,' she continued. He frowned; two "Steves" in two minutes; no "darling"? Her voice was barely audible and she turned away from him.

'I am sorry...but I think we can only be friends, we cannot be lovers anymore...I...' She stopped, obviously not knowing what else to say. The words had come too quickly, as if she wanted to get rid of them and forget them as soon as they had passed her lips. He stood there stunned and bewildered. He felt as if he'd been kicked in the belly.

He grabbed her shoulder more roughly than he intended and pulled her around to face him. '*Friends*? Why? What's all this about? What's going on? I thought...'

She lowered her head then looked up at him again. Her eyes were brimming with tears.

'You know how I feel about you…but my family…' she stopped, and this time she was unable to contain her emotions. The tears flooded down her cheeks; tears of anger mixed with unfettered frustration.

She didn't have to say anymore. Her family's reaction to him after the visit to Thanh Da was enough. As far as they were concerned he was "friendly" and that's all they wanted him to be to her…a friend!

'Well, what was all that about marriage, why the hell did you ask me?' he said bitterly.

'I am sorry, I had to ask you, but my mother, she wrote to me…about you,' she sobbed.

'What about your mother?' he said, his voice rising. 'For God's sake, what has she to do with this? I've never met her, she doesn't know me. How can she influence you?'

'She does not want me to marry a foreigner, she is North Vietnamese; she has bad memories of the war…'

Conway had heard stories of the ongoing hatred of Northerners toward foreigners but those he'd met in Saigon seem to bear no animosity. But it seemed Kim Anh's mother was of the old school and how could he blame her? Her part of the country had been bombed, blasted and fought over by foreigners for centuries: she had good reason to hate.

'Is that what you really want Kim Anh?' The question was rhetorical… he knew the answer. She shook her head and put her arms around him. He kissed the top of her head. Suddenly he was overcome with this terrible feeling of emptiness. He loved her, God how he loved her. No way did he want to lose her…ever!

What is it with her family? He had done nothing wrong! He had treated their daughter with respect. Couldn't they see how much he loved her? He had tried to show them he loved her and cared. They can't take her away from me! He tried to lift her head to kiss her but she turned and stood with her back to him.

'Here take this,' he said pulling a handkerchief from the pocket of his jeans. She took it with a muffled 'thank you.' He walked to the window and looked out for a few seconds then spun around and spread his hands wide in exasperation. 'Ok, I'll go to Hanoi and talk to her, I will change her mind! Darling, I'll get down on my knees if necessary.'

She shook her head. 'She will not listen, I know my mother; it is where I get my stubborn nature from. It is not just my mother…my friends and colleagues; they agree…they say…'

Conway exploded.

'Fuck your friends and colleagues…they don't know me either! It is you…you Kim Anh who knows me, not them! Are you going to let your feelings for me be dictated by people who don't even know me? That is just fucking stupid!'

She stood there head down, twisting the handkerchief in her hands. It was the first time he had used bad language in her presence.

'I am sorry…' her voice trailed off…

He looked at her open-mouthed shaking his head, his expression one of sadness and disbelief. This accounts for her mood all weekend in Vung Tau. She had obviously made up her mind and was steeling herself for this confrontation.

A sudden and surprising feeling of compassion came over him. How difficult this must have been for her. She had been given a choice; family or him? In Vietnamese society it was no contest.

'I'm sorry…I…you must hate my family,' her voice broke as she picked up the small bag of clothes she'd taken to Vung Tau from the settee and walked to the door. She stood with her back to him; hand on the doorknob for a moment. Then as if a big decision had been made, she opened the door and left without another word or a backward glance.

She never heard him say, 'no I don't hate them, I hardly know them… Kim I…'

He went to the door and stood looking out into the hallway. He could hear her footsteps echoing off the concrete walls as she hurried down the winding terrazzo stairwell to the entrance below and out into the street… then silence.

16

Conway lay awake trying to get his head around her words. He simply couldn't believe it. She had effectively terminated their relationship in just a few words; from lovers to friends in one sentence. He lay staring at the ceiling in the darkness. It was quiet, except for the soft swishing of the overhead fan. Memories of their time together flashed through his head like scenes from a movie, all so vivid, most of them precious.

How could he forget that memorable first day in Saigon in the bowels of the palace when he took her hand? She had told him later it was the most romantic moment of her life; the moment she had fallen in love. Their walks in the park at evening watching children at play; the kisses, the laughter; the sweet interlude in Binh Quoi; the romance of Vung Tau. He could hear her voice, 'darling, I can't imagine life without you, you are the most wonderful man I have ever met...I love you so much my Steve... please never leave me...I want you with me always...'

But there were also the sudden mood swings; the night at the Rex and Continental hotels. He recalled another occasion when she had disappeared from the apartment one night for no apparent reason. He had thought she had gone to the bathroom only to discover she had left the apartment. He had walked the streets trying to find her and given up, but on arrival back at his apartment received a phone call from her asking him to come to the Givral coffee shop.

There he found her sitting alone; her face hard and emotionless, stubbornly refusing to give any explanation for her behaviour. On the one hand, sweet, charming, caring and loving and yet she could be inordinately stubborn, uncommunicative and difficult. But then who was he to judge another? *He who is without sin cast the first stone.* She was his Kimmee, and he loved her.

He tossed and turned punching the pillow to make it softer and more comfortable but sleep would not come. He got up, poured himself a glass of cold water from the fridge and went out on to the balcony. It was a typical Saigon night; hot, humid and sticky, a sky without stars; and…a night without her.

He sipped the water and stared out into the winking lights of the city. From somewhere across the heavy, still night air drifted the soulful voice of Barbara Streisand singing *The Way We Were*. 'Jesus Barbara, that's the last bloody song I want to hear right now.'

Almost without thinking he put his hand in his pants pocket and withdrew something he carried with him everywhere. It was the small square block of pink quartz engraved with the words *I Love You* which she had given him at the airport the day he returned to Manila. He looked at it for a moment, shook his head and put it back in his pocket, then threw the last mouthful of water over the balcony and went back to bed.

He continued to lie awake his mind still seeing her, hearing her soft voice, her laughter when, floating in through the window from far away, came the sad, haunting strains of *Johnny Guitar*. '*Play it again, play it again, play it again, Johnny Guitar*'… Kinda fits my mood, he said to himself, tossing and turning for the hundredth time. Suddenly his phone rang! His heart leapt! He jumped out of bed not bothering to turn on the lights, rushing into the lounge to pick it up blundering against furniture in the darkness. 'Kim?'

'Steve, it's me Jumbo! You gotta get back here in a hurry man, there's a fire in the Down Under!' The sickening feeling in Conway's gut for one situation was replaced by another.

'What! How bad is it? Anyone hurt? Are the guests and staff ok, how much damage, where's the fire brigade?...Shit!' His words rushed out in a torrent.

'It's not good man,' replied Keyes between coughing fits.

'Sorry Steve, the smoke, it's so thick...we're clearing the hotel. Don't know about casualties. It apparently started in the kitchen. The staff are doing their best to fight it now but we need the bloody fire brigade man, they're so damn slow, thank God we installed a new sprinkler system but,' he began to cough again, 'there's a lot of shouting and noise...I can here the fire brigade now...gotta go buddy!'

Conway replaced the receiver shaking his head. 'My God, that's all I need right now.'

There were no flights out at that time of night but he'd catch the early morning daily flight of Philippine airlines to Manila and be there before lunch. He fell back on the bed hoping sleep would come. It didn't.

In her tiny bedroom in Thanh Da, Kim Anh lay face down, her head buried in a pillow to muffle the sound of her sobbing.

* * *

Marvin had tracked them to Vung Tau and back to Saigon. He'd caught the next hydrofoil and it hadn't taken him too long to spot them at Back beach or *Bai S*au, as it was known to the locals. This was the popular location in Vung Tau for Saigonese and expats, wanting a weekend retreat from the heat of the city and an obvious place for Conway and his "girlfriend" to stay.

He watched them come and go from their hotel to the beach, his military training allowing him to stay close but out of sight as they visited the market and other places. He was tempted to attack as they took their evening stroll along a deserted stretch of beach but a group of noisy Vietnamese, apparently on a company team building exercise, came charging down out of nowhere onto the beach at exactly the wrong time.

The following day waiting until the last moment, he boarded the same hydrofoil to Saigon and hid on the back deck behind the wheelhouse. On arrival in Saigon the cover of darkness allowed him to follow them from the port to Hai Ba Trung Street where they turned right into Nguyen Sieu Street.

He edged around into Nguyen Sieu where to his amazement and fury, found they had disappeared. He called to an old women selling coffee at the head of an alley a few yards into the street. 'Foreign man, Vietnamese lady?' he said, holding his hand high to indicate Conway. She stared at him for a few seconds then pointed to the end of the alley.

He walked past a group of young Vietnamese women in white tops and white mini skirts chatting. He asked the same question of one of them. She pointed to the entrance of a shop then turned her hand at right angles to indicate where they had entered. He grunted a 'thanks' and walked back to the street. He now knew where Conway lived. The next part should not be too hard. Unknown to Marvin, by the time he arrived for his stakeout the next morning, Conway's flight was on its final approach to Manila.

* * *

'Thank you for the flowers, they were beautiful,' smiled Kim, looking up at Dung who had sidled up to her desk almost immediately she had arrived for work on the Monday morning. He had arrived early and hung around anxiously waiting for her. He had asked himself a hundred times; 'did she like the flowers? Is she still mad at me?'

His heart leapt at the warmth of her words, his face twisted in a crooked smile. He shuffled his feet, 'er...I am very glad you liked them... *em oi*, maybe we can...' he got no further as her phone rang. Her smile got a whole lot wider as she quickly reached over to pick it. It was probably Steve. I can tell him how stupid I was and that to ignore what I said. 'hello Ste...'

The voice was Australian... her heart missed a beat. But it wasn't Steve. The caller was one of the Australian partners in the Waterworld joint venture. He needed Sales statistics for a certain period.

'Yes sir, yes, I will find this information for you and call you back,' she said, replacing her phone. Dung waited impatiently while she took the call and immediately it was finished, asked her if she would accompany him on a boat trip on the Saigon river the following Saturday.

'Thank you,' said Kim, her mind still on Conway, 'I'm not sure if I have free time but I will let you know, ok?' His sallow features, impassive while she was on the phone, lit up in a broad smile; at least she had not rejected him out of hand.

'Thank you Miss Kim Anh, I will wait your decision, thank you for your kindness,' he replied obsequiously, hating himself for his formality but desperate to show his good manners and be on his best behaviour. He returned to his desk now quietly confident. Finally it seemed there was a chance of winning her. Ngoc was right, persistence was the name of the game and despite the previous setback, this time, the roses had done the trick.

Kim sat staring at her phone. The urge to pick it up and phone Conway and tell him she was sorry and to forget what she had said was overwhelming, but pride and her stubborn nature would never allow that. That would be losing face. She returned to her computer screen to find the information for the Australian director her mind still on Conway.

'I wonder what he is doing? Where is he? How is he?' She remembered the distraught, bewildered look on his face a few moments before she left his apartment. She began to tap information into her computer but her emotions got the better of her and she was unable to see the screen through a veil of tears.

* * *

Conway and Jumbo Keyes sat in Conway's office drinking coffee and discussing plans for the rebuilding of the part of the hotel which had been destroyed in the fire. To Conway's relief, the fire had been largely contained to the kitchen and coffee shop area.

While there had been extensive damage to both, apart from a few rooms near the coffee shop, most of the guest rooms had not been affected seriously. No one had been hurt and there was little basic structural damage; water and smoke had caused much of the unholy mess to both areas forcing a temporary closure of the hotel. Guests had been billeted to other hotels in the area while reconstruction took place. Keyes had wasted no time and work had begun already.

'How long before the kitchen and coffee shop are operational Jumbo?'

The big American gazed up at the ceiling as if looking for divine guidance.

'My guess is around 2-3 weeks, give or take a week, hard to tell in this town. If we get the right workers, it'll be done quickly. Romy our maintenance guy is pretty good. I'm hoping he can keep the crew we have at the moment. Got the fingers crossed man.'

'Ok, keep me up to speed on it.'

Keyes stood up and headed for the door but then stopped and turned, 'something else disturbing happened while you were away Steve.'

'Oh?'

'One of our guards was found murdered...shortly after you left. Do you remember Roland?'

'Sure, nice young guy.' Conway frowned. 'What's the story?'

'We don't know the full details but he was found at the end of an alley off Adriatico Street. His body was hidden under a few sheets of corrugated iron. The smell was so bad a local guy went to investigate.' Keyes' face screwed up in distaste. 'The rats had got to him; it wasn't pretty the cops told me.'

'Any clues as to who did it and why?'

'No, but listen to this,' said Keyes lowering his voice. 'He was seen drinking in a cruddy little bar called *Madames*, and...he was with a big foreign guy, an American: "A white guy, a mean looking hombre" according to the owner of the place.' 'Steve,' Keyes paused again for effect, 'the guy fitted the description of Marvin.'

'What, are you sure?'

'Yes, from what the cops had been told; a big white guy, ugly sonofabitch, with a Marine haircut, and attitude. I'll bet a month's pay it was him. And there is something else...'

'What?'

'Mary, one of our girls on reception, who was a bit sweet on Roland, saw him talking to a guy fitting the same description out the front of the hotel the day before he was murdered. Now why would he do that? What was his game?' asked Keyes, his brows knitted.

'I know what his game is.'

'What? Revenge for being chucked out of here?' Keyes only half believed his question.

'It's much more than that. You don't murder some guy you don't know for being thrown out of a hotel, well, not as a rule. He's a psycho, and he thinks Sally has dumped him for me and that's why he wants me dead... and her as well.'

Conway leaned back in his chair and rubbed his chin. 'So...maybe he was pumping Roland for info about me, got what he wanted, then decided to get rid of him to cover his tracks.'

'Sounds feasible man...we know he's a head case but not a very smart head case, he's left a trail behind him.'

'He doesn't care Jumbo, as far as he's concerned the end will justify the means. Vietnam fucked his head, he probably doesn't care if he lives or dies.'

'I wonder where he is now Steve.'

Conway now had his own surprise for the American. 'He's in Saigon. He followed me there.'

The mouth of Jumbo Keyes dropped open like a trapdoor.

'What! So Roland must have given him the information and he's knocked him off to shut him up, but how did you know he was...'

Conway drained his coffee and placed the cup carefully on the saucer in front of him. 'I wasn't a forward scout in Vietnam for nothing. I noticed him when Kim and I went to Vung Tau for the weekend. He was wearing dark glasses, he's let his hair grow, he's got a moustache and trying to grow a beard, but it was him alright.' He looked at Keyes for a long moment.

'The arsehole probably thinks I didn't see him and I'm pretty sure he's not awake to the fact that I noticed him, otherwise he would have come out. Roland told him I'd gone to Saigon and he's followed me and somehow tracked me down.'

Keyes sat shaking his head slowly as Conway continued.

'It wouldn't be hard, it's a small town as far as expats are concerned, most live in District 1. He'd know that from his time in Saigon during the war. He'd be smart enough to hang around the few expat bars knowing sooner or later he'd spot me. You don't sit in your room all night in a town like Saigon. And it fits because,' he paused, looking Keyes in the eye, 'some bastard tried to kill me.' Conway related the incident with the black four wheel drive.

Keyes' eyebrows shot up. 'Holy shit!' He reached into his pocket and took out a large red and white spotted handkerchief and wiped his brow then leant forward in his chair. 'He knows your whereabouts, hired a car to keep an eye on you and when the time was right tried to run you down right?'

'Looks that way Sherlock,' grinned Conway. 'I can't think of anyone else who would want to kill me. After all, I hadn't been there long enough to make an enemy of a local, so who else could it be?'

'I wonder if he followed you back to Manila?'

'I don't think so. I checked outside my apartment when I left and he was definitely not around. But sooner or later he'll find out I'm back here and come looking for me again.'

'This is bad man. You better tell someone in the American embassy.'

'Sure, they need to know. I've already spoken to McGaw but they can't do anything because they've effectively got nothing on him. But,' Conway's voice hardened. He stood up and paced around the office.

'I've had a gutful of this bastard but I reckon he doesn't realise I'm onto him so I'll go carefully. If he tries anything I'll be ready...and how!'

Keyes frowned, he was worried; a lot more than he let on.

'For Christ sake buddy, you better be *very* careful. This guy was a Marine, and a psycho to boot. Who knows what he's likely to do. He's killed one person that we know of already and possibly others. I think there's no doubt now he's also the one who tried to shoot you in Del Pilar. Man, he's got to be caught...real quick!'

'I'll talk to McGaw at the embassy again, he's a good man, maybe he can come up with something...hopefully grab Marvin when he shows and hold him on suspicion. He'll know what to do.'

'Let's hope so. This motherfucker's got to be taken off the streets as soon as possible.' Keyes got to his feet and wiped his big black shiny cheeks …'like yesterday.'

'Before you go Jumbo…about Roland? I know it sounds like Marvin, but have the cops come up with anything to tie it to him?'

'None yet, they're "working on it" they tell me, but frankly to them it's no big deal. This is just another murder in a town where things like this are commonplace.'

'Yeah, I guess so, anything else?'

'No man, everything has been ok apart from the fire of course…oh,' the big man stopped again at the door and smiled, 'how's your Kim Anh?'

A shadow passed over Conway's face. He looked down for a moment then turned to stare out the window as if he was no longer aware Keyes was in the room.

'She's not my Kim Anh anymore Jumbo,' he said quietly.

'What! What happened Steve? I thought you two were…like…an item.'

'We were until last Sunday night,' said Conway bitterly. 'When we came back from Vung Tau she told me it was over…as far as lovers…we are now, according to her, just *friends* which means, romantically it's over between us.'

'I don't get it. Why the sudden change Steve?' Conway grimaced and shook his head.

'Family interference; she says her family do not want her hooked up with a foreigner. They're from North Vietnam and still harbour a few grudges. You know what it's like in Vietnam when it comes to family Jumbo…they come first, second and always. It's the Asian way.'

'Very true Steve. Remember I'm married to a Filipina. I know where you're coming from. Do you really think it's over man?'

'It seems the loving part is. She says we can be friends. Who wants to be a *friend* Jumbo? That sucks!'

'Maybe absence will make the heart grow fonder…I can see you still care for her.'

'Care for her! It's much more than care...I love her!'

Keyes knew that words didn't help, no matter how sympathetic they sounded. Conway was an upbeat guy but suddenly his whole demeanor changed, his shoulders slumped and he looked haggard as if he'd hardly slept in a week which unknown to Keyes was true. Hopefully they would find each other again because this girl had really got to him. In all the time he had known him, Jumbo Keyes had never seen Steve Conway so down.

After the American left, Conway sat staring out the window for an age before returning to the pile of paperwork on his desk but his thoughts kept drifting back to Kim Anh. He'd been back in Manila one week and had heard nothing from her. He wasn't sure if he ever would, she seemed so adamant the night she left his apartment.

He was sorely tempted to phone her at work and had picked up his phone a couple of times but decided against it. He still couldn't figure out how their love could end so quickly. Or had it? You don't turn a relationship on and off like a tap...or do you? It seemed Kim Anh could.

At the bottom of a pile of papers was a white envelope addressed to him. The writing seemed familiar but there was no return address. He opened it to find a one page letter from Sally dated a week previous.

Dearest Steve

I wonder where you are. Are you still in Vietnam? I miss you very much and hope you somehow get this letter soon. I am doing ok here in Isabella but it is very quiet. Do you know if they have caught Marvin yet? I will not rest until I know he is behind bars...or dead. I hate to say it but I would prefer him dead because I know if he catches up with me he will kill me. I have to bring my uncle to Manila for medical treatment next week but I am scared. I will not stay in Manila any longer than I have to. I hope it will only be for a few days at the most. I will be at the same number in Antipolo if you happen to be back from Vietnam please call me. I want to hear your voice again so much.

Love Always

Sally xxx

From the date on the letter, she would be now in Manila. He read it again tossing up whether to phone her or not. 'Not right now Sal'. He placed it back in the envelope and slipped it under a file in his top drawer.

* * *

Marvin was angry and frustrated. Where was this asshole? He'd staked out the entrance to the alley where Conway lived from across the square. It gave him a perfect view of the only exit from Conway's apartment into Nguyen Sieu Street. He'd kept it under constant surveillance for nearly a week now but there was no sign of his quarry.

He'd even gone to the trouble of paying a local female bread vendor to keep an eye out while he was away. She had some English and seemed to understand Marvin's description of the Australian. At least he hoped so, but was not too convinced at the smiles and vigorous nods she gave him when he handed her a fistful of dong.

Between the two of them he was sure he would catch up with Conway sooner or later. What he had to do was figure out *when* to kill him, *how*, was a minor detail. A quick thrust of a knife in the darkened shadows of Nguyen Sieu Street one night would be all that was needed. He would know when the time came.

Roland had told him Conway was in Saigon on a job. He'd not been there long and must surely be still in town, but where the fuck was he? Had he changed address in the dead of night? Had his vendor slipped up and been asleep when Conway had moved out? She started work early. Maybe he had moved out earlier…?

Marvin had tried to keep himself as inconspicuous as possible but for a man his size it wouldn't be long before the locals would be asking questions about this big, surly white man who lurked around the square across from Nguyen Sieu and Hai Ba Trung Street not saying anything to anyone, but obviously watching and waiting, for something, or someone. The police sooner or later would become interested.

Ok, enough is enough. He had to take a chance and find out Conway's exact whereabouts. He waited until 11.00 pm when things were quiet in the neighbourhood then quickly crossed Hai Ba Trung and stood at the edge of the front of the alley peering to the end and the opening he'd been shown where Conway was supposed to be living.

He made his way slowly towards it, stopping occasionally hoping to duck into one of the small shops which lined the alley if Conway suddenly appeared.

As he neared the opening he heard the yells and squeals of excited kids and the staccato ear splitting sounds of computer games. With his back to the wall he cautiously peered around into the entrance and found a row of young boys some teenage, most much younger, either side of a long, bare narrow concrete room bashing away at computer play stations. The noise from the kids and the games was deafening.

He made his way to the back where a frumpy, middle aged woman sat at a small table collecting payment from the steady stream of customers as they finished their games. Marvin signaled to her to come outside indicating with sign language that he wanted to talk. She looked up at him suspiciously then reluctantly, followed him out to the alley.

Marvin held out a handful of dong and said, 'foreigner, Mr Conway, you know him?'

Mrs Chong looked at the money then Marvin. 'I know him.'

'He's a friend of mine. I want to speak to him. Do you know where he is?'

Mrs Chong shook her head. 'Wait, he stay in apartment of my sister, I find out for you,' she said, hurrying back inside to a narrow hallway at the far end of her shop. Marvin waited nervously clenching his fists ready to attack if Conway suddenly appeared.

Ten agonizing minutes later, Mrs Chong reappeared. 'He go to Manila,' she said, licking her lips her eyes returning to the dong in Marvin's hand. Barely able to keep his temper under control; he wanted to strangle this fat piece of rubbish. Through gritted teeth he said, 'when…did he go to Manila? When is he coming back…do you know?'

'My sister say, she don't know, he don't say.'

In a fury Marvin turned and stormed off back up the alley.

'Hey you!...you give me money!' Mrs Chong shouted. Marvin ignored her and returned to his hotel in a rage.

His plans were now all fucked up. He couldn't fly straight back into Manila; there was probably a welcome party waiting for him. He'd have to think hard about how to re-enter the Philippines. The next morning he bought a large-scale map of Southeast Asia.

17

Kim Anh sat at her desk staring at her telephone. Should she or shouldn't she? Will she or won't she? What if he is cold and indifferent and doesn't want to know me? I couldn't bear to hear his rejection. What to do? Suddenly she had an idea. She dialed a number. A familiar voice answered almost immediately. 'Hello.'

'Hello *chi oi,* it's me, Kim Anh,' she said nervously. Kim wasn't sure what she was going to say but somehow she'd find out from Mrs Thanh how Steve was faring without letting on she hadn't seen him for over a week.

Before she could utter another word, Mrs Thanh ignored the pleasantries. '*Em oi* when is Mr Conway coming back to Saigon? And is he coming back at all?'

'Huh?' Kim was stunned, her mouth suddenly dry. What was she saying? Steve had left Saigon! She groped for words. My God! He must have been so upset after what I'd said he decided to go back to the Philippines. Oh how stupid I was!

'Wh…wh…when did he leave? Why?' she stuttered, her head spinning. She lost all thought of any pretext. What was happening? How could he leave without telling her?

'Just over a week ago, don't you know? He didn't tell you?' asked the landlady incredulously.

'Ah...er...no,' she said weakly, 'he didn't but, ah..I've been away. There...there...must be a good reason...what did he say to you?' Her voice became hoarse as she struggled to catch her breath.

'He didn't say anything, just left a note under my door saying there was a problem back in Manila and he had to return immediately.'

'And...he...ah...didn't say...how long he'd be away?'

'No, he didn't. He has paid up till the end of the month though, but I am surprised at Mr Conway.' The tone of the normally cheerful landlady was full of reproach. Not only was she hurt because her star boarder had taken off so suddenly and virtually told her nothing, but the fact he had not mentioned it to Kim Anh amazed and disappointed her even more. The poor girl was obviously devastated and hadn't a clue why Conway had left in such a hurry.

He seemed such a considerate and decent man. She had seen the way they looked and acted toward each other on the number of occasions she had hosted them for dinner. The deep love between them was obvious.

How could he do this to her? Is this the way foreign men treated their women? Vietnamese men were bad enough in the offhand, selfish and sometimes brutal way they acted toward their women, but she had always thought foreigners were generally more considerate. It seemed the stories she had heard were wrong.

'Kim Anh, please let me know as soon as you hear from him won't you,' said Mrs Thanh, her tone now soft and sympathetic.

'Yes...I will, I will, th...thank you...I...' Kim's voice broke as she hung up. She sat staring at the phone still trying to come to terms with what she had just heard. That's if I ever do hear from him again, which now seems highly unlikely, she thought.

Slowly anger and frustration began to replace the shock and hurt. So that's the type of man you are Mr Conway. You didn't even have the courtesy or manners to let me know you were leaving. I told you we were still friends, but you ran away like an immature child. To think I actually loved you!

Her thoughts fluctuated between positive and negative with the latter gaining ascendancy. One moment, he had good reason not to inform her, the next; there could be no excuse...

She looked across the office to see Dung speaking to one of the salesmen. At that moment he looked over the salesman's shoulder in her direction. She smiled and with a slight nod of her head indicated she wanted to speak to him. The salesman looked on open mouthed as Dung suddenly ignored him and almost leapt a desk on his way across the office to her side.

'You want to see me about something Miss Kim Anh?' he asked, trying to contain his excitement. 'Yes, Mr. Dung, I would like to accept your invitation to the boat trip on Saturday.' Dung nearly fainted with happiness. He was overjoyed but dare not show it. Instead, he simply returned her smile and replied in his usual formal manner. 'Thank you Miss Kim Anh, I am very honoured. The boat leaves the Binh Quoi jetty at 6.00 pm. Shall I pick you up at say...5.30pm?' For a moment her heart lurched. Binh Quoi. The memory of that sweet evening flooded back.

'Yes, that will be fine, thank you.'

Dung all smiles, returned to his office, his new jovial manner not lost on other staff, who knew him to be a rather aloof and churlish individual.

At her desk, Kim's thoughts were almost immediately those of regret. She loved Steve Conway but obviously he had turned away from her...it was all over between them. He had left her and returned to Manila, it was so hard to believe but now, she shrugged resignedly...she had no choice but to try to put him out of her mind and start a new life.

* * *

'Hi Sally, I just arrived from Saigon and got your letter. How long will you be here in Manila?'

'Oh Steve, it's wonderful to hear from you, thank you for calling. I hope to return to Isabella by the end of the week as my uncle's condition has improved a lot.' She hesitated before asking the inevitable question her tone anxious but hopeful. 'What about Marvin, have you heard anything?' Conway wasn't going to worry her unnecessarily and tell her about Saigon.

'No, not recently,' he said reassuringly, 'but as you know, the local American authorities here and the NBI are looking for him.' This was not strictly true. Although McGaw would have organized surveillance, he doubted if the NBI were involved at this stage. But he needed to boost her morale. It didn't help much. She was still very frightened.

'I pray to God every night that they will get him soon Steve, I am scared. I won't be happy until they catch him and put him away for good.'

'Don't worry,' replied Conway trying to allay her fears. 'They'll grab him, as soon as he shows his ugly head.'

'Can we meet, I need to see you again, I have missed you so much... please Steve.' He was about to say no but then...what the hell, it seemed to be over with Kim Anh...Sally had meant a lot to him in the past, so there was no harm in seeing her and giving some moral support was there?

'Sure, let's have dinner tomorrow night at Traders Hotel on Roxas Boulevard, you know it?'

'Yes, I do, what time?'

'Let's meet in the downstairs bar at 7.30 pm ok?'

'Wonderful, I look forward to seeing you then.'

Conway hung up and sat turning things over in his mind - there was plenty to think about. He'd phone McGaw tomorrow and give him an update on Marvin. Maybe the authorities in Saigon could pick him up and hold him on some kind of trumped up charge but realistically, it was unlikely, unless the guy had committed a crime, although in Marvin's crazy state of mind that was quite possible. I wonder what the bastard's up to now, no doubt planning to come back here. I'd better be careful.

* * *

Marvin sat on the side of his hotel bed studying a large scale map of south-east Asia and considering his options. He could try to re-enter the Philippines on one of his false passports; he'd come in and out of Manila as Philip Thompson, electrical engineer, even though he had changed his appearance somewhat, the risk was too great. For sure they were on the lookout for him by now.

The Philippine immigration system was still crude by world standards and had not yet been computerized but he wasn't about to take any chances. He needed an alternative point of entry, but where? It would be safer coming in from another country other than Vietnam. Singapore into Cebu was an option, maybe? Davao, perhaps, Zamboanga? The problem was finding an airline which could bring him into any of those places. Even if he found one, it was still risky.

He sat staring at the map going over the options. Which way? How? And there was another problem. Was it worth going back to Manila? How long would Conway be there? Had he given up here? Or was he coming back soon? Maybe he'd been recalled briefly for some kind of management meeting. These things happened in business all the time.

All these thoughts flew around his head. He had a closer look at the map and a plan began to form. He folded the map and was about to leave when there was a soft tap on his door. He froze then stepped quietly to the peephole to see the face of Li the chambermaid.

He opened the door to a dazzling smile as she glided past him carrying her bucket of cleaning materials. There was something about this girl that intrigued him. It was not sexual although she was an extremely attractive girl, just a whisper away from being beautiful; her complexion smooth, reminding him of the colour of burnished porcelain. She was a *mestizo*, the product of a union between Vietnamese and European.

He picked up the map and placed it on a small table on the other side of the room.

'Where are you from?' he asked as she began to make his bed.

She stopped stripping back a sheet and smiled that wonderful smile.

'Ban Me Thout in central Vietnam. Do you know it sir?'

Her English was good; the diction clear. This girl was educated; no ordinary chambermaid.

'I know it,' said Marvin quietly. He knew Ban Me Thout alright. He'd served between there and Pleiku in the central highlands. It was one of the hottest zones during the war. He'd lost his best buddy and many good friends in savage battles with the Viet Cong and North Vietnamese regulars in and around Ban Me Thout.

Li's eyes widened. 'Oh...sir, you know it as a tourist, or...were you in the war?' Marvin ignored her question. Something was eating him about her. What was it? She was tall for a Vietnamese. Her dark, glossy hair rested well below her shoulders shaping the flawless skin of a face which could easily, in another society, grace the front cover of any female fashion magazine. Despite the shapeless outfit of short sleeved light blue shirt and dark blue pantaloons, to Marvin she was one of the sexiest women he had ever laid eyes on.

She brushed away a wayward strand of dark hair with a delicate brown hand and continued to busy herself with tidying his room. For a reason he didn't understand, he had to know more about this girl.

'Tell me about your family Li, your parents, brothers and sisters,' Marvin insisted. She slipped a pillow into a fresh cover and walked around the other side of the bed so that she was now within a couple of feet of him, looking up at this tall foreigner with new interest.

He sounded American and was big. Big men frightened her. There was a cruel cast to his dark eyes which made her shiver but the fleshy features could not disguise the fact that he'd once been handsome.

He had never before uttered a word to her when she came each day to clean his room, just a nod and a grunt so these questions out of the blue surprised her. His manner was secretive and it appeared he'd dyed his hair dark brown since arriving, and allowed a moustache to appear above an incipient beard. He'd made a mess of the dyeing and there were streaks of dirty blonde among the brown. She preferred clean shaven men. But his white tee shirt was clean, if a little rumpled, and his kahki pants and brown boots looked almost new.

'I have no father and my two brothers are dead sir.'

'Killed in the war? What side?'

She replied, her face expressionless, as if she'd shed too many tears and it didn't matter anymore. 'Yes, killed...by VC...they ARVN.'

He nodded. South Vietnamese Army...so at least they were on our side.

'Your mother. What about her? Did she survive?'

'Yes, she survived,' replied Li grimly. 'But VC torture her, do very bad things, I don't know why she not die…I not know…' tears welled in her dark eyes. 'I work so she can have operation.'

'Operation…What for?'

She pointed to her groin. 'They do bad things, she has never had good medicine…she needs to come to Saigon for better treatment. She worked hard to care for me…she never get better, now I must care for her.'

Marvin nodded and paused before replying. There was a look in those hard eyes she couldn't understand, they seemed to have softened.

'Yes…VC did many bad things,' he said, but under his breath, 'but so did we. Your father, he was a foreigner?'

'Yes…he was American soldier…I don't know, I was a child, my mother only speak of him once, then never again.' Her head dropped and she stood looking at the floor.

Then something very strange happened. A feeling swept over him so foreign it confused and bewildered him. What was it? Compassion? Pity? At that moment he was overtaken by an overwhelming desire to hug this beautiful, simple, young Vietnamese girl. He lifted his hands and took half a step toward her but stopped and let them drop to his side.

'Yes, many of us did things we shouldn't have during that war,' he muttered. 'Do you know anything, anything about him at all, because I served there, I might know him or of him?'

She looked up at him with such pain in her eyes he almost looked away. 'She met him when she worked in American place. I think she called it a BX…PX, something like that.'

He knew the PX, everyone did. It was the canteen where servicemen could buy cigarettes, beer, ice cream and all kinds of American goods; a huge one stop convenience store away from home.

'What was his name, did she tell you Li?' There was desperation in his tone…'and to her surprise, she detected a nervous edge. She shook her head.

'She would not say his name…but she said…she loved him. She thinks he was killed. He left one day promising to come back…but he never did…They all died,' she said dully and turned away from him to face the wall, her head again bowed.

'What was her name?'

She turned, her head lowered. 'Her name was…Phuong.'

He closed his eyes and shook his head as if he didn't want to hear that name. There were a million Phuongs in Vietnam…it was a common name.

'She worked in the PX…I knew a Phuong,' he said almost to himself. 'There were many women, many memories, most unpleasant, every one of them he wanted to forget but meeting this girl now had brought them back and suddenly he hated her for it. He moved a step closer fists clenched as she took a postage stamp sized black and white photo from a tiny purse.

'This is my mother.'

It was a head and shoulders shot. Smiling back at him was a pretty girl no more than twenty. Long dark hair framed a pretty, heart shaped face. She was the image of Li. He took the photo and sat on the bed staring at it as if transfixed.

To her amazement, he suddenly led out a loud 'NO!' and began to rock back and forth his head bowed holding the photo to his chest. She stepped back, her whole body shaking with fear. He looked up and the agony on his face made her want to rush from the room.

She cowered holding her hands up to protect herself as he came to her, his eyes screwed up in anguish, tears rolling down his fleshy cheeks. She stiffened and closed her eyes. She wanted to scream but her voice caught in her throat, making it impossible to cry for help. She felt his arms upon her but there was none of the expected violence. He gently brought her head to his chest. She could feel the rise and fall of his chest as great sobs wracked his body.

As quickly as it had begun, it stopped. He handed the photo back to her, turned on his heel and left the room slamming the door behind him. Her legs gave way and she slumped to the bed open-mouthed, still trembling.

The following morning when she arrived for work, Ngan the front desk clerk handed her a thick brown A5 envelope. 'Mr LeGrand left this for you when he checked out this morning.'

Frowning, she took it to a small stock room at the back of the hotel. Frowning, she carefully slit open one side with a small penknife and stared in amazement at the contents. Inside was a thick wad of 100 dollar US bills and a one line handwritten note:

For your mother's operation.

With trembling hands she began to count. By the time she had finished, she was sobbing uncontrollably.

The envelope contained four thousand dollars.

* * *

Dung was pleased with himself. The boat trip with Kim Anh had gone well. Although a bit quiet at times, she seemed to enjoy herself chatting to him and some of the other guests who were colleagues from Waterworld, and despite a momentary flinch, had even allowed him to peck her on the cheek at the end of the night.

She had looked lovely, almost serene, in her pink and white *ao dai*, sitting on the deck in the moonlight as the brightly-lit river boat motored slowly along the turgid, slow moving Saigon River.

The occasion had been a birthday party organized for a friend of Dung, a Mr Lan, one of Saigon's social set and Dung had made a big deal of introducing Kim as his *friend*, with the inference she was more than that.

Mr Lan, a squat, flashily dressed individual in his forties, with gold around his fat neck and rings gleaming from stubby fingers, exuded an oily charm and bonhomie to all and sundry.

He was surrounded by a coterie of fashionably-dressed handsome young men and beautiful twenty-something women, hanging on his every word, but noticing Kim, he left them and weaved his way across the deck toward her. She shuddered when she saw this toad of a man in his white duck suit and white shoes approaching. His small black eyes roamed unashamedly over her body as he was introduced.

'She is charming,' he said to Dung, not taking his eyes off Kim. 'You must bring this lovely creature to my villa in Dalat, for a "nice" weekend,' he said with an exaggerated wink at Dung.

'Yes, we will be delighted to come won't we dear,' Dung replied, bursting with pride putting a proprietary arm around her waist. Kim said nothing and wished Dung would take her downstairs to the buffet on the lower deck and well away from this creature. He made her feel unclean. After more innocuous small talk, to her relief, Dung finally suggested they eat and Lan ambled back to his group of sycophants.

Over dinner he regaled her with stories about Mr Lan; how his family were from the North and how they had become very wealthy selling war surplus material left by the Americans.

'Lan says they left so much,' he laughed. 'Planes, helicopters, tanks, plenty of scrap iron. He did well out of our great victory.'

Kim listened impassively. Her family was dirt poor and there was no *great victory* for them. She had seen first hand the exploitation in the south by favoured Northern families like Lan's. It made her sick inside.

Dung continued to prattle on about what a clever and influential man his friend was and how one day he would be Secretary General of the Communist Party. Kim was singularly unimpressed and even less so when he hinted that some of Lan's other enterprises were not strictly legal.

'I don't like him,' she said.

This didn't faze her enthusiastic paramour. As far as he was concerned he was well on the way to winning Kim and to his secret delight…there had been no mention of the foreigner; yes, he was well satisfied with the way things were heading.

* * *

Chuck McGaw stopped writing, put down his pen and looked out from his third floor office of the American embassy perched on the shores of Manila bay. It was a peaceful scene. The sun shone from a cloudless sky upon a few small motorized vessels making their way across the smooth waters past anchored freighters and container vessels. Further out bancas glided toward the rich fishing grounds off Corregidor while inshore, a huge white luxury liner stood towering over the port area, disgorging excited tourists.

McGaw swiveled around in his chair and looked at Conway sitting opposite.

'Ok, I've got enough Steve,' he said in that deep, well modulated north eastern cadence. 'We can act now on your information... if he comes back into the Philippines.'

'He'll come back, I know it. He wants me...badly.'

They stared at each other for a few moments. The only sound was the whirr of the overhead fan. McGaw wiped his brow with a tissue from a box on his desk.

'Bloody air con's gone again, second time in a month, this heat's killing me. Next assignment I want is Alaska,' he smiled, leaning back trying to catch a non existent breeze from the open window.

'So what now Chuck...what's the procedure?'

'Well, I'll talk to my FBI guy here and see what he has to say then, we'll talk to the Philippine NBI. We'll post photos of him at every air and seaport but,' he said grimly, 'this guy's no amateur, he's probably changed his appearance and we know he didn't come into the Philippines as Marvin LeGrand so we've got a bit of detective work to do. We'll also keep an eye on you while you're here. When do you go back to Saigon?'

'Soon, maybe...' Conway replied absently. His disinterested tone surprised McGaw,

'You don't look with it buddy, is everything ok?'

'Huh, oh sure Chuck, just got a few things to sort out at the Down Under before I leave.'

'Not woman trouble is it Steve?' asked McGaw shrewdly.

Conway smiled crookedly. 'No, nothing like that,' he lied.

The American agent stood up and held out his hand.

'Ok buddy, thanks for the info on Marvin, we'll be in touch. If he hits this town again we'll grab him, but watch how you go.' They shook hands and Conway glanced at his watch. It was nearly time to meet Sally at the Traders Hotel.

* * *

Filipinos are notorious for being late and Conway found "Filipino time" to be a reality; but not with Sally. At exactly 7.30 pm she arrived weaving her way through the crowded bar. Conway's eyebrows lifted. She looked gorgeous. Gone was the pale, haggard look of a few weeks ago. Her eyes sparkled and she glowed with good health. Her long black hair fell freely to smooth, tanned shoulders which were shown to advantage by the décolleté of a simple white dress which revealed the upper slopes of firm, full breasts. She blushed as Conway gave a low whistle of appreciation.

'Dressed to kill eh?' he grinned.

'To kill you,' she smiled coquettishly, kissing him on both cheeks.

A smiling young barman stood waiting expectantly; Conway looked at Sally... 'drink?'

'Mango juice is fine darling, hard liquor makes me sin,' she laughed.

'I'm very disappointed in you Miss Sally,' Conway said with mock severity, 'I was hoping this was going to be one of *those* nights. But alas,' he sighed, 'I guess I'll just have to accept defeat and try to behave like a gentleman.'

'Mango juice for the lady and a San Miguel beer for me please.' The barman smiled and performed an elaborate bow, 'immediately sir.'

'Now my *maganda* Sally,' said Conway, using the Tagalog word for beautiful and anticipating her first question. 'I've spoken to agent McGaw at the U.S. embassy and we've got the might of U.S. law enforcement plus the NBI *and* the local police force on the case. They've stepped up their dragnet over the entire country. If Marvin shows so much as a toenail anywhere, they'll grab him and when they do, he'll be deported straight back to America, so you can rest easy darling.'

Sally still looked dubious. 'As I said before, I won't be happy until he's locked up...or dead, oh no, look who's just arrived.' Conway turned and there making her way toward them, chatting animatedly to a distinguished looking Filipino was...Lily Li.

At first she didn't notice them but her path through the crowd came within an arm's length. Conway was going to say something but decided to see if she would notice them. For some reason at that moment Lily stopped talking to her companion and glanced to her right and stopped, open-mouthed with surprise. She looked across at Sally and grimaced.

'Oh, hello Steve,' she said, her tone stiff and cool. 'I didn't realise you were back in town.'

In the past there would have been a gushing "hello darling" and extravagant gestures of hands and pretentious posing; but not this time. This was a different Lily. She had eschewed her usual flamboyant, sexy attire of low cut, thigh length dresses and gleaming jewellery, and instead looked almost puritanical in a sober, high collared black number which halted around mid calf.

'Same here,' smiled Conway, 'I thought you were still in Shanghai, how is it going there?' Lily flinched. Had he hit a nerve? She seemed about to answer his question but then ignored it and introduced her companion.

'Steve Conway, I would like you to meet my friend Alex Mendoza, who I am sure will become a senator at the next election,' her tone now almost the old gushing Lily. Mendoza bowed briefly and shook hands with Conway.

'Please to meet you Mr Conway, you are...I take by your accent... Australian,' said Mendoza, the voice, smooth and cultured. Conway figured he was probably around fifty. His tone, the styled, dark hair flecked with grey, the Armani suit, crisp white shirt, blue-striped tie and highly polished black shoes, bespoke the wealth and authority of a high born Filipino used to giving orders.

'Likewise, and yes, I am,' replied Conway evenly. 'Good luck with your campaign Mr Mendoza, hope you make it.' They continued small talk for several minutes. Mendoza asked Conway his situation and when told he was the manager of the Down Under Hotel back from Saigon to oversee reconstruction of his hotel, Mendoza produced his business card.

'If you need any assistance at any time, please do not hesitate to call me,' he smiled. 'But now I am sorry, we must leave you, my charming companion and I have something to discuss. Nice to meet you Mr Conway,' he said, nodding to Sally. Conway thanked him and returned the compliment with his own card.

Lily's poker face finally broke into something resembling a smile. She came very close and lightly pecked Conway's cheek. In a whisper which could not be heard by the others because of the music from a mariachi band in the background, she said, 'I'll call and tell you about Shanghai.' Then she slipped away through the crowd on Mendoza's arm. Conway turned to see Sally glaring at him.

'She is a bitch, so rude, I hate her,' she fumed. 'She treats me like I am a peasant, I want to kill her! Why didn't you introduce me? Do you think I am a peasant too?'

'Hey, steady on, kill me first. Yes, she was rude, but I know the feeling that exists between you two and I didn't want to prolong the conversation. I was waiting for the chance to introduce you but frankly, I was relieved when they left.' He reached over and put his hand on hers.

'Forgive me?'

'Of course I do, and anyway darling, you are with me…and not her. I could tell she was jealous,' she said triumphantly.

Later that night in bed, Sally did her best to revel in her triumph but Conway did not seem to share her enthusiasm. His lovemaking was passionate and tender as she remembered but her women's intuition told her something was wrong. She first noticed it at the restaurant. At times he seemed distracted and sometimes unaware of her conversation. There was a faraway look in his eyes. He was not the Steve Conway of old.

'Are you ok darling, there is something bothering you isn't there?' she asked. He'd been lying on his back saying nothing, staring at the ceiling. 'Huh…no, not really, well, there are a few problems at the hotel but nothing to worry about, sorry, I'm not much company tonight am I?'

He reached over for her. She knew he was lying. It was probably a woman on his mind and something told her it was not Lily. But Sally was a pragmatic lady and knew better than to spoil a mood, one she had wanted for so long. They made love again and this time sensing her disappointment, he did his best to satisfy her. He stole away quietly before dawn, leaving a note, promising to see her again before she returned north.

* * *

At exactly the same time, a large shadowy figure clambered from a dinghy on to the wharf along the Zamboanga waterfront.

18

'Hellooo sir, good evening, welcome back!' cooed Binky flashing her toothpaste smile as she greeted Conway at the door of Lily's mansion. 'I know ma'am is looking forward to seeing you,' she added, with her trademark impish grin.

Conway liked Binky. She was a devoted servant, the epitome of discretion and had been witness to a number of romantic hi-jinks between her boss and Conway over the years. She took him to the small ante room where he had waited the first time he had come to visit, several years ago.

'Please take a seat sir...ma'am will be here in a minute.'

Conway sat on one of the high-backed Brentwood chairs and reflected on that first time. Shortly after his arrival then, Lily had excused herself and re-appeared in a brief silk outfit which left nothing to the imagination. It was designed to seduce, and it worked!

He was still smiling to himself about that wild night when she entered the room quietly, wearing a wide smile and looking very different from the cool, detached woman in Traders Hotel...it was the temptress Lily of old.

Gone was the prudish outfit at the Traders Hotel replaced by a simple, low-cut, black, thigh-length cocktail dress, from which her over-full breasts were prevented from spilling by two gossamer-thin straps. The dress may have looked simple but Conway had no doubt it had probably come from some Paris or New York fashion house. Her lips were a bright red slash against the flawless skin of the high cheek-boned face, her feet shod in stylish, black strapped heels. Lily Li was again dressed for seduction.

She greeted him with her familiar "hello darling". He bent forward as she kissed him on both cheeks and gestured to follow her out a side door to the swimming pool. Again memories returned of their first night when they had frolicked naked in that same pool. No sooner had they sat at a small, white circular table on a deck just above the pool when Binky appeared with a magnum of champagne and two chilled flutes.

Oh, oh, thought Conway, here we go again. Binky poured the champagne with a flourish and disappeared silently into the interior of the house, not before, flashing a knowing grin at Conway over Lily's shoulder.

Lily lifted her glass, 'It is lovely to see you in my house again after all this time Mr Conway…ah…how do you say in Australia. Cheers, or bottoms up?'

'Cheers will do Lily, and what's this Mr Conway stuff? Have you forgotten who I am?' he said taking a sip of his champagne. It was French, and icy cold.

'Just teasing you darling,' she smiled at him over the rim of her glass. 'I wanted to get your reaction. How are you my lover and what are you doing here in Manila? I thought you were still in Saigon and…what about that woman I saw you with at Traders last week I didn't realise *she* was still in your life. There was a ring on her finger?' The reproof was obvious. It seemed the rivalry between Lily and Sally was still very much alive.

He took another sip, 'mmmm, there's no doubt about the French, they know how to make wine,' he said, parrying her question. 'Oh Sally? She's here on a visit from the States, we were just catching up on old times,' he said airily. 'I thought *you* were still in Shanghai? So…what did you want to see me about Lily?'

'Shanghai is over,' she said quickly. 'Sorry Steve.' She gazed into her drink. 'It's what I wanted to tell you about but…' her voice began to break and when she looked back up at him the happy façade had crumbled, replaced by one of dejection bordering on despair.

Conway frowned. What the hell was happening? Her mood had changed in an instant. Then to his amazement, she burst into tears. He jumped up and rushed around to her as she rose from her chair and fell sobbing into his arms.

Conway had always regarded Lily as a strong, self confident woman and in business, a tough uncompromising operator; he'd never seen her like this. After many minutes she calmed down and wiped her face with a handkerchief he handed her. She looked a mess. Her eye shadow had left streaks on her cheeks and her red lips were now smeared. The cool sophisticate had disappeared to be replaced by a distraught, vulnerable woman. Flustered, she excused herself and rushed away to repair her face.

When she returned, the cosmetics had done their job. Apart from the red rims around and slight puffiness below her eyes, she looked as before and had regained her composure except for the embarrassment lingering in those large brown eyes. Something pretty traumatic had happened in Shanghai.

Binky appeared again, this time more serious. She had helped her boss with the repair work. She replaced Lily's flute with a clean one, refilled it and glided away.

'Ok Lily...what happened in Shanghai?' Conway asked gently.

A grimace was followed by a long, unladylike swallow before she answered. Her eyes again glistened with tears at the memory, but therein was also a defiant glint. She placed the glass down in front of her and dabbed her lips.

'I'm sorry I had to leave Manila in such a hurry Steve, but I received a phone call from Shanghai to say things were not right with my restaurant and I should return immediately and...'

Conway refilled his glass and waited patiently for her to continue. She sighed looking at her glass again, and took a deep breath.

'I won't bore you with all the details but basically when I arrived back in Shanghai I found that my local partner had sequestered my share of the business, the bastard!' Like her tears, it was the first time he'd ever heard the elegant Lily Li swear.

In halting language, she described finding the restaurant locked and barred and of the meeting with her Chinese partner and how he'd arranged for the legal transfer of her share of the business into his company's name.

'Hang on Lily? He couldn't do that without your written consent… could he?'

She smiled grimly. 'You are not a naïve man Steve I'm surprised you asked that question. You know here in Asia money talks; anything can be done for the right price. Wang Ho is a powerful, well-connected man. He has friends in The Party, and the Judiciary. It was not hard for him to arrange things. What surprised me was that he already owns several hotels, even a shipping line. My restaurant was small fry compared to his other enterprises. I think in the "New China" he would be a billionaire.'

'Why do you think he screwed you?'

She heaved a deep sigh and toyed with her glass. 'Who knows?' she said bitterly.

'Probably greed, ego; it was a prime location in China's most exciting city. Some men can never have enough and there are many like him, too many…'

'Do you have any recourse in this matter? I suspect not,' Conway asked, answering his own question.

She shook her head. 'It would be a waste of my time even trying. I am afraid I will have to put it down to bitter experience. You know Steve,' she smiled ruefully. 'I never thought I would get caught like this, but…I was operating out of my environment which can often be fatal in this part of the world.'

Then surprisingly, her tone became philosophical. 'I have just been taught a lesson. A hard one for sure, but,' she brightened, 'all is not lost. I still have my restaurant here and here is where I will stay in future. And,' she added a smile, 'I still hope one day I will convince you to join me in some kind of business here. I have not given up on you Steve Conway.'

He smiled and raised his glass. 'There is a word to describe you in English, Lily dear, and it is…indefatigable…I toast you Lily Li, here's to your future success…here in Manila.' They had demolished the first magnum and Binky had brought out a second. It was now nearly empty and both were beginning to glow.

He looked across at her. She wasn't drunk, just pleasantly tipsy, certainly nowhere near the state she was in when they last had dinner together and…and there was that old familiar sinful gleam in her eye. Her breasts were heaving slightly. She often eschewed a bra when she invited Conway to her home and the movement caused her dress to slip a little, revealing a glimpse of the aureoles of her large pink nipples. The gossamer threads seemed to have given up the unequal contest.

'Tell me about Saigon darling, I know you went there on business… maybe funny business?' She laughed out loud. There was just a hint of a slur in her voice. Another glass and she would be well on the way again.

He shrugged, 'not a lot to tell. We are looking at a site to establish a Down Under operation there and it's still a work in progress. As yet we still haven't found anything suitable but I had to return because of a fire here in the Down Under. Fortunately, it wasn't a major blaze and the damage has almost been repaired. I hope to get back to Saigon soon.'

She brought the glass to her lips and looked at him shrewdly over the rim. 'You are a good looking man Mr Conway…and Vietnamese women are very beautiful…I am sure there have been temptations.'

Conway smiled. 'Too busy for pleasures of the flesh Lily and I have to tell you that while Vietnamese ladies are lovely, some stunningly beautiful, and certainly friendly, they are still quite conservative. You just cannot walk up to a Vietnamese girl and expect her to immediately be charmed. Respect, good manners and a smile breaks down the barriers though.'

Lily laughed. 'Ah, despite what you say Mr Conway to me you sound like the voice of experience. But you are right; those attributes work here too.'

He glanced at his watch. 'It's getting late Lily, I have to go. I'm sorry to hear about Shanghai but I know you darling, you'll bounce back.'

She got up, came around and stood behind his chair and put her arms around him.

'Please don't go darling, please, I've missed you and it's been such a long time, remember Boracay?' How could he forget their magical but brief, love tryst on that beautiful Philippine island?

She nibbled his ear and her heady perfume blended with the jasmine and hibiscus of the poolside gardens. It was a powerful and enticing proposition but why was this tiny voice in the far reaches of his mind saying…*Kim Anh*.

But another voice louder said *what the hell*. He pulled her down into his lap and kissed her...hard, as if he was trying to get even with her for something...or perhaps someone. She responded as savagely and it was many minutes before they broke the embrace. She pulled him to his feet. 'Come darling, please come,' she said. He shut off his mind and followed her willingly from the pool up the winding staircase to her bedroom.

* * *

Midnight in Zamboanga, a city on the south west tip of Mindanao in the southern Philippines; a city driven by ethnic and political hatreds for decades; a festering sore on the backside of the nation.

A combination of violence beginning with the Huk guerrillas after World War II led to the uprising by the Islamic Liberation Front who wanted recession from the Manila government. Then the communist New Peoples Army whose aim was to take over the entire country, had created a "Wild West" scenario in this beautiful part of the Philippines.

Marvin had arrived in the dead of night on a fishing smack out of Sabah. He'd flown to Kuala Lumpur then to Kota Kinabalu then endured an uncomfortable journey in an ancient bus up to Kudat on the tip of Sabah. From there money had changed hands in a dingy waterfront bar with Ali, the skipper of a ketch-rigged caique who agreed to take him, no questions asked, to Zamboanga.

'I can get you ashore, no problem with immigration and customs my friend, they will not see you,' he assured Marvin, his dark, weather-worn face creasing in a sly grin.

'Ok,' said Marvin. He didn't like the look of this guy, he had thief written all over him. But Marvin was becoming desperate. He'd spent two days trying to find a boat to take him to the Philippines with no luck until now.

Everyone else had cried off when they heard the details of the deal, so his options were now limited to trusting this guy. It was a long shot and if something goes wrong...I'll have to cross that bridge when I come to it.

'Now remember pal, I want you to take me back to Sabah when I have finished my business in the Philippines. How do I contact you to let you know when I'm back in Zamboanga?'

'No problem my friend, I give you the name and phone number of my cousin in Zamboanga,' smiled the seaman, showing a mouthful of broken, black and yellow teeth. 'You just let him know a couple of days before and he will contact me…don't worry, Ali will take care of you.'

Apart from a brief, terrifying tropical storm as they rounded the top of Sabah into the Balabac Strait between the Philippine island of Palawan and Sabah, the rest of the journey through the Sulu Sea was smooth.

Marvin kept to himself and made no effort to interact with the Muslim crew. They went about their business as if the bearded white man in the black baseball cap and dark glasses didn't exist, which suited him fine. He didn't trust them and noticed the occasional scowl from one of them, Haseem, a lean, angular young guy, early twenties, with a goatee and fierce eyes; not a man to be trusted.

One wrong move from you and you're overboard, thought Marvin. A light sleeper and alert from his days in the Marines, he kept aft with one hand on a slim, six inch blade he'd picked up in Kota. It was a relief when one night suddenly in the inky blackness he saw chips of lights far away on shore.

'Zamboanga,' smiled Ali rolling down toward Marvin perched in his usual spot.

'We there soon, but we not go in, we stop out a mile and take you in by small boat,' he said, pointing to a painter lashed to the deck. 'Sometimes customs come looking,' he went on anticipating Marvin's objection.

'Ok,' grunted Marvin, less than impressed with the arrangement. They could rob him and dump him at sea and be away before anyone knew they had even arrived. But then they could have done so during the voyage, he'd have to take his chances. One thing was certain; he'd take a few with him if they tried anything.

In the end, Ali kept his word and just before midnight a mile offshore, they lowered the small dinghy and with Haseem rowing and another crew member keeping watch they took Marvin in to the far end of a dock where roughly hewn, stone steps led up to the wharf.

Haseem and the other remained silent offering no assistance as Marvin rose unsteadily to his feet preparing to step off. The small boat rocked under his weight and the wash of the tidal surge. He was about to make his first attempt onto the slippery steps when Hasseem shoved an oar against the landing pushing them back out of reach. Marvin cursed and twisted around half bent, trying to keep his balance as the little boat continued to rock in the chop.

'What the fuck?' he whispered savagely to Haseem who sat looking up, his swarthy face wreathed in a cocky sneer. 'I want money white man, you give me money and you go ashore otherwise…' Marvin looked past Haseem to the other guy who sat expressionless. It was hard to tell if he was in on the shakedown or not.

Marvin sat down, now within a couple of feet of Haseem.

'Ok, you win, you want money, here take this,' he said, reaching into the back pocket of his pants. Haseem's grin got wider then changed instantly to one of terror as Marvin whipped out the blade and flicked it open at the seaman's throat.

'Take me back to those fucking steps motherfucker or this will go right through your skinny neck…now!'

Haseem yelped as he felt the prick of the blade and hurriedly manoeuvred the painter into the landing. Marvin stepped carefully onto the bottom step and turned to Haseem who sat looking up at him with unbridled hate in his eyes.

'Don't be on that boat when I come back motherfucker or I will kill you,' he hissed, holding out his arm the knife pointed straight at Haseem.

'That's a promise.'

Then he turned and slowly began to climb up to the wharf. By the time he had gone half a dozen steps the painter had disappeared into the pitch-black night.

At the top he stood not moving, carefully checking his surroundings. This end of the dock was in darkness. All he could see in the distance was the faint outline of what were probably bond stores and several merchant ships at anchor. Nothing stirred. Slowly and silently he crept, keeping to the shadows, stopping every ten feet to listen for any noise or activity from the warehouses or any of the vessels.

He was making good progress until he came to an ancient lamp above the door of a cargo warehouse casting a weak glow and bouncing shadows off a rusty Panamanian freighter. From the deck, came sounds of loud, drunken voices.

Marvin stiffened. There were three of them. They stood at the top of the gangplank their bellowing and laughter cutting through the still, humid night air. Marvin was within ten yards of the gangplank. He had no cover. If these guys left the ship now he would be discovered and awkward questions might be asked. He stood and flattened himself against a wall inching slowly away, step by step trying to put as much distance between him and the gangplank.

Their language was foreign, European but he couldn't pick the accent. It sounded German but was probably East European. They began to stagger down to the wharf. He felt something against his hip and left foot. It was an oil drum, one of several he hadn't been able to see in the darkness.

He eased himself behind it and crouched as the seamen passed, their drunken state making them oblivious to much around them. Then a thought came. This area was probably enclosed. There would be a gate somewhere and security where these guys had to pass and perhaps produce identification.

He cursed, what a damn fool he was to trust that little shit Ali! He could have brought me ashore on a beach, the stupid mother, anywhere but here! But now there was no choice. He stood up slowly and began to follow the trio his rubber soled boots making no sound on the concrete underfoot. These guys were seamen so they were probably looking for some action, even at this late hour.

He followed them for about 100 yards until he saw a small, brightly lit pillbox in which he could make out the uniformed figure of a watchman. He had an idea. He caught up with the seamen and called out.

'Hey guys!'

They stopped and looked around bleary eyed and blinking at the voice that had come from nowhere.

'Hey guys, where are you off to?'

He trotted up to them all smiles, his hands outstretched.

'Hey, I've just arrived, first time in Zamboanga, you guys look like you know where the action is, can you show a fellow sailor the way?'

Sober they may have had some suspicions about this big white man with an American accent, who had materialized out of the night, but in their boozy state, he just looked like another mariner eager to find a good time.

'Where you from friend?' asked the biggest of them. A hulking, individual sporting a bushy black beard, Zapata moustache and sideburns, wearing worn jeans and a dirty white tee shirt straining to accommodate his huge beer gut.

'Canada,' lied Marvin... 'you?'

The big guy sized Marvin up for a moment his eyes narrowing but not threatening. His trouble was focusing; a common problem following an afternoon on beer and brandy chasers. Marvin's answer seemed to be taking a few seconds to penetrate his brain.

'Ah...Canuk...good. I am Polska, my name is Viktor,' he said stretching out his hand. Marvin took it and was introduced to the other two; a solidly built, sandy-haired, middle-aged guy named Oleg, of sour mien with a face worn by the elements of many sea voyages and a skinny youth in a crumpled red tee shirt and baggy black shorts named Vlad who was leaning against Oleg for support.

'We go for drink,' grunted Viktor, 'you come too Canuk, ok?'

Marvin positioned himself in the middle of the happy trio as they approached the gate but he needn't have worried. The guard barely glanced at them as they passed by out onto an ill-lit secondary road devoid of traffic except for the occasional tricycle.

The Poles had been to Zamboanga before and made their way along confidently for several hundred yards before turning left into a busier thoroughfare which promised the kind of action they'd been looking for. A large flashing neon sign fifty yards ahead above the sidewalk declared *La Bamba Nite Club* and underneath in smaller letters, *Girls Girls Girls.*

'Ha Hah!' shouted Viktor turning to his companions, 'here we are my friends, let us drink, drink, drink and be merry!' Marvin stopped and excused himself. 'Get a beer for me I'll be with you in a few minutes,' he said, leaving them and crossing the street to an all-night drugstore.

He walked up and down the aisles until he found what he was looking for then picked up a couple of packets of chewing gum at the checkout and was about to leave when he turned to the sleepy young lad who had served him.

'Are there any short-time hotels or guest houses around here?' he asked gruffly.

'Two blocks down on your left you will find, *Mirandas*, that's where they go,' he said emphasizing the "they" obviously meaning the customers and their "girlfriends" from *La Bamba's*.

'What about the airport, where is it from here?'

The kid yawned and motioned to the door and then right. 'It's not far but it's closed till morning. A trike will take you from *Mirandas*, give him 30 pesos and he'll be happy.' Marvin grunted a "thanks" and threw him a 20 peso note.

Mirandas, a low set stucco brick hovel hadn't seen a coat of paint since the Spanish arrived. The desk clerk took 100 pesos and handed Marvin a key without hardly a word or a glance. He learned a long time ago never to show any interest in his "guests".

The room was a dingy sweat box lit by a weak overhead bulb. On the end of a lumpy double bed lay a threadbare white towel and a miniscule block of soap. In one corner a rickety sliding door led to a tiny bathroom. A black and white porn movie on the ancient television began almost as soon as he entered. Marvin switched it off and went into the bathroom. He opened the plastic bag from the drug store and withdrew a small cardboard packet of black hair dye. He needed to fix the previous botched dye job.

He cut the top off the tiny plastic container of dye and massaged it thoroughly through his now long hair and beard and waited for a few minutes for it to take effect before stepping into the shower. Marvin cursed as the weak dribble from the shower rose took ages to wash away the black residue. He toweled his hair dry and checked his image in the tiny mirror. He couldn't do anything about his build but the black bearded, wild looking face that looked back at him was a far cry from the clean shaven, buzzed cut blonde who'd arrived in Manila weeks before.

He stretched out on the sagging bed and made plans for the morning. First he would contact Ali's cousin then catch a flight back to Manila's domestic airport. He was confident no one would be looking for him coming in from Mindanao. He'd find a bolt hole somewhere, carry out his plan then slip back down to Zamboanga and escape to Sabah where he would hole up in some remote village for a while. The old bed creaked and threatened to collapse as he stretched out with his hands clasped behind his head and a crooked, confident smile on his lips.

Manila here I come and Mr Conway, you are history, were his last thoughts as sleep descended.

* * *

Dung dismounted from his motor bike and ran up the short flight of steps to the front door of Kim Anh's small apartment. Ngoc gave him a wide smile of welcome. She was not a demonstrative woman but she was over the moon at the way things were panning out between Kim and Dung. She was almost tempted to give him a hug, but not quite.

Kim came from her room dressed for their evening out and offered a small smile in his direction. He beamed and handed her a small posy of flowers.

'You are very kind Mr Dung,' she smiled, 'they are beautiful.'

'Wait,' said Ngoc. She left the room returning with a slim, white china vase. She took the flowers from her young sister and gently placed them in the vase, the smile on her face wider than ever.

Dung never noticed. His gaze was fixed on Kim Anh. He was delirious with joy. He still found it hard to believe that he had finally won her. She had been cool at first but as they began to spend more time together outside of work, she began to loosen up and he could feel her warming to him.

Tonight they were going to a concert at the Opera house and afterwards he had something very important to say to her. The thought of it made him excited but nervous, for tonight he was to reveal his true feelings and intentions toward her.

Kim had resigned herself to the situation. Dung was not such a bad fellow. He was clumsy at times, awkward in speech and a little immature but his love was obviously genuine. He had been promoted in his job at Waterworld and the word was that he would one day become a director. His credentials were first class and coming from a wealthy family, life with him would be comfortable, but a little voice in her head kept saying, *Steve Conway*.

She enjoyed the concert. A number of well-known singers, dancers and instrumentalists had come down from Hanoi to perform a mixture of traditional Vietnamese folk and classical music and dance. She had accepted his invitation with some misgivings, (she had never been to the Opera House before and to be among the Saigon social set made her apprehensive) but the night had turned out well, with one exception. They had run into Lan and his entourage.

'Hello Mr Dung and your charming companion, nice to see you both again,' he had said, giving his usual oily smile, at the same time undressing her with his eyes. Fortunately his seat was in the dress circle well away from theirs and afterwards she had encouraged Dung to leave quickly citing a headache.

They now sat under the stars beside the river in Thanh Da, not far from where she had taken Conway on that first night. They sipped soft drinks and made small talk until he finished his drink and placed it on the ground beside his seat. He slipped his arm around her and drew her closer. She allowed him to kiss her but stiffened and pushed his hand away when he tried to fondle her breasts.

'*Em* oi, you know how I feel about you, I want to marry you. I know maybe you do not love me now, but I am sure you will find that I am a good man who will look after you and be a good husband.' He sat breathing heavily, waiting with baited breath for her reply.

She put her hand on his and said softly, 'yes, you are a good man, and I thank you for your words, I will have to think about it, please give me some time, ok?'

'Oh, of course, I will, I will,' he said happily, reaching for her again and this time she did not resist as his hands roamed over her body.

***

Marvin woke early and had breakfast of pork adobo and coffee in a Filipino café next to the hotel. More enquiries led him to a shop selling discount clothing not far from his hotel and twenty minutes later he emerged wearing a clean shirt, underclothes, socks and cargo pants. He phoned Ali's cousin and made arrangements to meet him on his return to Zamboanga which he said should be within two weeks, at the most. He bought a small overnight bag from a general store and took a tricycle to the airport just in time to catch the first morning Philippine Airlines flight to Manila.

19

'So what do you think boss, almost good as new?' asked Jumbo Keyes, pointing to the newly renovated kitchen of the Down Under Hotel.

'They've done a great job to get it back in shape in such a short time,' agreed Conway.

'Once they finish painting those last two guest rooms we'll be fully operational again, better put a few beers on for them, they've earned it.'

'Gotcha Boss, it won't take long now, so long as these damn electricity blackouts stop for a while. We would have finished earlier except for them. They seem to have become more frequent in recent times. Will you join us, the boys would appreciate that?'

'Yes, blackouts, brownouts whatever they want to call them really are a pain in the butt. Who knows, maybe one day there'll be a change of government and someone will build a few power stations that work. As for tonight, sure, I'll be happy to join you guys but first I'm seeing Sally again.' He looked at his watch. 'In about an hour or so, she's back off to Isabella in the morning and from what she tells me, it's the last we'll see of her in Manila for quite a while.'

Keyes nodded sagely. 'A good move I think boss, especially while Marvin's still on the loose, any news on him?'

Conway shook his head. 'No, but no news is good news I guess. Ok, I'll leave you to it mate, got another mountain of paperwork to plough through I will...' just then the lights went out...another brownout. Thirty seconds later the hotel's ancient generators kicked in and the lights returned. Despite himself, Conway had to grin at his assistant manager.

'Never a dull moment in this place is there?'

Back in his office he sat stretching his arms and yawning giving the pile of work in front of him the evil eye. He was about to start checking suppliers' invoices when his phone nearly jumped from its cradle. Chuck McGaw, and he was excited!

'We've had a sighting of our friend Marvin.' Conway sat bolt upright and leaned into the phone. 'Where? When? So who saw him? What happened? Do you have any idea where he is now?'

'It was two days ago in the domestic airport on a flight from the south. A young airport cop noticed a disturbance just inside the door of the arrival hall. A big white guy was arguing with a security guard who had asked him for his baggage claim. He didn't have one because he only had one small item which he didn't need to check in. There was some misunderstanding; maybe the guard didn't like his attitude. Anyway, this guy got angry and pushed the guard, which started a ruckus.

The young cop intervened and sorted it out and the guy left but afterward the cop started to think about the incident. There was something about the big white guy that rang a bell. He had a full black beard, was wearing dark glasses and a baseball cap so it was hard to define his features but something nagged him about this fella. Back in the station he went through wanted photos but there was no one of that description.'

'So, what happened then, how does Marvin come into this?'

McGaw chuckled down the line. 'This kid will make commissioner one day. He persisted and got an identikit done of the guy, still no luck; then he went back through the photos and on a hunch fitted it to Marvin's pic and bingo! Jackpot! It fitted perfectly! Because it was a foreigner, he reported it immediately to the NBI.'

'Ok, so we know he's in town but did the cop see which way he went after leaving the airport?'

'Unfortunately not, but we know you are the target man. I'm putting men on you Steve. I'm a bit short of bodies so I'll have to speak to the NBI and borrow from them. This might take an hour or two so please lay low and don't do anything stupid OK? This guy is bloody dangerous but he will surface and when he does, we'll grab him. I'm sorry I didn't contact you before but I've been out of town and just got back an hour ago and there was a message to call the NBI about this.'

'Jesus Chuck, he's been here for two bloody days! I'm supposed to meet Sally tonight. I'll phone her straight away and tell her to get the hell out of here.'

'Do that and sit tight till you hear from me.'

'I'm not going to hide from that mongrel, if he wants me he knows where I am.'

'Steve, you heard me, don't be stupid. Do as I tell you, we want this guy as much as you do.'

'Yeah, ok,' Conway said, ending the call. Now, what to do? He didn't want to frighten Sally but he had to get her out of town immediately. He picked up the phone and dialed her number in Antipolo.

He felt sick in the stomach. Where the fuck was Marvin? He could be across the street from the hotel watching. He had arranged to meet Sally at the hotel. He had to stop her! It took nearly three minutes for her to answer, three of the longest minutes in his life. He was about to hang up when he heard her soft 'hello'.

'Sally,' he said struggling to keep his voice calm. 'You know where my apartment is right? Meet me there tonight, it will take you about 45 minutes from Antipolo, I'll meet you in the lobby ok?'

'Ok darling, I will see you soon,' her tone puzzled but happy. He put the phone back in the cradle. 'Poor little bugger probably thinks she's in for a candle light dinner.' He turned off the lights and stood beside the curtain of his window looking out into UN Avenue. His field of vision was limited. If Marvin was out there he could have a vantage point well away from Conway's line of sight.

His apartment was only a few minutes away. There was time to kill before meeting Sally. I need a drink. In the bar Keyes was chatting to a couple of guests. Conway took a local newspaper from a stand inside the door, ordered a beer and went to a banquette at the far end.

He couldn't concentrate. The newspaper was full of the usual "crackdowns" on scams, shootings and general chicanery. He swallowed the beer and called out to Keyes, 'off home,' leaving the same message with Annie as he passed by her switchboard.

She was busy on a call but as Conway disappeared through the front door she jumped up and called out, 'Sir Steve…I have something I must tell you…Sir! Sir!…' but he was gone.

As expected, Sally had not arrived at the apartment. He waited in the lobby pacing up and down, his fear growing as each minute passed. Shit! Why didn't he just tell her to get out of town immediately? But that would have panicked her. He owed it to her to ensure she left Manila safely and out of Marvin's reach. He would take her to the bus station and accompany her all the way to Isabella if necessary.

Then he noticed the guard at the front door was missing. Where the hell was he? These guys could be so unreliable. Maybe he was having his evening meal, but the rule was there had to be at least one on duty 24 hours. Then he recalled something about one of the other guards, Rudy, having been called urgently to a family problem in the province leaving them short-handed. Anyway, he told himself, that was the least of his worries.

Where was Sally? She should be here by now. The minutes slipped by. It was now well over an hour since they'd spoken. All kinds of possibilities for her delay whirled around in his head, Manila's notoriously heavy traffic being the main one. He didn't even want to think about the one which had his stomach in a knot; she'd somehow been snatched by Marvin.

'Hello darling,' came a familiar voice from behind him. 'Sorry I'm late the traffic tonight was just terrible!' He breathed a huge sigh of relief. She had come in by a side door looking beautiful, tanned and radiant in an off-the shoulder, tropical print dress.

She ran into his arms and gave him a huge hug then stood back smiling. Her happiness would normally have been infectious but when she saw his expression, the smile vanished to be replaced by one of concern.

'Darling, what's wrong? Why so serious?' she asked, taking his hand.

'I'll tell you in the apartment.' He went across to the elevator and stabbed the "up" button.

At the door of his fifth floor apartment he fumbled for a few seconds trying to find his keys. She stood behind him now frowning. He hadn't said a word on the way up. She suddenly had this cold feeling in her stomach. Conway was worried about something...she knew instinctively it was about Marvin.

She followed him in as he opened the door and switched on the light, then nearly collapsed in fright. Sitting in an armchair in the middle of the room facing them was a large, black-bearded guy in dark glasses and black baseball cap holding a revolver pointed straight at Conway's chest.

* * *

'What is on your mind *em oi* you seem so far away?' asked Ngoc reaching across the dinner table and putting her hand on Kim Anh's arm.

Kim blinked and shook her head. 'Oh, I'm sorry, I was just thinking of a problem at work, nothing really important,' she replied quietly, enough for Ngoc to disbelieve her.

'I think it is more than a work problem Kim Anh, you know you can tell me. Are you concerned about your relationship with Mr Dung? He is such a nice man,' she gushed, 'you and he will make a good marriage.'

'Oh for goodness sake *chi oi* I am not concerned about Mr Dung!' she snapped, getting to her feet and pushing her half-eaten dinner plate away.

'Excuse me but I am going for a walk.'

'Em please talk to me...you know you can tell me what is bothering you,' Ngoc pleaded, then, her tone changed. 'I hope you are not still thinking of that foreigner,' she said stonily, but Kim Anh was already half way down the stairs.

It was a cool night and Thanh Da was bathed in bright moonlight as she turned into the street toward the river. The same street she and Conway had once walked, not that long ago. She paused at the same market and got smiles of recognition from some of the vendors.

She returned their smiles but an overwhelming sense of sadness suddenly engulfed her. She walked on quickly lest they see the tears in her eyes. She passed the same families watching their children playing happily but couldn't bear to look. By now the tears were streaming down her cheeks.

The riverside on this night thankfully was quiet, without the usual couples around sitting astride motor scooters petting. She stood for a few moments in the cool breeze from the river, then went across and sat in the same small cane chair she occupied that night with Conway.

From the pocket of her jeans she took a handkerchief. She looked at it and smiled sadly. It was the one he had given her that night in Binh Quoi. She wiped away her tears and sat gazing out at the river remembering.

Oh, the beautiful nights they had shared and none more memorable than the first one here by the riverside in Thanh Da. It had been such a sweet interlude even though at that time they had only just met and were still just friends. What a lovely night it had been.

Just the two of them alone, sitting there, talking quietly; she telling of her life, and he listening politely and patiently, not interrupting as she poured out her heart. She recalled the look in his eyes; sympathetic, understanding.

Where is he now? Will he ever come back? Steve where are you? She looked up into the night sky, black and starless; a metaphor for her mood.

'Please God, tell me what to do,' she whispered.

She thought about her relationship with Dung and was unable to shake a feeling of guilt. It had blossomed, somewhat reluctantly from her point of view. He insisted on talking marriage and their future, encouraged enthusiastically by Ngoc, who never let an opportunity pass without telling her what a good "catch" he was.

She had to admit, it had taken time, but she had grown fond of him. He was clearly besotted with her, very attentive and caring, polite to a fault. Sometimes this irritated her but secretly, she enjoyed the attention.

And there was no doubt he had prospects both in his employment and socially. It was true that his family was well connected within the Saigon social scene. His father held an important position in the Party and was a man of great influence in Saigon, his mother often featured in the social pages of the newspaper for her charity work. Life with Dung would be more comfortable than that of the average married Saigonese girl.

But Kim Anh was a simple provincial woman; unused to trappings of wealth and position. She was ill at ease in such company; the pretention and confident self assurance made her uncomfortable and uncertain in their presence. In fact she found it all rather shallow. She never felt that way with Steve Conway. His easy going nature and broad smile had put her at ease the moment they met.

She sat for a long time her mind jumping from one conclusion to the next. If she accepted Dung, her family would be happy and her life it seemed, secure and stable; a union with Conway? It was hard to tell.

She had once asked him if he would consider marrying a Vietnamese and in reply he had told her that if he did so, he would not take her away from her family and environment. His words echoed in her head.

'I would stay with her in Vietnam because I see too many cross-cultural marriages fail when the Asian girl is taken into a Western society. I would live here and take her to Australia or the Philippines for a holiday.' She remembered also the words she had said to him on the night they had sat beside this river. 'I will only ever marry for love.'

By the time she returned, the streets were quiet. The vendors had closed up, the families and children had gone and the apartment was in darkness. She tossed and turned in her small bed and by the time sleep came, the first yellow and pink streaks of a breaking dawn appeared across the horizon.

* * *

'Ah, the happy couple, good evening, how nice to see you both again,' sneered Marvin holding the .38 Smith and Wesson rock steady. Sally's legs buckled and she lurched against Conway grabbing him to stop from falling to the floor.

'Oh my God...Marvin!' she cried in disbelief.

Conway stared down the black barrel of the revolver. His mouth suddenly dry, his heart almost jumping out of his chest! He swallowed and took a deep breath trying to calm his nerves, his eyes fixed on Marvin's trigger finger. Beside him he could feel Sally trembling violently.

'How did you find my address and how the hell did you get in here?' Conway asked, his voice coming out in a strangled gasp. Marvin's smile sent a chill up his spine.

'You have a very accommodating lady on the switchboard at your hotel Mr. Conway. I told her I was a great friend of yours from our service in Vietnam and I wanted to surprise you but preferred to see you in private at your apartment. She was very reluctant at first but in the end I convinced her of you being my best buddy and the stupid bitch told me where you lived. I gave the guard here the same story and persuaded him, with the help of a little *pera* (money) to let me in.'

'I didn't see any guard downstairs, where is he?'

Marvin's smiled mirthlessly and nodded toward the bedroom. 'He's in there, but I don't think you'd want to see him, not now anyway. But, I have to say, a very cooperative guy, he was kind enough to give me his gun.'

'He's dead?' Conway knew his question was rhetorical.

'Dead as...'

Sally began to sob uncontrollably. 'Oh no! Ma...Ma...Marvin... What! Where?...'

'Shut up whore! Another word and you're dead!' Marvin's trigger finger whitened and for an instant Conway thought it was all over but the ex Marine obviously wanted them to suffer. He held all the aces and was going to enjoy the situation for a while longer.

'What are you going to do with us?' asked Conway, trying to keep his voice steady.

'What do you think asshole? Take you for a stroll in the park, perhaps dinner somewhere? We'd make a cosy threesome wouldn't we?' His laugh was maniacal. 'I'm going to kill you both...asshole.'

'Why didn't you kill me in Saigon?'

'Huh!' Marvin's eyes widened in surprise; for the first time the gun wavered a little.

'What! You knew I was there? How? When?'

Conway allowed himself a thin smile. 'Never mind how, I spotted you in Vung Tau mate, you're not much good at shadowing people. They didn't teach you very well in the Marines.'

'Marvin, please...please! Let's talk,' sobbed Sally. 'I...I... was so scared, your moods, your behaviour, I couldn't stand it any more, I had to leave!'

Marvin exploded. 'I told you, not another word bitch!' he screamed, his face reddened, eyes dilated. He was now breathing heavily and the trigger finger whitened again. Conway's mind raced trying to decide whether to jump him knowing that realistically he had no chance.

'You left me to come back to this asshole...he's not going to have you, no one is bitch!'

'No! No! It's not like that at all, he's a friend, he's just trying...'

'Are you deaf bitch? Shut up!' Marvin's whole body was now shaking with rage but the hand holding the gun never wavered.

Conway knew their lives hung by a thread and could end at any second. Shit! What can I do? Two quick shots and it's curtains. But would he shoot them here? The noise would attract attention, he'd never get away. He must have something else in mind? He cursed himself inwardly. 'I should have waited for McGaw's men. Maybe they've already been to the Down Under and know where I am? But it wouldn't matter. If Marvin heard them coming he wouldn't hesitate to shoot, and even if he wasn't a Marine, he could hardly miss at this range.'

His eyes flickered around the room for some kind of weapon. There was nothing but a heavy 12 inch flashlight he used during brownouts, but it was on a sideboard, just out of reach. He'd be dead before he took one step toward it. He had to stall him somehow, keep him talking. Conway's mind raced. In a way we are both kindred spirits. Vietnam has affected us both, if I can just get him to relax...build some kind of a bridge. It's a long shot but...

'She didn't come back to me Marvin, she came back to escape from you. She loves you...or at least she did. You know that but won't admit it. You need treatment Marvin. I was in Vietnam too. I know what it did to guys who served there. The US is now looking after its Vietnam vets, haven't you seen a doctor?'

Marvin ignored the question. His wild eyes bored into Conway and for a second there seemed a flicker of interest. 'You were in 'Nam...Where? I don't believe you.'

'Phouc Tuy, between Saigon and Vung Tau. I was with 6 RAR, Australian task force. Before that I was with 1 RAR attached to *The Big Red One* at Bien Hoa.'

'Ah...ok but you guys were nothing, only small force.' The American's face twisted in contempt. 'You were just chickenshit. We were in all the big stuff.'

'Sure you were and got your arse kicked,' said Conway angrily. 'The VC didn't beat us pal! You ever hear of Long Tan? No, of course you haven't. You guys think you carried all the load but you didn't...not by a bloody long shot!'

Marvin's eyes narrowed the heavy brows came down; the frown deep and dark. For a moment Conway thought he'd gone too far. In truth, he had a lot of respect for the American military but wouldn't cop any aspersion on the Australian forces. Marvin waved the revolver dismissively.

'Nah, would've been nothing like what we went through. Anyway I'm not interested.' He stood up and backed out through the open door to the balcony where Conway could see two more chairs lined up beside the parapet. Conway's stomach knotted. He now knew what Marvin had in mind. He was going to stand them on the chairs and either, push them over the low parapet or shoot them so they would fall forward out into space. He desperately tried to keep Marvin talking.

'How do you think you're going to get away with this? If you shoot you'll wake the whole neighborhood. You won't get out of this building.'

'Who said anything about shooting dummy? I don't care what happens any more, my life ended in 'Nam. Ok, that's enough, come out here and get on these chairs...Now!'

Sally turned to Conway, completely panic stricken. 'Oh Steve...'

Conway gripped her right hand with his left and glared at Marvin. The revolver was steady, the face impassive.

Sweat poured down Conway's face, his shirt stuck to his back. He took a deep breath and slowly led Sally toward the balcony. He had to do something in the next few seconds. Marvin says no shooting but he'd be happy if I tried something. He'll probably shoot us anyway. They had taken one slow step toward the balcony when the lights went out!

Instantly Conway leapt forward and wrenched the heavy glass door across closing it and in the same action, pulling Sally to the floor as Marvin pumped two shots through the door shattering it and raining glass down upon them.

Marvin stood for a moment silhouetted against the night sky. Then he began smashing the remaining glass with his revolver, clearing a space to re-enter the room. They could see him but he couldn't see them.

Conway pushed Sally and grabbed for the flashlight but knocked it from the sideboard in his haste giving his position away. Another shot rang out and Sally screamed. He scrambled frantically and found the flashlight but Marvin was now inside and stumbled over him inadvertently knocking it from his grasp.

Conway leapt to his feet just as the lights came on again. Marvin was on his back looking up, his face a mask of blind hatred. He still had the revolver and raised it but Conway kicked his wrist and the American grunted in pain as the gun was sent spinning from his grasp.

A low moan from Sally caused Conway to glance to his left where to his horror she lay on her side, her face screwed up in pain. Blood seeped from her across the parquet floor. He spun around just in time to see Marvin clamber to his feet. In his left hand was a wicked looking 6 inch blade. He began to toss it slowly from hand to hand in the manner of an LA knife fighter.

'I'm going to carve you up into little pieces Aussie,' he snarled.

They circled each other Marvin thrusting, Conway dodging desperately. On one thrust he was not quick enough. He felt a searing pain as the blade bounced off a protecting forearm and sliced across his belly. He stumbled backwards, blood pouring from his forearm and beneath his shirt. Marvin charged again.

Conway was now backed against a wall. From a nearby shelf he seized a vase and threw it but Marvin ducked and it shattered against a far wall. As the enraged American came at him, in desperation Conway dived to his right and rolled away seeking refuge behind a settee which he shoved forward, frantically trying to stop the bull-like rush.

It didn't work. Marvin came over the settee as if it wasn't there and crashed on top of Conway who grabbed the knife hand just below the wrist, but he was now positioned awkwardly on his back making it difficult to get any leverage.

Marvin was at least ten kilos heavier and now had him pinned and unable to move. He jammed his left hand against Conway's throat and brought the evil looking blade, now in his right, slowly but inexorably closer and closer to Conway's chest. Suddenly he straightened and ripped his hand from Conway's weakening grasp and raised the knife high for a final plunge into the chest of his helpless foe.

* * *

Saigon like many Asian cities on Sunday is quiet and peaceful. To the devout, it is a time to visit a pagoda or church. Some will visit friends, while others like Kim Anh and Dung seek escape from the sweltering heat by spending the day in the wave pools and shady environs of Saigon's Waterworld.

The young female attendant in the ticket box at the entrance glanced up and waved them through with a bright, knowing smile. Dung held Kim's hand possessively, determined to make it plain to all and sundry, that she was now his…and his alone.

They strolled through the familiar surroundings stopping to chat to colleagues most of whom wished them well, while others looked askance but said nothing. Dung was not the most popular member of the Waterworld staff and it surprised more than one that these two different personalities should be together. The unspoken question on the mind of some was, 'where was the foreigner with whom she seemed so besotted?'

Dung was not a swimmer so they didn't venture into any of the pools. His sole intention was to show off his "girlfriend". He literally dragged her into the administration building stopping to talk and laugh with management and colleagues all the while keeping a proprietary arm around her, something which Kim Anh a basically private person, found embarrassing.

'Please Dung,' she whispered, trying to disengage his arm but he would not be denied. He was having too much fun showing her off.

They had lunch in the same small restaurant by the river, even sitting at the same table she and Conway had once occupied. The memory of that afternoon came flooding back, causing her to pick at her food almost oblivious to the non-stop chatter from the ebullient Dung. They left as the sun was setting. He gave her a mysterious smile as he mounted his motorbike. To her surprise, instead of taking her home, he took her to a small, shady park not far from Binh Quoi gardens.

'What are we doing here?' she asked as they dismounted. He grinned and said nothing. Then taking her hand he almost pulled her in his haste, to a secluded lotus pool shaded by a huge, flowering tamarind.

'It is very beautiful and peaceful here isn't it,' he said, the strange smile still hovering on his lips.

'Yes, it is, but…why are we here?' she said slowly, 'I am expected home soon for dinner, you know what my older sister is like if I am late.' He didn't seem to hear her words. He drew a deep breath and began what was obviously a prepared speech.

'Kim Anh, we have known each other for quite a long time both at work and in recent times more personally,' he stopped to take another breath. 'I am so happy these days that we have become…er, well…friends, *very good friends*,' he added hastily. 'In fact I believe we are now *more* than friends. You know how I feel about you. You know my wish is for us to be married but I must ask you,' he said nervously, 'what are…er…I mean,' he stuttered, 'how do you feel about me, can you give me an answer to the question of the other night?'

She looked at him her mind in a whirl. She knew this would come up again; it was decision time. Before long she would be thirty and to be still single at that age in Vietnamese society meant you had been "left on the shelf" something no Vietnamese girl wanted.

In some quarters this single state would attract pity and even scorn. He was no Steve Conway but she had grown attached to him. She had told Conway she would only marry for love, but what was love? Now all she wanted was a loving husband and a comfortable future.

He had been very kind and although a little possessive, had always treated her with respect and his manners on most occasions were impeccable. She had allowed some petting between them, but appreciated that he had not tried to take any further advantage. Her family liked him; a big plus and most essential in Vietnamese society if a relationship was to lead into marriage. Recently her mother had written again, apparently following a letter from Ngoc about her relationship with Dung, and had approved it in glowing terms.

She reached out and lightly touched his hand. 'Anh oi I care for you very much, you have been very kind to me, you are a gentleman and...I think we...' she was not sure what else to say. This was enough for Dung. He was now almost beside himself with joy. He turned away for a moment and when he faced her again his left hand was behind his back.

He took a huge breath and said slowly, 'dear Miss Kim Anh, I have something *very* important to say to you.' She glanced down at her watch. Ngoc would have her dinner on the table, and she hated it when Kim was late.

'Yes, what is it?' she asked quietly.

He whipped his left hand from behind his back and in it was a tiny square box of purple velour. He snapped it open and thrust it into her hands. Inside, sparkling in rays of the late afternoon light was a diamond ring. It momentarily took her breath away.

'Oh my God Dung! It's so beautiful! Where did you...?' She stood transfixed, gazing at the ring completely lost for words. She looked up into his face, now flushed, eyes wide and bright with expectation.

'Miss Kim Anh,' he said excitedly, suddenly switching to Vietnamese, '*em se cuoi anh?*' (Will you marry me).

To actually hear those words; words that so many girls live for and want to hear, left her stunned. In that moment, all the years of pain, heartache, sorrow, privation and despair came to an end.

She simply nodded and remained gazing in wide-eyed fascination and disbelief, as he slipped the ring onto the finger of her left hand.

20

'Say goodbye asshole,' screamed Marvin as the blade arced downwards for the *coupe de grace*. A split second later, the atmosphere in the room was shattered by the staccato blast of gunfire. Blam! Blam! Blam! The first bullet hit Marvin high in the chest. Its momentum carried him up and backwards his eyes wide, puzzled...uncomprehending. The second took him in the throat and the third missed and buried itself in the ceiling.

The knife clattered from his hand. He remained upright for a few seconds then slumped sideways across Conway. He was dead before he hit the tiled floor. Almost at the same moment the door of the apartment was smashed open and the room was suddenly swarming with heavily armed men in black, wearing flak jackets. Leading them, holding a Glock revolver held in a two-handed combat stance, was Chuck McGaw.

Conway pushed Marvin off, staggered to his feet and went across to kneel by Sally who lay on her back, eyes closed; Marvin's gun held loosely in her right hand.

'For Christ sake, get an ambulance! She's been shot!' he shouted, ripping open her dress.

'Steve, this guy's a trained paramedic,' yelled McGaw, above the pandemonium. 'Let him look at her.' One of the black clad individuals carrying a medical bag shouldered his way to Sally and began examining her.

McGaw looked from the spreading pool of blood oozing from Marvin's body and Sally to a bloodied Conway. 'Jesus Steve, this place looks like a mini charnel house and you need attention yourself. Hey! Put a sheet over that guy' McGaw said pointing to Marvin then began barking rapid-fire instructions into a walkie talkie.

'Sir, there's another body in here,' an agent called from the bedroom.

'That's one of the guards Chuck. Marvin killed him to get in here and took his gun. It's the one Sally shot him with.' Conway stood up and pushed his way through the crowd to the bathroom and took off his blood soaked shirt. Both wounds were shallow and the effect was worse than the actual injuries, but would need stitches.

He gingerly washed both, dabbed them with antiseptic, put on a clean shirt and rejoined McGaw. By this time two white coated paramedics were wheeling Sally out. She was still unconscious. Her face had a deathly pallor. Conway felt sick.

'How is she?' he asked one of the medics.

The guy looked at Conway dispassionately, professionally, but his eyes betrayed concern.

'She's lost a lot of blood, we've stabilized her sir, we're taking her to Makati Medical Center…I'm sorry sir, I can't say what her prognosis is at this stage.'

McGaw came across and put his arm around Conway's shoulder.

'Sorry Steve. I'm sorry we were too late. I phoned the hotel and they told me you had gone home. I'd called the NBI urgently to organize your protection and to their credit they had fast tracked my previous request from earlier today. We were on our way to talk to you when we heard the shots. What happened here?'

Conway explained how Marvin had found and talked his way into the apartment and how he intended to kill them. 'But guess what? You know what really saved us?' McGaw shook his head: 'A bloody brownout that's what! I'll never complain about another power outage as long as I live.' He wiped his hand across his face. 'Poor Sally, it's all my fault if she doesn't make it. I was a bloody fool. I should have told her to piss off straight away and take the first bus out of town...shit!'

'Take it easy Steve,' soothed McGaw. 'Makati Medical has the best doctors in the Philippines. If anyone can save her, they can. We'll clean up this place and in the meantime I'll take you to a good hotel tonight. I need you to get a decent night's rest, then I'll come and see you in the morning. You'll have to make a statement but don't worry, I'll cut the paperwork to a minimum, ok buddy?'

Conway stood staring at the blood stained sheet covering Marvin's body then his whole body started to tremble as the impact of the horror of the last hour began to take effect. McGaw waited patiently until he recovered his composure. 'Come on man, it's over, take it easy,' he said putting his hand on Conway's shoulder.

'Yeah thanks Chuck, Jesus Christ, poor Sally, that bastard...Ok, but take me to Makati Medical first. I want to check on her. In the morning we can do all the paperwork you want.'

'You got it guy,' McGaw slipped the Glock back into his shoulder holster. 'Ok, let's go, this is a crime scene. These guys have plenty of work to do here before reporting back to me.'

* * *

Steve woke next morning stiff and sore in every limb. The painkillers he'd been given at Makati Medical Center the night before had worn off and his arm and belly throbbed like hell. He eased himself out of bed, took a bottle of mineral water from the fridge and downed it almost in one gulf then went to the window and looked out over the Makati cityscape reflecting on the previous night's events.

My God, how close was that! He would never forget the hatred and madness in Marvin's eyes as he raised the knife in that last moment. He shuddered involuntarily. And Sally, if she dies, I'll never forgive myself.

McGaw had taken him to Makati Medical Center, waited while he was patched up then booked him into the five star Shangri La Hotel in Makati, promising to let him sleep in before a mid morning debriefing.

The adrenalin still coursed through Conway's body and despite a pill, sleep was a long time coming.

Around midnight he phoned the hospital to enquire about Sally's condition again but was unable to find out anything more than:

She *is out of surgery sir, but her condition is serious.*

He tossed the empty bottle into a trash bin and phoned Keyes.

'There's been some drama last night, meet me at the Shangri La for breakfast. I'll tell you all about it when you get here.'

He made another call to Makati Medical only to be told Sally's condition was unchanged but being monitored. Strictly no visitors would be allowed for at least another 24 hours. He showered, shaved and was reading the *Manila Bulletin* when McGaw phoned to say he would be there at around 11.00 am.

'How are you this morning Steve?'

'Bit shaky but ok, had a fair night's sleep. I see nothing in the paper about last night's little episode?'

'I decided to keep the press on ice until tomorrow. As I said last night, there's a fair bit of paperwork to do with an incident of this nature. We are working with the Philippine authorities and one of the most important questions we have to answer is, how the hell...and when, did he get back in to this country? Not to mention, trying to find kin of Marvin's although the records of the Marine Corps should answer that one. As you can imagine, this is a very sensitive matter to say the least, for us and our Filipino friends.'

McGaw stifled a yawn. 'Sorry, didn't get much sleep last night. There's also the situation as to what to do with the body...and reports to our embassy, the NBI, the local cops, you name it...yeah, heaps of things to do and complications, but it's all part of the job. Just hang in there Steve and I'll see you soon,' he said hanging up.

Over breakfast Conway explained what had happened to a wide-eyed Keyes.

The big man kept shaking his head in disbelief. 'You sure are one lucky guy, and to think a brownout saved you.'

'Not just the brownout, it was Sally who saved me in the end. I owe my life to her and now I don't know if she's going to pull through,' his voice cracked. 'She's a great girl…Jumbo, if she dies…'

'Hey, come on man,' said Keyes gently, reaching across the table and putting his hand on his friend's arm. 'She's in a world class hospital, they'll pull her though, you can bet on it.' His words held a conviction he didn't feel. Neither of them knew just how badly she'd been hit. Gun shot wounds caused terrible internal traumas to the body. They'd both seen the effects in Vietnam; it didn't give cause for optimism.

Conway stared at the plate in front of him piled high with bacon, eggs, hash browns and tomatoes. He pushed it away. 'Can't eat, no appetite, and the worst thing is mate, I can't see her until tomorrow, if there is a tomorrow…'

Keyes felt helpless knowing that words were useless. All he could offer was the time honored, 'Is there anything I can do for you?'

'As a matter of fact there is. Can you go around to my apartment and check it out? McGaw said his boys would clean up the place. There's glass, blood and shit all over the place. The glass door to the balcony needs replacing. They smashed down the front door; there's bullet holes in walls, get maintenance onto it. In the meantime I'll call Sinclair and let him know what happened. He needs an update on the repairs to the hotel after the fire anyway.'

'Ok, will do boss. Try and get some rest and I'll call you later. Hey! With all those bruises and bandages, you look like a traffic accident,' he laughed. Conway couldn't help smiling. 'Keep your pathetic humour to yourself Keyes and be off with you.'

* * *

The news of Kim Anh's engagement to Dung was greeted with great joy by both families, friends and colleagues although some secretly voiced skepticism about the union. Dung's condescending and superior attitude at times to staff at Waterworld had caused anger and friction among the ranks and some felt a popular girl like Kim could have done better.

No one however was more overjoyed than Ngoc who kept hugging both of them and looking at the ring, the night they arrived back at Thanh Da to break the news.

Ngoc was beside herself with happiness. 'Oh, this is soooo wonderful, I am so happy for you my little sister,' she laughed, almost crushing the breath out of Kim with a hug. She insisted on parading Kim and Dung around the neighborhood, showing off the ring and telling all and sundry what an important and great guy Kim's fiancé was.

'We must have a big party to celebrate mustn't we?' she gushed. 'We must start to make arrangements now. I will contact the family in Hanoi and our other relations in central Vietnam…oh…yes, so wonderful,' she clucked away to Dung's amusement. Kim looked on bemused and began to wonder who the celebrations were really for. She'd never seen Ngoc, a normally taciturn individual, so full of joy but she was genuinely happy for her older sibling who didn't have much to be happy about in her life.

She and her husband were desperately poor. A wartime disability restricted his capacity to work leaving Ngoc to be the main breadwinner with a couple of part-time jobs. One gave her a pittance for doing housework for several families which she supplemented by selling fruit and vegetables on Sunday at a local market. But by far the majority of the family income came from a good slice of Kim's monthly salary.

This engagement was not only a heaven sent distraction from her dreary, loveless daily life, but the advent of Dung and his wealthy family, promised a financial windfall for her brood.

The next few days where a constant round of visits to other family, parties and small celebrations with work colleagues and closest friends all very enjoyable, except those which involved Lan and his coterie. Kim resigned herself to Dung's friendship with the businessman but made sure she kept her distance from his lecherous advances.

In this suddenly euphoric atmosphere, for Kim Anh, life seemed one long celebration until one evening she received a phone call from Mrs Thanh which turned her life upside down.

21

Conway sat at Sally's bedside in the Makati Medical Center, holding her hand. It was a week since the incident with Marvin but she still looked pale and weak. Fortunately the bullet had not hit any vital organs passing beneath her bottom rib and exiting below a lung. But there was considerable internal damage and physical recovery would be months instead of weeks.

He had been allowed special visiting rights after pressure on hospital hierarchy from McGaw, and had spent hours each day with her. His presence brightened her considerably and doctors told him it was instrumental in restoring both her mental and physical condition.

'Some people never quite get over a trauma like that Mr Conway,' said the surgeon who operated. 'But, she is a strong, healthy woman and I believe physically she will recover well. But mentally Mr Conway...I am not so sure. She has been through a terrible experience and may need psychological help in future, only time will tell.'

Sally had been dozing. When she opened her eyes and saw who it was, she smiled wanly and reached up to take his hand. 'Hello darling, thank you for coming again. You have been so wonderful. It would have been very, very lonely without you coming to see me.'

'Hey,' he squeezed her hand. 'It's the least I can do for the girl who saved my life, not a small thing you know Miss Sally.'

'Oh Steve, it was horrible wasn't it? You were so brave, you know, you are my hero Mr Conway, you always have been. How is your arm darling? You still have that big bandage? Is it serious?'

'Just a scratch, nothing to worry about.'

'Steve, you never got the chance to tell me why you wanted me at your apartment that night, but now I realise, it was to tell me to get out of town.' She started to cough, her face screwing up in pain.

'Oh God, I hate coughing, it hurts like hell.'

'Take it easy love,' he said, stroking her hand. 'Any idea when they'll let you out of here and when they do, what are your plans?'

'I'm told another week at least before I can think about leaving,' she replied, taking a deep breath, the effort causing more pain. She grimaced and closed her eyes for a few seconds waiting for it to subside. 'As far as what to do next? Well, I have given it a lot of thought. To tell you the truth, I have changed my mind a few times but I think I'll go back to Isabella to recuperate then return to the States.' Conway looked at her with raised eyebrows.

'Permanently?'

She licked her lips. 'Would you give me some water please?' He filled a plastic cup from a container on a cupboard by her bed. She took a sip and put the glass back on the bedside cupboard.

'No, not forever, I will sell the house. It's in both our names so I don't know how long that will take. It may be complicated after what has happened, I'll get legal advice but Steve, I will come back here. This is my country, my home, and I feel I belong here.'

'I'm glad to hear that Sal.'

'Are you Steve?' There was something in her voice which made him look up.

'Yes…why?'

'First of all, let me ask you this. Are you going back to Vietnam?'

'Yes,' he nodded, wondering what she was driving at. 'I have unfinished business there. Why? I can tell by your voice, this is not just a casual enquiry.'

She paused. There was sadness in her eyes. 'There is, or was, a girl back there wasn't there?' He looked down at her for a long moment. The silence disturbed only by the low hum of the air con.

'How did you know?'

'Women can sense these things. Remember the last night with me?'

'Of course.'

'I knew you had something or rather, someone on your mind. I won't tell you how I knew, I just knew.'

'You are right, there was someone, was, meaning past tense.'

'I'm sorry.'

He looked away.

'You loved her very much didn't you?'

He turned back to her. It was the first time she had ever seen tears in the eyes of Steve Conway.

'Yes…I did…very much.'

She took his hand in hers. 'What happened darling? You know I should be jealous, but I know what it's like to lose a love, my heart goes out to you.'

'You are an extraordinary woman Sally…ah…the answer to your question is…I don't rightly know, all I know, it's got a bit to do with cultural differences. But it's over now I'd rather not talk about it.'

They again lapsed into silence searching each other's face for something to say. Both were afraid to express what was really on their minds. Finally, he stood up, leant over and kissed her on the cheek. 'Get well soon my sweet Sally, see you tomorrow.' He stood at the door for a moment then blew her a kiss as he closed it behind him. She stared at the door for a few seconds then burst into tears.

* * *

In the bar that night Keyes reported that work was well under way repairing the damage to his apartment and he should be able to move back in by the following weekend. They began to discuss Conway's imminent return to Saigon when in walked Chuck McGaw.

'Hi guys, who's buying?'

Conway signaled to Jackie, to give McGaw his usual Jack Daniels.

'What's happening in law enforcement Chuck, anything more on the late unlamented Marvin?'

McGaw stirred his Jack and took a sip. 'Yes there have been developments. We've traced relatives. His parents are dead but he has a brother doing life in a Kansas jail, apparently another psycho.'

'Runs in the family,' Conway said drily.

'Yeah, but there seems to be at least one sane member; a sister in Florida married to a retired oil baron. She's agreed to come and take his body back to the States. And,' he paused, taking another sip, 'we reckon we know how he sneaked back in to the P.I. We found a name on the passenger list from that Zamoanga flight which we reckon fits him. You'll never guess?'

'Elvis Presley?' grinned Keyes.

'Harpo Marx,' smiled Conway.

'Try, John Doe.'

'Oh, very original,' said Conway, 'so what was he doing in Zamboanga?'

'Well, there's no international airport so we believe, in fact we are pretty well 100 percent sure he came in illegally from Sabah by boat. It's happening all the time. The Moro Liberation Army uses it to smuggle in weapons. It's the nearest landfall to the south of here and a few dollars will get you passage on a fishing boat or something similar. There's a lot of small sea traffic down there. He could come in at night without too many problems.'

Conway thought about this for a few moments. 'Yeah, it sounds feasible I suppose. I wonder how long he's been here and where he would have stayed?'

'I'm glad you asked that my friend. The local constabulary in Ermita had a complaint from the owner of a small pension house about a foreigner not paying his bill. The cops weren't too interested, until the owner gave a description of the foreigner. They checked the room and found a small airline bag containing several false passports, US dollars and the name and phone number of someone in Zamboanga, methinks tied in with Mr LeGrand's entry into this country. This individual has already been taken into custody for further questioning.'

'I think that calls for another drink Mr McGaw…on me.'

'Thanks Steve. By the way, we took a statement from Sally. As expected, it confirms everything you told us, so as far as you guys are concerned, it's case closed. How is she by the way?'

'She's coming along well. The doctors are happy. She'll be released next week then go back to Isabella and later to the States but eventually will come back here.'

'Good, a real nice girl…pity about her choice in men…er, sorry Steve. I mean husbands.' Conway joined in the laughter.

'To you Chuck.' Conway raised his glass in a toast.

'Hear, hear,' agreed Keyes. 'Here's to the good ole U S of A.'

'When are you going back to 'Nam Steve? I'm gonna miss you buddy. I'll have nothing to do with you out of the country. You could find trouble blindfolded,' grinned McGaw.

'In a few days Chuck, just as soon as I can tidy up a few things here, I will…'

'Call for you sir,' said Jackie, leaning over the bar. Conway excused himself and picked up a phone at the end of the bar. He rolled his eyes when he heard the smokey tones of Lily Li.

'Hello lover,' she crooned, 'I've missed you.'

'Yeah thanks Lily, what can I do for you?' asked Conway, slightly irritated at being taken away from his discussion with McGaw. Lily ignored his tone and came straight to the point.

'Darling, I'm putting together a consortium with Alex Mendoza to look at building a resort on Boracay, I thought your organization might be interested, I see it as a sensible extension to your operation. That island is booming, tourists are flocking to the place. Your organisation has a captive market and you could offer good deals to your guests…it would be a win win situation darling.'

Conway leant against the bar and turned his back to the guests lowering his voice.

'Sounds interesting Lily and makes sense, but as you know at the moment we are looking at Saigon. Have you done any feasibility study? I know the place is booming but is there enough room in the market for one more? Have you costed anything? There are so many things to consider, and Boracay has a difficult reputation for start ups. I thought you would be a bit wary after your Shanghai experience?'

'Darling,' she replied soothingly, 'I'm on my home turf. It's early days and just in the planning stage. We have a site picked out but I agree with you, there is much more to be done.'

Conway thought about it for a moment. 'Ok Lily, you know I cannot promise anything but I'll run it past some of our guys and if they're interested I'll let you know. I have a full plate at the moment and have to leave for Saigon in a few days, leave it with me ok?'

'Sure darling, thank you. I will keep you up to date with developments, and I may even come to Saigon to do just that. Maybe we can have some more fun darling, like we had on Boracay.' She gave a little giggle. Conway couldn't help smiling.

'Ok, thanks Lily but you better give me some notice ok? Gotta go now busy boy, bye bye.' He replaced the receiver and thought about her offer. It might be ok but would need a lot of careful consideration; more than one foreigner with big ideas had been burnt on Boracay. Right now Saigon has first priority. He rejoined Keyes and McGaw and stayed late. The atmosphere was right, the mood festive; a night for wassail and song.

* * *

The next few days were spent on phone calls back and forth to Australia. James Sinclair warmed to the Boracay project but said it had to go on the back burner for the time being.

'We need you back in Saigon Steve.'

Conway couldn't agree more. The thought of seeing Kim again somehow made him feel a bit like a nervous schoolboy about to call up a girl and ask for date. I wonder what her reaction will be when I get back, he thought. I hope she's changed her mind about this "friendship" thing.

He had stayed out of touch not just because of the events in Manila but because the finality and abruptness of their parting convinced him it was better to keep his distance and give her time to hopefully, reconsider.

He had been temped many times to phone and once had lifted the receiver to call her replacing it at the last moment. The nights were the hardest. He had lain awake staring at the ceiling in the darkness thinking. I wonder how she is. What she's been doing? Has she missed me? I hope absence *does* make the heart grow fonder.

He visited Sally who was starting to look more like her old self. The colour was back in her cheeks. Her hair had been styled by a visiting hairdresser and she looked lovely lying there in a pink silk nightgown Conway had bought her. Her eyes lit up when he walked in carrying a huge bouquet of flowers. She was overwhelmed and tried to lift her face for his kiss.

'Darling, I would love to kiss you but I am not quite up to stretching yet, but thank you so much, they are simply beautiful.' He stayed for two hours during which they spoke of many things, including the first time she had seen him.

'I remember the day I first saw you, when you came into the Black Jack bar with Mr Keyes, and,' she giggled, 'you nearly strangled Sir Groyne my boss when he insulted you, it seems so long ago now...' her voice dropped and tailed off. They continued to reminisce until he glanced at his watch and realized he was overdue for a management meeting. It would be hard to leave her.

'Sorry darling,' he said, leaning over and kissing her cheek. 'I have to go. Please keep in touch.'

The smile she gave him was forced. The lump in her throat made speech difficult.

'I will...I will miss you so very much darling...please, take good care of yourself,' she said, tears welling in her eyes. He walked to the door and stopped for a moment, then turned and smiled. She looked away. When she looked back, he was gone.

Twenty four hours later a Philippine Airlines flight with Steve Conway on board, lifted off into a cloudless blue sky morning, banked left and headed westward for Saigon.

'I am coming back Kim Anh, but will you be waiting?' he whispered softly.

22

Dung leant over Kim Anh's desk and playfully pushed documents she was typing away from her. 'Please dear,' she smiled, 'I'm trying to work and this report is urgent, it has to be on the Director's desk within the next half hour.'

'Ok my love,' he grinned. 'I would hate you to get fired, but then maybe we could both leave this place and live happily ever after somewhere, ha ha ha. Don't forget our date tonight darling, I think you will like the place we are going. You know I don't spare any expense when it comes to you,' he said smugly, swaggering off in his ten-to-two walk.

She was about to continue the report when her phone rang. She reached over and picked it up to hear the excited voice of Mrs Thanh.

'You must be so happy now Kim Anh.'

'Oh…yes, I am, thank you,' replied Kim puzzled. How did Mrs Thanh know of her engagement? She hadn't told the landlady and Dung had no connection with the Thanh family.

'I am so happy for you,' said Mrs Thanh. 'I want you both to come for dinner on Saturday night, will you come please. My husband and I look forward to seeing you both very much.'

'Ah, yes, I think that will be ok…but…I will confirm it with you,' Kim said slowly.

'Oh, that will be wonderful; you know you are lucky to have found such a lovely man.' 'Oh really? I mean, yes he is nice, thank you.'

'Oh Kim Anh, you know, he kept apologizing for leaving so suddenly but it was because of the fire in his hotel, and you know Kim Anh, the poor man, his arm is bandaged and there are some bruises on his face, but he said it was just an accident and wouldn't say what happened,' she rattled on. 'Oh I am so pleased…are you still there Miss Kim Anh?'

Kim sat stunned looking into space, the phone limp in her hand. It wasn't Dung she was talking about…Conway was back! She struggled to find something coherent to say.

'Yes…I am here, er, sorry but I have been away…when did Mr Conway return?'

'Oh, what a naughty man, he hasn't been in touch? Well, he only arrived yesterday. I am very sorry if I spoilt the surprise, I'm sure he will phone you, please ask him to accept our invitation, bye bye, I…we, look forward to seeing you both Saturday night.'

'Ah…yes.' Kim replaced the receiver in a daze trying to get her head around what Mrs Thanh had said. What was this about a *fire* and an *accident*? She looked down at the sparkling ring on her left hand and a wave of nausea passed over her. Her hands began to tremble.

Oh my God! What have I done? What a fool I've been. What am I going to do? I thought he left in a hurry because he was so upset with me for telling him we were now just "friends" and decided to go back to Manila and forget me. How stupid I am! I have given myself to a man to please my family and Vietnamese culture.

She picked up the phone and called Mrs Thanh back and explained that she was busy at the time and could the dear lady tell her more about what Conway had said regarding his sudden departure, his accident and anything else he may have mentioned. For example, did he mention her name during his explanation of events?

The landlady went into more detail about Conway's need to return to Manila, how important it was for him as the boss to be there and supervise reconstruction etc. She told Conway of her surprise that he had not informed Kim Anh of his departure.

'He said he was very sorry about that and would explain everything to you when he saw you again. And yes Kim Anh, he did ask if I had heard from you and seemed disappointed that I hadn't.' Her voice was tinged with reproach. Kim was about to angrily reply that Conway hadn't contacted her the whole time he'd been away, but thought better of it.

There was no way she could explain her engagement to Dung. Just the thought of the landlady's reaction made her shiver. She thanked Mrs Thanh and hung up, her head spinning. Another wave of nausea came over her and she just made the bathroom before throwing up.

It was twenty minutes before she was able to return to her desk still pale and ill. Her phone rang again. This time it was Vy on the switchboard.

'Mr Conway is on the line,' she said brightly. She had seen Conway with Kim and thought they made a nice couple. Like many of her co-workers she found it hard to understand why Kim had become engaged to someone like Dung and not "handsome Mr Conway". 'I will put him through now.' To her surprise Kim refused.

'Please tell him I am busy, I am not here. Tell him anything, but I cannot speak to him just now,' she said sharply.

'Oh, ok if that is what you want,' replied Vy, miffed and surprised by Kim's unexpectedly curt tone. Conway phoned again three times and received the same answer.

For the rest of the day Kim worked in a haze. The report for the Director was returned to her for correction twice causing him to ask if there was anything wrong. Kim Anh was the most efficient secretary he'd ever had and mistakes from her were rare and very much out of character but like everyone else, he was aware of Kim's recent engagement. 'It must be love,' he told himself.

Five o'clock could not come quick enough. She logged off her computer, tidied her desk and went to Dung's office to call off their date, but he was out. Ok, I will phone him from home she thought, and left the office her head in a whirl.

She walked around to the back of the building where her motorbike was parked with those of the other staff. It stood at the end of a row hidden by a number of trees. It was a shady spot and she often came to work early in order to claim the space. As she approached her bike she heard voices.

One of them she recognized as her fiancé's. She stopped and stood behind one of the trees and looked across to an outbuilding where two men stood talking beside a parked black four wheel drive. What was Dung doing meeting someone in this area? Why not in his office? The other voice was that of Lan's driver. They were standing close together, their manner conspiratorial; their voices low.

She frowned and edged a little closer. It was difficult to pick up the exact conversation but she froze when she heard the word, *Conway*. She drew back quickly as both men looked around furtively, checking to see if anyone was watching. Satisfied they were alone, the driver handed Dung a white envelope. They shook hands. The driver then climbed back into the four wheel drive and sped out through the main gate.

She watched as Dung tore open the envelope and withdrew two sheets of folded white paper. One he began to read. When he finished, he glanced at the other sheet then put both back into the envelope and returned to the administration block, a smirk of satisfaction on his moon face.

She phoned him from home but he was still unavailable. She replaced the receiver unaware of what she was doing, her mind in utter turmoil. The phone call from Mrs Thanh and hearing Conway's name during the conversation between Dung and Lan's driver left her bewildered and sick with worry.

What would she say to Conway when inevitably they met? How could she explain her engagement and what had Dung been up to? The body language looked suspicious. What would he have to hide?

Dung arrived just before 7.00 pm with flowers and wouldn't listen to her pleas and excuses for cancelling their date. Instead he became childish and said he had booked a table at an expensive restaurant and would lose face with his friends if they didn't show; maybe she didn't love him; perhaps he had made the wrong choice of fiancée, etc, etc. In the end to keep the peace, she agreed. It wasn't exactly a blissfully happy couple who set off that night for District 1.

* * *

It was early evening. Conway sat staring gloomily out the window of his apartment sipping coffee. His worst fears had been realized. Kim Anh had rejected him completely. To all intents they now weren't even friends. It was bad enough not seeing her smiling face waiting at the airport, but her refusal to take his phone calls left him dejected and sick at heart.

It seemed he had paid the price for his lack of contact and negligence. When he thought about it, he could hardly blame her. But it had been her call, what was he supposed to do? Beg and ask her to reconsider? She was the one who had made the decision to change the relationship.

He picked up the phone and thought for a moment. Who to call? Ah, yes, Jack Malone. He badly needed a drinking partner and someone to whom he could pour out all his troubles. A knockabout like Jack, who'd had his share of broken relationships in Vietnam, would be just the right guy.

Several minutes later there was still no answer so he hung up and phoned Mrs Linh. She answered almost immediately. It brightened Conway a little to hear her warm, friendly voice.

'Oh, you're back Mr Conway, it's so nice to hear from you again and your timing is good,' she said in her immaculate English. 'I have some news for you.'

'Well can we meet for dinner and discuss it tonight Mrs Linh if you are free. I am in need of some company?' There was a slight pause before she answered.

'Oh really, I thought Miss Kim,' she said hesitantly, 'ok, do you like Chinese food Mr Conway? I can recommend the dim sum the Caravelle Hotel serve in their ground floor restaurant.'

'Sure, what time?' What he needed more than food though was companionship; anything to avoid sitting alone in the apartment brooding and he did need to hear what Mrs Linh had to say. She was a nice lady, pleasant, intelligent and the Caravelle was only a few minutes walk from his apartment.

'Would 7.30 pm suit Mr Conway?' The question was rhetorical and at 7.30 pm on the dot Conway sat in the Caravelle's Chinese restaurant with the slim, smiling Mrs Linh looking lovely in an eye-catching white silk *cheong sam*. Before ordering their meal Conway asked for the wine list and was delighted when she agreed to eschew soft drink in favour of a bottle of *Du Tetre Rouge,* a luscious red from Bordeaux.

The wine came and Conway raised his glass in a toast: 'To success!'

'*Salute,*' Mrs Linh replied demurely. They sat engaging in small talk when Conway asked about Jack Malone. 'Have you seen him recently?' Her face fell and she put her glass down and drew a deep breath.

'Poor Mr Malone, he's not with us now,' she said slowly shaking her head.

'What? Is he dead?'

'No, no, not that I know of, but he became very ill and had to be flown to hospital in Bangkok about ten days ago. I have heard nothing since. I am very worried about him.'

'Have you any idea of what it was?'

'I heard it was a brain haemorrhage, I think they call it an aneurysm.'

'That is the correct term, my father died of the same ailment,' said Conway. 'Poor Jack, it needn't be fatal but it's not good, let's hope he pulls through.' He leant across to refill her glass then nearly dropped the bottle.

Coming across the foyer and up the few steps to the same restaurant was Kim Anh, hand in hand with a short, plump, well-dressed Vietnamese guy with a pencil moustache, whom Conway recognized immediately as the one who had stared at him with hate-filled eyes in the *Allez Boo* restaurant. Neither looked happy.

Mrs Linh followed his gaze then looked back at him frowning. 'Isn't that…your… girlfriend?' Conway was too dumbfounded to reply. He put the bottle down and slumped back onto his chair feeling sick.

He watched as they were led to a table in their direction. Suddenly Kim Anh saw him. She stopped in mid stride and put her hand to her mouth in shock, her face turning a whiter shade of pale. Her sudden halt caused Dung to stumble and turn on her angrily.

Conway jumped up from his table, and strode across purposely stopping in front of them preventing further passage. Dung tried to walk around him but the Australian put the flat of his hand against his chest.

'Stay,' he grated. He turned to Kim who had her head down.

'What is this?' he exploded, 'what the hell are you doing with this… this guy?'

She said nothing. 'Do you know who this piece of excreta is?' he said his voice choking with rage. She remained silent. 'He's the one who was looking daggers at us in *Allez Boo*. Now I know why you suddenly wanted us only to be "friends" you've been playing with this creep behind my back,' shouted Conway. 'What kind of a woman are you? Jesus, what a bloody fool I've been and I thought you loved me. Is this how Vietnamese women behave? If this is your bloody culture you can stick it!'

Other diners began to turn and look in their direction. Kim began to cry. Conway turned to Dung with clenched fists and for a moment it looked as if there was going to be violence. The disturbance had now caught the attention of the *Maitre 'D* who began to advance accompanied by several waiters.

Dung went pale. His bowels were about to open. He tried to speak but nothing came out. Then in an attempt to gain the initiative, he grabbed Kim's left hand and held it up in front of the furious Conway's face. It worked. The Australian's mouth dropped open. He stared in disbelief at the diamond ring on her finger.

'I have no idea what you are talking about but I can tell you now white man,' snarled Dung, 'Kim Anh is mine and we are going to get married,' he said triumphantly. 'So go away and leave us alone or I will call the police.' He pushed past, pulling Kim with him, leaving Conway speechless.

They went to a table on the far side of the restaurant. As Kim passed Conway she kept her head down, shame, confusion and hurt written all over her face.

The approaching staff withdrew as Conway stumbled back to his table in a daze and sat down heavily. Mrs Linh reached over and took his hand.

'I am very sorry,' she said softly. Conway said nothing. He sat with downcast eyes.

He looked up and across to Kim and Dung who were being attended by a waiter. As Dung ordered, Kim lifted her head slowly and looked across at Conway. Even at that distance he could see the pain in her eyes.

He met her gaze and shook his head. She lowered hers again.

'Let's get out of here,' said Conway angrily. He paid the bill and made a show of taking Mrs Linh's hand as he escorted her out. Bloody childish of me, he thought, but what the hell! A moment before they passed through the huge glass front doors, he turned and looked back, to see Kim's eyes still following him, her expression one of anguish.

Mrs Linh asked the concierge to bring her car around. She put her hand on his arm.

'Mr Conway, you are a very nice man and I realise what you have just seen has devastated you. I think you should not be alone tonight.' Conway was unable to speak.

'Please,' she said kindly, 'I would like you to come home with me tonight. Oh, don't get me wrong,' she added hastily, 'I am not trying to seduce you Mr Conway, I am sure you would not be interested in a women my age,' she said, 'but I have been hurt in love and I know what you are going through right now.'

Conway was about to refuse, but when he looked into the eyes of this small, quiet Vietnamese woman he saw a depth of compassion, honesty and tenderness that made him want to hug her.

'Thank you very much, I would be happy to Mrs Linh,' he said dully, 'and let me tell you, you are much too modest. Believe me, you are a very attractive woman and many men would be very happy to have you on their arm.'

She smiled at the compliment. 'You are very kind Mr. Conway and please...call me Hoa.'

'Only if you call me Steve,' he said, forcing a smile in return.

She lived in a three story, rambling old French villa in the Chinese area of Saigon known as District 5. She ushered him up several stone steps through a vestibule into a cosy lounge room bedecked with photos of her family and yellow *mai* blossoms.

The walls were hung with original watercolours and Han prints. Expensive antiques and porcelain figurines decorated shelves and inside glass fronted cabinets. A large round coffee table of black mahogany stood in front of a red velvet chaise lounge; high on one wall a Buddhist shrine was bathed in gold from the light of a small candle. The room, with its subdued lighting, objets d'art and expensive furnishings, exuded elegance and class; much like the lady herself.

Conway waited on the chaise lounge while Hoa busied herself in the kitchen returning a few minutes later with a tray containing a silver pot of steaming coffee, two cups and saucers of Spode china and a plate of *banh chung*, sticky rice cakes. He had no appetite but took one to be polite and sat munching something he couldn't taste, staring at his cup as she poured the coffee.

She sat beside him and took his hand. When she looked up into his face the pain in his eyes made her turn away for a moment.

'Would you like to talk about it? It might help Steve,' she murmured. He took a sip of his coffee. 'This is very good, thank you Hoa.' He put the cup back on the table and turned to her.

'Yes, maybe it will, maybe it won't but I need to talk about it, you're Vietnamese maybe you can make sense of it, because I sure as hell can't.'

He leaned forward and put his head in his hands. 'My head is crazy at the moment, so bear with me if I rave on a bit.'

She patted his hand. 'Talk, tell me anything about her, I'm a good listener,' she said gently.

He explained the reason he had come back to Vietnam and how he had met and fallen in love with Kim Anh. He spoke of their happy times together in Saigon, their letters and phone calls, the intense feelings between them which led to romantic interludes in Binh Quoi, and Vung Tau. He paused often when the memories became too painful. All the while, she sat quietly saying nothing, occasionally refilling his cup. She offered more rice cakes but he shook his head.

'And then one day, she decided it was over, just like that! One moment we were lovers, the next she told me I was just a "friend".'

'Did she give a reason?'

'Sort of,' he said, closing his eyes for a moment. 'I can't remember exactly because it came as such a shock but she said it was mainly a cultural thing.' The words were coming more quickly now as he relived that evening.

'Her family are from the North, apparently they don't like or trust foreigners, they want her with a Vietnamese. Her mother wrote her a long letter giving her all kinds of reasons why she should not hook up with me and get this Hoa...she has never bloody met me!' He shook his head in utter bewilderment.

He took a deep breath and continued. 'To make matters worse, her older sister feels the same way. I know she has filled Kim's head with crap about me! But you know Hoa, when I look back I should have seen it coming because she never once invited me to meet her friends or colleagues socially and, I never got another invitation to the family home in Thanh Da.' There were tears of anger and frustration in his eyes.

'I think she was bloody ashamed of me! I honestly loved her Hoa, and believe me...I treated Kim Anh and her family with the utmost respect. I have done nothing to give them cause to hate me but I guess being a foreigner is good enough reason,' he said bitterly.

'I believe you Steve. It is obvious how much you loved her,' she said sadly, 'but it is the Vietnamese tradition, especially for some of those from the North who are still very conservative and steeped in such things. It would be very hard for Kim Anh to go against their wishes. She might even be cast from the family, something she could not bear and I am sure you would never want that to happen.'

'Of course I wouldn't, but...'

He sipped his coffee and let his words hang in the air. It was quiet in the room except for the ticking of an antique clock on a mantel piece. She poured him more coffee and gently handed it to him.

'Steve, I have seen quite a few cross cultural marriages in this country and I often wonder how many succeed. Apart from the obvious difficulty often of a language barrier and conflicting thought processes, there are wide gaps between our cultures; sometimes insurmountable. We are in many ways so different from the West and often these differences are not apparent, especially in the first bloom of love.'

She refilled his cup and continued in that soft, warm voice. 'Certainly, we share the same desires and objectives of a happy family life, and the desire to be successful in our work and communities but we express ourselves differently and go about things in ways which sometimes confuse and annoy those of another race and culture. For example, our manners and courtesies are different. It is so easy to misunderstand and offend each other, unwittingly. I know, I have seen it, it happened to me a long time ago with an American.' She paused for a moment with a faraway look in her eyes.

'I respect the Western way of life very much but the fact is, family relationships are very close here and I think given our poverty, there are more expectations for our children to marry well and be successful in life. I also think perhaps we put too much pressure on our children but it is our way. I am sure with your experiences in South East Asia you are aware of this.'

'Only too well,' he said ruefully, looking at the floor. He looked up at her fiercely.

'They can't do this to me. You see that little germ she was with? He followed us to a coffee shop in Pham Ngu Lao and sat glaring at us. Kim didn't see him but if looks could kill...hey!' Suddenly, he stood up, walked a few paces and swung around looking as if something had just dawned on him.

'Maybe it *was* him?'

'What are you talking about, what about...who?'

'That guy she was with tonight!'

'Please, you are speaking in riddles.'

'There was an incident shortly after I came back here looking for a Down Under site. I was knocked over one night crossing the street after having a drink with Jack.'

Her eyes widened in surprise. 'I didn't know that, he never said anything about it.'

'I never got around to telling him. Fortunately I wasn't badly hurt and at the time I put it down to a drunk driver, because it was inconceivable that anyone would want to kill me, after all, I knew no one here other than Kim Anh. I remember thinking how deliberate it seemed to be but dismissed it. It had to be an accident but now...'

He smacked his right fist into his left palm looking down at her, revelation on his face.

'Hoa, it makes sense now! I remember Kim telling me about this guy who worked with her, a real possessive individual, desperate to be her boyfriend. Apparently he was insanely jealous of any male she even spoke to at work or anywhere else. For sure it was him in the black four wheel drive that tried to run me down, exit Conway and he had a free run.'

'But you have no proof?'

'No, I don't...shit! But I know I'm right. Somehow I have to nail that little prick. He's taken her from me and they got bloody engaged in the short time I was away. Can you believe that?' He shook his head as if the full impact of what he had seen in the Caravelle was beginning to dawn.

'After what she told me about him, how the hell did she agree to such a thing Hoa? I didn't even know they were seeing each other. What a complete mug I've been! I knew she wanted marriage but my God...'

She stood and took his hand. 'It's getting late dear, I think we should get some sleep. I have a spare bedroom you can use unless you...' He nodded, and she led him to her bedroom.

* * *

They hardly spoke during the meal. Kim, her face tear-stained, picked at her food while Dung ate his in between shooting baleful glances across at her. He smiled weakly at a table of socialite friends nearby he'd hope to impress by showing he finally had a girlfriend, but after the incident with Conway they studiously ignored him.

He raged inside, that dirty foreigner had ruined the night and I can tell she still has feelings for him. The bastard, I will make sure he can never have her.

After the meal she begged him to take her home saying she was very tired, but keeping his rage inside, he smiled for the first time all evening and gave the impression that everything was now ok and back to normal.

He insisted with a sly grin, they go to his apartment in District 3. She knew what he had in mind but he had always been a gentleman and restrained himself taking their love making no further than a kiss and a clumsy grope. Hardly knowing what she was doing, followed him out of the hotel where he summoned a taxi.

When they arrived he dragged her into the apartment and up to his bedroom on the first floor where he dropped the pretence.

'You are mine now Kim Anh and you will do as I tell you, you know it's the Vietnamese way,' he snarled, pushing her roughly onto the bed.

The sudden change in his manner bewildered her; this was a completely and different Dung. A side to him she had never seen, and it frightened her.

'No, you are wrong, this is *not* the Vietnamese way anymore, times have changed,' she cried staring up into a face now twisted with hate. Who was this person? Where was the kind, loving man she had accepted as a future husband, the man who said he loved her and had promised so much? The horrible realization dawned on her. His true personality was now being revealed in that room, at that moment.

She tried to sit up but he pushed her back down. He was going to make sure that foreign bastard would never have her. He tore away her blouse and skirt and ripped off her bra. She cringed and turned away, 'please no! Dung, please don't,' she cried, putting up her hands to fend him off, but he ignored her pleas and reached down and ripped off her panties.

'You are mine and will *always* be mine Kim Anh,' he gritted, quickly shucking off his own clothes. She now began to shake and sob uncontrollably but nothing was going to stop him.

He pinned her on her back and spread her legs. She bucked and screamed for mercy as he entered her but her pleas went unheeded.

23

Conway woke and felt a weight across his chest. He looked sideways to see a tousled black head and suddenly remembered where he was. The weight was Hoa's arm. She was still sleeping peacefully with a smile on her lips. Her arm remained where she had embraced him last night before they slept.

He leaned across, lightly kissed her forehead, carefully lifted her arm and trying not to disturb her, slipped out of bed. He dressed quickly and went to the kitchen to put on the kettle for a cup of tea. A few minutes later he returned to the bedroom and sat on the bed beside her.

'Are you awake?' he said quietly.

She stirred sleepily, opened her eyes and smiled when she saw him sitting there. 'This is for you dear Hoa,' he said, handing her the cup of tea.

'Oh, my goodness, what a lovely surprise thank you so much. What a gentleman you are,' she said, sitting up. She savoured the tea. 'Mmmm, I love a cup of hot tea first thing in the morning dear.'

He sat watching her drink, occasionally pausing to give him a lovely smile. It made him feel so good, for a moment he forgot why he was with her.

She placed the cup and saucer on the bedside table and lay back in the bed smiling up at him. 'Thank you my gallant knight, no one has ever done this for me before. Kim Anh is such a silly girl to give you up...oh, I am so sorry,' she said, quickly realizing how insensitive her words were.

He waved away her apology. 'Please don't be Hoa, I just want to thank you for last night. I needed someone and you were the perfect person, I am very grateful,' he said sincerely, but his expression and tone couldn't hide the depth of his sadness.

She looked at him with sympathy she hadn't felt for anyone in a long time. This was a *good* man. He didn't deserve to be hurt by some capricious woman. Inwardly she was surprised. Kim Anh seemed neither capricious nor shallow. There had to be a very valid reason for the change in her behaviour toward Conway.

What she had observed was a lovely, quiet, provincial girl who was probably subject to strong family pressure not to become involved with a foreigner. Sadly, as she had told him, this situation was not uncommon in cross cultural relationships in Vietnam.

'I should thank you Steve Conway. It has been a long time since I was with a man.' She looked away then up at him again and there were tears in her eyes. 'You were so gentle and tender you made me feel like a real woman again.'

He smiled at that. 'Hoa, you *are* a beautiful woman, it's not flattery...it's the truth. I simply can't understand why you are still single.' He glanced at his watch. 'I better go and oh, by the way,' he gave a wry smile. 'You didn't get around to telling what that information was you had for me.' She slipped out of bed, put on a robe and walked out to the front door with her arm around him.

'Oh please forgive me. After what happened it completely slipped my memory. I have a few appointments so please give me a call in a few days dear and I will tell you over lunch. You can be sure, I will certainly do all I can to help you. In the meantime, if you want to talk again, I am here for you.' He gave her a peck on the cheek. 'You are a real gem lovely lady, see you soon.'

He caught a passing taxi and as the cab pulled away he turned and looked back to see her small figure still standing at the door waving until she was lost in the heat haze of the Saigon morning.

* * *

Kim Anh took several days off work after the incident with Dung. She lay on her bed weeping for much of the time. She kept reliving the horror of the night in his apartment and the terrible mistake she now realized she had made. Cultural compatibility, family unity and keeping the peace could not forgive what he had done and to hell with his wealthy family. It might have been acceptable in the past for Vietnamese men to beat their women, but not in this day and age.

The hate in his eyes terrified her but what was far worse and unforgivable; he had taken her virginity. He had raped her. There was no other word for it. An extremely conservative girl, she had kept herself waiting for the right man and now Dung had ensured no respectable Vietnamese man would ever want her. Conway to his credit had promised never to dishonour her. He had kept his promise and she had thrown his love away.

She began to cry again. She had said nothing to Ngoc who believed her sister was down with the flu and continued to waltz around the house smiling and asking when she and Dung were going to set a date for the wedding. Kim largely ignored her and stayed in her bedroom trying to hide her misery, only coming out occasionally for meals.

What was she to do? To call off the engagement would mean a huge loss of face for Dung and his family, and hers. It would cause a terrible hullabaloo and the reaction of friends and colleagues was not worth thinking about. I should have become a nun, at least one has peace, spiritual, physical and emotional....She fell asleep praying for an answer.

* * *

Conway was still in shock several days later. Mrs Thanh had waddled up to him smiling and asking if he and Kim would come to dinner on Saturday but he mumbled something about *not being sure,* and left her standing open-mouthed at his door.

He couldn't think about his work. He was unable to sleep and found himself drinking beer in the early hours of the morning staring out into the darkness of a sleeping city, broken hearted, disillusioned. He kept seeing Kim on the arm of that fat little man. And the engagement ring! How could it happen in such a short time?

He simply could not get his head around the situation. He had been head over heels in love with Kim Anh. To think she had done this to him after the sweetness of their relationship was beyond his capacity to understand. His only conclusion was that she had betrayed him and had been carrying on with this guy behind his back. A slow burning anger inside him began to build.

One morning he remembered Mr Loc and phoned Michael at the Le Le Hotel and asked him to contact Mr Tam. He wanted to visit his old friend again and hopefully see Mai. It might help to take his mind off the situation for a while. The hotel manager promised to have Mr Tam contact him as soon as possible.

Twenty four hours later Conway was seated in Mr Tam's battered old chariot as it rattled and backfired its way out of Saigon bound for Mr Loc's village. 'I must be a glutton for punishment,' he smiled to himself as they turned south from Thu Duc towards Baria/Vung Tau.

His thoughts drifted back to the last time he had taken this journey. What a difference! Then, he couldn't wait to return to Saigon, because she was there waiting for him…with love. Now incredibly, in the space of a few short weeks she had left him and become engaged to another man. What a fool I was. I believed her love was deep, honest and true. He couldn't make sense of it all. So many questions all without answers, threatened to drive him crazy.

* * *

Mr Tam dropped him off at the same spot and lit a cigarette. 'I wait for you sir,' he said as Conway headed off across the rice paddies. The same group of men hadn't moved from where Conway had last seen them sitting outside the small, tin-roofed cafe. They were still gossiping, drinking and eating, except this time there were nods and smiles of recognition. The scholar rose from a small rickety table and left his bowl of *Pho*, hand outstretched to Conway.

'Welcome sir,' he said, in heavily accented English, 'nice to see you again.' Mai must have been giving him English lessons thought Conway, shaking his hand.

'Miss Mai?' asked Conway.

'Mr Steve how wonderful of you to come back to us,' cried a familiar voice. He swung around to see a delighted Mai running toward him with arms outstretched, her unfettered, long, black hair swinging freely in the afternoon sun. He'd rarely seen a more beautiful and welcoming smile. She seemed slimmer, darker, indicating long hours out in the fields but if anything, she looked even more beautiful. She ran into his arms. 'You do not know how happy I am to see you again.'

'The feeling is mutual Mai, you look lovely, how is your life, and how is my friend Mr Loc?' She stiffened. From the look in her eyes he knew.

'Mr Loc died two weeks ago,' she said softly.

'I'm so sorry Mai.' He rested her head on his chest.

She stepped back still holding his hands. 'Would you like to see his grave?'

'Yes, I would.'

She led him away from the village along a track into the jungle. A green canopy shielded them from the burning heat until fifteen minutes later they emerged into a peaceful glade.

They walked across to a small, rectangular upraised mound beneath a spreading tamarind tree on the far side. It was bordered by white washed stones and at the head stood a simple white cross. Fresh flowers adorned the grave. They stood, heads bowed in prayer.

'He was a nice man I liked him very much,' Conway said. She looked up at him tears rolling slowly down her cheeks.

'He liked you too Mr Steve. He often spoke of you with affection. "Australians very good",' he used to say. 'He was so happy after your last visit. Mr Steve, he was very kind, he was like a father to me, I miss him so much.'

They strolled slowly back to the village and sat at the little café eating and drinking the dark, sweet Vietnamese coffee. She asked him about his work in Saigon but he was more interested in what she intended to do in future.

'Your English is very good Mai, have you ever thought about going to Saigon to look for work?'

She put down her chopsticks and dabbed her lips with a tissue. 'Yes, but I have no money and I don't know anyone there, my only relatives are in the central highlands.' She placed some more lemongrass into her *Pho* and deftly lifted another mouthful of noodles to eat before continuing.

'Mr Steve I would like to take a course in office work but how does a country girl with no knowledge of the city begin? What is your advice please Mr Steve?'

'Get me a pen and paper Mai. I think I know someone who can help you.'

She turned and said a few words in Vietnamese to an elderly man behind the counter. He rummaged around and produced a worn ball point and a crumpled piece of white paper. Conway scribbled something and handed it to Mai.

'This is the name, phone number and address of a very good friend of mine, a Mrs Linh. She is a good woman, I'm sure she will help you find work. I will speak to her when I go back to Saigon and tell her to expect a call or better still, a visit from you, ok?'

'Oh, oh, Mr Steve.' She looked down at the piece of paper and back at him, her eyes shining. 'I don't know what to say, you will make me cry again.'

He stayed until sunset. She put her hand in his and walked with him to the outskirts of the village where they had said their goodbyes on the previous visit. They stood in awkward silence not knowing how to say goodbye. They both knew that this could be the last time they would ever see each other.

The rays of the setting sun behind her created an almost ethereal halo around her heart-shaped face framed by her shoulder length, blue black hair. The large almond eyes were brimming with tears. He gently placed both hands either side of her face and kissed her tenderly.

Unlike the last time when she was totally unprepared, now she held him tightly and met his kiss with passion. It was several minutes before they broke away. She stood looking up at him, her breasts heaving.

'I have never met a man like you before,' she gasped. 'I don't know if you have a woman, but if you do not, I hope you will keep a place in your heart for me. I will pray that we will meet again one day.'

He looked down at this beautiful Vietnamese girl; so innocent, so genuine, so good and kind, so utterly without pretension. He pulled her to him again and held her for a moment unable to speak. This was heart wrenching. He had been betrayed by the woman he loved and here in his arms was someone so sincere, why had it not been Mai...?

'I hope so too,' he replied stroking her hair. 'I also hope that one day you will find a good man. A man who will love and cherish you and give you the happiness you deserve Mai. And yes, there will always be a place in my heart for you.' He kissed her again. She stood watching until he disappeared into the gathering dusk then walked slowly back to the small thatched hut she once shared with Mr Loc.

* * *

Kim Anh was dreading returning to work. She knew there would be another confrontation with Dung. He had not been in touch, possibly ashamed of his behaviour and she was enormously relieved to find he had gone to Da Nang on business for several days. Fortunately, her family was in bed, when she arrived home that night after the terrible incident with Dung.

She had violently refused his offer of a lift home. After what he had done how could he think she would still want to be in his presence? She had dressed quickly and panic-stricken, rushed out into the darkened street.

She looked back fearing he had followed her but there was no movement or sign of him. She began to run and hadn't gone more than fifty yards when to her relief, a taxi came from an adjoining street. Frantically she had waved him down and fell into the back seat gasping, 'Thanh Da... please...hurry!'

* * *

She sat at her computer her head in turmoil trying to figure out what to do. Dung's actions were unforgivable, but then a strange feeling came over her. Was it really all his fault?

Conway had confronted them and caused a great loss of face for Dung. He was her fiancé; she should have stood by him. If anyone was to blame, it was her! She had hurt Dung. She had hurt Conway and caused great pain to both of them. But please God, I never meant to. Why do relationships have to be so complicated and painful?

She was so confused. Why did Conway have to come back? What a shock it was to see him in the Caravelle, of all places in Saigon, why did he have to be there that night? She would have met him sooner or later and explained everything. Sure, it would have been painful for both of them but Conway was a mature person, he would have understood, wouldn't he? Oh what a mess! The awful part of this whole fiasco was the realization that she knew she still loved the Australian, but it was too late. Despite what Dung had done, she had made her commitment.

And there was something else. Whatever happened, she could not continue to work in the same company with him. While all these thoughts rushed around in her brain, it started to rain, a monsoon storm.

Thunder boomed and the sky was ripped with frightening, jagged flashes of lightning and fierce winds began to buffet the wooden admin building. The heavens opened and onto the tin roof thundered rain so heavy staff had to shout at each other to be heard.

Pandemonium reigned. As one, they all stopped work and rushed around frantically closing windows as the tempest blew documents from desks and rain poured in threatening to damage furniture, phones, computers and other electrical equipment.

Kim ran to Dung's office closing the windows and drawing the curtains. The wind had blown a correspondence tray from his desk and the floor was littered with invoices, advertising brochures, memos and other sundry documents. She knelt down and began to scoop them up and put them back in his tray.

One of the last items was a blank, white envelope which had been torn open. She stared at it for a few moments and a light came on in her head. She glanced back into the general office to see if anyone was looking in her direction but they were all too busy closing other windows, picking up material from the floor, rearranging their desks and mopping up rainwater.

She opened the envelope and took out two sheets of white paper. One was an invoice for repairs to a motor vehicle, the other a note addressed to Dung. As she read her eyes opened wide with horror and disbelief.

It was a request for Dung to pay for the attached invoice and an apology for not being able to "finish the transaction" and a regret that *your fee is non-refundable*. But it was the last sentence that was the source of her horror and the sickening realization of what the note represented.

I too would want to eliminate any foreigner who tried to take my woman, but you got her in the end my friend so it all ended in your favour.

It was signed by Lan.

She felt sick and her hands began to shake. She remembered the word "Conway" during the conversation between Dung and Lan's driver and this was the envelope she had seen handed to Dung that day.

She read the letter again and the terrible truth dawned on her. The hit run was no accident! Dung had tried to kill Steve Conway and had hired Lan or one of his men to do the job. She took the envelope back to her desk on unsteady legs and sat with her head in her hands. How much more can I take? Conway's return, Dung's brutality and now this…but through the pain and haze, a plan began to formulate.

At lunch when the staff filed out to the canteen she photocopied both documents, folded the originals carefully and put them back in the envelope and placed it in Dung's intray ensuring it was near the bottom, well hidden by other material. Then she wrote a letter of resignation, effective immediately and placed it on the Director's desk.

* * *

The day after his visit to Mai, Conway phoned Mrs Linh and arranged to meet the elegant Vietnamese woman for lunch and discuss the information she had regarding a site for the Down Under. She listened carefully to

Conway's glowing character reference of Mai and assured him she would look after the young provincial girl when she came to Saigon.

'Your recommendation is good enough for me, Steve. Miss Mai sounds like a true Vietnamese girl and I would be delighted to assist her to find a job and help fund her studies. In return she could help with some duties around my home and I could do with some companionship.' She gave an uncharacteristically girlish giggle. 'Ha ha ha, maybe, I would prefer your companionship instead.'

'That might just be an offer I can't refuse,' laughed Conway, 'but thank you Hoa, I know you will love Mai, she's a real gem.' He had hardly replaced the receiver when the phone rang again. He picked it up to hear the deep voice of Jumbo Keyes.

For a moment Conway thought, trouble, but Keyes allayed his fears immediately with his cheerful tone. 'How goes it in Ho Chi Minh land boss? I just wanted to catch up to see if you were behaving yourself,' he chuckled.

Conway was puzzled. Why Keyes had rung so soon? He's possibly concerned about my welfare but I know there's something else. The big man then revealed the true purpose of his call.

'How is Kim Anh buddy, have you patched things up?'

Conway told him of the incident in the Caravelle and from the long silence on the other end it was obvious his friend was gobsmacked. When he had recovered the power of speech all Keyes could say was, 'Jesus Christ, she moves quick doesn't she?'

'That's an understatement! There must have been things going on behind the scene I wasn't aware of. I know there was family pressure but it simply blew me away to see her with this creep. And when I saw the engagement ring, it was just too much…'

'Shit yeah Steve! I don't know what I would have done in the circumstances but murder comes to mind.'

'It crossed mine too,' Conway said, only half joking.

'So what now boss? The Saigon "Down Under" is it still on?'

'Yes, of course it is, that's what I'm here for. I'm not paid to give up just because a local floozy gives me the flick.' He regretted his words as soon as he uttered them.

'Ah, I shouldn't speak about her like that. I really loved that lady. She might be many things but she sure isn't a floozy.'

'Steve you wouldn't be human if you weren't bitter, buddy, I know how much you cared for her. By the way I just remembered something that might cheer you up. Take heart buddy, you're still in demand. Sally came to the hotel and left a present for you before she returned to Isabella and the redoubtable Lily Li phoned me and wants your address and phone number.'

'I hope you didn't give it to her.'

'No way! I told her I would have to clear it with you. After the Marvin debacle, all staff were issued a memo telling them that your whereabouts are not to be disclosed to anyone at anytime and to do so, means instant dismissal.'

'Good. Right now I don't want to see Lily or any other female socially. I have a good contact here now and she and I will have lunch today, strictly business. She has a site she thinks might be just what we are looking for.'

Conway asked about several operational matters then finished the call. He glanced at his watch. James Sinclair would be up and about but I better wait until I've heard what Hoa has to say before I phone him.

He made a couple of phone calls to Vietnamese contacts he'd been given but one was out of the country and the other was in hospital after a motor bike accident. He looked to the heavens. 'It just ain't my week is it God?'

* * *

Kim sat at dusk beside the river reading the note again and again. With each reading the sicker and angrier she became. It was now obvious what she had to do. She had no choice but to bite the bullet and call off the engagement and the first thing she had to do was show this note to Ngoc. She steeled herself for the upheaval to follow, and wasn't disappointed.

Ngoc at first refused to believe the note referred to Dung. Kim had to sit her down and firmly explain the entire circumstances. She told an increasingly amazed Ngoc of the hit run which she now knew was an attempt on Conway's life, and of the exchange between Dung and Lan's driver.

'For God sake *chi oi,* Steve could have been killed and this note tells it all. I saw this being given to Dung with my own eyes,' she said desperately. 'Look what it says on the bottom!' She snatched the paper from Ngoc and thrust it back under her nose, her finger stabbing at the last sentence. Ngoc reluctantly read it again.

'Now,' Kim pleaded, 'take your head out of the sand for once and don't be so pig headed! This man paid someone to kill Steve Conway. It failed but it is attempted murder! I will not marry this man and I do not care what you, mother, or anyone else says, it is over! Do you hear me...over!'

Ngoc stood up her face sullen. 'So now you will go back to the foreigner!' She spat the words. Kim went to the kitchen and stood with her back to Ngoc both hands on the sink in front of her.

Then she turned and raised her fist. 'You caused this! You never wanted me with Steve, you and your stupid Vietnamese culture, your inbred hatred of foreigners. He never did anything to hurt you,' she shouted. 'He treated you with a respect you *never* deserved! I hate you!'

Ngoc stood rooted to the spot white faced and trembling, she'd never seen Kim in such a rage. 'You didn't care about me,' she continued. 'It was you, you! It had to be your way! You wanted Dung because of his rich family. Your objection to Steve had nothing to do with culture. You just wanted to get out of this rathole. You didn't want me to marry Conway because you thought we would go to Australia and you would still be stuck in this rotten dump!'

'You are wrong! Wrong!' Ngoc screamed. 'You do not know how foreigners live and how unfaithful and uncaring they are. They think we are shit! Do you know why our mother was so against you and Conway?'

Ngoc didn't wait for a reply. 'She once loved a foreigner, an American who promised her the world. And do you know what happened?' Ngoc took a step toward Kim and raised her own fist. 'He got her pregnant and one day he went away and never came back. He left her penniless. He left her...and the baby died at birth!' She glared at Kim her face flushed and twisted in rage the equal of her younger sister. 'And something you never knew *em oi.* I too had foreign boyfriends and all they wanted to do was fuck me!' she said viciously. 'You can have your foreigner for all I care and I will never speak to you again!'

Both women stood chest to chest. For the first time in their lives, these two who had always lived for each other, were within an instant of coming to blows. Kim stepped back and lowered her voice. 'At least Steve Conway never raped me.'

Ngoc's mouth dropped open and her eyes widened in disbelief. 'What! What! Rape! What are you talking about?' She went pale struggling to grasp what she had just heard.

'Dung raped me.'

'What! I don't believe you! You are making this up! He would never do that!'

Kim pushed her down onto a chair. 'Shut up! Shut up! For once Ngoc just listen to me!'

Kim related the episode at the Caravelle and what happened afterward at Dung's apartment. She went into detail, leaving out nothing, emphasizing the brutality of Dung's attack.

When she had finished Ngoc sat slumped in the chair. She held her head in her hands and began to weep, her shoulders heaved with great wracking sobs. Kim put an arm around her shoulders.

'You don't have to worry about Conway. He will never take me back now.'

'Oh I am so sorry my darling sister,' Ngoc cried, pulling Kim down onto her bosom. Tears flowed in a torrent from both of them for many minutes. Then the anger and hate drained away and all that remained was their innate love for each other and hatred for the man who had dishonoured Kim Anh and their family. Ngoc took Kim's hands in hers.

'You cannot marry Mr Dung now…I will stand by you.'

Kim breathed a huge sigh of relief and hugged her. 'Oh thank you so much. I need you now more than I have ever needed you. I will have to tell him and I know it will cause terrible trouble, so please, please help me through this awful time.'

'Do not worry little sister, I will explain to our mother and the other relatives and friends. What we have to do is decide where and when to tell this man he will never be part of our family.'

24

Conway strolled along Le Loi Street deep in thought. Mrs Linh had dropped him off on her way home after they had visited a site she had in mind for the Down Under. It was a run-down three story apartment in District 4. The basic structure was sound and there was plenty of room for a bar cum restaurant on the ground floor and accommodation on the top floors, but Conway had reservations.

The Chinese owner Mr Chen haggled about the lease. Conway wanted a minimum of 15 years with an option to renew because the property would require a substantial amount of capital for renovation to bring it to a standard capable of satisfying foreign tourists. Mr Chen shook his head and mumbled, 'ten years, maybe.'

Then there was the question of the cost of the lease right and monthly rental which staggered Conway. He wished he'd sent Hoa to negotiate alone. Too often he'd seen this problem before in negotiations in regard to property involving foreigners. The foreigner appeared; and the price suddenly jumped.

The main drawback in the Australian's eyes was the location. Tucked away behind a number of tower blocks, the street was narrow and dimly lit, hardly appealing to foreign tourists. It was also an unacceptable distance from the central business district and tourist enclaves of District 1 and Pham Ngu Lao. Somewhere in Thi Sach or Thai Van Luong in District 1 would be much more suitable. Still, to date his search hadn't turned up much so it had to be considered.

These thoughts were spinning around in his head when from behind, he heard the high pitched cries of a Vietnamese female. He took no notice until the voice suddenly changed into English. 'Stop thief! Stop! Stop that man!'

He spun around and racing toward him through the lightly crowded sidewalk was a skinny, barefoot youth wearing a black tee shirt and jeans. In his right hand he carried a white handbag. The handbag's owner was well back waving her arms frantically. The youth sidestepped and weaved through startled small groups of tourists and locals, bumping them out of the way in his haste to escape. Nearing Conway he accelerated and swerved to his right seeking a passage through a gap between the Australian and the marble wall of a tower block.

In his rugby league playing days Steve Conway had earned a fearsome reputation as a crash tackling inside centre. This situation didn't call for such violent action, perhaps something more subtle, but just as effective. As he came level, Conway took a small step to his left and thrust his hip into the side of the youth. His timing was perfect. The gentle nudge was enough to unbalance the thief and propel him sideways into the rock hard wall in a tangle of arms and legs. He cannoned off the wall and skidded face first along the sidewalk. The handbag flew from his grasp and Conway scooped it up in one motion and made a grab for the youth. But fear lent wings to the kid. He was up in an instant and off like a jackrabbit out of sight around the corner into Nguyen Hue.

Conway turned as a breathless woman appeared at his side, her breasts heaving with exertion. It took her a good minute before she recovered enough to speak, but he recognized her immediately. It was Juliette, the beautiful French/Vietnamese owner of the restaurant he and Malone had visited the night of the hit run accident.

'Thank you, thank you so much sir, these damn thieves in this town, they drive me crazy,' she gasped as Conway handed her the handbag.

When she had caught her breath she said. 'Excuse me sir, but your face is somehow familiar?'

'I ate at your restaurant some weeks ago, nice food, great service,' he smiled. She looked at him more closely and recognition dawned. 'Ah, yes, I remember you now sir, you were with another man that night, am I right?'

'You have a good memory,' smiled Conway. 'Yes a friend of mine, another Australian, a Mr Malone.'

'Oh yes, I have seen him there before. So, you are Australian? I have many Australian guests in my restaurant from the embassy, local Australian businessmen and of course tourists. May I have your name please sir?'

'Steve, Steve Conway and I know your name, Juliette.'

'Oh, aha, you know my name,' she said in a wonderful French lilt.

'Yes, I have to admit my friend Mr Malone told me,' grinned Conway.

'Oh, so you were interested in me no?' she smiled impishly.

'Er, well, as much as I am interested in any beautiful woman Juliette,' he replied, a little wrong footed by the French woman's direct manner and self assurance but an assurance by no means offensive. He found it refreshing and captivating.

'That is very gallant,' she said with the accent on the last syllable, 'Mr Conway…'

'Steve please, may I call you Juliette?'

'Steve, yes of course you may. What I wanted to say was that you have done me a great service by stopping that bad boy.' She held up her bag. 'This contains so much that is valuable and would take a lot of replacing, some of it personal and simply irreplaceable.'

'I thought all women carried in those things were lipstick, powder and the kitchen sink,' laughed Conway.

'Oh you are a joker Mr Steve.' Her face lit up with that megawatt smile he remembered.

'Seriously though, I have the usual, money, credit cards, licences, etc., but there are also personal business documents and my grandmother's wedding ring. It is a family heirloom beyond price, so you see I have much to thank you for Steve.'

'Glad to be of service Juliette. I love this city but you are right. These damn young thieves; you can't drop your guard for a moment.'

'Yes,' she sighed, 'I am sorry to say that is true. Now, Steve, I want to offer you a little more than a simple thanks...I want you to have a meal at my restaurant free of charge but, I hope it will be soon because I have the place on the market. I shall be returning to France when it is sold.'

'Thanks that's very kind of you Juliette but that won't be necessary, I'm just happy you recovered your bag.' He turned to leave but she reached out and touched his arm.

'Please, do you have a few minutes? I have given myself the night off, the least I can do is buy you a coffee.'

'I was crazy to reject your first offer for sure I'm not going to pass up the second. I know a nice place on Nguyen Hue, why don't we go there?'

'Lead me to it my charming knight,' she said, linking her arm through his. A few minutes later they sat facing each other across a small round table in *El Primo, a* crowded, dimly lit, Italian style coffee shop on Nguyen Hue, not far from Saigon Port.

Despite the crowd the service was quick. A pretty young waitress in a white ruffled blouse and ankle length, black skirt, brought two cups of espresso and a plate of pastries.

'*Sante,*' said Conway raising his cup in a toast. 'To you my saviour,' replied the French woman graciously. They gazed at each other for a few moments saying nothing. She took a sip of her coffee, eyeing him from over the rim of her cup. 'Steve, may I ask, what are you doing here in Saigon? I presume you are here on business and not on an extended holiday...mai oui?'

Conway briefly explained his purpose and that he had just come from visiting a prospective site. 'That's quite a coincidence,' said the French woman, 'As I told you my restaurant is up for sale, would you be looking for something like it, or...?'

He shook his head, 'No, I'm sorry Juliette, your place is very elegant and has wonderful atmosphere but we are interested in a larger site which will allow accommodation. We are looking to replicate our Manila operation which has accommodation, bar/restaurant, travel agency, effectively a one-stop shop for travellers.'

She nodded and nibbled a pastry. 'I understand and wish you well. It sounds the kind of operation that could be successful here.' She took a sip of her coffee. 'I hope you do not think I am presumptuous but …may I ask you a personal question Steve?'

Conway grinned. He knew what was coming. 'Be my guest.'

The deep sea-green eyes twinkled, 'you are a handsome man, and I can see, quite a gentleman, there must be someone special in your life non?' He looked down at the table for a moment and back at her.

'There was.' It was impossible to miss the pain in his eyes.

'Oh I am sorry cherie,' she said, reaching across and touching his hand.

'Don't be Juliette. I guess it happens to all of us at least once in our lives. Would you care for another coffee?' he asked, indicating his tiny cup was empty. She nodded, 'yes please.'

He ordered another two and looked into those beautiful eyes. 'I doubt you would have had any disappointments in love?' The question was probably rhetorical. The thought of any man rejecting this stunning creature seemed beyond comprehension.

She sipped the last of her coffee and looked at her cup for a few seconds before carefully placing it down in front of her. 'Have I been disappointed in love?' she repeated the question then paused and grimaced. 'Yes…I have lost in love, more than once, it is the worst pain one can experience.' There was a long silence. She sat nursing her cup. The twinkle in her eyes had been replaced by a faraway look.

'There was someone, a long time ago in Paris,' she said, her voice barely above a whisper. 'I was just eighteen and he, nineteen. We were so much in love, oh, we had wonderful dreams, there was talk of marriage, but we knew we were too young. We had no money, only our dreams. We were both at the Sorbonne and life was a mad mixture of long days of study and equally long nights of fun, but there is always a price to pay isn't there Steve?'

Conway nodded.

'Of course, it was too good to last and then one day,' she took a deep breath, 'I missed my period. A doctor confirmed I was pregnant. I was distraught, we'd been so careful. The shame, the social and family implications in those days, was too terrible to contemplate.'

'What happened?' he asked gently.

'I had an abortion, but by then he had run away and joined the Foreign Legion; so much for love,' she said bitterly. 'Then there was an affair with a married man. Of course I didn't know he was married until his wife appeared at a restaurant one night and caused a scene. Oh yes, I've been hurt Steve, and I still carry the pain; and you? What happened with you dear Steve? I find it hard to imagine a woman would reject you.'

The waitress arrived with their fresh coffee. He waited until she had served them before replying.

'Thanks but they seem to find it pretty easy. It's not the first time and probably won't be the last. I was never very good at the game of love. I don't want to go into all the gory details but essentially it seems to have been a culture thing. Her family, from the north, conservative, wanted her with a Vietnamese; there was a guy in the wings, bye bye Steve. That's it in a nutshell.'

She nodded sagely. 'You have to be very careful when choosing a woman in this country.'

'Tell me about it.'

She leaned across and put her hand on his, her face only a few inches away, her perfume subtle and intoxicating, like the woman herself.

'I have heard your sad story more than once before here in this country, but,' she said brightening up, 'let's not speak of lost love. The world is a wonderful place and there are millions of beautiful women out there who would love to put their slippers beneath your bed.'

He joined in her laughter then glanced down at his watch.

'You are wonderful company Juliette and I have enjoyed this very much, but I have an early start, tomorrow.'

'I have enjoyed it too, and yes I have to call in on my restaurant before I go home. Where do you live Steve?'

'Nguyen Sieu, two minutes walk from your restaurant.'

'Oh wonderful, we can walk together, you can protect me again.'

They said goodbye outside the alley that led to his apartment. As she was about to leave, on an impulse she took his hand and kissed him on both cheeks. 'Thank you for a lovely night Steve. I am so happy that bad boy tried to steal my bag…please will you come to see me again?'

'Of course I will, but there is a question I have been meaning to ask you. The ring on your left hand, it's a wedding ring?'

She held up her hand. 'My late husband, I never take it off. He was a good man, and like you with your girlfriend, I miss him terribly.'

'Juliette, there is one more thing…'

'What is that my dear?' she asked, still holding his hand.

'You said you would return to France, when you sold your restaurant.'

'Yes, that is my plan.'

'Will you ever return to Vietnam?'

'Oh yes, this is my home now. I shall only return to France to visit my parents, they are now very old and I have not seen them for a very long time.' She looked at him shrewdly. 'You would like me to come back cherie?'

'Yes I would…very much. I am not sure if I will still be here but certainly I do not want to lose touch.' It was his turn to be impulsive. He took her in his arms and held her close. She didn't resist. The temptation to kiss her was almost overwhelming but he stepped back.

'Good night Juliette.'

They stood for a few moments staring at each other. She smiled and squeezed his hands.

'Good night my dear Steve.' He stood watching till she was at the corner of Nguyen Sieu and Thi Sach where she turned and blew him a kiss. He lifted his arm to wave but she was gone.

* * *

'What is this nonsense?' Dung screamed down the phone line. Kim allowed him to continue raving and said nothing. 'I arrive back at work and find you have resigned! What is this? You did not tell me before. What is your explanation? We have to talk.'

'Yes, you are right, we have to talk. We must meet now. I have things to say to you,' she said calmly. Her reaction surprised him. Her tone was cool, no fear, no remorse, she seemed different.

He paused then continued his tirade. 'Yes we will talk today and you can give me an explanation. You know I must be consulted about these things and…'

She cut him off. 'I want you to come to my house tonight and we can discuss everything, 7.00 pm,' she said hanging up. She smiled to herself. He would hate what she just did.

There would be fireworks tonight.

Dung arrived a few minutes before 7.00 pm. He jumped off his motorbike and stormed towards Kim's apartment. He'd been seething all day after the phone call. He was not going to tolerate such behaviour and she better have a good excuse.

A few metres from her front door he was surprised to see a grim-faced Kim emerge, flanked by her equally grim-faced family. In her hand she held what looked like note paper.

Something was wrong. He didn't like the expressions on all of their faces. This was not the welcome he was used to, especially from Ngoc, his great ally, who if anything, looked the grimmest of all.

'Stop there,' commanded Kim. He opened his mouth to say something when Kim thrust the piece of paper under his nose. 'Explain this.'

'What? What is this?' he said, snatching it from her. He began to read his eyes widening and by the time he'd finished the colour had drained from his face.

'What is this?' he repeated, licking his lips nervously. 'I don't know...'

'You should know...it's addressed to you, you...' said Kim, her voice shaking with rage.

'I...er...do not know what this is, where did you get this?' he stuttered. The hands holding the paper trembled.

'This is a copy of the note Lan's driver gave to you at Waterworld. I saw him give it to you, but you...you did not see me, you low life scum,' she shouted. Dung took a step backwards, his knees shook and his bladder opened. He felt a warm trickle down the inside of his trouser leg.

For a moment he thought she was going to hit him. His mouth opened and closed but no words would come. Finally he regained a little composure and tried to take the initiative.

'I do not believe you. I do not know where you got this from or what you are trying to do. You are my fiancée let us discuss this somewhere in private,' he said waving his arms. 'There seems to be a misunderstanding.'

She shook her head violently. 'There is no misunderstanding in these words Dung.'

I too would want to eliminate any foreigner who tried to take my woman but, you got her in the end my friend, so it all ended in your favour,...and...your fee is non-refundable. 'It is all there, Dung. It was you, you! who tried to kill Steve Conway! I cannot believe it! You even paid someone to do it and you are a rapist as well. I hate you! I hate you! I hate you!' she screamed.

Dung stood frozen with shock. 'But...but...I...I...' he stuttered. 'You are my fiancée, don't you see I love you, I love you Kim Anh. I did it for you. You would never be happy with a foreigner, only I...'

'You are not my fiancé, not any more,' shouted Kim taking off the engagement ring and hurling it at his feet. 'There! That is where it belongs, in the dirt with you, you bastard!' Then she broke down.

Ngoc shot Dung a look of pure hatred. 'Come *em oi*,' she said, putting her arm around her weeping sister's shoulder guiding her back inside the house.

'Please,' cried Dung, attempting to follow them, but backed off when Ngoc's husband made a threatening gesture.

He stood there wild-eyed then on all fours, scrabbled around in the dirt for the ring. He found it and stood looking at it shaking his head in disbelief. He walked slowly back to his motorbike and looked back as if expecting to see Kim come back out again.

Her front door remained closed. He looked up at their front window on the first floor flinching at the hatred he saw in the eyes of the small group looking down at him. He shook his fist at them, mounted his bike and roared off toward the city.

That night he made a phone call to Lan. 'Can you get me a gun?'

'Yes, I want a gun, and I want it now! I have a score to settle.'

* * *

'Terrific meal Juliette, compliments to the chef,' said a grinning Conway about to leave *Le Figaro*. 'Thank you kind sir,' she replied with a theatrical curtsy. 'You must come again.'

'I will, but on condition you allow me to take you to dinner one night, ok?'

'As you would say dear Steve, an offer too good to refuse,' she laughed. 'Oh, I meant to tell you, I have had a firm offer for this place. A good one, it's now a question of finance which I am assured will be no problem, so I have my fingers crossed it will be soon.'

'How soon?'

'Maybe a week or two.'

He took her hand again. 'I will miss you Juliette.'

'I will miss you too cherie,' she said quietly. 'Let's make that date soon.'

* * *

The night was balmy as he walked back to his apartment, much like the night of the hit run. He stopped at the same spot and looked both ways. There was no black four wheel drive tonight only a couple of motor bikes which he let pass before crossing over. As he climbed the stairs to his apartment he was surprised to see Mrs Thanh standing outside his door.

'Good evening Mr Steve,' she said. 'May I come in and speak to you please?' her tone a little nervous. She was not the jolly lady he knew so well. They went in and he asked her to take a seat on his lounge. She did so and was about to say something but he cut in.

'Mrs Thanh, I am very sorry for not coming to dinner the other night, it was kind of you and I was most impolite, please forgive me.'

She rose from the lounge and took his hand, her round, motherly face serious.

'I understand Mr Steve and...I know why you and Miss Kim Anh did not come to dinner.' His eyebrows shot up.

'You do?'

'Yes, please sit,' she said, taking her place back on the lounge and beckoning him to join her. 'Mr Steve,' she took a deep breath, there was a long pause before she continued. English was not her native tongue and she seemed to be thinking carefully about what to say.

'I have been speaking to Miss Kim Anh and I know everything. She has been with me all afternoon.' She inclined her head as if waiting for his reaction. He said nothing.

'Mr Steve, she told me she thought you had left her and gone back to Manila, never to return and Mr Steve, she did something very stupid. But you must understand her position and our society. Please do not blame her.'

'If you know everything Mrs Thanh,' he said harshly, 'you must know she left me and became engaged to another man as soon as I left Saigon. I am sorry I was unable to tell her why I had to leave in such a hurry, but my God, I am no sooner out of sight than she falls into the arms of another guy, bloody unbelievable!'

'Please, listen to me Mr Steve,' implored the landlady. 'As I said, she thought you had gone out of her life. This other man made her an offer. She loved you Mr Steve and was heartbroken when you left so suddenly. She accepted this man because she just wanted to get married and have a normal life. She admits it was foolish what she said to you before you left and even more foolish what she did afterwards, but it is the simple wish of any girl to settle down and have a family. Can't you see?'

'Of course I see, but why tell me all of this? It's over between us and I have lost her. She is with someone else. I don't need to be reminded.' She patted his hand and said softly, 'it is not over, unless you want it to be over Mr Steve.'

He looked up sharply. 'What do you mean?'

'She still loves you, very much.'

'So what,' he replied bitterly. 'If she loved me she would not have left me for that other guy.'

'She is not with that guy any more.'

'What? Over so quickly?' he sneered, 'she's like a bloody kangaroo.'

'Mr Steve, she found out something terrible about that man. She has parted with him. You should give her a chance to explain.'

'Why the hell should I?' He jumped to his feet and looked down at his sad-eyed landlady. 'You have no idea how much she hurt me, why should I listen to her, let alone forgive her?'

'Because I know I made a big, big, terrible mistake,' said a quiet voice at the door. He whirled around and his mouth dropped open. Standing there, her face drawn and tear stained was Kim Anh. She looked at him and began to cry.

He jumped up and ran across the room and took her in his arms. She leaned into him and put her arms around him sobbing uncontrollably. He was unable to stop tears trickling down his own cheeks. Mrs Thanh rose and quietly went back to her apartment, her face wreathed in a huge smile. Kim Anh did not return to Thanh Da that night.

25

'Penny for your thoughts darling?' asked Conway, as they sat at dinner in *Lemongrass* restaurant off Dong Koi Street in District 1. Kim Anh shook her head and smiled. 'Nothing really darling, I was just thinking how happy I am. It is so wonderful to be with you again, I can't believe I was so stupid.'

'Forget it darling, it's past now. I think it was a lesson for both of us and…' he reached across and put both his hands on hers. 'The next time the Down Under is on fire, I promise you will be the first to know,' he grinned.

'Oh Steve, please don't say that. I don't want your hotel to catch fire and I don't want you to ever leave me again.' A week had passed since that night in his apartment when they had sat up until the early hours talking about recent events and the misunderstanding that had lead to their parting. Now they would start again and this time there would be no talk of "friends".

She had told her family in no uncertain manner that Steve Conway was "the one". Ngoc was reluctant at first to accept this news but warmed after a bouquet of flowers and a visit from Conway. In the end she succumbed to his charms and (to his great relief) gave her blessing to the relationship. Kim's mother was harder to convince so Conway and Kim accompanied by Ngoc, flew to Hanoi and took a local bus to her house in a small village just outside Hanoi.

Kim's mother first looked at the foreigner suspiciously, but turned out to be a sweet, gentle woman who gave Conway her approval following a long animated, round table discussion between herself and her daughters. When she finally turned to the Australian with a wide smile, he knew it was mission accomplished.

Mrs Hoang insisted they stay for dinner and they all dined royally on *Pho, Bun,* rice cakes, spring rolls and tea. The old lady held Conway's hand for a long time when he said goodbye and it was a very happy and satisfied trio who returned to Saigon the following day. Thankfully there had been no sign of Dung and it seemed that he had got the message.

Kim had successfully applied for a job as a secretary with a French company and was to begin at the end of the month. Conway had found a site in District 1 which met all the requirements for a Saigon Down Under Inn and Bar. It would have been impossible to find two happier people in Saigon that night.

He had begun to court Kim Anh in earnest and each time they went out together, he insisted on picking her up from Thanh Da and delivering her home in a taxi despite her protests about the expense.

'No more bumpy motor bike rides for me across that bridge into Thanh Da thank you Miss Kim Anh,' he had joked.

After the meal at *Lemongrass* they joined a large crowd to watch a cultural display of ethnic dancers on the steps of the opera house for a while then strolled down Dong Khoi checking out the elegant boutiques, restaurants and souvenir shops, unaware they were being observed.

After dinner they often went back to his apartment for a quick cuddle before returning to Thanh Da but on this night, he surprised her by hailing a taxi and taking her straight home.

She was puzzled, but sat contentedly holding his hand during a journey taken almost in complete silence. What intrigued her was the smile hovering at the corner of his lips. He was up to something. No doubt all would be revealed in due course.

Another surprise awaited her on arrival at Thanh Da. Instead of giving her a quick goodnight kiss and returning to his apartment, he paid off the driver and led her across the grass verge outside her house to a number of waiting cyclos. Then came surprise number three. He lifted her up into the nearest cyclo and said to the driver. 'Binh Quoi.'

'Darling, what are we doing going to Binh Quoi at this time of night?' she asked, as they rolled slowly down the narrow dark road toward the place that held such a special memory for both of them. He just grinned and said, 'wait and see.'

Except for a few lights in the trees, Binh Quoi was in darkness when they arrived. Perfect thought Conway, it was just the romantic atmosphere he was hoping for. He told the cyclo to wait. Taking Kim's hand he led her into the gardens to the same small bench beside the big brass gong where they had sat and kissed on that wonderful first evening.

It was just as he remembered it. The moon again shone like silver on the same pool; a gentle breeze wafted gently through the trees cooling their cheeks. Anyone observing the scene would see them as two silhouettes facing each other in the moonlight. He took her in his arms and kissed her long and lovingly.

'I never want us to part,' he said softly. 'You are the love of my life, I cannot express in words the love I have for you my darling Kim Anh.' She looked up at him, her eyes shining.

'And you are the love of my life too my darling Steve. I want us to be together…forever.'

'I have something to say to you,' he said, kneeling down in front of her. She looked down at him open-mouthed as he said, 'Miss Kim Anh, will you do me the honour of becoming my wife? I will love, cherish and protect you for the rest of my days.'

'Oh my darling. Yes! Yes! Yes!' she cried, throwing her arms around him as he regained his feet. From his pocket he produced a small square velvet box and opened it. A diamond ring encrusted with sapphires gleamed in the moonlight. He took the ring and gently placed it on the third finger of her left hand. She stood looking at it unable to speak.

At that moment a shot rang out.

The bullet crashed into the side of a palm tree just above Conway's head. Instantly he grabbed Kim and threw her to the ground. Another shot whistled past and tore through bushes beside them. Whoever it was,

was no marksman. He could feel her shaking with fear on the ground beside him. He placed his hand gently over her mouth and whispered. 'Sssshh.'

They had landed beside a small garden bed and as he felt around in the darkness his hand brushed one of the small round stones that bordered the garden. He carefully and quietly gripped the stone, listening for any movement from the shooter.

There was nothing for what seemed like an age then a footstep crunched on the gravel path nearby. It stopped then moved slowly off the path onto the grass in their direction. It was getting closer…too close, but in the darkness Conway was unable to yet make out the location of their attacker.

In the time-honoured manner of the movies he tossed the stone away to his left where it bounced off a palm tree bringing an instant volley of shots. Conway's military experience told him this was no cool professional, but someone inexperienced and panicky.

Kim was still shaking violently beside him, flinching as each shot rang out shattering the eerie silence. Conway threw another rock in the opposite direction. Their attacker whirled around and blasted three shots in the new direction, the the muzzle flash this time, giving away his position.

It was hard to tell but to Conway it sounded like a .357 magnum which he knew held varying numbers of bullets depending on the model. He hoped it was the 8 shot, and if so, it would be now close to empty. The guy might have another clip but if I can just get close enough and jump him before he reloads, thought Conway. But this was all supposition. Attack was now the best form of defence. Conway pushed Kim down and whispered, 'stay.'

He slowly got to his feet, a rock in both hands. He threw one to the left and a few seconds later threw another to the right. Both drew fire until there was a click…the magazine was empty. Conway had seen enough of the gunman's outline now to know exactly where he was…about ten feet away facing the other direction. Conway charged.

He was almost on top of the gunman when he stumbled on the edge of a garden bed, causing the dark figure to turn and whip the weapon in an arc catching Conway across the jaw. He staggered back, his hands to his face and the attacker hit him again and again connecting with each wild swing. Blood spurted from the Australian's nose and one side of his face. He dropped to the ground on all fours and the gunman kicked him hard in the ribs.

He rolled away as another kick aimed for his head missed. He staggered to his feet to be met by another savage blow to the belly and another to the head. He stumbled back his hands up trying to protect himself, but his attacker was frenzied and continued to rain blows on him.

Conway's strength was ebbing fast. He swung in desperation and missed, paying for it with another savage blow to the side of the head which dropped him on his back. He tried to roll away but copped another vicious kick to the side of his body.

As he lay almost helpless, a bolt of lightning lit up the sky followed by a crash of thunder; the unpredictable storms of the Saigon rainy season. The lightning flash identified his attacker...an out of control, wild-eyed Dung! He stood over Conway his eyes blazing. He lifted his boot to smash it into the face of his defenceless foe.

In desperation, Conway reached up and grabbed the descending foot twisting it, throwing Dung off balance. The realization of who was trying to kill him filled Conway with renewed strength and rage. This was the guy who had taken Kim Anh from him and was now doing his best to kill him and probably her as well.

He got to his feet and stood balanced and ready for his foe to come again. As the Vietnamese scrambled to his feet, Conway aimed a kick to the side of his head but didn't quite connect. Dung stood for a moment then rushed at Conway uttering a spine chilling scream.

Conway went into a boxer's crouch with knees slightly bent, and threw a perfect straight left. It smashed into the nose of the onrushing Dung stopping him in his tracks, causing him to stumble backwards as the cartilage in his nose collapsed. But it didn't stop him. He came again, now completely off his head. Conway let him get within a couple of feet then took one step forward and kicked him between the legs. Dung's mouth opened in a silent scream of agony. Conway bent his knees again and threw the best uppercut any boxer ever let go. It straightened the Vietnamese upright, sending him staggering to the edge of the pool where he teetered for a second before falling backwards arms outstretched, down into the murky depths with a loud splash.

Conway got to his feet, looked down and waited. He didn't reappear. Dung was no swimmer.

'Goodbye bastard,' muttered Conway. He went looking for Kim and stepped on the weapon Dung had used. He picked it up and hurled it across into the middle of the pool.

* * *

Dung's body came to the surface several days later to the horror of a courting couple. The police were called but no one knew how he had come to be there and although there were signs of a scuffle, they had no leads and the case became another on the unsolved register. Conway decided not to tell a distraught Kim who tried to kill them. She'd already had enough drama with her ex fiancé.

Not surprisingly, the cyclo driver doubtless hearing the gunshots, had taken off, leaving them to walk most of the two kilometers back to Thanh Da until a taxi returning from dropping off a fare past Binh Quoi, picked them up not far from Kim's house. The driver made no comment at the appearance of the dirty, bloodied foreigner with the shirt almost ripped from his back and his weeping female companion. His only reaction was a smile when they told him the destination. District 1 was a good fare.

Kim in deep shock was in no condition to be taken home. He took her back to his apartment and phoned Ngoc, telling her Kim was not well and he would take care of her for a few days before taking her to Nha Trang for some respite by the sea.

The next morning Conway had his badly bruised ribs strapped and allowed Kim to sleep, which she did for most of the day and night. By the time they flew to Nha Trang on the coast of central Vietnam the following evening, both had recovered somewhat from their frightening ordeal.

Conway's other injuries had begun to heal and Kim Anh's emotions, much to Conway's relief, had settled down considerably.

Now they simply looked forward to enjoying their engagement and to a few days at an upscale hotel beside the golden sands of Nha Trang's beautiful beach.

Weatherwise their luck was in. It was idyllic. Days of blue cloudless skies and nights of gentle tropical breezes made for the perfect romantic getaway. They lazed by the pool, walked hand in hand along the beach on sunset; dined on superb Vietnamese cuisine at great little restaurants and Kim for the first time in her life drank exotic cocktails for which she expressed an instant liking.

At dusk one quiet evening, after a day of sightseeing and shopping, they sat holding hands on the balcony of their hotel, sipping the inevitable cocktail, gazing out to sea watching the fishermen bringing in the day's catch.

'Darling, I have never been so happy in all of my life,' she said, turning to him, her eyes shining in the evening light. He leant over and lightly kissed her cheek. 'Kimmee, I simply do not have the words to tell you how happy I am. I honestly did not think I could ever feel this way again, it's impossible to explain. But, now I know what love is.'

The idyll eventually had to end and it was a reluctant but happy couple who boarded the Vietnam airlines flight back to Saigon several days later.

* * *

Early one morning Conway was woken from a booze induced sleep by the jangling of his ancient telephone. The night before had been a long one in a restaurant in District 3; an all male affair involving much drinking, mostly of beer and some weird local concoctions proffered him by a group of Kim Anh's relatives from Central Vietnam, down to celebrate her engagement.

To say Conway had a raging hangover would be an understatement. 'How can they drink this crap?' he had asked himself as each seemingly endless round was preceded by shouts of "Yo!" the Vietnamese version of "down the hatch".

One particularly evil looking beverage was the blood of a cobra. 'Good for your sex,' a smiling uncle told him with a wink; more likely to ruin it thought Conway, as he struggled not to gag on the warm, thick liquid. The night had ended in the early hours after much singing, patting on the back, hugs and all round bonhomie. Conway could not remember leaving or how he got home. It was both a night to remember and forget.

He stumbled out of bed and picked up the receiver. 'Yeah,' he said wearily.

'Hey Steve, how is my man in Saigon? Bloody hell you don't sound too well my boy,' came the ebullient tones of James Sinclair. Conway closed his eyes for a second.

'Oh Jesus, this is the last person I want to hear from right now,' moaned Conway to himself. Sinclair, never one to beat about the bush, came straight to the point.

'Steve, we're going to have a shareholders' meeting in Manila next weekend. All shareholders have promised to attend. I know you haven't been back in Saigon long but we'd like you to be here and give us an update on the prospects of the operation there. Can do?'

'Sure James,' replied Conway nearly gagging. His head felt like it was about to explode and keeping his voice anywhere near normal was a huge effort. 'Things look promising here and I have some other interesting news for you...but I'll keep it for when I see you in Manila.'

'Mmm, sounds mysterious, good news I hope?'

'I think so James. I'll prepare a report and discuss it with you prior to the meeting, ok?'

'Sure, Steve, see you then mate, bye now,' said the MD hanging up.

No sooner had he put the phone down when it rang again, this time, Kim Anh, her tone frantic.

'Darling, my God, I've just heard about Dung, you knew it was him, who tried to kill us. Why didn't you tell me? We just got a call from his mother. Oh Steve, she's crying so much, it was hard to tell what she was saying at first. Oh it is so terrible...' her voice faded.

'Did you say anything?'

'No, of course not, but I am afraid they will find out, it was you who killed him, oh my God!'

'Calm down. It was self defence Kim, remember that. I can't say for sure but I think this was the second time he tried to kill me. The only one who knows we were at Binh Quoi that night was the cyclo driver and he left anyway. No one deserves to die, but it was him, or us. He would have shot you too, you know that don't you?'

'Yes…I know you are right, but I will have to pay my respects and go to the funeral.'

'I understand that, and in fact I am sure it would be expected. I am sorry but it is something we will just have to deal with and get over ourselves. I am sorry darling but it is best you say nothing. No good will come of telling anyone anything about what happened. Trust me, it is for the best.'

'Yes, ok darling,' she said slowly. 'He really meant to kill us both and I can tell you now that it *was* Dung who tried to run you down that night.'

The one thing she had not mentioned that night in Mrs Thanh's apartment was Dung's attempt on his life in Thi Sach. She now told him how she had found the note from Lan and the events that followed.

He listened without interrupting. When she had finished he lay there shaking his head.

'Ah, so it *was* him after all…and no accident. After what happened at the Caravelle I put two and two together and had him in the frame but couldn't prove it. At first I felt it had to be an accident and yet it seemed so deliberate. But I could never be sure because I couldn't figure out who would want to kill me. I knew no one here but then of course my love, I didn't know you had this paranoid boyfriend.'

'I am so sorry darling. But I agree with you, let us put this terrible time in our lives behind us. My love, I nearly lost you on two occasions and he ruined what should have been the most beautiful night of my life so far, but we still have each other so let's thank God for saving us.'

'It is the only thing to do darling. Now I have some other news for you.' He told her of Sinclair's phone call. 'But don't worry I will only be away for a few days, a week at the latest and when I come back, we can set the date for our wedding, ok?'

'Oh yes my Steve, I will count the minutes you are away from me and in the meantime it will give me time to make plans with Ngoc for our wedding. Do you know darling, she really loves you now?'

'Thank God for that, I thought at one time I would never win her. Ok my beautiful Vietnamese girl, I'd better go and begin this report for Mr

Sinclair, see you tonight. Let's have dinner at the restaurant beside the Ben Thanh market, ok?'

* * *

Conway spent the next few days writing and redrafting his report with facts and figures explaining in detail the viability of the proposed operation and the site he'd found until finally one evening, he put down his pen satisfied that all bases were covered.

'That should give them the picture,' he yawned, getting up from his desk and stretching. He phoned Kim and they had their usual thirty minute conversation spiced with "I love you" before calling it a night.

She came with him in the taxi to the airport on Saturday morning and for the first time allowed him to kiss her in public before he entered the departure lounge. He could still see her through the glass windows waiting and waving frantically as he mounted the escalator to immigration on the first floor. He blew her a kiss and she mouthed 'I love you,' a moment before she was lost to sight.

* * *

He received a great welcome from Sinclair, Keyes and all the shareholders and staff on his arrival in Manila and his presentation to the meeting of the Saigon operation was applauded by all and sundry and declared, "a goer".

That night Sinclair held a dinner in a high class Manila restaurant for the shareholders with Conway and Jumbo Keyes as special guests. The great efforts in Conway's absence of the popular black American had not gone unnoticed. When the meal was finished and most were enjoying a convivial ale, James Sinclair got to his feet and called for silence.

'Our esteemed director and Manila Manager Mr Steve Conway, has a rather important announcement to make,' said a beaming Sinclair. Conway rose, cleared his throat and announced his engagement to Kim Anh. 'The most beautiful girl in all of Vietnam,' he proudly told the gathering

The news was greeted with a spontaneous roar of approval from all present. Among much genuine congratulations, shaking of hands, pats on the back, there was also dire advice and good natured banter from some of the married for the surprised and delighted Conway.

'Make sure you wear the pants mate...another good man lost to the cause,' etc.

Jumbo Keyes in particular was delighted for his friend. Conway had filled him in on what had happened as soon as he returned to Manila otherwise it would have left his assistant manager scratching his head. As far as he knew Kim Anh was engaged to a Vietnamese, the change in circumstances had left him wide-eyed and amazed at first. Now his joy was unbridled.

He gave Conway a massive bear hug and shook his hand until it hurt.

'I couldn't be happier for you man,' he said with Conway's hand gripped in his massive paw. 'I know how much you truly love that girl. I've never seen you so happy Steve. It couldn't happen to a nicer guy. You are the best my man and I can't wait to meet your darling. Please bring her here as soon as you can. We all want to meet her now.'

The outpouring of goodwill and joy was getting to Conway. He was becoming a bit emotional. 'Thanks mate, you and I have been through a lot together Jumbo and I count you as my best friend. Yes, she is something special, you will love Kim Anh...and she will love you too buddy, of that I have no doubt.'

The celebrations continued long into the night until in the early hours Conway collapsed thankfully into the welcoming bed of his Manila apartment.

It seemed his head had hardly hit the pillow when he thought he could hear a phone; must be a dream. It was no dream. He woke, blinked and shook his head. It *was* a phone...his. He dragged himself up and staggered out in the darkness. He had to stop the incessant jangle of the phone it was driving him crazy. I'm going to get this bloody phone put next to my bed when I come back here. Who the hell would be phoning at this time of night?

'Hello, this better not be a wrong number,' was all he got out when through his addled brain, he recognised the voice of Mrs Thanh. She sounded overwrought.

'Sir Steve, Mr Conway, it's me, Mrs Thanh, you must come back to Saigon immediately, please!' He was now instantly awake. A chill ran up his spine. Something was badly wrong.

'Mrs Thanh, what is it? What?'

'Sir Steve, it's Kim Anh, you must come back now, she is very ill. She is in the People's hospital in District 10.'

'What? When? What is wrong with her? Please Mrs Thanh, tell me more,' he pleaded. 'I cannot tell you much but she was admitted to hospital last night with a very high fever. They are not sure what it is yet. Her sister Ngoc phoned me just now and told me to contact you and tell you to come back to Saigon straight away. The doctors say Miss Kim Anh's condition is very, very serious.'

Conway's mouth went dry, his hands began to shake. My God, this kind of illness could be anything, malaria, meningitis, dengue, anything. In Vietnam there were tropical diseases that the West had never seen. Oh God, this sounds bad.

He phoned a groggy Sinclair and explained the situation and got the approval to be on the first flight to Saigon in the morning.

'Steve, I'm shocked to hear this please let me know what happens as soon as you can,' said the managing director, his voice changing from irritation at being woken to one of extreme concern.

At 7.30 am next morning PR 591 with a very worried Steve Conway on board headed for Saigon.

26

Conway's flight arrived at Tan Son Nhat airport just after 10.00 am. Mrs Thanh and Ngoc were waiting and waving frantically at the barrier as he ran from the arrival hall to meet them. They grabbed a taxi and rushed through the heavy morning traffic to a public hospital in District 10.

The first impression of this hospital didn't instill him with a great deal of confidence. It was an old, ramshackle wooden structure in urgent need of renovation. This confidence was further dented as they hurried along corridors with paint peeling from the walls, frayed curtains and the pungent smell of disinfectant and urine. The wards with their old fashioned cast iron beds were clean, but shabby and run down. The whole place exuded an air of despair with families sitting gloomily beside loved ones. It smelled of death.

They were taken to a long narrow ward where Kim Anh lay in a bed at the end near a window. His first sight of her shocked and sickened him. Her usual tanned, healthy complexion was ashen. She wore a simple sleeveless white cotton gown revealing dark red marks which looked like bruises on her uncovered arms. Her eyes lit up as he approached her bed but she could only manage a weak smile. His beloved Kimmee was ill… very ill. He took her hand and leant over and kissed her on the cheek.

'Hello darling, what are you doing, trying to frighten me like this?' He tried to joke but wanted to cry. She smiled wanly, and reached out her left hand, his ring gleaming in the dim light.

'Hello my darling...sorry you had to come back so soon. I...I...didn't want to ruin your meeting.' Her voice was low and ragged. It took an effort for her to speak. It frightened him. She was too sick to engage in a conversation of more than a few words.

A nurse brought him a chair after a sharp few words from Ngoc, and he sat holding her hand. He stayed praying all day and through the long night and the next day. The nurses came frequently to sponge her trying to reduce her temperature. Their faces were sombre and what worried him terribly, was he detected tears in *their* eyes. Not a good sign from people who were often immune to suffering. What did they know they were not telling him?

A tall, thin, white-coated Doctor Tham came to check her temperature, pulse and other signs. He took one of the nurses to one side and spoke quietly to her. She looked across at Kim with a worried expression shaking her head. They continued speaking for another minute then she returned to Kim's bedside, wiped her burning forehead and changed the drip in her arm.

Conway took the doctor aside and tried to ply him with questions but he had little English and it was left to Mrs Thanh to translate. Her condition had them puzzled but the consensus of medical opinion was that Kim had contracted the worst strain of dengue, haemorrhagic fever and her immune system was not coping. Despite their efforts, her condition was deteriorating.

What further frightened Conway was the knowledge that there was no cure for this particular strain which occurred when a victim had been infected more than once. It was known to be often fatal.

'Jesus Christ,' stammered a wild-eyed Conway, 'as far as I know dengue doesn't kill. I know it's bad, and I've heard it called "Breakbone Fever" but here in Vietnam with all the mosquito born diseases, they *must* know how to treat this kind of thing,' he said desperately.

'Yes, they are very experienced with these types of diseases Mr Steve,' replied Mrs Thanh kindly, trying to reassure him. 'It is not usually fatal, but sometimes I'm afraid it can be. She is very sick as you can see, but they are doing all they can for her. Ngoc told me she developed a very high fever one night and vomiting. This was followed by a terrible headache and sore stomach so they rushed her to hospital. She has been given saline drips, medication and has been under constant care. But Mr Steve, we can only pray. She is in God's hands now.'

At a few minutes past 10.00 pm on the fourth evening as an exhausted Conway slumped by her bedside, Kim Anh woke from an intermittent coma, her face and neck shiny with perspiration; her eyes now sunken and glazed. It seemed almost as if she was not aware of her surroundings. She looked terrible. There was no improvement, if anything her condition had worsened. His stomach knotted and he prayed silently, trying not to show her how worried he was. 'Please, please Kimmee, get better...please.'

She reached out weakly and touched his hand. 'My darling, you know you are the love of my life. I love you more than any person I have ever known.' The effort of speaking was now almost beyond her. She closed her eyes for a moment then opened them and looked up at him with an expression of such sadness it made him want to cry out.

'I know I am going to die,' she said in a voice barely above a whisper. It didn't register at first. When it did, he stood up and shook his head wildly.

'No! No! No! Darling, you will not! I will not let you die, please hang in there Kimmee darling, please! You, me, we can beat this! I love you darling, please, don't leave me,' he cried. Tears poured down his face. She gave him a smile he would remember till his dying day and tried to lift her head but the effort was too much. She looked up at him with tears slowly rolling down her pale cheeks.

'Goodbye my darling, *em yeu anh*,' (I love you) she whispered. Then she gave a deep sigh and closed her eyes. Conway screamed. Nurses and doctors came running. But it was too late. Hoang Thi Kim Anh, the love of Steve Conway's life, his soulmate...had gone. A stunned Conway unable and unwilling to accept what had taken place let out a long loud moan more like the wail of a wild animal in distress...'NO! NO! NO! KIMMEE!'

He reached down and pulled her limp body up to his chest. 'OH DARLING, PLEASE DON'T LEAVE ME! DON'T LEAVE ME...

PLEASE!' he bawled, hot tears blinding his eyes and spilling onto her cheeks. He wouldn't let anyone take her from him for many minutes until finally, the kindly Doctor Tham and two nurses eased her from him and gently laid her back down onto the bed.

'I'm so sorry sir,' Doctor Tham said quietly as he covered her still form with a white sheet.

Conway stood staring at the sheet. His whole body was shaking uncontrollably, his chest heaved, tears continued to flow unabated down his cheeks. In a daze he was unable to comprehend the magnitude of the situation. His beloved Kim Anh, his beautiful, wonderful Kimmee was gone…forever.

He would never again see her smile. Never hear her voice, her laughter or her tears. He would never again hold her in his arms and feel the sweetness of her lips. She would never see his face, hear his voice, feel his arms around her, see another sunset, or hear a baby cry. So much they would never again share. He was overwhelmed with unspeakable sorrow and at that moment, something in Steve Conway died.

* * *

Light rain was falling softly from a leaden sky the morning she was laid to rest. It captured the sombre mood of the group who gathered at the graveside in Da Phuoc cemetery south of Saigon. She was buried wearing a white wedding dress, his ring on her finger. Her mother and immediate family, other relatives from north and central Vietnam attended as did friends and colleagues from Waterworld. Mrs Thanh and Mrs Linh were there; even James Sinclair and a distressed Jumbo Keyes flew in from Manila. An utterly broken Steve Conway with head bowed tears rolling down his cheeks, said a short prayer in a halting voice and placed a single red rose on her coffin as it was lowered into the earth.

The world of Steve Conway was destroyed. Consumed with grief he could not function properly. He spent hours sitting alone in his apartment staring at her photo. He had no appetite and stopped eating. He was unable to sleep properly, waking up frequently in the night, crying out her name.

He rarely shaved and his appearance began to change. His face became thin and haggard, the eyes permanently red-rimmed. His clothes hung on him as he started losing weight.

His grief worried Mrs Thanh. She had loved Kim Anh deeply and thought the world of Steve Conway. The kindly landlady brought him food but it was left untouched. She tried to console him but he was inconsolable.

One day when she came with food he looked up at her from his bed and said.

'Why Mrs Thanh? Why did she have to die? She was so young. It's not fair…she had so much to live for! I don't understand Mrs Thanh, why did God take her? She didn't deserve to die! What will I do without her? Life means nothing to me now…' Mrs Thanh placed the bowl of *Pho* by his bedside and left hurriedly, her eyes blinded by tears.

Mrs Linh also visited but fared no better, coming away worried and saddened for a man she had grown to care for, more than he ever knew. In an effort to cheer him up, she said Mai had now come to live with her and had been enrolled in one of the best hospitality management schools in Asia. She was proving to be an excellent student and Mrs Linh had high hopes for the lovely provincial girl.

He was glad to hear this but it did little to ease his grief and the terrible ache in his heart. Word filtered through to him that Juliette had sold her restaurant and returned to France. If there was one person who might have had some chance of consoling him it was Juliette. But now even she was gone.

Weeks passed with him rarely leaving his room. Phone calls were ignored and memos from Manila went unanswered. The once strong, fit body now almost skeletal, and he had aged almost overnight. Steve Conway was deteriorating physically and mentally. One morning after yet another sleepless night he woke and in a rare rational moment, decided to leave Saigon.

He wrote a long letter of explanation and apology to James Sinclair suggesting that Jumbo Keyes take over the promotion of the Saigon Down Under; Keyes with his management skills and Vietnam experience would be an ideal replacement.

Sinclair understood and immediately agreed. Conway would return to Manila and resume his management duties.

* * *

Late one evening he returned to Thanh Da and took a cyclo to Binh Quoi. He sat on the bench in the darkness beside the huge brass gong. He didn't know how long he stayed staring into the pool shimmering in the moonlight, but it was all just as he remembered. The precious memories of that wonderful evening so long ago flooded back.

That first night when they had sat by the pool so much in love, holding each other as if they were afraid someone would come and tear them apart. It seemed like yesterday. He could still taste the sweetness of her lips, see her small shoulders heaving as she sobbed into his chest because he was returning to Manila the following morning.

When he looked back on the day they first met, he realized he had fallen in love with her on sight. He never knew what it was that attracted her to him but there was an honesty about her, a sincerity, he had not found before in other women. He remembered the eager anticipation of seeing her each evening, and sometimes during her lunch hour; just being with her, seeing her smile and listening to her conversation, was a simple joy.

He had found her intelligent, yet in so many ways, heartbreakingly innocent. There was no pretension, so often the province of Western women. It was when they were apart, even for a short time that he realized how much she meant to him. And now she was gone…

He felt the hot bitter sting of tears. His shoulders slumped and he sat with head bowed in the silence of that precious place. It was after midnight when he rose slowly and took the quartz stone she had given him from his pocket, and walked to the edge of the pool.

He looked down at it for a long moment. The moonlight glinted on the words engraved within. *I love you.* Almost reverently, he gently tossed it into the water where it made a soft 'plop' and disappeared.

'*Tam Biet* my precious love,' he whispered, then turned and walked out of the park down the road toward Saigon.

He'd missed the last cyclo to Thanh Da.

- 283 -

Epilogue

Two Years Later.

The walls echoed with his footsteps as he slowly climbed the dark, winding, narrow terrazzo stairs to the second floor and stood outside the big oak door of the apartment he once rented; the one she had found for him. He looked at the closed door. It seemed to symbolize everything that had happened between them. It was dark, impenetrable, unyielding, telling him, you are not allowed in here Conway…it's over!

The memories of the golden days they had shared came back and once again he felt the familiar lump in his throat threatening to choke him. He shook his head trying to shake these memories, make them go away. But he couldn't. They remained like the flashback of a movie…a movie he wished he had never seen.

He stared with unseeing eyes at the door and remembered…she used to knock softly on that door then hide. As he opened it and looked around, she would jump out laughing and throw her arms around him and they would kiss passionately. He could see her again, hear her, feel her. His throat was constricted, his chest heaved; he had difficulty breathing.

It seemed like only yesterday he had returned to Saigon. She had met him at Tan Son Nhat airport, smiling that shy smile he had come to love, wearing again in his honour, the green *ao dai*. There was the taxi ride from the airport to this apartment. She, sitting quietly beside him; he, not knowing where they were going but trusting her judgment.

He remembered their arrival when they had been met by the smiling, landlady, Mrs Thanh who had organized his luggage to be carried upstairs by her husband and a sweating youth. The one bedroom apartment proved to be just what he wanted; clean, tidy and well-furnished. The memory of the sun streaming through the bedroom window that evening filling it with a golden glow was as vivid now as it was then. She had looked at him expectantly and sighed with relief when he gave it the thumbs up.

Again he heard the words of Mrs Thanh. 'She came here many times sir,' she had laughed, looking at Kim. 'She wanted to make sure it was a good place and comfortable for you.' He recalled the long, sweet kiss he had given her when the landlords had left.

This was to be his new home ...a home he would share with his new woman. The future looked so bright. He had found his soulmate. That day there was no happier man in Saigon.

On this day, there was no sadder man in Saigon.

Tears of unspeakable regret rolled down his face...for what might have been. He bowed his head in prayer for many minutes then walked slowly downstairs into the bright sunshine of Nguyen Sieu Street. There he stopped for a moment and looked back down the narrow alley where a part of his life had begun in joy...and ended in grief. Then he walked away and didn't look back.

The city was ablaze with flowers. Like a new bride at her most beautiful, bustling, boisterous Saigon was welcoming in the New Year celebrating Tet, Vietnam's most important and joyous celebration.

He began to walk across Lamson Square toward Nguyen Hue, the broad boulevard in the heart of the city where huge crowds were admiring the magnificent floral displays. He had walked this way with her many times to Givral coffee shop opposite the Continental Hotel for lunch or snacks at night before she went home to Thanh Da.

Suddenly, he felt a tingle throughout his body. He could feel her presence. She was there! He heard that soft, familiar voice. 'I am here my darling Steve, I am always here beside you, I will walk with you always. You have not lost me.'

He stopped and looked around. 'Kimmee! Where are you? Kimmee!' There was no one.

She watched with a smile he would never see as he continued on past the Caravelle Hotel, across Dong Khoi Street to Nguyen Hue where he turned and looked back one last time, before becoming lost in the milling crowd.

'You can shed tears that she is gone,
or you can smile because she has lived.
You can close your eyes and pray that she'll come back,
or you can open your eyes and see all she's left.
Your heart can be empty because you can't see her,
or you can be full of the love you shared.
You can turn your back on tomorrow and live yesterday,
or you can be happy for tomorrow because of yesterday.
You can remember her only that she is gone,
or you can cherish her memory and let it live on.
You can cry and close your mind,
be empty and turn your back.
Or you can do what she'd want:
smile, open your eyes, love and go on.'

David Harkins

Also by John Pullinger

The Last Jeep to Baclaran

More details here:
www.vividpublishing.com.au/lastjeeptobaclaran

Praise for John Pullinger's debut novel
The Last Jeep to Baclaran

'With this first book in a trilogy, local Maleny author John Pullinger, has produced a gripping yarn of corruption, lust, greed and the brutality of the drug trade which permeated the dying days of the Marcos regime in the Philippines He has captured the excitement and colour of the night life, the bar scenes, corrupt officials, prostitution driven by poverty, the futility of alcohol fuelled Australian ex-pats eking out their lives in Manila.in an action packed story led by the hero with all the sexual prowess, skills and luck of a James Bond. A real page turner' – Jack Wilcox AM DSc (h.c)

'The more pages I turned, the harder it was to put down, the tension and twists and turns of an intriguing plot built chapter by chapter. Slick writing, highly professional research and free flowing dialogue. An irresistible travelling companion or a new best friend to snuggle up with on a lazy afternoon' – Glyn May-International journalist, feature writer

'Damn! Damn! Damn! I didn't get to sleep till 2am. I just had to find out how it ended. It really had me intrigued, it's a real page turner and I loved the humor interspersed with the drama.When is the movie coming out, Hugh Jackman would make a great Steve Conway' – Gerard Loth-Australia

'This is a page turner, with each page packed with action. Steve Conway is another 007'- Martin Dockery –New York

'I was totally absorbed by the characters and events that weave through this enthralling tale. The story builds to a climax of mystery and intrigue, where corruption is rife and greed is the driving force behind the powers that be. A thoroughly enjoyable read....I look forward to the sequel' – Marg Elkington-Australia

'A simply great read' – Mary Ann Owen -Las Vegas

'It kept me enthralled to the intriguing end. I just had to keep reading. Steve Conway is a hero with all the best qualities a man may possess. It would make a great movie' – Elena Meysak – Moscow

'A thoroughly enjoyable book with a good mix of characters, subtle humor and a bit of history.' – Steve Lovell - Saigon

Steve Conway returns to Bangkok

The Last Tuk Tuk to BanG Na

John J Pullinger

Intrigue, Murder, Deception n Romance

Steve Conway returns to Bangkok to run the local operation and saves the life of a beautiful Thai girl during a shoot out on arrival at Bangkok airport.

A romance develops but Conway doesn't realise her family is the target of a Romanian drug gang intent on killing them because of a crackdown by her father, a police general. His association with Pim attracts the focus of the gang and attempts are made on his life.

Conway is drawn further into this dangerous web of intrigue when he learns of a plot to kill Pim's father at an award ceremony to be attended by the King of Thailand and a shocking revelation about her family. When his source is killed Conway is then hunted by both the Romanian drug gang and Thai police seeking revenge.

Conway and Pim are captured by the gang and what follows is a desperate race against time as he tries to clear his name and prevent the assassination against the backdrop of an imminent military coup.

In true Conway style he once again confronts murderous foes, exotic women women intent on his seduction including a Thai female boxer in this tale of intrigue, murder, deception and romance.